Harbor Town Seduction

A Wild Chance Hogan Ride

by K. Randall Ball

BOOK 1

5-BALL, INC.

– 2010 –

First published in the United States in 2010 by 5-Ball, Inc.

First published in paperback 2010

Copyright 2010 by K. Randall Ball

The first Chance Hogan book is published by 5-Ball, Inc. We grant discounts on the purchase of 12 or more copies. For further details, please write to:

5-Ball, Inc.
200 Broad Avenue
Wilmington, California 90744
Or Bandit@bikernet.com
www.Bikernet.com

Printed and manufactured in the United States of America

First edition: January 2010

Cover art by Jon Towle, Aubrey L. Selden and George Fleming
Copy edited by Bruce Snyder and Trent Reker
Interior design by David G. Barnett/Fat Cat Graphic Design
www.fatcatgraphicdesign.com

Library of Congress Catalog Card Number: 99 97428

For Nyla Olsen and my mom, the two women who understand, I think.

-1-

Standing In Line

Los Angeles, a sea of lights from the splashing Long Beach coastline, to the Malibu hills bordering Ventura County. It's a 13-million-plus sprawl of humanity and concrete, with congested lines everywhere, from airliners jammed in a long elevated corridor entering LAX. There are lines at movie premieres, on the freeways, restaurants, theaters, at Disneyland and at the city's 4,000 Jack in the Box restaurants. Not to mention the white lines on glass mirrors in the Hollywood hills, lines of cars in the streets, and lines of carts in the supermarkets. But the worst line for Chance Hogan was in the massive art deco San Pedro Post Office where he lived from a small P.O. box.

Standing on the granite floor of the '30s-era, five-story building, he towered above the others in line. He stood 6-foot-4 and weighed 228 pounds. His sandy blond hair and chiseled features, coupled with a week of stubble, made his appearance questionable. Was he a seaside bum or cool? In Los Angeles, his appearance could mark him a writer or park-living homeless. Smell would answer the question and he didn't stink.

Chance was a life-long biker. He wore Wrangler jeans and shitbrown Justin cowboy boots with "In The Wind" stitched in the oil stained flanks. He strapped a $65 Harley-Davidson watch on his big boney wrist, and slipped a gold motorcycle-wheel ring on his calloused right hand. It was a wedding ring from his distant past, when he married a biker-broad, then his fourth wife installed a diamond in the center. She, too, was gone.

A faded green bike-event sweatshirt with a rusty-brown riding vest thrown over it covered his muscular torso. He shuffled while waiting to pick up a package, because he was too cheap to rent a larger box. He'd recently endured the ravages of his fifth divorce, gave up his 13-year job and home, due to his weakness for redheads, one in particular. Chance was starting over 60 miles from his last home base in the San Fernando Valley.

Three overdue bills and a wad of junk mail hung loosely in his worn sheepskin-gloved hand. He didn't dare step out of line to shit-can the junk mail. It would cost him an hour, and maybe a fistfight and jail time. It was the middle of December and the lines were even more formidable than usual. He was supposed to meet his riding partner, Vince, for lunch. He didn't like the nagging reminder his watch was giving him, 10:15 a.m.

Chance wasn't mastering an upwardly mobile career climb, but that came with his nickname. He took chances, rolled the dice and lived life, one risky adventure after another. He made a good bargain from time to time to keep himself out of serious debt, but he wasn't rising financially toward executive levels. It was the way he liked life, easy, so he could flow with the wind. He took opportunities fate dealt him. He was a chip off his dad's block in some respects and soaked up the adventuresome, creative spirit from his mom.

Those who knew his dad called him Dice Hogan. The elder Hogan was a gambler, constantly playing the odds and generally losing. A player, he ran with the high-roller crowds from Reno to Vegas, Atlantic City and back to the coast for a couple of decades. He finally drank himself to death. Chance rolled a different, softer set of dice. He didn't drink much. He was a loner and a lover. Chance enjoyed selective iso-lation between women. No one saw Chance on a regular basis, except Vince and girls. Chance looked at his watch again, 10:26.

Chance fell in love with motorcycles early in life. He came to dis-trust groups and enjoyed the solitary biker roll, flying through traffic to find a new woman, his addiction and downfall. He learned to weld so he could rake motorcycle frames. He was taught strong work ethics from his depression-era mother and the Royal Machine Shop on Signal Hill, where he worked in high school. He treated tools with respect, new acquaintances with a wary eye, and adored women, but he roamed. When the routine became stagnant, he shuffled his tattered riding boots toward the door.

Chance stood still as three culturally diverse patrons absorbed the postal workers' attention at three barred windows. After waiting an endless amount of time to reach a clerk, each patron stood comfort- ably against the marble facade and chatted, as if they had the whole fuckin' day. Time crept past, as if the clock ran in 60-weight motor oil for the remaining patrons, as the attended-to jawed with the invisible postal workers behind the marble exterior.

Chance shook as his anxiety increased. He was nervous and twitching. As his mind wandered, a psychotic redhead crept to the forefront. She destroyed his marriage and almost ruined the company he worked for. He moved to the harbor town of San Pedro for a fresh outlook, a new dose of freedom, but he wasn't sure she was history. The junk mail in his hand burned and he removed his gloves. Just as he thought he'd lost his mind completely, a small child burst into tears after cutting her lip on the steel railing.

«« — »»

Across town, Vince rolled his Street Stalker, a Harley-Davidson Softail, out of the garage and fired it to life. The bike was a used wreck he'd rebuilt and slapped a Street Stalker kit on for a tough, bobbed look. It was jet black. Everything was blacked out, even the wheels. Most of the chrome was gone except the stainless handlebars, the primary, the shift lever, and the Bartels' Harley-Davidson per- formance pipes. The Southern California dealership installed a BP-40 cam, shaved the heads and ground performance into the valves. The bike sported a modified CV carburetor with a Thunder jet and a Thunder slide installed by Departure Bike Works in Richmond, Virginia. The custom-painted scoot was black, with traditional yellow scallops, hand pinstriped in red. It sounded as bad as it looked.

Vince rode his custom Harley like Billy the Kid handled a Colt revolver. It was a part of him. He threw his muscled leg over the saddle and molded his jet-black, bruised, and scraped leather pants into the seat. His black gloves became an intricate part of the handle- bars as they wrapped around the black vintage-style grips, while he snapped the throttle.

Vince was 5-foot-10 and strong for his size. He had long, black, wavy hair and a goatee that framed his olive skin. With his menacing Italian heritage, he terrified most men and attracted plenty of women. At 30, his eyes were sky blue and brilliant, and his smile was wry. He was confident without being egotistical. He couldn't pack a lot of ego in an empty bank account, but he reeked sarcasm. No one knew his last name, not even Chance. But then, no one knew Chance's real first name, either. They were both anonymous to the outside world.

Both men worked out regularly at Gold's Gym in Venice, and Vince had an extensive martial arts background. He even taught others from time to time, but, like Chance, he was currently out of work. They met at a magazine publishing company. Chance was an editor of a small custom motorcycle magazine, and Vince pitched a story so wild, it shook the motorcycle industry.

Chance respected Vince's writing abilities and creative endeavors, but otherwise, he was a loose canon. Vince buttoned his black leather shirt over Patagonia thermal underwear. The final layer was his black Little Joe's leather vest that fit like a glove. He threw a black leather satchel strap over his shoulder and gunned the engine, while releasing the choke. The satchel held a finely cleaned and cared for .45-caliber Heckler & Koch automatic, two magazines, two protein bars, and a 65-page screenplay.

Vince headed across town to pitch his movie notion to a Santa Monica producer. Everyone rode in the '90s, but when it came to promoting screenplays, the old bad biker stereotype prevailed. Every studio Vince approached showed him the door. Bikers were still scary to wimpy Hollywood types.

Vince was involved with a naïve, tall, lanky German blonde, Nicole, who could have been a supermodel but she couldn't speak enough English. Vince, being an overprotective, paternalistic and possessive sonuvabitch, scrambled many of her relationships with agents. He scared them half to death. He grew up in Kansas, on a ranch where he rode bulls until most of his bones were broken at least once. Sort of a riding, irate postal worker, he was a serious gun zealot, with weapons placed in strategic locations in every room of his Palos Verdes apartment.

As a college student, he was attacked twice by gangs and beaten badly. A switch went off in his brain. He heavily armed himself, went on a violent bent and prepared to use whatever means it took to settle any threatening situation, quickly and efficiently—like that insane postal worker.

Vince rode out of the alley where he lived with Nicole and blasted onto the Pacific Coast Highway. The PCH had a sexy reputation, one of gentle curves, sparkling nightclubs, and the lapping ocean.

Winding through Redondo Beach, Manhattan Beach, and on toward Santa Monica, Vince passed a sea of junk food restaurants, car washes, gas stations, car dealerships, strip malls and barred windows.

He skipped through traffic as if it was a parking lot, darting past a sea of four-wheeled stationary obstacles. Stoplights peppered the famous highway every four blocks. He added 15 mph to the 35 mph limit, which timed them to remain green. At 50 mph, he was golden, making time like a scared rabbit on an open trail. He had an appointment in Santa Monica, then he'd jet south on the 405 freeway to Long Beach for lunch and a game of pool with Chance. They were both writers of differing sorts. Vince wrote copy for national television ads and Chance scribbled pure motorcycle, romance, and whiskey prose.

Vince split lanes past Manhattan Beach Boulevard, making two lanes fit two four-wheelers and one fat-tire motorcycle. Ahead, he faced another quick-spurt intersection, while a teenager stood on the corner chewing a fist full of gum, a senior staggered in the crosswalk, and a compact made a right turn into his lane. Like a rattlesnake crossing a path in the desert, Vince visually evaluated every metal threat and human movement. He was certain the compact driver looked directly into his charcoal-tinted shades.

The senior lumbered across the side street predictably. The car people edged into the crosswalk. The teen bounced a ball light-heartedly against the curb.

Vince zinged into the intersection at 50 mph, when the woman in the car edged into right-hand lane directly in front of him. He stood on the brakes. The rear tire broke free, the bike began to slide, and he backed off the rear brake pedal, while pulling firmly on the blacked-out handlebar controls toward the left lane. The 16-inch stern Avon tire grabbed at the harsh pavement. He wasn't going to T-bone the cheap hunk of old tuna cans. He bore down on the rear brake again and the wheel broke loose, sliding graciously toward the left rear fender of the compact, but he had the next lane in his sights. He aimed at the open lane between the obstructing vehicle and a truck coming the other direction.

At the crucial moment, he released the rear brake, nailed the throttle and spit the bike forward into the left lane, thinking, praying, and predicting that the dark-haired car person would remain in the right-hand lane.

Not so. She continued into the left lane and caught his frame just below the shotgun exhaust system, popping it into the air. The bike lurched to the left directly into the heavy steel bumper protecting the grill of a Ford F-150, shattering the fiberglass headlight cowling on the blacked-out Street Stalker. Vince launched into the air like a rag doll and slammed to the pebble-gray asphalt. A flying sack of bull-riding cement, his lower back impacted first, whipping his torso down against the unforgiving surface.

For a moment, his world went into a Twilight Zone of slow motion and surreal images. He could see the horrified look on the car person's muted face. He saw the squealing, smoking, rear Ford truck tires as it veered into the opposing lane to prevent additional contact. Vince's limbs slapped the pavement next. He felt something crack in his right elbow and a charge of pain rushed up his arm and down to his fingertips. The impact reminded him of his bull-riding days. He rolled to his right in searing anguish. His shoulder took the upper torso impact, head snapping to the side, pulling against his adrenaline-packed muscles. For minutes he laid as still as a bronze sculpture, looking peaceful. Sirens wailed.

«« — »»

In the post office, Chance answered his cell phone.

"You don't know me," said the anxious voice. "I ride a Ducati and was chasing your friend down PCH when a woman pulled in front of him and he went down."

"What?" Chance snapped, startling the people around him. "Is he all right?"

"I don't know," the rider, Tim, said breathlessly. "He just mumbled something about his briefcase. Somebody's got to come and get it."

"I'll take care of it," Chance said. "Where are they going to take him?"

"I don't know, but I'll find out."

"Call me back when you know," Chance said and hung up.

He would have rushed to Vince's side, but L.A. forms a vast 13-million strong quagmire of obstacles. He knew it would take him almost an hour to reach the other side of town. He dialed Nicole's number and let it ring.

No one picked up the phone in L.A. Fax machines and the Internet were created to enhance communication. Most people just let the phone ring, watching the caller I.D. code for a reason not to answer. If Nicole recognized Chance's cell number, she wouldn't answer the phone for two reasons. Girlfriends and wives hate single riding buddies, especially tight ones. The other reason had to do with Chance's green eyes. She had a weakness for them and it wasn't a healthy one.

When the answering machine kicked in, Chance said, "Goddamnit Nicole, answer the fucking phone. It's about Vince. Call me, goddamnit, on my cell." He hung up.

One patron left a post office window and the line moved a foot.

His cell jiggled in his pocket again. "Yeah?"

"What do we do with the bike?" Tim asked, still gulping air.

"I'll take care of it," Chance said and hung up.

He called the Marina Del Rey Harley-Davidson dealership and asked for Ron. "The Street Stalker is down," Chance said.

"Where is it?" Ron asked.

"On PCH, not far from you," Chance said.

"I don't have a truck," Ron said.

"You don't have a truck? What kind of fuckin' dealership..."

"Excuse me, excuse me," a voice came from behind Chance. He spun to face a massive, middle-aged Slav who was wearing a dirty set of royal blue overalls with "Roy's Towing" embroidered above a pocket full of pens.

"What the hell?" Chance barked. "My brother was just in an accident and you're in a hurry?"

"I own a towing service, dipshit," the man said through crooked teeth. "Where is he? I'll send a truck."

"Sorry. He's at PCH and Marine. Hurry, will ya, and haul it to Bartels' on Lincoln."

The man dug into his stained uniform, came up with a smudged cell phone and dialed. "Joey, get the flatbed over to PCH and Marine to pick up a Harley, and take it to Bartels'."

Chance finally took notice of the long line of people staring at him as he barked into the cell phone and the big mechanic behind him followed suit.

"Excuse me, sir," a feminine voice called out from the line.

"Yeah?" Chance said, dropping his voice to an acceptable level.

"I'm a nurse." She was a short, round Hispanic woman with caring eyes and long black hair tied in a ponytail. "Don't let them take your friend to the county hospital. Ask them to take him to Sisters of Mary in Santa Monica. They will take good care of him."

"Cool, thanks," Chance said, hoping the phone would ring again. It did.

"It's Tim. The EMTs are here. He's rolling in and out of consciousness. Where should they take him?"

"Sisters of Mary in Santa Monica," Chance spat with confidence. "I'm trying to get in touch with his girlfriend to get the briefcase. Just keep it out of the hands of the cops, if you know what I mean."

"Yeah, I got it," Tim said.

Chance was distracted by a tugging on his sleeve.

"Hold on, Tim," he said.

As he turned around, he noticed a small kid dressed in black, carrying a full-faced helmet and wearing a fluorescent yellow vest. The Chinese kid with a milky clear complexion and scraggly Fu Manchu mustache looked up at Chance and held a bright yellow card in his free hand. He didn't utter a word.

Chance took the card, which read "L.A. Courier Service. Safe, Fast and Secure. Tommy Pagoda." A light went on in Chance's overloaded brain.

"You know where he is, kid?"

The kid nodded.

"Bring the briefcase to the Blue Cafe in downtown Long Beach at lunch."

The kid nodded and turned away, then abruptly turned back, handing Chance an 8-by-10 envelope sans postage.

Chance nodded, "I'll take care of it."

"Tim," Chance said into the cell, "Tommy Pagoda is on his way to pick up the case."

"All right, I've got it," Tim said. "The cop looked in it for Vince's ID, but now I've got it."

A chill went up Chance's spine. "Did he find anything?"

"He looked a little startled, then said something about it not being in there and handed me the case." Tim said. "Damn, that thing is heavy, though."

They exchanged numbers and hung up. Chance called Nicole again. The phone rang four times before the answering machine picked up.

"Nicole," Chance barked into the phone, startling the post office patrons again. "Listen, Nicole, the next time I call you, answer the phone, or I'll come over and ring your Kraut neck. Got that?"

Chance was still behind six people with packages. Another half-hour passed. The cell rang again.

"Hey," a gravely voice stumbled through the airwaves.

"Who the hell is this?"

"It's Vince."

"What's happenin'? You still going to make lunch?"

"I don't know, brother." Vince struggled to say. "Do me a favor and don't call Nicole. She'll freak."

Chance nodded without saying anything.

"Ya see, her brother was run over by a car last week. She's a bit sensitive about bikes and the car people," Vince said.

"You gonna make lunch or not?" Chance asked, ignoring the Nicole subject. "We've got shit to talk about."

"I've got a concussion and can't see or balance too well," Vince said. His voice seemed to fade out like the signal on a cell phone running through traffic, but it wasn't the phone.

"You're not dead, right? Then you'll be getting hungry shortly," Chance said.

"I'll do what I can, brother, but the bike's a mess."

"I'll call Ron and get back to you," Chance said and hung up. He called Bartels' again.

"Ron, as soon as the bike gets there, give me a call. We need that thing running. We don't care what the hell it looks like."

"No problem, Chance," Ron said.

Chance tried Nicole again. No luck. Another patron was helped and the line moved another foot. Murmurs circulated about the lousy level of service, the plodding clerks and the wait. For a while, the drama on Chance's cell kept the zombies occupied. Some asked about Vince's condition?

Chance kept thinking about a particular waitress at the Blue Cafe. She was way tall, with jet-black hair that hung softly around her shoulders and curved upward against her skin. Her hair-do was the shape of a bell. She was well proportioned for a tall girl, with ample breasts, pouting lips and supple hips. She was hanging with a local bouncer, but what the hell? Thoughts never hurt anyone.

The phone rang again. The connection was bad and Chance pressed the receiver hard against his ear.

"Brother?" Vince's voice was drawn and strained.

"I can't hear you," Chance said as another patron was helped and the line moved another foot.

"It's me, Vince." Was he talking from a coma? "Not sure I can make it to lunch on time. Got a concussion, chipped a bone in my elbow, bruised all my ribs and my spine."

"So, I take it ya can't ride," Chance said. "And I called Ron and told him to hurry. Can't get a hold of your wandering wanton woman either. What do you suggest?"

"Hooooow about breakfast in the morning?" Vince asked hesitantly. His voice was strained and distant.

"Breakfast?" Chance said raising his dirty blonde eyebrows. "Breakfast? You know the rule, the code. If you say you're going to do something, ya gotta do it."

It was 11:15 on the clock above Vince's hospital bed. Time was running out.

"I know, I know," Vince said, "but without wheels or Nicole, I'm shot."

"Do what you can, brother," Chance said. "No one will get shot if you don't make it." He hung up.

The line moved again. Chance stepped up to the window just after eyeing the speeding deco clock on the wall. 11:30. He slipped the yellow postal form up to the thin black woman behind the counter.

"What's the box number, sir?"

Chance gave her the number and watched her hips sway past the other tellers into the area behind the post office boxes. She returned with one crushed box leaking red syrupy fluid, and a certified letter. The box came from his mom, who had made some sort of fruit jam and the post office crushed it. The envelope contained an eviction notice.

He turned and faced his fellow post office inmates. With his leathered arm outstretched, he dropped both items into the adjacent waste paper basket and shrugged.

A short surfer-looking girl with her arms filled with shipping boxes stepped around the tow-truck Slav. She set the boxes on the cold deck and stood up. Chance was taken back by the size of her tits, pushing hard against her white T-shirt printed with bold black letters, "Celeb Limo."

"You might be able to help," Chance said and wrote, Vince, Little Sister of Mary and Blue Cafe on the back of his card and handed it to her. "Can you set up a pick-up?" Chance asked and headed for the door.

"Of course," she said and smiled as wide as a breaking wave. "I'll call the Santa Monica office."

Outside, he mounted his stretched Harley-Davidson chopper, fired it to life and blasted toward the Los Angeles harbor. The frame was a used Indian Larry unit, all-nasty, and rigid with terrific stretched lines. His stroked Evolution engine sat in it like two atomic silos coupled to the rear wheel through a Baker 5-speed transmission. The pipes swooped toward the pavement, a combination of 1 3/4- and 2-inch pipe with a turnout that could only be described as the tongue of the devil lapping fearlessly at the asphalt. His seat padding was almost non-existent, a thin layer of foam, with a thick slab of leather stretched over it.

The gas tank was pure stretched evil, with a hint of H-D Sportster. The front end was a narrow traditional Springer extended 12 inches, and between Indian Larry, from New York City, and Chance, they had fashioned the narrowest pair of drag bars on earth to Custom Cycle Engineering dogbone risers. The rear fender was a small chunk of sheet metal, just enough to cup the 180 Avon tire. The paint was metallic coffee brown with floating red dice painted on the tank sides and etched into the leather seat. It was a two-wheel, 100-horsepower dart thrown by the devil himself. He called it the Dicey Evo.

Chance dropped his dream machine into gear and ripped over bridges and Terminal Island towards downtown Long Beach. He slid into the parking lot of the Long Beach blues joint, the Blue Cafe. The silent courier sat at a table in the outdoor patio. Chance paid the kid, and he zipped out of the parking lot on a flat-black rice grinder, doing a wheel stand for half a city block. Chance was broke, but he ordered a Corona with his last twenty.

A half hour passed before a black stretched limo rolled onto Broadway Boulevard and pulled over. Vince struggled out of the limousine, stumbled and grabbed the outdoor patio railing. His head was bandaged, but he pulled off the bloody gauze wrap and shit-canned it. He struggled to the table where Chance sat sipping the icy Corona.

"'Bout time you got here," Chance said.

"Fuckin' car people!" Vince said, dropping into a racing green plastic lawn chair. As soon as he hit, he came out of the chair like a rocket.

"Think I'll just stand." Sweat poured off his reddening brow.

"What's the matter? The Vicodin hasn't kicked in yet?"

"I don't take that shit," Vince said. "Took a handful of aspirin before I left the hospital. Where's the briefcase?"

"Right there," Chance said, "but don't bother opening it. The screenplay's gone."

"Whatta ya mean?" Vince asked in a pained voice. "Is the H&K still there?"

"Yep," Chance said.

"What kind of problem will it cause?" Chance said.

"What kind would you like?" Vince said, "If it gets in the wrong hands..."

"We'll deal with whatever," Chance said looking at the menu. Their banter was all bullshit confidence. Neither rider knew how he was going to cover the rent, but they always had a good time fuckin' with each other.

Grabbing for the edge of the table, Vince lost his footing and fell abruptly to the concrete deck and moaned like a sick dog. Waiters and busboys ran to his aid. Chance pushed the light plastic table aside and looked down at his brother. "You ready to order?"

-2-

THE SPOT

A couple of weeks passed and Vince healed. Over in Marina Del Rey, Bartels Harley-Davidson finished Vince's repairs, and he and Chance rode to San Pedro for the first time.

It felt damn good to feel the chill of the coast as he rounded each curve on the hopped-up Softail. It danced along the sheer bluffs like a showgirl at the edge of a Vegas stage.

They pulled into a parking lot that bordered a single-story, corner stucco harbor saloon, and chained and locked their bikes. The bar sported one flickering sign that said, "The Spot," with a dartboard painted under it and a peeling, striped dart pointed at the bull's-eye. The box of a building housed WWII sailors and fist fights in the '40s and was finally refurbished in the '70s. It rotted ever since. The street-lights cast an amber hue on the sparkling motorcycles.

Inside, a group of young Hispanics leaned against the bar drinking beer and speaking in their native tongue. Three bikers played darts. An enormous blonde stood at the pool table in contrast to her skinny 8-ball partner, an older rail of a man in Levis and a pressed flannel shirt. Her shooting was so abysmal that Chance finally got up from his stool and gave her a simple, aim-the-cue pointer. She sunk her next three balls. Suddenly, her pudgy features glowed. She searched the darkness beyond the scratched and dented pool table to find Chance and thank him.

Chance sipped his whiskey and turned to Vince.

"I need to make some money and you need to find that script. Plus, I need to get laid. It's been too long."

"We're not going to find any girls around here," Vince said.

One hot babe roamed into The Spot the first time they showed, but never again. Harbor girls were small, multi-cultural and just under blue collar. Maybe the dank port water stunted their growth? They didn't seem to have a lot on the ball, either.

Chance nodded as he watched the only decent looking chick in the joint dart up and down the bar pouring drinks. She was the bartender, a short bubbly blond. She exuded a natural ability to spill her entire emotional condition with a turn of her lips. Fortunately, they indicated good weather most of the time.

"You're right," Chance said as if admitting defeat. "We could go to Hollywood."

"We need to make some coin, brother," Vince said. "We need to deal with my stolen screenplay, to sell that movie deal, and you need to sell some bike parts or write a freelance tech article for some bike rag before we go play in partyville. We need a plan."

They were both running on empty. Vince wrote for an ad agency until his account evaporated and he was fired. He was non-stop integrity, honor, and creativity, like a biblical time bomb. He didn't take bullshit, under-handed deals or anything but high moral principles. Discussed with slippery, dishonest ad agency antics, he wrote a searing anti-big ad agency screenplay. He didn't care if he made a living. He was devoted to revealing over-priced tactics and setting the record straight, but he would surely catch heat.

If the screenplay found its way into the wrong hands, Vince would never work for an ad agency again, or worse. Nicole, his leggy German blonde, flew to the east coast for modeling work. Vince packed his Malaga Cove apartment and readied to shovel everything into a storage locker, and the year was only beginning. His bank account neared bottom, but he was as confident and cocky as a Princeton grad.

Chance, who was usually upbeat, looked at the shattered wood shutters that once protected the saloon windows and wondered how anyone could keep a business in such bad disrepair. He compared the bar interior to his disheveled life. He was horny and broke, but he wasn't unhappy. His new adventure was only beginning. He was living on the coast, had a few prospects for income, his motorcycle ran strong, and he liked the small Spanish home he moved into overlooking the harbor. Life was good, albeit uncertain.

"This place needs a hand grenade," Vince said, patting his leather satchel that carried his .45-caliber H&K, two extra magazines and another violent goody or two.

The comment smacked Chance in the chest like a slap to the face. He grimaced. He looked at Vince's armament bag and didn't ask what it held that Friday night. It was best not to know.

The front door, littered with busted deadbolts and locks, sprung open as three young hotties strolled in, giggling and playing grab-ass with one another. They slid up beside Chance and whispered to each other through clouds of cheap perfume. Chance turned to face a bubbly brunette with shoulder length waves of softness. Her face was unnaturally hard for such a young broad. Her skin was soft and freckled, but her features were mature, her brown eyes direct and tough. Maybe it was the dark eyes and heavy untrimmed eyebrows.

"I'm Chance. What's your name?"

"Suzanne. What kind of name is Chance?"

"A bullshit one," Vince said. He nudged Chance, whose eyes were cemented to the girl's.

"We'll see," she said, turning back toward her friends at the bar.

Her tits were small and her legs long. Chance overheard her girlfriend say, "Let's get out of here."

The girls picked up their gear and Suzanne turned to face Chance as they headed toward the door. "Will you be here in a half-hour?"

"If you will," Chance said.

She nodded and said, "I need to take care of a problem with an old boyfriend, but I'll be back." She strolled out the door leaving a fragrant trail.

Vince spun on his rickety stool to face Chance. "It's always a dangerous proposition with you, isn't it?"

Chance shrugged his shoulders and ordered them another round of drinks. "We could leave."

"You won't leave and you know it. You'll play the card and take your chances, you bastard."

Vince was right and twice as cocky as Chance. Thirty minutes passed before they finished their next drink, then 35.

She danced in the door in a black mini-skirt, a tight blue velvet top and a long leather trench coat. Those same dark eyes bore into Chance as he stepped off his barstool to meet her.

"I told you I'd be back," she said in a quick burst of Arnold Schwarzenegger-like confidence.

Chance looked at the long legs disappear under the thin short skirt and thought better of reminding her that she was five minutes late.

"What'll you have?"

"You," she said and tossed her purse on the bar.

"We'll get to that, but wouldn't you like a drink?" Chance said.

"Don't drink much, but I like hot chocolate," she returned.

"Hot chocolate?" Chance was floored. Suddenly he wondered how old she was, but he didn't ask. Vince pushed everything, while Chance allowed his sensual cards to unfold. He was quiet and observant, while Vince was a bullhorn.

"How about Baileys and cocoa?"

She shrugged and Chance placed the order. She seemed to enjoy the sweet coffee flavor, so the deal was done and the bartender shuffled off to brew some cocoa.

"How about a ride?" she said. Her leather trench coat spread open like a satin curtain on a mystery movie and the shapely mistress became much more intriguing.

"I'm sure we can work something out," Chance said, feeling the growing need to press his body to hers.

"I'm sure we...," she muttered in a whispery voice that rolled out of her mouth like a midnight harbor fog and engulfed Chance. She took a step closer and slipped her hand around his trim waist.

"Let's go to my place," she said in his ear and followed it with her moist tongue and hot breath. He didn't need to answer verbally. His body responded.

The bright-eyed bartender returned with a steaming cup of cocoa seriously laced with Baileys. The mixture, about a thousand calories a drop, swirled around in the cup like some treacherous swamp of chocolate daring anyone to wade in. Someone coincidently tuned the jukebox to play, "I Think I'm Going Out of My Head," by Little Anthony and the Imperials. The words poured out and encircled the couple.

Chance pulled Suzanne onto the tiny chipped parquet dance floor. They smashed their bodies together in a screaming grind.

"Come on, let's get outta here." she said and ground her hips against his. He didn't need to answer verbally.

Vince looked at the two, shook his head, and returned to the bar and the slow banter he'd started up with the blond bartender. When he turned around to check on his brother, they were gone. Only the swinging bar door gave away their departure. Then he heard Chance's motorcycle fire to life, rattling the filthy saloon windows. The rumbling pipes spit hot exhaust at the pavement, sending cigarette butts and San Pedro grime up against the drab stucco.

Like the scream of a banshee, the chopper peeled out of the parking lot and into the night. Suzanne's coat flapped wildly in the wind, her hair like flames behind her head. A short mile away, across from an elementary school, surrounded by tall chain-link fence, Chance pulled his sizzling metallic chopper between two 1940s clapboard duplexes and shut it off as lights flickered on in the other units.

He and Suzanne crashed through her front door in a fiery blaze of hormones, ripping at each other's clothes. Chance came out of his cowboy boots, socks and Levis, then stood above her and removed his shirt. She seemed to flow effortlessly out of the trench coat. Her pantyhose disappeared while their faces pressed together in one long, daring kiss. Steam seemed to drift off their bodies as they slipped into the small bed like long-lost lovers.

Their tongues dueled in desperation to find something they never would. Chances' hands flowed over her flesh like an addict's straw over a fresh mound of cocaine. She felt good, real good, too good. She tasted better than Jack Daniel's, an indescribable flavor that just says yes or no. It said YES.

Their animal lust was interrupted by a knock at the door, then a more persistent pounding. Chance pulled back and could see the longing in her bright eyes. Her expression turned from fiery passion to concern, then fear.

"I didn't tell you," she said, panting. "My last boyfriend is a cop. We broke up months ago, but he keeps coming around."

The pounding shook the door.

"Suzanne! I need to speak to you." The ardent voice broke the barrier of the rickety wood door.

Chance jumped out of bed. He searched the cluttered deck for his Wranglers. For the first time, he noticed the interior of her one-bedroom bungalow. The joint was a disaster. There were art projects, kids' toys, stacks of papers and photographs everywhere. It smelled of chocolate-chip cookies. He quickly slipped into his denims and opened the door. A tall, dark-haired man, with a pockmarked face, in a windbreaker, tried to look past him to the interior. Chance blocked his view.

«« — »»

Back at the bar, Vince sipped his drink and watched the tall, thick, blonde play pool. She was young and fresh-looking, with soft skin and a clear complexion, but she had let her body go the way of her pool game. Her ill-fitting clothes were another indication of her stormy life. A cardigan sweater hung at an awkward angle around her shoulders, partly covering a smudged white T-shirt. She must have weighed over 250 pounds.

Vince slipped a quarter onto the table and sat back as she missed another shot and proclaimed, "I'm no pro." As if that announcement somehow freed her from any competitive responsibility.

Her scrawny partner wasn't much better. The audience consisted of one slightly buffed youngster with a crew cut and high-water jeans. Next to him sat an equally buffed partner. They must have been from the nearby military base, and he drank one MGD after another. Clean-cut, he scoffed at the players' lack of abilities, yet never put up a quarter.

Next to the youngster sat the oldest seafaring drunkard on Pacific Avenue. All gray, with flowing hair and a long scraggly beard, he watched intently, occasionally getting up to point a crooked forefinger at the edge of a ball, the blonde intended to hit, as if he was her coach.

Finally, the game was over. The blonde consumed a barstool with her ass and sipped at her beer. Vince approached the table and picked up his quarter as his gaunt foe chalked his cue meticulously, eyeing the dark-haired biker suspiciously.

The muscled kid in the T-shirt jumped up from his stool, knocking it over as he approached Vince.

"It's my turn, asshole," he said.

Vince didn't budge, but leaned down to scoop up a handful of balls. "Where's your quarter?"

"Well," the kid said, reaching into his pocket, "I was going to play next."

"Put your quarter on the felt there, and you can play next game. It's the Code of the West," Vince said, leaning down for more balls.

"Fuck!" The kid snapped and almost ran to the bar for change.

Vince racked the rainbow of balls, eyed the kid warily, and the game was on.

«« — »»

"I want to speak to Suzanne," the middle-aged off-duty cop said, his eyes full of peaking anxiety.

"You can't," Chance said, acutely aware of the man's discomfort.

"She's in there, isn't she?" he said. "How long have you known her?"

"Listen, buddy, I'm cold," Chance said. "I barely know this girl, but you've got to go."

The young broad burst onto the porch under Chance's naked arm and started screaming at her ex-boyfriend.

"I told you we were through, now get the hell out of here!"

Chance listened to the sudden harsh tones, looked at the broken middle-aged man, and wished he was back in the bar.

The cop's shoulders drooped and he moseyed slowly down the narrow path toward the gate, muttering, "I guess it's over. I see now."

"You're goddamn right it's over!" Suzanne shouted from the door.

Chance went back inside wondering how long ago she made the break-up announcement. He sat on the edge of the bed and tried to find his boots in the rubble on the floor. He smelled the tattered musty apartment and the notion that he was somehow being used to end this relationship. He wanted no part of it.

"Where you going?" Suzanne's voice softened like metal rock suddenly becoming R&B. Chance pulled on a cotton gym sock and rolled the scenario around in his mind. He was witnessing the gamut of a woman's emotions in a one-hour period.

"I don't like cops," Chance said, pulling on a boot. "I don't trust the system, they've got too much power, and I just moved into this town. Besides, I don't like witnessing a broken heart."

"But you don't understand," she returned. "I haven't been seeing him for..." She was naked again, pressing her tits against his back. "Just stay for a little while, please."

«« — »»

Vince played 8-ball with the tall longshoreman, took the game handily, and downed another shot of Jack. He stood back from the table and waited for the young punk to return.

Vince ordered another drink. As he lifted the tumbler to his lips, someone walked into him and the harsh amber liquid splashed down his leather shirt. Spinning as the kid passed, Vince planted his black cowboy boot carefully between the kid's legs, then tightened. The kid stumbled and fell to the floor soaked with every imaginable brand of liquor and sprinkled with 20 years of boot grime and cigarette ash. Vince returned to chalking his cue and paid little attention to the kid scrambling to get up.

"What the fuck do you think you're doing?" the kid asked as he pushed his chest out and drove it against Vince's wooden cue.

"What the fuck is it to you military boy?" Vince said, eyeing the raging bull. "Did someone loan you a quarter? Rack the balls."

The kid fumed. He stormed around the table, grabbed the rack and tossed it onto the nicked felt surface. He grabbed the balls and dropped them onto the table, making no attempt to organize them or with any concern for the precision slate surface.

"There motherfucker, break!" he snapped.

Vince eyed the punk warily, leaning down to take his shot. He took quick strokes at the alabaster ball, sniffed the violence building in the air, then his arm tensed and he lunged with the cue. It struck with such force that the cue ball smacked the racked balls, lifted off the table, and struck the punk in the chest. Stunned, it forced him to stumble backwards against the wall, and he dropped his cue. The old man leaned toward the dank deck and retrieved the ball, placing it back on the felt.

The muscled kid stormed around the table. He stood eyeball to eyeball with Vince shouting, "You sonuvabitch! You did that on purpose."

Vince looked him straight in the eye and said, "Lousy rack. Your shot." He had a gunslinger's confidence, fueled by whiskey.

«« — »»

Chance lay back down on the bed and she curled around him like a boa constrictor wraps its silky smooth body around its prey. He felt the answer to his addiction return. A woman's yearning touch, her softness, and gentle curves were like heroin to a junky.

The cop at the door had distracted Chance. The situation wasn't kosher. He thought about the rubble-strewn apartment, the screaming woman and the steaming chocolate she never touched, then he felt his body start to respond again, and again the clothes fell toward the filthy floor. Soon they were clamoring all over each other. Chance's weakness was a passionate woman, no matter what the circumstances.

Tomorrow, he could handle whatever life dealt. Tonight, he would bet on her passion and his growing lust. With his lips brushing her taught nipples, the cop became a distant intrusion. As his rough hand slipped up her smooth thigh, the condition of her apartment became unimportant, and as his tongue slipped deep into her mouth and his hardness into her wetness, her harangue fell on deaf ears. He'd gone to heaven once more, and nothing would interfere with the natural bliss of it all.

She writhed against him on the tiny bed, as if they were making love on a mountaintop and the whole world was far beneath them.

«« — »»

Vince adjusted his peripheral vision to include every angry move the kid made standing in the corner as he sunk one ball after another. The kid was drunk and hated bikers, but that wasn't Vince's problem. He loved a fight. With each carefully calculated shot, the kid tensed. His thick young arms twitched to Vince's pool cue cadence. His spine stiffened and eyes narrowed. Finally, Vince missed a shot and the tight-lipped crew around the table took a tentative unified breath. The sigh and the missed cue eased the tension.

Vince stood back as the kid glared, a vehement gaze capable of melting steel. The kid desperately searched the table for a shot. Vince carefully positioned the alabaster ball as to prevent most any reasonable trajectory.

"Fuck," the kid snapped and turned toward Vince, his hands shifting on the cue to a baseball bat stance. Vince eyed the kid with his slick surly deadpan, Italian mug, as if he had no idea what the kid was upset about, which infuriated the youngster even more.

"That's it, mother fucker! I've had it with your biker shit! I'm takin' a piece of you!"

Vince ignored the comment.

"Wait mastermind," he said. "I think you have a shot on the 13 ball. Look."

Again, the tension surrounding the table peaked as the kid nearly took a swing at Vince with the cue, then hesitated. The gathering crowd sighed while Vince pointed out the shot. The kid's dark military partner folded his bulky arms and stared at Vince. Beads of sweat built on his brow. He wanted to leave.

Red-faced, the player's eyes flashed at Vince, then at the table. He saw the shot in the barroom din, difficult as it was, but his machismo wouldn't allow him to back off. He was blind to the rest of the table. All he could see was the 13-ball partially hidden by the grass-green 6-ball. If he was able to slice it finely, he could pass Vince's ball, clip his and make the shot. But it pissed him off that the biker in all black was manipulating him at every turn. He fumed, found the chalk and rubbed it so hard against the padded tip of the cue that it cracked and shattered into several pieces.

The kid's palms were damp and sticky. He could smell beer oozing out of his pores and felt it permeating his thin T-shirt. The wetness made him uneasy. He downed another MGD and hoped it would somehow be Popeye's Spinach. He leaned over the table, stared down the over-used, bent, barroom cue and aimed. He wanted to prove he could sink that 13-ball, then he wanted to kick this biker's ass more than anything in the world. The cue moved awkwardly in his hands. Beads of sweat built on his forehead like bubbles floating to the surface in boiling water. The tension surrounding the table heightened.

The old man, on the stool next to the table, scratched his beard and his yellow eyes brightened with back street terror. Suddenly, he saw the trap Vince set up, plus he was sure that if the kid didn't make the shot, there was going to be a fight. The big blonde backed into the corner of the room and whispered to her lanky friend. The kid's eyes darted around the dark, smoke-filled room nervously. He stroked the cue, stopped, wiped the sweat from around his eyes and tried again.

Finally, his patience gone, he was forced shoot, no matter what happened. Straining his cracking composure, he shot. As planned, he clipped the 13-ball. It bounced against the cushion prematurely, missed the pocket, but the cue ball didn't. Scratch shot.

«« — »»

Suzanne lay spent on the edge of the bed. Chance kissed her cheek tenderly and pulled the covers over her nude form. A crooked smile formed on her lips. She tried to say something then decided that the moment was too perfect to disturb with verbal communication.

But Chance had to move. He slipped out of bed and dug through the crap at his feet to find his clothes.

He left quietly, watching for the cop outside. He wiped the moisture off his bike seat, pulled on his gloves and looked at the sky as if to find an answer to the wonders of life. Why are the true joys in life absolutely free, like sex, a brilliant sunset and a starlit night? It was cool around him as the bike rumbled to life, but he was floating on air as he popped the chopper into gear and slipped into the street as quietly as he could, his straight pipes slapping the pavement.

It was less than a mile back to The Spot and the motorcycle ran effortlessly, in tune with Chance's ecstasy. He enjoyed this situation many times, but each was like the rush of heroin in a junkie's veins. He couldn't get any higher, more at ease with the world and at peace with himself as he blasted into the parking lot alongside the bar and skidded to a stop.

Shoving his tan deerskin gloves between the risers, he stepped off the two-wheeled freight train, just as a 13-ball crashed out a window and rolled under a car. Shouting followed.

Suddenly, Chance was back in the rude reality of the barroom scene. He wondered why the hell everyone didn't just go home and fuck. They'd have a much better time. They'd spend less money and snatch fewer DUIs and fights. He bounded into the dingy bar as the young Marine charged Vince with a swinging pool cue.

"He knew it was a scratch shot!" the kid screamed, tearing around the pool table toward Vince.

Chance instinctively knew what was going to happen as he turned to hear Vince's side of the story, while the other patrons ducked for cover and backed against the wall. Vince pulled his leather fanny pack around until it rested under his belt buckle and unzipped it. Vince was cocky beyond belief.

"No!" Chance shouted, rounding the corner of the table.

Vince yanked a massive .45-caliber H&K from the leather-tooled sack, in a practiced defense motion. The semi-automatic cannon was loaded and cocked. He crouched slightly, shifted his feet into a firing position and dropped two spare clips onto the pool table, as if preparing for a running gun battle. The fat blonde screamed.

Vince calmly released the safety. The kid charged, drew the cue stick back in a blind rage and let it rip. Chance cut in front of Vince pushing the muzzle off target. The gun went off and shattered bar-back bottles and the window behind the bartender. The bent cue whistled in the air until it smacked Chance's left palm with a nasty slap. Chance hit the kid in the throat with the web of his free right hand. The kid's forward movement halted, and his knees buckled. Chance looked back at Vince as the patrons screamed and dove behind the pool table. The youngster gasped and fell to the seedy deck.

Vince spun the opposite direction and scanned the joint for the Marine's partner. He was nowhere to be found.

Chance yanked Vince upright. "Goddamnit, you're fucking with my vibe!"

"It was self-defense," Vince said while the patrons kissed the molding carpet around him. "He threw a pool ball at me, and would have hit me with that cue."

"I don't give a fuck," Chance hollered. "We've got to get the hell out of here."

A siren could be heard in the distance.

Vince knelt down to retrieve the clips, slipped them into the sack at his waist and stood casually. Watching for any movement on the other side of the table, he backed toward the door.

They hurriedly fired their bikes and blasted into the street.

"What's for breakfast?" Vince hollered over the screaming machines.

"Pancakes," Chance returned, looking in his vibrating rear view mirror for cops and angry boyfriends. "In Arizona!"

-3-

SURROUNDED

The lingering full moon dipped below the harbor's horizon as the duo crept into Chance's fenced backyard and shut down their bikes. It was 3:30 a.m. The cops watched the streets of San Pedro for Chance and Vince after the fireworks at The Spot. Drunk, they scooted through alleys and side streets to the rented stucco pad Chance called home.

Chance enjoyed the industrial seaside community where he moved less than six months before and rented a 1937 bungalow. San Pedro housed the Port of Los Angeles, the largest port facility in the world. Nearby was the competing Long Beach Harbor, which kept 'em both on the move. But San Pedro wasn't like the other high-dollar beach cities adjacent to L.A. that would have the two riders constantly cited for loud pipes, beanie helmets, no turn signals, you name it. San Pedro was an old union town, and most of Chance's neighbors enjoyed the protection a couple of gun-toting bikers offered the street-gang-riddled neighborhood. A wheelie on a loud locomotive chopper, down the length of the narrow street wouldn't render a report to any white-bread citizens' safety league. If a community group existed, their agenda would focus on gang gunshots tallied every night.

As a kid, growing up in Long Beach, Chance heard talk of San Pedro stabbings. It was the place to hang for violence. Stevedores, long-shoremen and merchant marines made small Spanish bungalows their homes in the early '30s. Now, most of the one-bedroom clapboard build-ings, stacked side by side like mining tenement houses, were homes for young, stubborn, single, uneducated mothers trying to make ends meet.

After a couple of cups of coffee, Vince planned to slither north along the jagged coast to his apartment.

"I'll bet ya $20 you won't make it," Chance said, watching Vince pull his bike out of the tall-fenced backyard.

"Fuck it," Vince said, patting the .45-caliber H&K in the satchel on his hip. "That's a bad bet, you babe-chasin', broke bastard. We don't have 20 bucks between us, but I'll make it."

He did a burnout and shot across the sidewalk, off the curb and into the street.

"I'll call ya later," he hollered, and blasted up the street, rattling windows with his exhaust.

Chance shook his head as he rolled his long chopper in the side door to the garage. He'd modified the rickety old garage to hold only his bike. He buttoned up the garage doors facing the street so bike thieves wouldn't have easy access. They'd be forced to break into the yard first, where he could lay down a clear line of fire from his riot pump shotgun. They'd be trapped like dogs stumbling into the city pound.

He thought about wild-assed Vince's love life. Vince and Nicole were a most unlikely pair. Yet even though he never seemed to shut up and she could hardly speak any English, they got along.

"I don't cares," she muttered when Vince suggested that he might start a harem. An oddball chemistry existed between them, like something black and white, they represented good and evil.

The mating gene eluded Chance. He wanted to find a woman who fit him, wouldn't fight him, rode with him instead of on him, enjoyed pinto beans, jalapeños and tequila on cold nights, and could keep up and contribute when there was shit to do. He locked up the garage and meandered into his kitchen from the rear of the house.

He walked through the dining room and opened the dilapidated front door for a view of the harbor and noticed a note taped on the door: "Sorry about the cop. When will I see you again? —Susanne." As it turned out, she worked at a local fish and chips joint down the hill from Chance's Pedro ghetto home.

He crumpled the message in his hand but didn't throw it into the trash-strewn gutter. It wasn't because of his civil consciousness. He couldn't let go, even though he had known her less than a couple hours. They spoke fewer than 25 words, but her taste, smell and wispy softness stuck to his senses. He had a thing about women. He liked the connection.

He went back inside his project home. It needed a great deal of work.

Chance threw his jacket and gloves on a chair and wandered outside to retrieve the mail from his Sportster gas tank mailbox. He added the bills to the ever-growing, knee-high pile in the corner, then came across a greeting card sporting feminine handwriting.

Setting everything else aside, he opened the card. The words floated on a cloud of perfume drifting off the page. "Hello darling, it's been so long, I thought I would fly out to the coast. I know you don't remember, but my birthday is on Friday. I'll call you. My dream is to spend all day in bed. Love, Karen."

It was Tuesday morning and there was still a mist on the harbor. Soon the sun would crank up its throttle and burn off the nighttime moisture. Chance thought about his constant dilemma with women. He wasn't a bad looking guy, but he wasn't Tom Selleck, either. He loved romance and wanted to find a woman who would share the adventure but not destroy his freedom. Until the day the marrow in his bones melted at the sight of his woman, he would test the waters, search and experience. Trouble was, each woman who entered his life left her mark on him. He'd collected too many sexual tattoos to count.

The phone rang as he pondered the week, looking forward to Karen's arrival.

"Hey, wonderful. Whatta ya doin'?"

Chance recognized the voice immediately. "Alison, how are you?"

"I'd be better if we could spend a few hours together," she said.

"Of course, baby. What's on your mind?"

Alison was a hot model from Marina del Rey. She had been through a bout with cancer and lost her career as a dancer. She picked up a gig at a car dealership to assist as she paid off her medical bills. Chance helped her out as long as he could. She was crazy for him, in spite of his indifference. She always thought she had a chance with him. She, too, was looking for love.

"I'll see you tonight," she purred and hung up.

Chance was going to say, "I might not be around," but she was already gone. He made his way down the hall and turned into a small closet housing his fax machine, computer printer and CD player.

"Music, goddamnit!" he barked at his cat, Gumba, and flicked on the power. Oldies spilled out and slithered from room to room on the hardwood floors.

While turning to leave, he noticed that his fax machine was blinking and bent to retrieve a sheet of paper from the tray. The note began with a twist: "I can't stand the snow any longer. I must leave. Will you still be there for me? Can I come to visit?"

Chance was confused, then realized who sent it, a buxom brunette from Wyoming who worked with a chain of women's spas. After years of being trapped in an ugly marriage, she broke away, scooped up her two teenage girls and kicked off a new life. For the last couple of years, she'd done an admirable job of making the most out of each day. Step by step, she built a clientele selling products to spas. Then she bought her own salon. Chance met her on his way to Sturgis, South Dakota, one year and they had been in touch ever since.

Chance sat on the edge of the bed and began to remove his boots when he heard a banging on the front door. He rushed to see who it was. With one hand on the door knob and a snub-nosed .38 in the other, he peered through the glass block adjacent to the jam. Suddenly he let go of the knob. The banging intensified.

"I know you're in there!" the woman shouted, her flaming red hair dancing around her shoulders. She was tall, with just the right amount of ass coupled with perfect double Ds.

"You sonuvabitch, come out! I know you were seeing someone else and I can prove it."

Chance backed away from the door. She was his nemesis, the terminator of his heart. He never saw another woman as long as he was with her, but her jealous rages drove a wedge between them, like a semi-truck between two scooters. For some strange reason, the fire still raged, but Chance knew this one could literally kill him like a .45 slug between the eyes. He took another step back and wondered why he was so attracted to her. He knew deep down he could never have her. Although he'd once felt she was the one, she wasn't. He'd put 60 miles between them, but it wasn't nearly far enough. It wasn't over.

He'd left his last wife for her, but it didn't work. If only they could have fixed the electrical charge between them, like yanking the cable off a car battery. If only...

Chance sat on the edge of his tattered couch and listened to her batter the door. He couldn't open it to acknowledge her screaming or argue with her. It wouldn't work. For all his power and passion in other circumstances, he was out of his element, out of control, at sea and rudderless with this woman. His mind slipped from woman to woman. He was lost, in love with them all, wishing one would fill his every dream and wondering if he could ever be satisfied with only one.

For all his passion, Sheila was a psycho, a madwoman with the tits and chemistry to destroy men. It took Chance two years, half of everything he owned, and his last marriage to realize this rip tide would never fade into calm seas.

«« — »»

Vince screamed along the coast as amber streaks cut the darkness and lit the splashing waves slapping the rocky cliffs. The streaks of gold bounced off the vast ocean like the roar of his pipes against the unforgiving asphalt. The rich coastline was jagged and wandering. The farther he pulled away from the San Pedro side of the point jetting south along the Pacific, the higher the home prices became.

In the dwindling darkness ahead, he spotted a series of bright lights. There was only one traffic light in five miles and occasional lights from homes, so the blinking emergency lights were unusual. He studied them through narrow tinted glasses. It could be a fire or a seaside accident. He rounded another curve and could make out the blue lights of a police car, then another and realized he was heading directly for a roadblock.

His thundering exhaust caught the ears of the officers and they shifted into full alert. Vince downshifted and leaned inland at the next street. Sirens wailed in the distance as he aimed the black Softail toward the hills and scrambled to escape. He goosed the throttle as the black-and-whites rounded the corner at the bottom of the hill. He knew immediately that if he tried to outrun them, they would call in helicopters and he would be finished.

He rounded a strip mall, zipped along the dark storefronts, then between two buildings and behind a dumpster. He skidded to a stop, shut off the bike and walked into an all-night grocery store. He found the pay phone and called Chance. His answering machine picked up.

«« — »»

At that moment, Chance faced daunting troubles of his own.

"I know you're in there, you biker piece of shit!" the redhead shouted. Her lipstick was smeared at odd angles, obviously applied in a fit of crazed anger.

Chance stood at a distance and gazed through the muted glass at her tattooed-on eyebrows and fake boobs. He gritted his teeth. He hadn't seen her in months. What the hell was she mad about? On one hand, he wanted to open the door and embrace her. On the other, he would just as soon knock out all her capped teeth. He backed away from the door, away from the insanity of her psychotic passion.

Chance moved down the hall as the phone rang. He collected his Bandit's Bedroll, stuffed some clothes in it and opened the bedroom window. He tossed the bag outside into the weed-coated yard separating the garage from his dinky home. Just before leaving, he picked up the phone and dialed for messages. He had two. He pressed one.

"Hi honey, I called to tell you I just got my boob job and I want to come visit. We need to try 'em out."

Chance recognized the voice as his blond, 22-year-old connection from Northern California. "Please call me," she said and hung up.

He saved the message as the beads of sweat built on his forehead.

The second message began as abruptly as the hammering on the front door.

"Chance, it's Vince. You were right; we've got to get out of town for a while. I'll meet you on the Vincent Thomas Bridge at 90 mph at 5:40."

The phone went dead.

Chance needed to get out of town for a lot of reasons, including too many women. Some would be angry, and one would always be crazed. A few he would attempt to make amends to, but he needed to ride and ride fast. He threw on his leathers, tossed his gloves into the yard and climbed out the window. He made his way through the foot-high weeds and opened the garage as quietly as he could.

He pulled his bike onto the concrete and spun it around to face the gate, which led to a sidewalk directly past the front door. He had no choice. He opened the gate and propped it open silently with a stone. He returned to his wild steel creation. Still warm, it fired immediately.

He tore out of his back yard, leaving the startled, angry redhead screaming on the cracked front porch. Flying off the curb, he thundered down the bluff to Harbor Boulevard, slid to the stop, hung left and cranked.

«« — »»

Vince waited for a half hour, then rumbled quietly out of the back of the mall. Along side streets and through cluttered alleys, he backtracked across town to Chance's stomping grounds near the port. He gradually picked up speed as he neared the street that would take him to the sweeping on-ramp of the Vincent Thomas Bridge, toward the federal prison on Terminal Island.

Chance flew along the harbor heading for the bridge that guided a constant line of 18-wheelers from the west end of the city to the docks on Terminal Island. "Terminal" rolled around in his mind like an omen. Whereas Vince was chased by every San Pedro cop, Chance's problems involved the fairer sex. He looked in his rearview mirror and saw a smoking Jeep Cherokee sliding onto Harbor.

"Damn," he muttered and pulled on the throttle. The 98-inch S&S motor barked and he wheelied through a red light. The crimson Cherokee was fast approaching. In the distance, he could hear the thunder of another motorcycle, the Street Stalker, its shotgun exhaust system barking through the mist. Then he heard a siren. Chance rotated the throttle harshly, like a whip to the devil's steed.

Vince, his jet-black hair streaming behind him, ducked into an alley, trying to evade the cops, then onto Gaffey and down the long ramp to the Vincent Thomas Bridge. Chance swung into the left turn lane on Harbor, sliding sideways, the Cherokee still coming. He blew through the light and up the ramp where a sweeping right would launch him onto the bridge. Leaning low and right into the curve, his footpeg ground hard against the pavement, sending up a shower of sparks. He sensed the fast-approaching black beast, Vince's bike, but something else was in pursuit. A black and white, siren blaring, lights flashing, tore after Vince. Chance poured more coal to the fire, crossing the guiding line, and moving into the number two lane, just as Vince pulled alongside of him. No time to acknowledge each other, they pressed their chests against vibrating tanks and hauled ass.

The Cherokee, which was being driven by the psychotic redhead, hit the on-ramp at breakneck speeds. Frightened by the lifting motion of the top-heavy vehicle, she mistakenly hit the brakes. The lumbering 4-door lifted onto two wheels, banged over the curb-medium and dove onto the bridge sideways, directly in the path of the police cruiser. Mayhem ensued.

Chance and Vince ignored the crashing sounds of twisting metal and breaking glass as they sped away.

Flying over the bridge, the brothers glanced at the shimmering sea beneath them, then flew down the opposite side onto Terminal Island.

The ancient prison facility on their right reached out to them. Two miles and they would slip up over the Darryl Desman bridge onto the Long Beach Freeway, heading inland to the 91, to the 10 and....

"We need a break," Chance yelled to his longtime riding partner over the thundering screams of the two machines.

"Phoenix," Vince shouted back and they turned up the heat.

-4-

Escape to the Desert

Vince, the deacon of street-fighting discipline, never varied his course, not even to catch the golden sunrise just southeast of their direction. He never altered his gaze from the strict and rapid surveillance of the tarmac ahead. He shifted into fifth and blew through the intersection leading to the Henry Ford Bridge inland to Wilmington.

Off to the right, the sunlit sky portrayed a rejuvenated downtown Long Beach, which once housed nothing but sailors, bums and run-down businesses. Vince and Chance swung off to the right and entered the only seaside freeway in the world to house more 18-wheelers than passenger cars. The right two lanes of the Long Beach Freeway testified to the years of abuse with ragged cracked concrete every foot of the way.

The two riders' teeth rattled as the worn pavement struck their rear Avon tires like karate kicks. They quickly navigated into the free zone in the left fast lane. They poured the coals to the two machines. Vince's blacked-out Street Stalker Softail bounced across the lanes like a thoroughbred angling for an inside track. Chance's stretched rigid chopper was 150 pounds lighter than the Softail and the light weight and additional torque blew past Vince. The frame was stretched enough with the long front to flex across the lanes, but it was comfortably at home on a freeway scooting along at more than 90 mph.

Time to roll, and maybe not. Chance and Vince had both danced through two decades as freethinking bikers, hard workers who were tough on women and always on the move. They both were confronting crossroads in life as they thundered out of the seaport area, past the oil fields, now hidden from view, and into the garment district on the outskirts of downtown L.A. At the connector to the 10 Freeway, the brothers nodded at one another as they leaned side by side onto the ramp at 85 mph.

The most deadly force on earth, thousands of careening automobiles, surrounded them. Some 44,000 folks die in car accidents in a year, yet only 5,000 die in motorcycle accidents and just 800 soldiers died in Iraq in a year. The fearless pair played a deadly game of traffic dominos, slithering between tons of jagged steel. Few handle the dangerous steel blades of the car people the way Vince and Chance did, like two Vikings wielding broadswords in a field of an armed enemy. As they moved with traffic, Chance felt something sting his skin. Then a rapid succession of droplets began to smack them. Almost in unison, the two brothers shouted, "Fuck!"

No one heard their swearing above the drowning hum of the zillion wheels driving against unforgiving asphalt. The two-leathered monks hunched over their handlebars to dodge 70 mph raindrops. Visibility diminished as they attempted to escape Los Angeles commuter traffic for the open road leading into the desert.

Los Angeles, like a plague on the golden coastline, spread farther and farther from its roots by the sea, until tentacles reached across the desert to collide with Las Vegas in a shower of neon and pornography, street gangs and movie studios. The eastern limbs reached Palm Springs and beyond, nearing the Arizona border. Chance looked at his chromed front wheel and at the wedge it was driving in the growing pool of water on the grated concrete. It didn't look good, yet they were forced to press on.

If they could maintain a near-hydroplaning speed, they could beat the traffic into the desert and be free of the congestion for the remainder of the ride to the Arizona border. The fresh rain raised grime and oil from the 65-grit surface, which enhanced treachery by reducing traction. Unprepared for the onslaught, they pulled off at a sprawling truck stop at the intersection of the 15 and the 10 freeways. They dodged an 18-wheeler traffic jam as they steered to the pumps and refueled.

"This can't keep up," Vince said, shoving the hose into the 5-gallon fatbob tanks.

"If you kept that fuckin' .45 in your pocket, we wouldn't be a couple of drowned rats running from the floodgates," Chance said.

He unzipped his bedroll and pulled out a sweatshirt and scarf.

Rain already seeped into the roll and small patches of his sweatshirt were damp.

"Fuck it, let's eat," Vince said, "maybe this shit will blow over."

Vince was aware of his violent nature, his unrestrained desire to fight, shoot, and kill. He had survived several near-death experiences. While on his father's Kansas ranch, he nearly lost an arm in a chainsaw accident. And more than once, while riding competition bulls, he was nearly crushed by 2000 pounds of angry muscle.

He joked about the falls, the hospitalizations and the surgeries, but each horn or hoof that nearly split his skull left an emotional mark. Why was he still alive?

Crowded with truckers of all shapes and sizes, the terminal was bustling with activity. Whether it was the traditional pot-bellied driver in a T-shirt and bib overalls, the intrastate shipper in a plaid flannel shirt and Levis rolled up at the ankles over his industrial boots, or the button-down couple studying their charts and spread sheets, they all looked at the dripping wet grungy bikers with disdain.

"Not the day for a ride," said a stout, elderly driver as he sipped his coffee and pulled on the bill of his ball cap.

"Nope," Chance said, pushing Vince toward a booth. They both ordered egg whites and a short stack and stared out the window.

"Where the fuck are we going, water boy?" Vince asked.

"Phoenix," Chance mumbled. "We'll hang out with Myron for a week, until things cool off."

"That's how far?"

"Little over 300 miles from here," Chance said.

Outside, truckers covered their heads with plastic trash bags and ran for their cabs. The two chops were parked within view, as the Code of the West dictated. What began as a gradual, mild rain escalated into a downpour. The sky darkened and drivers turned on their headlights as they pulled away from the station.

"We better hit the road and see if we can outrun this shit," Chance said. "I hope you have some cash."

He paid the tab with a stack of $1 bills. Gas prices were making it hard to be a cheap-livin' biker.

"Fuck," Vince muttered, looking out the window. "We may end up dancing with the Tarantula tribe."

A passing trucker dropped a couple of fresh hand towels on their Formica table.

"You may need these," he said, eyeing the two soaked bike seats under an ever-increasing deluge. Vince looked at him suspiciously, not uttering a word.

"Thanks," Chance said. "Next we'll need trash bag ponchos."

The two bike brothers got up from the table and went to the head, put on every piece of clothing they carried and walked out to the bikes. Their gear was no match for the driving torrent they faced on the interstate. They wiped down the seats, donned their shorty helmets, wrapped bandannas around their faces to prevent the stinging of the rain against their mugs and pulled into the street. It was one of those rare times when, as riders, they didn't think about breakdowns. A breakdown would have been a welcome respite from the water torture that lay ahead.

They rolled tentatively onto the freeway and gradually picked up speed. Visibility was short, but Chance noted a break in the cloud cover. His hopes skyrocketed as the road dried a half-hour later and he nestled in for the 180-mile stretch to Blythe and the Arizona border. Warmth crept through the wet outer layers as they traversed 50 dry miles and were confident that the road ahead was clear.

It was Mother Nature's evil ruse to trap them into thinking the storm had lifted. Almost 200 miles from the city, the tempest jumped them with both feet. Gale winds peeled across the desert freeway, throwing tumbleweeds and sand into the wet mixture. Now they were in a gauntlet of biker hell, reaching for the next safe haven.

Hunkered down against their tanks and with water running off their glasses, further limiting visibility, they tried to make time pushing 85 mph on the two-lane highway. With visibility at a maximum of 50 feet, they pressed into the fold. Chance moved out in front as he approached an 18-wheeler. The turbulence behind the massive, rolling container truck tossed his front wheel from side to side. As he neared, he began to draft the truck. The pocket behind the truck was protected and warm, but riding less than a bike length from a 75-mph semi was as terrifying as returning to the city to face that redhead. It sucked him closer like she would, given half a chance.

Chance moved to the left corner and into a turbulent zone. Suddenly the spray off the wheels consumed the bike and reduced visibility to a short 5 feet, and the spray from the cab ate the remaining visibility. He squinted, he couldn't see any more than a few feet ahead, until he cleared the rumbling cab and was once more tossed by the desert cross winds.

He had no choice but to twist his quick throttle and pray that nothing happened before he cleared the massive front wheels. With every truck he passed the wind hit home as he rounded the steel rear corner. Chance whipped back and forth, as he held his breath, squinted and rounded massive 23-inch diameter wheels capable of hauling 80,000 pounds of cargo, then the gale was suddenly blocked by the thundering vehicle. Chance's-500 pound monster stood up straight as storm gusts were momentarily abated, only to be engulfed with the spray from the cab wheels.

His quivering speedometer indicated nearly 90 mph in a blinding downpour. Quickly, the thundering stroker passed the trailer and the bike was windblown to the left once more, only to straighten again behind the cab. Then slapped with wheel spray and smacked with gale force winds again, he pulled into the open and improved visibility. He survived one more of hundreds of trucks to be passed ahead.

Vince mentally crossed himself as he passed each semi. He wasn't religious, though his parents were Catholics. Yet the thought of crossing himself gave him hope when entering a notoriously rough rider zone, where one false move could thrust a biker into a blender of careening metal and rain water.

Some 70 miles out, Chance sensed that he had lost Vince and pulled off the freeway. Vince showed up five minutes later and they rode to a gas station.

Stumbling into the store, Chance looked at a display of white socks. He bought a pair and struggled to pull off his soaked leather cowboy boots. He tossed the old holey socks into the trash and donned the new ones, sitting in front of a gas stove. For a few moments, Vince and Chance felt the comfort of heat against their frozen feet, but they couldn't thaw.

Time was clicking and they had to make Phoenix and catch Mad Myron, who owned the Billet Bar and a bike shop on Scottsdale Road. He was their only hope for shelter. If they missed him, his crew couldn't catch the stocky weight lifter until the next morning and the two drowned rats would become Phoenix homeless.

They rolled out of the station and back into the freeway mayhem. It wasn't long before they were slipping tires at 90 mph and watching out for 18-wheelers. Chance wasn't concerned about the truckers. He had always found their driving habits to be consistent and predictable. It was the stoner in the compact, packed with enough camping and hiking gear to last him a decade in the wilderness, who worried him. A lump in the road and a paranoid driver with a cell phone in one hand and a doobie in the other could send Vince and Chance dancing in the cactus.

With some relief, Vince peered over his narrow sunglasses, as a state billboard along the freeway reported only 7 miles to Blythe. Blythe was the last bastion of desert misery before they jumped off California near the Big Maria Mountains and crossed the narrowing Colorado River into the nothingness of the Arizona desert and the Eagle Tail Mountain Range in the distance. One of the largest deserts in the world, the Mojave extended from California through Arizona and Nevada.

Vince indicated that he was leaning off the freeway and the two riders rolled to the right and into a Mobil station. Their new socks were already soaked. Their feet were frozen, fingers numb, and faces pale from the chill of the constant rain. Cold was beginning to penetrate their bones as they pulled into the station lot and 15 inches of water. They had little choice but to step off their riding pegs into the gray pool.

Their motors sizzled as water reached hot crankcases. They filled the bikes quickly and darted into the station to pay. Vince spotted trash bags and suggested that they cut holes in the bottoms to form ponchos. Sloshing through calf-deep water, they mounted their steeds and rolled back onto the freeway. Ponchos made of trash bags worked but only if duct taped to the rider's torso. At 90 mph, with some 160 miles to go, the green plastic flapped wildly in the wind. Shortly into the ride, the plastic shredded, slapping the riders in the face. Regardless, there was no stopping at that point.

The weather and visibility deteriorated, the traffic slowed and the temperature dropped. Chance could feel the water in his Justin boots splashing from side to side, but the one thing that never gave an inch was his Dicey chopper. It hummed a defiant tune at the pavement, screaming at the rider to keep the throttle twisted on hard. It was as if the motorcycles were challenging the riders to stay glued to their saddles for the final miles.

Traffic bunched up 50 miles west of Phoenix, and Chance and Vince felt the onslaught of another metropolis rearing its ugly head. Drivers unaccustomed to wet weather swerved, braked and drove too slow. Both Chance and Vince felt the numbing effects of hypothermia as they reached the outskirts of the desert city, then tried to navigate the flooded side streets. The water ran up and over their boots at every intersection.

At the next stop, Chance looked over at his workout partner. Vince was pale and tired, his eyes distant.

"Wake up, goddamnit!" Chance shouted and slugged him.

"What?" Vince said, his eyes brightening.

"We're not far, brother," Chance shouted above the roar of the traffic, the pelting rain and the thunder of the powerful v-twins. "Hang in there, goddamnit."

Ten minutes later, they pulled into the parking lot of the Billet Bar. Legs stiff, the bikes wobbled. Vince slipped up beside him and kicked out his kickstand. Stepping off the bike, he almost fell into 3 inches of water flooding the parking lot. Chance struggled to get off his bike as a buffed brute emerged from the Billet Bar.

"What the fuck?" Myron shouted. "Get your asses in here!"

Chance sloshed inside. As he shook Myron's hand, he looked over the weight lifter's stout shoulder. The bar was empty except for a girl in the corner drinking a margarita on the rocks.

Chance was wet and chilled to the bone, and as the girl looked up, he felt himself begin to shake. She turned on her barstool, her red hair sparkling under the halogen bar spots.

"Thought you could get away, didn't you?" she said.

Chance spent New Years with Sheila in Phoenix two years ago, but he couldn't figure it out. Why would she go to these lengths?

Chance's eyes widened and he slowly backed out into the rain, terrified.

"What's wrong?" Myron asked.

"She's here," Chance said.

As Chance turned slowly, not knowing what to do, a police cruiser slammed into the lot. Flashers blinking in the dismal gray, a blip of siren startled the riders. Two officers jumped from the car and grabbed Vince, who was trying to take the bedroll off his bike and get out of the rain. The officers shoved Vince against the stucco building and scattered his belongings onto the wet pavement.

"People are looking for you, asshole," hollered the officer with a sizeable beer gut.

Chance looked back at Myron. "Nowhere to run, nowhere to hide."

-5-

ARIZONA IMPOUND

Chance stood outside the Billet biker bar in the driving rain, wondering which way to turn. Myron, the stocky, weightlifting bar owner, stood aside as the fuming redhead strode directly into the deluge, shouting at the top of her lungs.

"You did it, you bastard. If it wasn't for you I wouldn't have slit your girlfriend's tires."

On the brink of hypothermia, surrounded by cops, nearly broke and standing in the rain, Chance was lost. He licked the moisture building in his bushy mustache and spit it on the ground.

Myron talked to the cops while they loaded Vince into the back of the cruiser, but his words had little effect. He knew several local cops, but it didn't help this time. Shortly thereafter, a tow truck pulled in and loaded Vince's bike for a short ride to the police impound lot.

Chance ignored the screaming bitch and said to Myron, "We don't have a dime. I can't bail him out."

"Any interest in selling your rigid?" Myron asked. He was a retired outlaw, had owned a couple of World Gyms in the Phoenix area, then a bike shop, and more recently, a bar. He knew how to make money.

"Ya know," Chance hesitated and looked over at his shiny chopped pride dripping a constant stream of rainwater, then back at Myron. "I suppose. Anything for a brother, right?"

"I may know someone who'd jump on it."

Chance was soaked to the bone. He shivered with cold and fatigue. Sheila saw her opportunity and ran to his side. He took a step backward and stumbled over the parking lot block, almost falling through the picture window in front of Myron's bike shop.

"What do you want?" Chance asked as she wrapped her arms around his neck and tugged him against her slim form. The effect was enhanced by the dark streaks of running mascara.

"You know what I want!" Her eyes pleaded but her mouth turned to rage. "It's all your fucking fault," she spat and pounded her small fists against his chest. "I could never trust you. I hate you. I hate you!"

He leaned against the rough stucco, his shades dripping rainwater.

"If you hate me, just leave me alone," Chance muttered.

He was still attracted to her, but her furious outbursts were too much bullshit. He knew they would only escalate. He was his own man and had never taken abuse from any woman. This constant harangue was all new to him.

She stormed back into the bar, grumbling about Chance being unfaithful, and grabbed her purse. Myron, behind the bar, using the phone, spotted the revolver in her handbag and hung up. She marched out the door of Myron's recently remodeled bar. He followed her and locked the door. "She's nothing but trouble," he said to himself.

Chance pushed himself for weeks to find solace and separation from this woman. He couldn't understand her effect on him. In the past, if a relationship went wrong or soured, he went his separate way, done deal, move on. But this woman held fast like a lingering addiction, and he found himself smack in the middle of an emotional low. He had to cut a dusty trail before it was too late.

Sparky, the mechanic, punched Chance in the shoulder. "Wanna get that sled out of the rain before it floats away?"

"Yeah."

"Is it unlocked?" the gray-bearded mechanic asked.

"Yep," Chance said. "Ready to ride."

Sparky looked the big man over, saw a graying in Chance's usually warm skin tone and noticed how his legs buckled from time to time.

"Better get Chance a hot shower and a bed before he falls down," he muttered to Myron, and pushed Chance's bike into the service area.

Myron shoved Chance and their gear into a lowered Chevy pickup and watched Sheila climb into a rented SUV. He drove the back streets of Scottsdale until he was confident she wasn't following, then found a small motel. He registered the big man, tossed him the key and shoved him into the drab stucco room with his bedroll.

Chance managed to mumble, "Thanks," as Myron closed the door and left.

Chance peeled off his rain-soaked jacket and it fell to the deck like a Pacific seal flopping alongside a tide pool. He stripped out of his clothes then noticed that his bedroll was completely wet and so were all the clothes.

He called the manager's office. The cleaning staff was gone. He took a hot shower, then another one. He discovered that he was so cold that while he allowed the hot spray to thaw his front, the rear was shivering. He shifted back and forth, then again, until he heard a knock on the door.

A short, dark-haired Hispanic girl stood at the door, the rain still pelting the asphalt behind her. She suspiciously eyed the tall, muscular, man dressed only in a towel, then a smile crossed her face and her dark eyes opened wide.

"You have clothes to dry, señor?"

Chance tried to focus on her dimpled cheeks and smooth complexion. The penetrating warmth of the shower had enhanced his deep fatigue.

"Uh, yep, you're right, come in," he said, not realizing that he was nearly nude.

She hesitated and followed. Quietly, she gathered up his belongings and Vince's and left.

The phone began to ring between the two beds and Chance flopped down to answer it. "Yep?" he said.

"Hey, it's me," Vince said. "You've got to get me out of here."

"I'm working on it," Chance said. "What's the bail?"

"I need a couple of grand," Vince said from inside a polished corridor without windows. He was in the Phoenix City Jail.

"What's the deal?" Chance said.

"I don't know," Vince said. "They didn't have anything on me until they booked me, but I'm fuckin' wet and cold."

"Whatta ya mean, until they booked ya?"' Chance snapped.

"Well, these cops started pushin' me around, so I popped one. Then they worked me over and stuck me in this cell with this thug who started asking a lot of questions. I refused to answer so he started to get rough, and we went at it. I held my own, but now they want to press more charges. Maybe he was an informant."

Vince's voice was anxious. "You've got to get me out of this fuckin' place."

"I'm working on selling my bike," Chance said.

"Fuck, that's no good," Vince said. "Oh, fuck, I've got to go," and the phone went dead.

Chance hung up and it immediately started to ring again.

"Yeah?" Chance said.

"The bike is sold," Myron said. "I'll have the cash in an hour."

"I'm waiting on dry clothes and we've got to get him out," Chance said. "Call me in two hours, I need some sleep."

Myron hung up and Chance began to pace the small room. The phone rang again.

"Yeah?" Chance said.

"You can't hide from me!" The shrill voice was like a dagger to Chance's inner ear. "It's your fault all of this happened."

Chance listened but he couldn't believe what he was hearing. What did she want from him? She didn't say, she never did. She screamed, threatened, blamed, but there never was a solution.

"Leave me alone, Sheila."

She'd been a hot lover, but not much of anything else. Parting seemed to be a problem. She knew where he was staying. Chance figured there would be more trouble and soon. He was so tired he could barely reach for the phone again, but inside panic wrestled with the fatigue. He called the front desk.

"Can I speak to the girl from housekeeping?"

The operator connected him with the extension. The phone rang and rang. Nothing. He hung up the phone and passed out. Two hours later, Myron called back.

"The cash is here."

Chance awoke with a start and mumbled a cotton-mouthed response, "Oh, OK, I'll be along."

He called the desk again. They transferred him to housekeeping—nothing. He waited, nervous and tired, trapped in a towel, in a bland motel room. He knew the redhead was coming. He could sense her evil spirit.

There was a knock on the door. Chance jumped, then tried to read the knock. Was it aggressive? Was it malicious? Was it the tender knock of a soft-eyed Hispanic girl with ample breasts and a brilliant smile?

He opened the door with a jerk and prepared for the worse. He saw the Mexican girl standing before him, her arms stacked high with the neatly pressed and folded clothes. He whisked her inside, paid her bill, tipped her heartily and showed her to the door. She looked disappointed.

Chance opened the door as a SUV pulled up in front of the motel lobby and slid to a stop on the wet pavement. It was Sheila. Chance pulled the girl toward him. She spun and her chest smacked his bare skin. Their eyes met. If only this happened under different circumstances.

"Do you have a car?" Chance asked and looked over her shoulder as Sheila jumped out of the driver's seat and entered the small lobby.

"Si," the girl said, looking deeply into his eyes.

"Can you give me a ride, quick? I just need to put on some clothes."

"Si," she said, her smile broadening. Her dark nipples became aroused and pressed stiffly against the fabric of her uniform.

The little Mexican girl with the long, flowing dark hair ran to her car as Chance pulled on his Wranglers, a sweatshirt, his wet cowboy boots and his soaking vest.

She met him in front of his room in a small pickup. Chance jumped in and ducked as Sheila climbed into the SUV and peeled out, looking for his room. The young girl attempted to leave, but the speeding truck tried to run her into the motel shrubbery.

"Dios mio!" the young girl said, avoiding a crash by inches and speeding into the street. Chance tried to stay down and out of sight.

"Senorita, su loco esposa?"

"No, she's not my goddamn wife, and won't ever be my wife. What's your name?"

"Maria," she said.

Chance sat up and gave her directions to the shop.

"I will see you tonight, no?" Maria said.

"What's your number?" Chance said. "I'll call."

Chance kissed her on the cheek and uncoiled his lanky form from the compact truck.

"I've got the cash," Myron said and they jumped in his truck for the cop shop at the far end of town. When the two riders arrived, Vince was standing on the corner in the drizzling rain.

"What's up?" Chance shouted as they pulled to the curve.

"Seems they cut me a deal," Vince started. His olive features were lumpy with cuts and bruises.

"No charges, clean slate in exchange for my motorcycle. If not, the bail is $100,000 and I sit in jail until trial. I've got to get the fuck out of here!"

"What?" Chance said in dismay as Myron pulled his lowered truck away from the police station. Vince sat in the back rumble seat still cloaked in wet clothes. Out of shouting distance from the headquarters, Chance said to Myron, "Pull over."

"What?" Myron said.

"Pull over, goddamnit," Chance said, gritting his teeth. Chance turned in his seat and faced his brother in the rear of the extended cab. Vince looked beaten and cold. He was dejected and distraught. The cops had twisted the charges until he was convinced that his life was gone, to be spent for decades behind bars. As a felon, the attack on the officer and his cellmate could constitute a three-strikes offense. He could be forced to spend the rest of his life behind bars.

"So," Chance said, cross-eyed with anger, "I sold my motorcycle to get you out of jail and you trade your own bike for freedom. You realize that we're both out of bikes."

"I'm sorry, brother, but I didn't know what else to do. They were throwing the three strikes beef at me. What the fuck could I do?" The wise-ass Vince felt the fangs of justice around his neck.

"How about call an attorney, for one?" Chance said.

"I can't afford an attorney," Vince said.

Chance got out of the truck and stood on the drying pavement.

"I've been in fucked-up situations before, but this one takes the cake."

"I may be able to get your chopper back," Myron said to Chance and started the truck. "It's still at the shop. The new owner hasn't picked it up. I'll see what I can do."

"Best news I've heard so far, today. Then we've got to get that Street Stalker out of impound," Chance said, turning to Vince. Vince looked at him, a hopeless expression crossing his dark mug.

They drove along in silence, heading back to the shop. Chance looked out the windshield at the dark clouds moving quickly away from the long, Valley of the Sun. Chance brightened.

"I've got it. I remember a story a Hells Angel told me about how he got into a jail to visit a brother."

"Did it do him any good?" Myron asked.

"Nope, got a free donut and pissed off the captain," Chance said. "But the plan is a good one. We just need a licensed repo man. Know one?"

They pulled up to the shop and Myron returned the cash to the safe minus $200, which he split between Vince and Chance. He handed the chopper registration to Chance. Relieved, Chance returned to the service area to make sure the bike was still in Sparky's care.

"I knew you'd be back for it," Sparky said, wiping down the coffee-brown stretched rigid with the dice painted on the tank.

"I rolled the dice this time and they came up seven," Chance said, and patted the wet leather seat.

Myron called some ex-partners and quickly a rider/repo man showed up at the shop in with a flatbed tow truck.

"We've got to move fast," Chance said, looking at the burley rider's repo business card. It had an official Phoenix Police shield emblazoned in the corner and said CDI in the center with his name beneath it and the title "investigator."

"I don't want to go into that yard," Big Al said emphatically to Chance.

"Do you ever go into that yard to pick something up?" Chance inquired.

"Nope," Al said, "just make deliveries. Oh, once I had to get a car. I hoisted the wrong one."

"You work with the cops, don't you?" Chance asked.

"Yeah, and once in a while they need to move a vehicle that needs to be fingerprinted," Al said, his eyes beginning to sparkle with inspiration. "I'm not sure, though."

"We don't have time to ponder the downside, we need that bike this afternoon," Chance said. "Let's get to Kinko's."

Ten minutes later, Chance was back with a laminated official-looking card. He pulled his hair into a ponytail, put on a clean shop mechanic shirt and headed to the tow truck.

"What can I do?" Myron asked.

"Vince will take my bike back to the motel, get cleaned up, and load the bike. He can ride it to where Scottsdale Road intersects the freeway and wait for me," Chance explained. "If I'm not back in one hour, you may need to sell it again for my bail. Otherwise, we'll be on our way out of town. We need to get across the border into California before the cop with the busted nose knows he didn't score a bike. Myron, watch for that redhead."

"She's not a problem," Myron said with a glint in his eye. He'd rather slap her around than look at her.

Chance jumped into the cab next to Al.

"You won't have to do or say anything until we get to the bike, if it's there. If anything goes wrong, just blame the situation on me."

"I'll be holding my breath," Al said.

"Do you know the guy at the gate?" Chance asked.

"Usually," Al said.

"Then just be cool and familiar," Chance said as they pulled up to the impound yard.

They rounded the corner to the gate, the large flatbed diesel jerking as Al stumbled nervously through the gears. The truck screeched outside the guardhouse. An officer came out of the office.

"Nothing to deliver, Al?"

"Nope," he said. "We need to pick up the Harley that was delivered a couple of hours ago, for fingerprinting."

"There's a lot of interest in that bike," the officer said. "Some detectives have already been over a couple of times to look at it."

"That's right," Chance said, "the owner may be going down for the final time."

"Who are you?" the officer said, looking directly at Chance.

"Milfred Hogan, CDI," Chance said and handed him the laminated card.

"All right Al," the officer said, "another biker down. It serves those bastards right."

The clanking gate rose and the truck lurched
forward, Al's gears grinding.

"We need to move fast," Al said. "He may call the station and confirm."

"I'll jump out and ready the bike. You get this puppy in position," Chance said.

Chance leapt to the asphalt and looked around at the dusty, muddy array of vehicles waiting for their guilty owners to pay for their freedom. The black Street Stalker stood proudly, surrounded by rusting hulks. Even after 400 miles of rain, the bike glistened. Chance pulled on the handlebars, his worst nightmare realized. The bike was locked.

"Fuck!" he said. The sharp word stung at Al's back and he turned.

"The bike's locked," Chance said. They were burnin' daylight and his nerves were on edge. "Bolt cutters?"

Al turned and tossed something to Chance. The bolt cutters landed at Chance's feet. He snatched them off the damp pavement and bent to take care of business while the compressor spun and the air pressure system tilted the bed of the tow truck.

Chance pushed the Harley to the center of the bed, then backed up and pushed it onto the ramp. With the rear wheel a few inches onto the slippery grating. Chance pulled the front brake lever hard to hold it in position on the greasy diamond plate surface. But the oily surface wouldn't hold and the bike slid off the ramp.

Al couldn't help. He had to operate the controls behind the cab. Chance pushed again and this time the front wheel slid an inch sideways and the bike almost went down. The desert sun's heat intensified as the afternoon reached its Arizona peak at over 90 degrees. Both men began to sweat profusely. The officer in the office opened the door and looked in their direction.

Chance backed the bike off slowly, trying desperately to appear professional as he attempted to push the bike onto the ramp once more. Inside, panic was getting on the emotional elevator and pushing the button for the penthouse suite.

"Don't you ever clean this sonuvabitch?" Chance muttered under his breath, as the officer stepped into the sun 25 yards away.

"Yeah, I do, but I picked up a wrecked Mercedes this morning and it dumped its entire oil supply onto the bed. Didn't have time to steam-clean the bastard."

Chance pushed with all his might, holding the bike dead center and straight. The front wheel impacted the grating and rolled straight up. As the rear wheel hit, Chance threw his right leg over the saddle and sat down while applying the front brake. "Hit it!"

Al threw the lift lever. The front wheel jerked, slid an inch on the oily steel surface, then stopped.

As the bed leveled, Chance dismounted and moved the Softail forward and secured it with a wooden chock. Al moved swiftly around the bike, tossing Chance straps that he adeptly fastened while Al cinched each fiber tie.

The officer stepped several paces from the air-conditioned office and stopped. He could see the men working efficiently around the flatbed. The impound duty was one of the worst on the force, and he couldn't wait for his time to end. It was a boring, uneventful job that took little effort, no intelligence, and generally was a slap in the face. He wanted to move into the detective ranks quickly and this station wasn't furthering his career. Besides, he didn't need to work up a sweat in this rare Arizona humidity. He turned as he heard the phone in the office ringing.

Chance and Al both boarded the truck simultaneously and Al shoved it into gear. They rolled to the gate and Al waved at the officer as he reached for the phone. He picked up the receiver and said, "Hold please." Then he pushed the button to open the gate and Al pulled into the street.

«« — »»

Vince showered, changed clothes, loaded Chance's chopper and hit the pavement for the rendezvous point. The rigid felt strange to Vince after riding the Softail for two years. He pulled into the gas station with his bedroll strapped to his back.

Moments later Al drove the tow truck behind the station. They unloaded the Stalker quickly. Al watched from the cab as the two men switched and loaded their bikes. They refueled the motorcycles, put on their jackets, vests, gloves, and shades, and fired them to life.

"No where to run, nowhere to hide," Vince said straddling his bike.

Chance fired the rigid to life and pulled alongside the tow truck cab. "Al, we couldn't have made it without you."

He waved and dropped the stroker into gear. Without waiting for a response, the two riders dropped out of the station and headed toward the freeway.

Al was two miles from the station when the Phoenix police pulled him over.

-6-

DESERT OASIS

It had been a rough couple of months for the two riders as they hit the hot desert freeway heading south then west away from Phoenix, rolling toward the California border. Although they were running from the Phoenix P.D., a psycho broad and the San Pedro cops, Chance was anxious to find something. His first thought was to jam back to the coast, but that wouldn't work. He needed to pay his rent and there was no job waiting in the harbor.

Vince looked at his vibrating watch, then at his speedometer. They cruised along conservatively, just above the speed limit, unlike their usual brazen selves. They were tired and uncertain. They'd been beat on, rained on, shoved around, almost lost their bikes, and they instinctively knew that heading back to Los Angeles was a mistake. Yet they had little money and choices were limited. Mexico perhaps?

Chance's bike sputtered 35 miles west of Phoenix. They were almost to Tonapah, a dried-up truck stop in the middle of the flat, vacant desert.

Vince looked over at Chance, then back at his watch. He needed to call Nicole and let her know what had happened to him. Chance shouted against the hot wind, "What's the deadline?"

Vince shrugged and Chance's rigid coughed again, then died completely. He raked the throttle back and forth, and the bike sputtered to life. They could see the turnoff looming ahead in a haze of heat shimmering off the asphalt, a traveler's oasis rising out of the sand.

Just as soon as the bike fired and Chance accelerated, it coughed again. He jerked the throttle like it was a fishing rod. It sputtered, revived momentarily, then died just as they leaned toward the off-ramp.

Out of the way of screaming 18-wheelers doing 85 to 90 mph along the desolate stretch, the two bikers pulled to the side of the road. Vince slid off the side of his bike and looked at his watch. It was black to match his all-black outfit. The late afternoon sun split the waning clouds like an axe through marshmallows, searing the two riders. It could reach as high as 115 degrees before sundown, and with the morning monsoons, the humidity was kissing Filipino highs. Soon, the wetness would be gone and the sun would suck the life out of anything left unprotected.

"Why do you keep looking at your watch?" Chance asked as he knelt beside the ticking stroker, bewildered at the symptoms.

"I need to call Nicole, you half-witted barnacle. What the hell's wrong with that out-of-date piece of wrought iron? I told you two years ago not to build a rigid."

Chance shook his head. "At least you haven't lost your sense of humor, and the cops didn't beat it out of you. But what's with the watch? You can call her whenever. There are no fucking deadlines out here."

"That's the point. I tried to call from the jail and no one answered. I'm looking at my watch for a clue," Vince said. "We can't go back to L.A. We're broke. And now your shotgun on two wheels has a round jammed in the chamber."

Chance took the gas line off the tank and turned on the petcock. Gas splashed against the hot primary and ran down the side of the bike and onto the smoldering pavement. He reattached the line and disconnected it below the fuel filter with similar results.

"Catch that pussy grinder on fire and we'll be stuck in the desert only to die of heat exhaustion or scorpion bites," Vince said. He walked to his Street Stalker, where he sat sidesaddle and looked at his watch.

"Feels like a fuel problem," Chance said.

Vince pushed his bike another 6 feet away from Chance, took off his vest and his black leather shirt, and put the vest back on over his tanned muscles. Then he strapped his leather fanny pack holding the .45 and spare mags back to his waist. The bruises from his jailhouse beating showed in purple patches.

Chance glanced at Vince and grimaced. He pulled a crescent wrench out of his bedroll and undid the brass fitting on the bottom of the float bowel. Again, gas spilled over the engine and onto the ground between Chance's ratty brown boots. The engine pinged in the sun as an 18-wheeler screamed past, throwing dust, and gravel in all directions. The explosion of 18 tires, and 80,000 pounds slapping the pavement caused Vince to recoil.

"While you're dousing yourself in fuel and praying for that redhead to roll past and throw a match, I'm going to the station to check it out. Remember, the cops are still looking for me, and that insane seductress is looking for you," Vince said.

He spun on his ass to face his bars, flicked the kill switch on, and hit the starter button. In a shower of gravel, he blasted to the top of the overpass and made a left to the Triple AAA Truck Stop on the other side of the freeway.

Some truck stops look professional and well-kept from the freeway when you're tooling along at 90 mph. When an unsuspecting motorist rolls up to refuel, he discovers the true faded and chipped colors. That was the case in Tonapah. The massive neon sign seemed to glisten with franchise quality and plastic luxury from the lanes of the I-10, but on closer inspection, Vince discovered a has-been truck stop with hand-painted, cracked and faded signage. The equipment was in disrepair, the restaurant abandoned, and the shop area a junkyard. The business was obviously hanging by a thread.

Vince pulled up out front, went in the store, and bought a couple jugs of water and a package of Slim's jerky described as "Hotter than the sun, and spicier than her panties," on the outside of the plastic container. Vince cringed and paid for it with change.

The woman behind the counter was Indian and Mexican, and she didn't say much, probably because no one could hear her for the rattling swamp cooler banging against the tin roof over head. Her cash box was still manual and half the keys were busted, but she seemed to know what she was doing. Vince glanced at the half-stocked shelves and thanked the woman.

As he headed for the door, he eyed his watch again, then turned back to the woman. She was handsome for 30 years of sun. She wore a white dress with a gathered top and a ring of Indian embroidery at the bottom. She didn't smile and a hint of a bruise surrounded her left eye.

"Do you know the date, and do you have a pay phone?" Vince asked more loudly than usual.

She shrugged and pointed at a calendar hanging askew on the wall in the service department. It was a stained and abused nudie calendar from 1996. Not exactly what Vince was looking for.

He found the wind-battered pay phone booth outside. It was like a Japanese POW sweat box, perfectly designed to sap the very will from a man's bones. The sand-blasted aluminum and cactus-scratched glass had a Pac Bell sign above it. He dropped in a handful of change and dialed her cell phone number.

"Hello?" the voice answered. It was Nicole.

"You all right, baby?" Vince asked.

"Vin, Vin, is dat you?" she asked in her shattered English. "I'm worried sick."

"It's OK, baby. I'll be back in a couple of days."

"Vin, I'm going to Germany," Nicole said. "I'm bored."

"What? I thought you hated that place and didn't ever want to go home."

"You not doing it for me," Nicole started to explain. "We're broke, I have no friends. I need to go."

Vince was shocked. He thought they were inseparable.

"I've got to go, Vin." She hung up.

"Wait, what do you mean?" Vince said to the dial tone.

He looked out the dirty glass door to the gas islands and the waves of heat, and didn't relish going back outside. His will dwindled like the blood from a run-over jackrabbit. He pushed and the door creaked its discomfort. Then something made a cracking sound inside the store. There was a terrible screech and something was falling.

Vince opened the door to the store and immediately ducked, almost knocking over the half-empty rack of faded area maps. The swamp cooler broke free from its rusting mounts and a corner popped through the corroded galvanized steel roof. Thick, rust-filled water poured from the twisted contraption onto the floor below. The Indian woman crouched behind the counter, and when she emerged, a tear ran down her cheek. Vince looked at the cooling unit, which was coasting to a stop, then at the woman, and finally toward his partner at the overpass.

"I'll be right back," he said. His words echoed off the sheet metal walls. She looked at the ceiling and at Vince, then at the floor.

"Gracias, senor."

Vince jogged to his bike with the water bottles and the pack of jerky, and fired the reliable Street Stalker to life. In a minute, he was beside Chance, who was pushing his bike up the off ramp toward the over pass.

"I need to get out of the sun," Chance said, his shirt soaked with sweat.

He never took off his vest, even in the heat. Vince tossed him the water bottle. He stopped just long enough to break open the jug of chilled water and guzzled the entire quart.

"I take it that rough-hewn nut-hook you call a motorcycle is not fixed," Vince shouted over his shoulder as he turned his bike around. "We may have a job here, though."

Vince spun the black Softail around and came up behind Chance. "Wanna push?"

"Not from you," Chance said, huffing toward the top of the ramp. "Whatta you mean, a job?"

"Nicole is leaving me," Vince said.

"I knew that would happen sooner or later," Chance huffed pushing his 480-pound chopper, "but what about this job?"

The closer they got to the station, the more evident it was that it needed to be bulldozed, not repaired. Besides, repairs in the heat would be next to impossible.

"What?" Chance asked. He was puffing against the thick high-temp air and the effort to push the rigid.

"This broad's air conditioning is out. I told her you could fix it."

The three service bays were vacant except for a '52 Ford truck missing its wheels. No mechanics, though there seemed to be an impressive array of tools, welders and a small bench lathe in the corner.

In the window next to the door was a faded, plastic sign that read: "Help Wanted, Inquire Within." Chance rolled his bike into one of the bays and parked it. He drank more water. It was almost too hot to breathe, let alone work on his motorcycle or consider employment.

Vince went back inside with the woman. "My friend can fix your cooler. How much can you pay us?"

She was visibly excited that he returned, but leery of his tall, dirty blond friend. The store had become extremely hot in just the five minutes since Vince left.

"No mucho dinero," she said, looking skyward as if for help.

"Senor aqui?" Vince asked, wondering where the man of the house was. She seemed to jump and look around. Visibly shaken, she tensed.

"No mas aqui, I hope."

Vince looked at the purple hue around her eye as she recoiled, covering the wound with her hand. Her eyes darted around the floor as if a mouse was loose. She was scared to death. Questions rushed through Vince's mind. Did she own the joint? Will the old man be back? He made a sweeping gesture of the entire facility and asked,

"Esta su casa?"

"Si," she brightened, "mi padre owned it for 30 years."

Chance came in and gazed at Vince and the woman. She was striking, with dark skin and flowing black hair. Chance reviewed the dilapidated store. Most customers opened the door with trepidation, paid their bill as quickly as possible and left. He spotted the tilting swamp cooler and turned back toward the service bay.

"What's the deal?"

"I don't know much," Vince said. "She has an old man, but hopefully he's gone. But he probably took her money. This is her place. She speaks some English. She can pay us something, but not a lot."

"I meant Nicole. What's happening with Nicole?" Chance's green eyes flashed in his direction.

"Haven't the slightest, you meddling old man," Vince said, but his eyes went to his black boot tips. "Ya got me. She says she's going back to Germany. She's a broad. They're all maidens of Mercury. If ya can't buy 'em a new vibrator or a television once a week, they dump ya."

"I'm going to fix my bike," Chance said, shaking his head.

"Wait a minute!" Vince shouted. "We've got to help this woman, besides you're the sex sucker for helping women."

"Two things," Chance said as he turned to face his brother.

"It's gonna be dark soon. If her ol' man returns and doesn't want us around, I want to be able to hit the road, and I can't work on that cooler until the sun goes down."

Vince stood dumbfounded and Chance went back to his bike.

"See if it's all right if I use some tools," Chance said.

He sat on the edge of a greasy lift and pulled off his air cleaner. He ducked under the carb and found the mid-range jet. He removed it with a small socket while he wiped sweat from his brow. He tried to look through the hole, which was the size of a sewing needle, then blew on it. Nothing. It was clogged.

He sucked on the other end. Something popped, and he had a small grain of rust lodged in the back of his throat with a drop or two of gas. Chance choked and gagged, spitting and coughing.

"Jesus, that tastes like shit!" He reached for his jug of water.

Chance replaced the jet, cleaned the float bowl, the air cleaner, and started the bike. He rode it into the sweltering sun, down the frontage road and back. It checked out. Then he pulled back onto the melting asphalt of the truck stop and into a service bay.

"Hey, Vince," Chance shouted.

Vince appeared at the door, sweating profusely. An Arizona Highway Patrolman was rolling up the hill.

"Better move that fuckin' motorcycle."

Vince darted into the sun and jumped the solo seat like a cowboy mounting his horse from behind. He hit the starter and blasted around the building as the officer hesitated at the stop, then rolled across the intersection to wait for a speeding motorist. The officer's window was rolled up tight; the air conditioning on full blast and his radio bleeped and squawked. He never heard the motorcycle.

Behind the station was an extension of the junkyard, containing a myriad of vehicle carcasses, parts and scrap iron. There was also a small home with a Spanish tile roof and sun-bleached plaster surrounded by a grove of sturdy pepper trees that did a half-assed job of shielding the bleak home from the harsh sun. The flaming hubcap in the sky was beginning to head for the another hemisphere and long shadows from the rusting cars and tall cactus reached out across the desert as if the sun's wicked fingertips were trying desperately to hold on and give the dry earth just one final blast of hot breath.

Vince parked his bike under a pepper tree. The news of Nicole's departure was just beginning to seep into his subconscious.

Chance pushed his bike deeper into the service bay, then went inside the store. He pulled the bandanna from his back pocket and shook it out. He noticed the woman react to the flick of his wrist with fear. Chance was dog-tired and could hardly respond. He put the water bottle on the counter and pulled out some cash.

"Do you speak English?" he asked.

"Some," said the woman, who said her name was Rosa. "But I understand what you say."

"Well," Chance said, looking at the tittering swamp cooler still dribbling rusty water on the chipped linoleum floor. "We're dead tired. I'll fix your cooler once the sun goes down, if we can have a bite to eat and a place to sleep tonight."

"I don't have much, but what I have is yours," she said, a glint returning to her eye. "Gracias, senor."

"If you don't mind," Chance said, "I want to make one phone call, and then lie down for awhile."

"Si, si," she said, pointing to the old cradle phone behind the counter.

Chance called the fleabag motel in Phoenix. "Hey, is Maria Cruze in?" There was a long wait, then a young voice came on the line.

"Chance?" she said.

"Yeah," Chance said.

"I heard about the trouble with the law."

"We're okay and we're not far," Chance said.

"Can I help," Maria asked. Her youthful voice revived Chance.

"There's a crazy woman," Chance started

"Where are you?" Maria asked anxiously.

"Baby, did she come back?" Chance asked.

"I haven't seen her."

"Watch yourself and I'll call you tomorrow," Chance said.

"I'm staying with my folks tonight," Maria said.

"That's good," Chance said. "I just wanted to check on you."

Rosa led Chance into the house. The place was simple and neat, with antique furniture and desert landscape paintings. The house was dark to retain what coolness could be captured in the cracked lath and plaster walls. She started another swamp cooler in the back, and soon a cool breeze drifted down the hall. Chance rested on a single bed and was asleep within five minutes. He'd barely removed his boots and vest before he fell asleep.

Vince drank a beer with Rosa in the station and helped her straighten up before going into the house to crash. He, too, was out before he knew it.

They both awoke at 10 p.m. to the smell of refried beans, chorizo, and eggs. They had slept like two dead dogs for five hours. Their bedrolls were neatly placed on the chairs beside their beds. Outside, their bikes were carefully covered with sun-dried tarps. The night was as clear as freshly polished crystal and every star in the galaxy was on display in full multi-watt brilliance. Stillness hung in the air as if the world had stopped rotating and the only sound was the drone of cars and trucks on the highway at the bottom of the bluff.

"Whatta ya gonna do?" Vince said to Chance as the tall man came out of the bathroom. Chance turned toward Rosa.

"Do you have any overalls and a ladder? I need to get on that roof."

She went quietly down the hall to the back of the house and returned with two pairs of overalls. Chance took one pair and threw the other at Vince.

"Get dressed," he said.

He turned to Rosa. "If it's OK with you, I'll fix that cooler with your help finding me tools, and Vince will begin a spring cleaning of this joint. We may be here a couple of days. Whenever we decide to leave, just pay us what you can, OK?"

She looked fresh in the evening coolness, although it was still 80 degrees. Her long black hair was tied in a bun, which pulled it off her shapely neck. She was wearing a floor-length white nightgown that hung off her ample breasts and contoured her supple thighs.

When Chance returned from the bedroom, he took Rosa aside.

"Are these your husband's?" he asked, pulling on the ballooning fabric of the stained overalls.

"Si," she said, her eyes drifting to the floor.

"He must be a monster of a man," Chance said. He tied the vast waist with a chunk of rope and the inseam was almost long enough.

"Big drinker?" he asked.

She cringed. "Yes."

"Been gone long?"

"No," Rosa replied.

Vince sat in the chair and watched the exchange. He thought about Nicole, his Germanic blonde. What happened to her?

Chance and Vince surveyed the front of the shop and hatched a plan. Vince would move the crap away from the front of the shop and into the back, straighten up the service bays, and clean the refueling islands as best he could.

Chance gathered the tools he thought he'd need in a bucket, and with rope in hand, scaled the ladder to the roof, and man-handled the swamp cooler back into position. The support structure had rotted, rusted and crumbled. He made a new one from an old angle-iron bed frame and fastened the cooler again. He oiled the bearings and checked the water fittings. He tightened and tweaked, then slithered down the ladder. It took him a couple of hours.

Inside the store, the two men rearranged the stock and helped Rosa clean the mess from the cooler mishap. By the time they were through polishing the floor, cleaning all the racks, and restocking where they could, the store looked presentable inside.

They closed the service doors and decided to crash for the night. The station was dark. Vince, Chance, and Rosa sat at the breakfast nook, sipped cheap wine, and discussed the next day's projects. They planned to fix Rosa's old pickup. Her husband took the drive gear out of it, so she couldn't leave to buy supplies or even groceries. At 2:00 a.m. they turned in.

At 4:00 a.m. a flatbed tow-truck pulled into the station lot. An enormous bald, farmer-type in bib overalls crawled out of the cab and headed for the last service bay. He scoured through his keys looking for the padlock match.

A grating steel noise awoke Chance. He nudged Vince in the next bed over.

"Get dressed and grab your shit," Chance said.

Chance knocked on Rosa's door tentatively. "Yes?" Rosa said.

"Does your husband carry weapons?" Chance asked.

"I don't know," Rosa said. "He doesn't have much—the drinking."

Vince shot out the door, his hands grappling for the zipper on his fanny pack. He jogged to the back of the tin building and crouched on one knee while pulling the big H&K from its holster.

Chance walked out onto the porch and listened; someone was in the service bay near the pickup. Chance ran to the left and the opposite end of the back of the tin building, and around the corner to the front of the station, as Vince moved stealthily along the side of the service office to the front. Chance was armed with only a Beretta knife.

As they reached their respective corners of the building, they both looked around simultaneously and found a mountain of a drunk releasing tow chains from the back of the flatbed. He was obviously going to attempt to pull the pickup off the lift sans its wheels and onto the diamond plate bed of the truck. The man swayed in his hazy mission to steal the truck. Obviously drunk, he knelt down to coil the chain around a cross-member of the frame under the old truck bed.

That's when Vince couldn't restrain his vigilante presence any longer. He released the safety on the cannon of a pistol, aimed it skyward and fired.

The blubbering idiot stood bolt upright, spotted Vince rounding the distant corner of the building and moved behind his flatbed. Vince stepped out of the shadows and pointed the smoking gun at the man's head.

"What the fuck do you think you're doing blubber-gut?"

Chance pulled his knife and scratched the stubble that covered his face in silence. He was close behind the escaping man and moved closer, silently toward the pickup. He knelt and unchained it from the tow truck.

"Fuckin' bitch lied to me," the big man blathered. "She said I'd make a lot of money out here. She owes me the truck."

Vince was usually loose and easy with his rantings, but he tensed. The big man appeared frightened, but he moved along the bed toward the cab.

Chance stepped out of the darkness as Vince moved in for the kill.

"You dirty, foul-mouthed maggot-pie. I'm gonna put a 180 grain hydro-shock hollow point right between your dilated pupils and bury your alcohol-soaked brain in the desert."

The man, who must have weighed 350 pounds, hesitated as he reached for the door of the cab.

Chance stepped out of the shadows.

"Brother, you okay? This fat chunk of whale lard is nothing to us. Remember the hassle you caused the last time you shot at someone?"

Vince looked as if his destiny was at hand as he squeezed the gnarled pistol grips. His eyes were sharp and focused on his target.

"Come on brother," Chance said. "He's not worth the powder to blow him to hell, as my pappy use to say."

The man didn't respond to the dialog, so Chance moved toward the flatbed.

"You fuckers ain't gonna get my place," The man said and yanked open his driver door. He ducked and reached under the seat

"Mister," Chance perked up, "my riding partner here is awful mad right now. He just lost his girl and he hates liars. He might just move here with Rosa. I suggest you get in your truck and leave here forever."

"Fuck you biker trash," the man said, and pulled a cannon of a revolver out from under his seat.

Chance liked knowing what he was up against. He weighed it out, part drunken bravery, laced with hate. The man ground his teeth and stumbled as he attempted to aim the weapon.

Slow and lumbering he turned toward Vince, and Chance moved out of the shadows, as Vince followed around the stern of the truck, with the H&K ready for action.

Chance hit the big man in the jaw with all he had, grabbed his gun hand, and twisted it out of his grasp. The whiskey effects wearing off, the broken man stumbled and reality returned.

The bulky man leaned against the cab door, as Vince rounded the bed and leveled his .45 at the drunk. It was one of those moments in life that could turn to shit in a blink on an eye, even a drunk one.

"Time out!" Chance said, as he showed the big .44 magnum to Vince. "That's enough of this bullshit."

Chance picked up the tow chain and threw the 25 feet of forged links onto the back of the flat bed. Vince kept moving, cat-like with his .45 was squarely on his target. Chance returned, searched the man, took his wallet, and keys, then returned the truck keys to him.

"Get in and get the hell out of here. We're going to be here awhile. If you so much as cruise by, we'll take your truck the next time."

Chance looked at Vince then back at the old man.

"I know you've been drinking, but did you hear me? My partner's on edge and I don't want anything to happen that either one of you will regret, forever." Then he spotted a set of vintage wheels, with new tires mounted, strapped to the back of the cab. "Just what we need."

The guy's eyes lite up, but Vince was on top of him now and the cannon was still aimed directly between his eyes.

Vince never said a word and Chance was concerned. The notion of Nicole leaving might hit home, and he could snap and unload the .45 into anything that moved.

"Vince, goddamnit, focus" Chance said. "Unstrap those wheels. We need them to get Rosa's truck running." It worked, and Vince's focus altered from a death-ray stare to the classic truck wheels. He snapped the weapon safety to "On."

"Thanks, you're right," Vince said. "I hate to admit it, but fuck it."

Even as the vehicle lumbered out of the lot, Vince pointed his weapon with deadly accuracy at the cab. Slowly, the tow truck disappeared onto the freeway and the two brothers faced one another.

"I could have killed him," Vince said. He was shaking.

"You mean Nicole, don't you?"

Vince was silent. For the first time in the three years Chance had known Vince, he was shaken. He uncocked the weapon and cleared the chamber.

"I could have killed the sonuvabitch," Vince muttered again as he slipped the H&K back into his fanny pack.

"Let's see if Rosa can muster some shots of tequila," Chance said, putting his hand on Vince's shoulder.

-7-

MIXING DREAMS AND DEVASTATION

Vince and Chance woke to the rich aroma of strong black coffee and huevos rancheros. Chance hit the head and showered in the luke-warm water creeping out of the rusting spigot. It was going to be another blistering day in the desert.

Vince awoke with several sailor knots securely tied in his stomach. He jerked and a cold sweat beaded on his trembling fore-head. He sat up abruptly and looked around at the faded plaster walls and scratched hardwood floors. He wanted to reach for a phone, but no such luck.

The room was dark. It had a single window adorned with faded shades and curtains drawn to prevent the sun and its ensuing heat from creeping into the room. A small dresser stood against one wall and a diminutive western lamp rested on the nightstand next to the two double beds.

His mind raced with thoughts of Nicole. What had happened to her? He felt as if someone had worked him over last night and all the jabbing punches were directed at his abs. He could sense the smells from the kitchen, but his mind raced in other directions. He had to leave Chance and rumble back to Los Angeles. Just as soon as he made that unwavering decision, he felt somewhat relieved. He felt that he could solve the problem, if he could just sit with Nicole and talk it out.

"It's about time you got your ass up and rolling," Chance said as he wolfed down spicy refried beans smothered in cheese, eggs, and salsa. Steam rolled out of his cobalt blue coffee mug.

"Please sit," Rosa said, rising from the table to fix Vince a plate of food. Vince didn't look into Chance's direct gaze as he pulled up the simple wooden chair in the small breakfast nook.

"I'm going back to L.A.," he said, looking at the plate of food. He had no appetite.

"I knew it," Chance said. "You've got to do what you've gotta do, brother, but don't forget that the cops are still after your ass, and your agency clan doesn't want your movie produced."

"No problem," Vince said, sipping the onyx coffee. He couldn't seem to swallow. His thoughts were on one thing—getting to Nicole before she left the country.

Chance looked at Vince and noted the tell-tale signs of a man whose heart was breaking. Vince was pale, the blood drained from his angular features. His lack of concentration was evident in his hollow stare. Chance could feel the pain. He'd been there, broken way too many hearts, and had felt the pure devastation of having his own heart broken.

"Maybe Rosa can give your broken-hearted self enough cash to keep your tank full and get you a burger on your way back," Chance said.

The darkened adobe home kept the simmering sun at bay, but the full blast hit home as Vince opened the door and all three ventured outside. Vince loaded up the Street Stalker and refueled. Without a word of goodbye, he fired up the black monster and headed onto the freeway. Rosa stood beside Chance as they listened to the smooth running 80-incher disappear into the desert.

"Do you need to go with your friend?" Rosa asked. Her voice was down; as if she was afraid she might lose Chance.

"Nope," Chance said. "This is something he needs to handle on his own. We've got work to do around here."

As he turned toward the station, Rosa stopped him in his tracks.

"Thank you, Chance," she said looking up at him with a more than a warm gaze.

Chance looked into her dark eyes, at her full red lips, at the night-gown hanging loosely over her substantial breasts, and his mind filled with tender thoughts. He wanted to hold her, but he thought about his first wife. The one he left for the young nasty biker chick.

Chance left too many women and the emotional scorecard was full. He felt guilty about every one he'd devastated, and the guilt was beginning to wear on him. He couldn't settle down with one woman.

There was always the next satin attraction luring him to more fertile ground. He couldn't figure it out, but with each failed relationship, another chip was clipped from his heart. Besides, the recent escapade with Sheila still haunted him.

He looked into Rosa's eyes and sensed goodness that he didn't dare shatter with his vagabond love. He cupped her soft face in his rough hands, kissed her gently and said, "We better get to work."

«« — »»

A crack split the air in the small Phoenix strip motel. There were no tenants on that Monday morning, just the owner, his fat wife working in the office, and the janitor bent over the pool filter. Just a backfire, the owner thought.

An SUV was parked outside room A12. Alongside the chipped door was the maid's cart. A redhead emerged from the room in a nervous jog, stuffing something into her purse. She threw a small black bag into the passenger seat, got in the cab, and started the vehicle. Spinning the wheel, she headed for the entrance, spitting a shotgun blast of gravel in her wake.

Half-hour later, the motel's owner discovered the body of Maria Cruz in a pool of blood in the bathroom of room A12.

«« — »»

Vince raged along the hot asphalt. With full 5-gallon tanks, at 30 miles to the gallon, he was good for another 150 miles. He planned to gobble as much of the landscape as he could. He would be nearly half-way home before he needed to stop and refuel.

Riding gave him a sense of emotional solace, and he let the tears flow as his vibrating speedometer pegged the 90-mph marker. Even in the heat, he shook with emotional chills. Usually cocky and self-assured, Vince didn't realize how much he loved Nicole until she pulled the plug.

Vince ripped past one lumbering 18-wheeler after another. He couldn't figure out his feelings. He'd lived with Nicole for a couple years, helped get her situated in the states, but he hadn't been the affectionate lover he could have been – no, should have been. Vince was generally too macho to pay attention to his soft partner.

He was a man on the move, writing, training, working on his bike, and blasting from one insignificant project to another. Women just slowed him down. He took her for granted until she said those words. Suddenly, he was nothing without her.

As he thought about Nicole, a small compact pulled out from behind an eighteen-wheeler and tried to pass. Vince floundered in a pool of muddy emotions and his reaction time was hindered. He didn't fully recognize what was happening until his front end was about to kiss the rusting compact's bumper.

He lifted his foot off the footboard and reached for the rubber-capped brake pedal. The screaming motorcycle smacked something hard in the lane and his foot slipped off the pedal. Mud-slow, he reached for the front brake and squeezed. The telescopic front forks collapsed and the bike bore down toward the abrasive asphalt simmering against the brake rotor and tugging the tire alongside the road surface. It began to break free as the front end came precariously close to the rear of the compact.

The driver, a middle-aged alcoholic, rock collector, glanced in the rearview mirror too late to avoid his action. He was already centered in the left-hand lane when he discovered the black motorcycle bearing down on him fast. He was laid off from the gravel plant where he'd worked as a forklift operator for 15 years. Since then, he'd lived off Social Security and beer. Instead of putting his pedal to the metal, the threat of impact by the 500-pound rocket ship roaring up his ass caused him to release the pressure on the gas pedal. The compact slowed. There were just two asphalt west-bound lanes surrounded by sand and dry creosote bushes.

Vince usually would have looked for a slim lane between traffic, to the outside, or swerved around the car and been gone in the blast of hot exhaust, but not this time. The bike wobbled after impact with a slice of shredded retread and came within inches of the slowing compact and its gawking driver before Vince found the brake pedal with his cowboy boot. The bike squealed and slid to the side.

Vince's brain finally shifted into gear as he remembered his recent deadly encounter with the car peeps on the coast. His eyes widened behind the dark sunglasses and he tensed as he had a hundred times on 2,000-pound bulls. He was called to action.

The alert professional in the big rig saw the accident unfolding in his convex rearview mirror and immediately pulled his thundering truck to the right to allow a safe path between the vehicles. Instinctively, Vince found the opening and shot past the compact. Alert and angry, Vince's normal mode of operation, he pulled back in front of the compact and hit both brakes. The taillights of the black beast lit up and the tires smoked—revenge.

The driver of the compact panicked and drove into the sandy median, mowing down tumbleweeds, yucca plants and scattering roadside debris. Vince kicked the Softail in the ass and was gone in the blink of an eye and the rap of thundering exhaust.

«« — »»

The redhead in the SUV spun out of the gravel motel parking lot and onto Scottsdale Road. Her mind raged with anger and vengeance. She met Chance several years ago. They had a hot and desperate love affair, but she couldn't seem to hold on to him and it drove her crazy. She grew up in a broken home with only her schizoid mother and a sister who felt the same pangs of disconnection with men. The broken home, the absence of men in her childhood, the crappy jobs her mom had and her bizarre upbringing set the stage for an unstable woman. Add to that a narrow waist and ample, bolt-on tits and she was a sexual nightmare.

Her father moved to Europe to escape her mother, and she had no brothers. At one time, in the eye of the relationship storm, Chance spoke to a psychologist who explained that women who have no men in their families don't know, understand, or trust men. They have no point of reference. He thought it was strangely coincidental, but there was nothing he could do but set her free. Chance understood freedom, she didn't, and as the months passed, her level of aggravation grew.

She pulled out onto the freeway as the police skidded into the parking lot of the motel, followed by a news van.

«« — »»

Chance donned stained overalls and continued to clean the service area, moving junk into the backyard, sorting crap from useful parts and supplies as the sun blazed overhead. Rosa went into the sundry store and waited on customers.

As the day turned into a blistering inferno, the faded red paint on the building appeared to lose even more pigment. The red became lighter and the white letters cracked under the unrelenting rays. Chance could smell the heat and was pushed against the pavement every time he stepped into the sunlight from the shade of the corrugated service bays. But even the shade surpassed 100 degrees by noon. Rosa's swamp cooler purred in the heat and cooled the store. She busied herself unpacking new supplies.

For the first time in a year, she had some hope that her family business would flourish again. She hummed to the new Carlos Santana tune crackling from the radio. Another customer ducked in from the heat to buy bottled water. At noon, Chance came into the cool interior for a sandwich and soda.

"If we could paint this joint, repair the signs and slurry-coat the asphalt, this place wouldn't look half bad. What are the chances?"

Rosa glowed with the expectations of what Chance was saying. He spoke as if he wasn't going to leave and that pleased her.

"I have a compressor and spray paint equipment, but the signs are something else," She said

"I can prep and shoot the paint, but I'm not a sign painter. Let me think about that one. Do you have a portable sandblaster? And what about the asphalt?"

"Look in the back," Rosa said, wiping her hands and coming around the counter to be closer to Chance. She looked up at his green eyes and at the ridiculously baggy overalls. He wasn't bad on the eyes.

She came up close to him and tugged on the overalls. "Do you think you could live in such a place?"

Chance looked in Rosa's eyes. He thought about Rosa and life in the desert. There was something remote and intriguing about it, but he was a city boy from the beginning. Could he handle the seclusion? He enjoyed his home on the harbor. He questioned himself. It wasn't likely that Rosa's situation would work; yet, there was a chance.

«« — »»

Vince was re-energized by the close call and kept his throttle pegged for another 100 miles before he pulled off the interstate for gas. The heat was excruciating as he dismounted. But his emotional malaise seemed to make him impervious to the elements. Vince paid for the gas, drank a bottle of water, jumped back on the motorcycle, and split.

On the highway, he dissected every word Nicole said in their last conversation for hidden meanings. He hunted through the labyrinth of his emotions for a release valve. Chance was the one with the checkered past when it came to women. He had the reputation of being a romantic and an unmatchable catch. Vince didn't see Chance as a womanizer. He had lots of them but didn't overtly chase them or use them. He was just hard to hold down for the long run, and not a man to put up with much crap.

Chance was the type to fall head-over-heals and get his heart broken. Vince was tough and aloof. He didn't understand what was going on inside him, the tugging, the tightness in his chest. He didn't see himself as a mighty lover or a skirt chaser. He was too busy breaking heads and pumping iron.

He cut through Palm Springs like a torch through tin, blazing into L.A. The air cooled slightly and the traffic increased as he neared the coast. He took the 10 Freeway until it dumped his ass onto the Pacific Coast Highway, where he turned south through the Santa Monica suburbs, through Venice, Manhattan Beach, Redondo Beach and finally into Palos Verdes. He twisted his petcock to his reserve tank as he skirted the bluff overlooking the vast Pacific only a mile from home. As he pulled into the alley behind the apartment complex where he lived, a lump grew in his throat.

He hadn't given much thought about his first words to Nicole. For some odd reason, he was sure when their eyes met that some cerebral explanation would be evident and all of this nonsense would be over. He parked the bike in the garage, but no one came to greet him. He jogged up the stairs from the underground parking lot to the front apartment. As he reached for the door, he discovered it was ajar.

Bursting into his apartment, Vince found several half-packed boxes. He was relieved, she hadn't left yet. Something was out of place, though. His favorite chair was knocked over. He called out, but only his desperate words reverberated off the walls. Then he noticed it. His laptop was missing. The home for all his writings, his screenplay, his heart was gone. Something was wrong, really wrong.

-8-

Hollywood Traps and Desert Tarantulas

Vince stood in the center of his Palos Verdes apartment and wondered what the hell had happened. It looked as though Nicole was packing when someone splintered the doorjamb with a heavy boot and ransacked the joint. Whoever it was may have taken Nicole with them. Vince had a sinking suspicion why—his screenplay.

A year ago, he lost his job with a major ad agency, writing slogans and copy. He drew a serious salary, but he didn't fit the mold of the advertising executive. He wore his black vest over tight black T-shirts and kept his black hair shoulder length. He didn't hesitate to pull a knife in the middle of a client conference and literally slash a lame proposal to shreds. He scared the shit out of most of his co-workers. Whenever he reached for his waist and the fully dialed-in H&K he kept there, the room immediately cleared. He was a frightening guy to those who didn't know him, so management let him go.

Vince was pleased to take his walking papers and follow his dream of writing screenplays. But while he was busy investigating the Hollywood ad agency underworld for a movie concept, his girlfriend became disconnected.

Vince erupted from bed each morning with a pulse-pounding agenda that included pumping iron, training, and hitting the keyboard. He wrote with wild abandon and tried to shove his concepts down the throats of numerous studios. Unfortunately for Vince, his point-blank tactics failed to ingratiate him with the Hollywood elite.

Finally, someone read his first attempt at a movie script and word spread. He wrote his scathing script with the cut-throat ad agency community as a backdrop. He exposed gross over-pricing in an industry where TV ads were produced to sell the creative minds and production resources of the agency, not the product. Ad spots that cost $10,000 to produce were sold for millions. Suddenly Vince, without fully recognizing the ballpark he was playing in, was again proving the adage, the pen was more powerful than the sword.

Then the phone rang and Vince jerked back to reality. "Yep."

"Vince?" the male voice inquired.

"Who is it?" Vince said.

Then Nicole was on the line. "Vin, Vin, vat happen?"

"Nicole," Vince clenched the receiver. "You OK, baby?"

"I hate you, Vin. You ruin my life. I vas leaving. Vhat's dis?"

"Nicole...?" Vince tried to ask.

"I don't know what's up between you two," the male voice returned, "but you know the drill, punk. Lose that screenplay or you won't see Nicole again." The phone went dead.

Vince slammed it into to its cradle, cracking the plastic case. He picked up a wicker chair and threw it against the brick fireplace in the center of the room. Grabbing boxes, he tossed them against the walls. His rage tore the apartment from furniture to toothpicks. Every fiber in his body wanted Nicole, and every intellectual cell that pulsed within him wanted his computer back. It was the cache of his work.

«« — »»

Chance worked throughout the day, prepping to paint the roadside gas station, while Rosa waited on customers and kept the books. As the sun blazed, he quit sanding and turned his attention to the old pickup in the garage.

Within an hour, Chance replaced the wheels and checked the wiring, fluids, and hoses. Rosa's ex had put some time in the restoration, but when the relationship went sour, he didn't want to give her any means of escape, so he disassembled the '52 Ford. He couldn't bring himself to destroy the parts, so everything was housed in the shop, rebuilt and ready to be installed into place.

Chance fired the truck to life. He backed the pickup to the pumps to gas it up and check under the hood. The truck ran smooth as a baby's ass, and Chance, although more experienced with motorcycles, was proud of the rumbling flathead Ford.

The truck was primered and ready for paint, but Chance was finished for the day. It was still in the 90s as the sun drifted from sight and he was beat. Rosa ran to the side of the truck as she saw it pull to the pumps.

"Chance, Chance, my truck! It runs!" She burst into his arms and held him with all her might.

Chance lifted his tired and grease-soaked hands to her wrists and tugged. "I've got to get a little sleep, then I'll hit it again for a few more hours while it's cool."

"I understand," she said, backing away after planting a big wet kiss on his cheek. "You all right?"

"No problem, baby," Chance said. "This is a big joint and there's a lot of work to do. I've got to pace myself. I just need a break from this heat."

«« — »»

A flaming redhead in an SUV screamed out of Phoenix at breakneck speed. Sheila stared at the hot pavement ahead. She was consumed with hatred for a man she never really knew. She blamed her pathetic life on him. He was the reason for their broken relationship and her rage against the young Mexican girl. Specks of dried blood stuck to her cream-colored blouse and fingernails, her thinning hair was matted to her head. The woman drove like there was no tomorrow. She was oblivious to any thoughts of being caught.

To her, men were all the same - womanizers and wanderers. But Chance had touched a chord in her and made her happier than ever. She wanted him, wanted it all to be different. He would belong to her and never abandon her like her father had. But her manic-depressive grasp of reality was fleeting and she turned on him as soon as his history with women sunk in. She could never trust him.

Chance was an easygoing guy with a large portion of wanderlust mixed with his romantic spirit. The redhead had put the touch on him in a weak moment, during a dry spell with his wife, and Chance fell head over heels. He ignored the little voice in his head that warned him of her evil nature. He fought the romance, breaking up with the girl over and over, only to return. Ultimately, the affair destroyed his marriage and he wandered into the fray with the devil woman, knowing full well it would never last. He couldn't tolerate her outbursts and he split, but she would not give up. She turned vicious. When he walked away from her in Phoenix, it infuriated her. He thought if he merely disappeared, she would tire of the pursuit and drift into another relationship.

She drove south of Phoenix, then west on Interstate 10 until she reached Buckeye, where she drove through every fast food joint, and gas station looking for Chance's motorcycle. She knew he had to be moving toward Los Angeles.

Her fatigue caught up with her and she pulled into a Motel 6 and rented a room. She bought some fast food and curled up on the bed. In an hour, she was asleep, grinding her teeth as her eyes fluttered. Her purse lay open on the nightstand with the butt of the .38 protruding from the gold-plated clasp.

«« — »»

Chance awoke at 8 p.m. to the smell of spiced Carnitas sizzling on the stove. He sat up, his long sandy-blond hair mussed and tangled. He felt a sense of calm and accomplishment. He stretched and walked in his boxer shorts to the bathroom, where he ran a shower and shaved.

What the hell, he thought, may as well clean up for dinner. As he scrubbed his body down he felt the tightness in his muscles from a day of physical labor, and his mind drifted to the beautiful Mexican woman waiting for him in the kitchen. In an instant, he wanted her. He wanted to run his hands under her cotton nightgown and feel her silken thighs and pendulous tits. He cringed and felt himself begin to harden.

It had been a while, but his sense of guilt rode him hard. He sensed that this could never be; yet, she deserved something. His mind reeled with the responsibility of love, but he knew as well as she did that love is what love gives. Expectations conflict with the realities of life and she should be aware of them. Most women weren't, and a harlequin romance novel was never the premise of love, something he knew all too clearly.

Chance climbed out of the shower and toweled himself dry. He pulled on his Levis and a T-shirt. As he strolled into the small kitchen, Rosa popped the top off an icy Corona. She had limes sliced perfectly to fit the mouth of the cold glass and spun to meet him. Her smile was one of pure joy, a calm that a perfect world can bring to the eyes of a woman in love. All was at peace in her world. She could envision every element of her life coming together with this big Prince Charming in leather at her side. She pushed the biker aspect of the equation out of her mind.

"Cervesa, senor?"

"Muchas gracias, senorita."

The Spanish rice and tortillas were already on the table and the smell was intoxicating. Chance leaned over and kissed Rosa on the forehead, and she set the wooden spatula on the edge of the stove and hugged him.

"I'm so happy you came along," she said. "I appreciate everything you're doing."

Her face glowed and Chance could not contain himself. He kissed her. It was like a spark to the desert tumbleweeds and creosote setting a valley ablaze. Rosa's apron fell away and they embraced against the table. Her hand groped his crotch. The frosty beer bottle fell to the floor, the foamy liquid spilling onto the hardwood. She turned off the flame under the food and fell backward toward the table. Chance pushed the checkered tablecloth aside and the ceramic salt and peppershakers fell to the deck. She yanked off her nightgown and lay down on the table. The wooden legs rattled as Chance pulled her to him and they made love. Rosa responded like a thoroughbred hungry for the starting gate. He gave her what she wanted.

Spent, Chance stood sweating beside the table. She reached out to him. He picked her up and carried her down the hall to her bedroom, trying not to trip over the Levis bunched around his ankles.

Chance placed her gently on the bed, then disappeared. He returned with another beer and shared it with Rosa. As she drank, he removed his pants and crawled into bed. It wasn't until midnight that they peeled out of bed and ate quietly in the afterglow of their lovemaking.

"I want to start painting this joint tonight," Chance said, heading for the door.

He pulled the compressor out of the service area and mixed the paint. The compressor whirred and jiggled as Chance cleaned and prepped the first island and went to work. By 4:00 a.m., the first island was painted and it was time to sleep. Tomorrow would be another long day.

Rosa was already tucked into her queen-size bed when Chance slipped in beside her. She rolled to meet him. He lay back against the smell of fresh linen and she curled up against him. She was warm and soft and he could sense her nakedness.

For a long moment, he laid there, contemplating his situation in the desert. For the first time in his life, he was away from the city, from splitting lanes and the hectic lifestyle, of streets lined with beer cans, panhandlers, and gangsters. The desert had its dangers, but this woman was the solace. He was in heaven again. Chance drifted off, but awoke an hour later with a start.

"What's wrong?" Rosa whispered, half-asleep.

"Nothing, baby; go back to sleep."

But he had heard the radio report about the girl found shot in the motel room while they were eating dinner. And suddenly it dawned on him that it could have been Maria. He questioned his exact words to the young woman. For an hour, a cold sweat washed over him. Had he told her where he was? He couldn't sleep.

«« — »»

Vince woke to a feeling of loneliness and loss. Someone was banging on the door. He recovered his senses, grabbed the .45 off the bed stand and darted to the door. He opened it with a snap and shoved the barrel of the automatic against the sunlit sky. There was no one in sight, just the L.A. Times lying at his feet. He thought he heard a car speed away, but when he reached for the paper the message hit home. An envelope slipped out from the folded newspaper. He snatched it off the bricks and opened it: "If you ever want to see Nicole again, drop the movie project."

His knees buckled and his heart hardened. He instinctively reached for the phone to call Chance, but it was broken. He looked around the apartment. Nothing looked orderly. He grabbed his clothes, dressed and marched to his Street Stalker. He had only two trustworthy entities in his life — Chance and the motorcycle.

About to leave the apartment, Vince stopped and looked around. His bull-riding photos hung from the walls, but there was nothing left to collect. Nothing but stucco walls and cheap furniture. He could call an ex-girlfriend to pick up and stash his ammo can and CD collection. He packed fresh clothes in his bedroll and headed out to the bike.

He rolled north on PCH into Redondo Beach and pulled into the Portofino Hotel in King Harbor. He ordered breakfast and wondered what the hell he would do next. With less than $200 to his name, Vince looked longingly at the boats docked in the marina. He wondered why some people had money and others constantly struggled for enough to stay afloat. Then his heart grew heavy and a rush of emotion engulfed him. Nicole may have hated him, and she was abandoning him, but she didn't deserve to be fucked with. Vince was in shock. He didn't know who to go after or who to run from.

-9-

COLLIDING LOVE

Sheila McBride awoke at 6 a.m. as 18-wheelers thundered past her motel room. The racket grew steadily during the last hour as the trucks barreled down Interstate10. When she finally gave in and sat up, the previous day's nightmare returned with the force of a desert flash flood.

Her palms grew moist despite the air conditioning as she caught a visual of the young cleaning girl pleading for her life. She jerked as she remembered the crack of the .38 and the life draining from the girl's young body. Sheila reached across the nightstand and retrieved the .38 from her small leather purse. Something stirred in her loins. The thought of the whimpering housekeeper brought a level of excitement to her and she began to stroke the weapon.

She spread her long legs to reveal a partially shaved pussy. She put the gun's snub-nosed barrel to her clit, flinching at the touch of the cold, hard steel. In her mind, Sheila saw the innocent face of the Mexican girl, tears running down her rosy cheeks as she swore that she didn't know where Chance was.

"Of course you do, you little no-account toilet cleaner," Sheila said before pistol-whipping the girl. She'd became turned on when she saw the girl's pear-shaped breasts jiggling under her torn white uniform.

Sheila also felt a sense of doom, as if this would be her last climax. She was sure she'd be apprehended. Perhaps it would be best to off herself at the moment of climax. She shoved the barrel inside herself, her finger wrapped around the trigger. Her other hand held the cylinder and thrust it inside her. It hurt, but she kept doing it. She rocked her pelvis and looked at her wickedness.

She climaxed and couldn't prevent the desire. All the fear and hatred she contained bounced off the walls of the small motel room. No one would ever hear the gun over the trucks rushing by outside. The hammer of the pistol left its carriage as she arched her back, thrusting her silicone boobs forward and rocking her pelvis to meet the iron intruder. The firing pin rocked back as she spasmed, then it settled again in its steel cavity as her climax dissipated.

A sheen of moistness covered her body as she pulled the .38 from her pussy and threw it on the musty carpet. Tears exploded from her eyes as reality struck home.

«« — »»

Chance awoke with a start. Police all over Phoenix were looking for a woman in connection with the shooting.

"Is everything all right?" Rosa asked in a dreamy voice as she nuzzled against Chance's nude body.

It wasn't. Guilt ran through his veins instead of blood. He was a woman's outlaw. He was the epitome of what Sheila feared. She had fallen in love with her nemesis. She knew it, feared it, hated it, and worst of all, couldn't control it. Chance was afraid for Rosa.

He rolled over and kissed Rosa on the lips, then did what he did best, making love to her like there was no tomorrow. He made her feel like she was the center of his universe and the only reality was their two bodies coupled as one.

How could he dismiss a 30-year past of breaking hearts, one after another? How could he ignore all the tears and make love to another woman? He didn't know the answer. It was simply his existence. At one time, it was exciting; now death accompanied the photo album of broken hearts, and his tender, romantic nature was as deadly as the venom from a Mojave rattlesnake.

Rosa climbed on top of Chance and bobbed up and down on his cock, driving herself to one climax after another until she thought she'd pass out. No man had unleashed her steamy sensuality as Chance had. She felt so free. When he finally climbed on top of her, she spread her legs willingly and hoped that his tender thrusts would never end. They lay side by side for long moments as Chance caressed her moist form.

The sun was already melting asphalt outside and they were soaking the bed in sweat. As Chance rose, Rosa admired his muscular back and thighs. She had only known Chance for a couple days, but she knew he would never physically hurt her. She sensed it in his touch, the caring manner in which he did things. She also surmised that he would not stay.

Chance returned with a small bowl of ice and a damp washcloth. He wiped her down gently with the cool rag and teased her luscious tits with the ice cubes.

"Could you live here, Chance?" Rosa asked again.

"I'm not sure, baby," Chance replied, "I just don't know anymore. I have a place in San Pedro."

She dropped the subject.

"What's on the list for today?"

"Well, I hope to finish painting the pumps and move to the exterior of the building, if the paint supply holds. When it's too hot to work in the open, I'll finish checking out your truck. It should be good to go."

They got up and showered together. He enjoyed the tenderness of her touch under the lukewarm spray. He wished he could tell this woman he would remain by her side for the rest of his life, but it wasn't in him. Then he remembered Sheila.

"Rosa," he said, "there's something I need to tell you."

«« — »»

While Vince stirred the eggs on his plate, his whole existence came into focus like a laser beam. He gnashed his teeth thinking about the self-serving bastards he worked for, about the studio low-lifes who knew nothing of the streets and tossed writing careers around like olives in a drink at the country club, eating the exterior and spitting the pits in the dirt.

Vince jumped up from his breakfast beside the marina. He grabbed the toilet key from the waiter and bolted to the head where the boaters went to shower. He had never fallen in love. He didn't know how to act, or how to treat a woman, and now she was gone. He was a good guy but passionate to the point of being over the top. He was effusively obsessive about everything in his life except Nicole. He assumed she would always be there.

Vince pulled the high-tech .45 automatic out of its home in the leather fanny pack and laid it on the counter. He pulled out the two spare magazines and studied them. Both full, nine rounds apiece. Then he ejected the magazine in the weapon and studied it. It was missing two rounds and it pissed him off. He kept a handful of spares in a zippered compartment within the fanny pack. He thumbed in two rounds, reloaded the mag, snapped it back into the handle, and pulled the slide. Locked and loaded, he flicked on the safety with his thumb. Vince barreled toward the door, knocking aside a flabby, middle-aged boat owner in white pants and a navy blazer.

Vince did things in a John Wayne sort of way. There was no conservative ground, no casual demeanor. His eyes blazed as he mounted the Street Stalker and cut a dusty trail across town toward the Wilshire district. He rode like hell possessed through the busy streets, onto the 405 Freeway and off at Santa Monica Boulevard. When traffic thickened, he split off onto little Santa Monica, into the land of high rises and marble sidewalks. His front end bounced as he rode the blacked-out bike onto the sidewalk and into the foyer of a 40-story high rise. Before security could react, he walked into a waiting elevator and pressed the button for MacIntyre and Levensol Advertising.

He burst out of the doors and into a bare room that contained an odd-shaped mirror and a silk plant. The area was stark, yet refined, with hardwood floors leading to a set of double doors. Vince jammed through the doors like a man on a mission – which he was. His narrow shades were planted securely on his face, and his black, shoulder-length hair was mussed. He wore a black T-shirt and vest with black Levi's and boots. He was one nasty-looking character.

To his left was a richly paneled divider that hid the sharp-looking receptionist wearing a telephone headset and staring at a computer screen.

"May I help you?" she asked, one hand poised above the button to call for security.

"They're expecting me," Vince said. He stormed through a maze of account rep cubicles, digital graphic artists, photo retouchers, and Internet geeks until he reached a wall of glass offices overlooking Los Angeles. He wanted Barry MacIntyre, as he reached for his fanny pack and the H&K.

Employees spotted the mad biker and murmurs spread around the myriad of small cubicles. A young exec reached for his phone. Vince snapped the blued weapon in the direction of the scared face, and the man dropped his phone. Vince marched down the lane of offices, looking into each one until he came to a private conference room, where he kicked open the door.

MacIntyre sat at the head of the table. He'd sported his share of shady deals, any one of which could have drawn a hit. But the world seemed shy of the necessary hit men to rid the planet of the shysters who scavenged off the unsuspecting and got away with it. MacIntyre was 39, fast-talking and good-looking. The man was highly intelligent, but misguided.

Levensol, the Jew, sat next to him, his eyes directed at the balance sheets on the glistening oak conference table. He was the perfect partner for MacIntyre—rich and pliable.

Vince aimed the .45 at MacIntyre.

"What the hell do you think you're doing?" MacIntyre shouted. Once he recognized that it was Vince, he wasn't as afraid. Vince yanked out his pistol on a regular basis to make a point.

"You have Nicole, you sonuvabitch." Vince fired a round shattering MacIntyre's gold-embossed coffee cup, exploding the hot liquid all over his chest and Levensol's paperwork.

"I'm going to kill you and your Jewboy, just for the fun of it."

The acrid smell of gunpowder filled the room as Vince slammed the door with his boot. There were two clients in the room who dove under the conference table in terror. They didn't know the mad biker in black, and didn't want to.

"Where is she?" Vince shouted, preparing to fire again, when the phone rang. There were two phones on the desk, one at each end. One of the many buttons was red for emergencies and major deals. MacIntrye's instructions were strictly enforced: Don't call me on that line unless it's a high-dollar client. He couldn't fathom why a call would be coming through on that line now.

Barry hit the speakerphone.

"Vince," the voice barked, "Vince, it's Chance! Pick up the phone!"

Vince was stunned. How would Chance know he was there?

"Pick up the phone, Vince!"

Vince picked up the receiver from the other end of the table with one hand, keeping Barry covered with the .45 in the other.

"Don't say a word, Vince," Chance said. "Get the fuck out of there quick. Ride fast away from downtown. Don't say a word to those guys. Just get the fuck out, now! Ride to Century Motorcycles in Pedro. We'll deal with this shit later."

Perplexed, Vince put the phone down and backed out the door. He darted for the entrance and dove on the first elevator. Chance's advice was invariably on the money. Vince knew he was a hothead, and that he was better safe than sorry.

The elevator seemed to take forever to reach the ground floor. Vince leapt as the doors crept open, and he discovered a tow truck parked in front of the building. The driver was talking to the building's rent-a-cop.

Vince ran to his bike in the lobby, snapped on the ignition switch and hit the starter. It fired immediately, the crisp exhaust note reverberating off the marble and granite interior, the smell of high-test fuel filling the foyer. He dropped it into first and the rear wheel spun against the polished marble floor. A bystander startled by the commotion opened the door and Vince shot through it, leaving the security guard slack-jawed.

Vince was out in the street in a second, peeling through the back streets of the Wilshire District, Hollywood, then onto the Santa Monica Freeway, and then the 405 toward San Pedro. He spun off the freeway at Crenshaw and took Western into the harbor.

Vince shot down Pacific Avenue to Century Motorcycles and rode into the old service entrance. Century was the Boot Hill of motorcycle shops. Cindy, the old broad who took it over from her father never sold a thing, but she had a heart of gold.

He stashed his bike in the junkyard service department and Cindy came back to see what the commotion was. She loved Vince—his wry grin, sharp wit, baby blue eyes, and angular features. She stayed in the business for the men, although she was well past her prime with her pudgy features and wild dyed-red hair.

《《 — 》》

"Is that what we needed to talk about?" Rosa asked as Chance hung up the phone.

"Nope," Chance said, pulling her down on the small, tattered couch. He rapidly became attached to this woman, but he wasn't sure whether it was love, sympathy, a longing for something he wished he had accomplished in his past, or penance for all the bad shit he had done.

"Listen, there's this woman I once went out with who hates me enough to kill to find me. Remember the girl killed in the Phoenix on the news?"

"Yes," Rosa said.

"This woman could have done that in her psychotic rage."

"Does she know where you are?" Rosa asked.

"No, she just knew I wasn't far," Chance said. "I met her at a motel. She was the cleaning lady."

"What do we do?"

"I'm not sure," Chance said. "I could leave and never come back, and hope that she continues to follow me away from you."

Chance could feel her grasp tighten on his arm.

"Or I could stay and we could take our chances that she doesn't stop in Tonopah. If she did come in here, I would be close by."

"I like that option," Rosa said, holding him tight. "I would rather you were here."

《《 — 》》

Sheila sat in a vinyl booth at a Denny's, studying a map of metro Phoenix. Two highway patrol officers strolled into the restaurant and took seats in an adjacent booth. She lowered her head, sipped her third cup of coffee and ate some fruit and cottage cheese.

Sheila decided to backtrack and look in Avondale, then try Litchfield, Goodyear, Buckeye, and then Tonopah. Chance's one-off custom sled wouldn't be hard to find.

She tossed the exact change on the table and slipped out of the restaurant.

-10-

THE COAST CALLS

Vince stood at the door to Century Motorcycles and felt the cool breeze rolling off the Los Angeles Harbor. The gusts blew his dark hair, which was as unkempt as his life. He was down to his last few bucks and had no place to stay. Grinding his teeth, he stared down the street toward the harbor and wondered what the hell he was going to do next.

"Hey handsome," hollered Cindy. Vince turned without answering.

"There's a phone call for you," Cindy said, eyeing him up and down like a hungry cat.

"What?" he said into the phone.

"Vince, it's Chance."

"What the hell do you think you're doing?" Vince asked. "How did you know where I was?"

"Remember McIntyre's receptionist?" Chance said. "We never went out, but we did swap numbers."

"What makes you think those ad execs didn't snatch Nicole, Detective Marlow?" Vince snapped.

"I don't know what's going on with Nicole," Chance returned, "but I had a hunch I needed to find you, before you broke something or someone. I had to get you out of that building."

"Man, I could have taken out that entire agency and still gotten out of there. I would have sent a message to anyone involved that I don't take prisoners. I don't negotiate when it comes to Nicole. I'm going to discover who snatched her and make lunchmeat outta the bastard.

"Listen, hot-head, you're a mess. I've got something I need to deal with here, then I'll be back and we'll clear that up. Can you hang on for a couple of days? Stay outta site, use my place."

"Not sure I can hang for 15 minutes. I'm chewing my nails, tooth-picks, and parking meters. I'm wound to the stops," Vince said, chewing a pencil from Cindy's desk.

"Go to Harold's Saloon and get a drink. Calm the fuck down. Clean up your bike, relax," Chance said and hung up.

Rosa grabbed at his sleeve. "You're not leaving, are you?"

"Not just yet," Chance said. "We have our own project to deal with. I don't want to leave, but I may need to jam to LA and help Vince before he cracks."

Rosa was relieved but concerned. She reluctantly lived the life of a desert recluse and she knew her chances of hanging on to the wandering biker weren't great. Chance finished his Diet Coke and went back outside where he painted her gas station exterior. Her profits had already climbed. Chance cleaned up the outside of the shop, painted the pumps and islands, and restored her truck to running condition. Besides making mad passionate love to her, he had changed her life for the better. She didn't want the rush to end.

"I need to go to town for groceries," Rosa said. "Can I use the truck?"

"Gimme an hour," Chance said, leaving his duty station adjacent to the service bay where his portable compressor clicked and pumped to keep the air tank full.

He sandblasted the corrugated tin walls and spray on a coat of fresh red paint. He scoured the stainless steel on the pumps and nozzles to free them of rust and years of sloppy paint. What once looked like a dilapidated business beyond repair was beginning to shine once more.

Chance opened the vintage truck hood and pulled the charging cables off the battery. The truck was ready for new paint, with fresh new wood panels installed in the bed. Chance checked the timing, fixed the wiring, and fired it up. He drove it around the smoldering black asphalt to check the brakes, then went a little farther until he was confident the truck would make the 40-mile trip to the nearest grocery store.

He beckoned for Rosa to come out and drive the truck. It hadn't run for several months and he had only been on the job three days. He didn't know if she was handy with it or not.

He watched as she walked into the sunlight from the station sundry store. The desert was her home. Her Mexican and Indian heritage tanned her skin and her long black hair looked comfortable in a ponytail. She always wore white dresses with a touch of colorful embroidery. Her smile glowed in the sun.

Chance opened the door for her and she slipped in, depressed the clutch, and fired the straight six to life.

"Just take it around the block," Chance said, "I want you to test it first."

She shifted the gears like they were second nature to her and returned in a jiffy. Chance checked the fluids once more and sent her on her way. He waved as she rolled out of the station lot and watched her accelerate onto the freeway, heading east toward Phoenix. She was sharp, sexy, and passionate, but Chance wondered more about himself. He walked out of the stifling heat into the first service bay, pulled up a shop stool and tore the canvas off his bike. She was motion on two wheels, and just to look at her filled Chance with wanderlust.

«« — »»

Sheila McBride twisted the knob on her rental SUV air conditioning unit to high. Nervous energy coursed through her blood. Everywhere she turned there were cops, but she vowed to find Chance if it was the last thing she did. She cruised every truck stop and gas station on the outskirts of Phoenix.

She pulled off the freeway in Avondale. While she was checking out the Denny's parking lot, she came face to face with an Arizona Highway Patrolman. The officer was too busy trying to catch a glimpse of her cleavage to notice her nervous, angry demeanor. From Avondale, she hit Goodyear, a truck stop, and Buckeye.

Her anger grew with each stop. She dissected the last time Chance made love to her. She cringed at her explosive behavior, pushing him away. She wanted him so badly she would kill anyone, including him. The freeway was hot, over 100 degrees, as she headed west, frustrated with her inability to find her man.

Tonopah was the last stop before the 81-mile stretch to Quartzsite, just 16 miles from the California border. She pulled off the freeway with a vengeance. Sweat beaded on her forehead and her palms were clammy as she turned left over the freeway to the only business in the area, Rosa's Truck Stop. Adjacent to it was a restaurant that had been closed for years and sat rotting in the sun. Sheila skidded up to the gas station and looked inside. No one was visible.

Rosa was in Buckeye, buying groceries. Chance stepped out back to retrieve another gallon of exterior paint. He heard the car screech out front and turned to investigate. As he rounded the corner of the building, he spotted the SUV.

Sheila unclasped her safety belt and turned off the ignition when she spotted something in the service bay. She fired her SUV to life and backed up a couple feet, then turned the wheel and aimed the rumbling Explorer at the first service bay. There was Chance's ride, glistening in the streaming sunlight.

She couldn't believe it. She'd found him. Now what? Run over his motorcycle? Her hands tensed on the wheel. There had to be another woman involved—Rosa's Truck Stop.

Chance ran around the corner. Was it Sheila? Had she seen the bike? Sheila turned the SUV around and peeled out of the parking lot. Chance visually followed the Explorer as it roared onto the freeway heading east.

Chance stood still sweating in the sun, his Daytona Bike Week T-shirt growing damp under the arms. He wiped his brow with a red bandanna and replaced it in a hip pocket. Staring at the desert 10 Freeway, he knew if it was Sheila, she'd be back. He had to protect Rosa.

Sheila pounded the steering wheel as she drove away, spitting angry words from her silicone lips. She knew where he was. She knew in her black heart that there was another woman, and this time, she would take care of them both. She wouldn't allow another woman to have the happiness she longed for. She knew now, she could never have him back.

《《—》》

Vince marched down old Pacific Avenue and into the run-down Harold's Saloon. Promotional Jack Daniel's posters were nailed over holes in the ceiling. The felt was nearly gone from all three pool tables, and there wasn't a straight cue in the joint. But Rachel, the young chubby waitress with streaked hair and a crocked smile, poured the meanest drink in town. She never used a jigger and didn't overdo any drink with too many ice cubes.

Vince sauntered up to the bar wearing all black, as usual. He had a strange habit of wearing his black riding gloves with loose gauntlets inside bars. He even wore his gloves while he played pool. He wasn't a great pool shark, although athletically he was a powerful, agile man. The glove thing always irritated someone in the bar. Some half-sloshed local would make a comment and there would be hell to pay.

Three young Mexicans played pool in the main parlor. One of them noticed the biker straddle a stool and order a stiff Jack Daniel's on the rocks. Rachel picked up a large tumbler, scooped up four ice cubes, and turned to the lineup of liquor bottles. The Jack Daniel's bottle was always handy. She pulled it from the arsenal of intoxicants and began to pour in a circular motion as if she was a soda jerk putting hot fudge on a sundae.

She was almost to the top of the glass when the bottle ran dry. Rachel yanked off the bar nozzle and tossed the empty fifth in the trash. She reached under the cabinet where several fifths of Jack were lined up like shells in an artillery magazine. She cracked the seal, and, without installing the tapered nozzle, topped off the amber liquid.

"That'll be $4.50, handsome," she said to Vince.

"Hey," a voice broke the stillness in the bar above the dense rock 'n' roll. "You, biker boy. Something wrong with your hands?"

Vince gazed at the drink on the slippery bar. He was still mad as a female lion missing a cub. His muscles twitched. He looked forward to sipping the drink and trying to think, but this fat Mexican leaning on a bent cue ruined that plan.

The other two Mexicans, in their early 20s, pointed at Vince and laughed at their buddy's remark. Vince picked up the drink, took a small sip, so as not to lose any, then sloshed the cubes around in the glass. He put the tumbler to his lips and downed the four-shot drink. Rachel stopped in her tracks and watched in awe.

Vince abruptly stood and eyed his opponents in the cracked mirror above the bar. He slammed the fluted tumbler on the bar, took one step backward and picked up his barstool. Spinning, he launched the stool across the bar at the two laughing Mexicans, who were at one end of the table. Then he stormed to the other end.

The Mexican leaning against the cue stepped back, tossed the cue to the side, and reached for a knife sheathed at the back of his dungarees.

He no sooner had the knife in his hand than Vince drove his fist into the young kid's throat. Vince slammed the youngster against the chalk stand, splintering the base and sending an explosion of chalk bits and dust around the room.

Vince pulled him away from the wall and threw him on the pool table. Reaching for a pool ball, he noticed one of the man's cohorts swing a cue in his direction. Vince side-stepped the table, grabbed the cue, and yanked it from the thin assailant's hand. He spun and slammed the cue upside the young man's head. He dropped like a sack of potatoes.

The other kid picked up a chair and threw it. Vince snatched the chair and drove it against the man trying to get up off the table. The man collapsed and groaned. The young man on the floor scrambled to his knees and charged Vince's legs. Rachel screamed at the top of her lungs for Vince to stop, but he didn't hear her. The impact of the wooden chair split the prone man's skull and blood flowed readily onto what was left of the felt.

The young man who had attempted to tackle Vince was unaware that he easily squatted 600 pounds. When Vince didn't budge, the kid rolled away, but not before Vince caught him alongside the skull with an engineer boot. He got up screaming, blood running down his face, and ran for the door.

The youngster in baggy denims bumped into a man in a dark suit strolling quietly through the door. He was slick and out of place. The bar was in pandemonium when a silenced gunshot split the air, then another. Vince stood up straight at the foot of the pool table, where he had slammed a 5-ball into the skull of one of the Mexicans.

The first shot center-punched Vince's chest; the second left a neat hole right between his eyes. He was dead before he collapsed on the beer-soaked carpet.

The shooter calmly holstered his pistol, stepped back into the afternoon sun, and drove off in a late-model BMW.

-11-

BAD EGG IN THE SAND

Chance watched the Explorer barrel onto the eastbound freeway in the blazing afternoon sun. He assumed that she spotted the chopper sparkling in the service bay, and that she would return with a vengeance. He wiped his brow with a tattered bandanna, but the sweat continued to pour. He stepped out of the sun and wondered what the hell he was doing. Rosa was in danger if he stayed, and even worse off if he rolled back to L.A. to help Vince.

Half-heartedly, he went back to work, cleaning and painting the building while taking breaks to help customers who dared to compete with the heat to refuel. Chance replaced the burned-out bulbs that illuminated the signs around the station, repainted the lettering, and replaced floodlights around the property, making the truck stop more visible at night. Business improved, even in the couple of days that he'd been there, but they couldn't compete with the franchise joints popping up at every turn-off.

The place had class, though. It rapidly became an antique, a relic of the service station past with dated pumps and truck-sized service bays surrounded by corrugated tin walls.

Chance worked his ass off all day. Whenever customers weren't pumping gas or buying snacks, Chance worked and thought about the crazy redhead. He tried to evaluate the alternatives. He could stand fast and defend himself and Rosa. He could go after her, but he would stand to lose either his life or his freedom if it didn't go down perfectly.

He didn't want to murder her, but how could he convince her to leave forever? She was like a shark in a pool of bait. As long as there was prey, she would stay. It gave Chance the chills.

As the sun settled over the distant freeway, Chance scrubbed the windows on the sundry store. It felt good to be productive.

«« — »»

Sheila fumed all the way to Buckeye 15 miles away and pulled off the freeway. Perspiration ran across her throbbing temples as she cruised the rapidly growing one-horse town, looking for a hardware store. Buckeye grew from 8,137 population in 2000 to 29,000 in 2008 as a Phoenix suburb in Maricopa County. It was just 18 miles east of Tonopah.

Sheila was incensed that Chance was with another woman so quickly. She pounded her steering wheel furiously, screaming at the top of her lungs, "I hate you!" as she pulled into a Rite Aid lot next to a grocery store. She parked next to a restored '52 Ford pickup and got out, slamming the door. She stormed into the drug store and ran into a pudgy Mexican clerk.

"Where's automotive? I need a gas can," she snapped at him.

"Aisle three, ma'am," he responded, dusting himself off. "Can I help you find anything else?"

"Rags," she spat, her narrow eyes boring into the young man.

He took a step backward. She was good looking. Her big tits strained against the cheap elastic top printed with a series of tattoos. Her denims clung to her ample hips and swept neatly over her curvaceous ass. Her long legs were too long for the pants and he saw her skinny ankle protruding from cheap vinyl boots. He took in the shapely package, but it was her angry demeanor that made him cringe.

"Same aisle, ma'am," he said.

"I'm not your ma'am, fuckin' wetback," Sheila snapped.

She stormed down the aisle, grabbing a 5-gallon plastic gas can and a dozen shop rags. She didn't know what the hell she was doing, but her anger forced her on. She grabbed a box of wooden matches and headed for the checkout counter.

The notion of the Rite Aid fueled her anger. She couldn't stand the gaudy advertisements, the flashy labels and the multicolored aisles. It was as if she was having a bad acid trip. She couldn't contain herself. She muscled her way in front of a large Hispanic woman with a brimming cart and two whimpering children.

"I'm in a hurry," she spat.

Rosa was also in Buckeye at the grocery store. She was floating on air, buying groceries for the first time in what seemed long months. For awhile, she couldn't leave the truck stop. Her truck was dismantled and her jealous, drunkard old man was nearby. She couldn't risk leaving the station unattended. Then Chance came along.

The truck ran better than ever, the station was making money, and her life was complete. She glowed as she glided up and down the aisles, picking up supplies and pondering what Chance would want to eat. She stopped and looked at the magazine stand and flipped through a couple of woman's magazines, pausing to look and some of the sexier outfits. She could still sense his sex inside her and it made her blush. She finally got into the checkout line and picked up a copy of Cosmopolitan.

She paid for the groceries and rolled the shopping cart out into the 100-degree air, stopping to pick up a newspaper. She loaded the perishables in the cab and the rest in the bed of the old truck.

Suddenly a woman was screaming at her. "Excuse me, I'm in a fuckin' hurry."

She turned abruptly, answering without hesitation, "Oh, I'm sorry."

"Fuck sorry, just get the hell out of the way!" Sheila kicked Rosa's cart aside, opened her tailgate with a remote beep and tossed the can, rag and matches inside. She pushed her way past Rosa and climbed into the SUV, firing it to life.

Rosa looked at the sweating woman in awe and moved around the front of her cab. Sheila put the car in reverse and screeched out of the parking space, hitting Rosa's rear fender on the way out.

Sheila was jarred by the impact but not put off by it. She stopped behind the old truck and rolled down her passenger window.

"You should learn to park in your own spot," she spat. Sheila rolled up the window and peeled out of the parking lot.

Rosa jogged to the other side of the truck to assess the damage. The wild woman had creased her right rear fender. She turned to see the SUV nearly collide with another vehicle as it attempted to enter the parking lot, and Sheila careened into the street.

It was nearing 3:00 p.m. and Chance continued painting the exterior. He took a break from prepping and spraying due to the high winds in the afternoon, and painted trim instead. The building was beginning to take on a new look, and Chance built a sense of pride, but Sheila was nagging him. He couldn't get her out of his mind. He sensed she'd be back. He could close the place up and go after her, and he began to think he was being selfish for not doing just that. What if she came back and harmed Rosa? He couldn't stand that. He worked faster.

He wanted Rosa to know if something happened to him, that he tried to leave her with the building in good shape, and it was. Finally, he couldn't stand it anymore. He knew that Sheila was at a nearby motel and he'd find her. He rolled his stroker into the sun, grabbed his vest and gloves and fired it to life. He put up the "Closed" sign and locked up.

Just before he left, he went inside to write Rosa a note. He didn't want to panic her. He stared at the slip of copy paper for a long time, finally writing, "3:30, Baby, I'll be back in a couple of hours. Almost done with the exterior. Love, Chance."

He fired up the dicey beast and rolled out of the station and onto the dusty freeway heading east.

Sheila stopped at the Mobil station near the freeway onramp and filled up the Explorer and the 5-gallon container. She careened out of the station and past the lumbering pickup containing Rosa and her groceries. She hit the passing lane at 90 mph, her air-conditioning turned to the max, the Four Tops preaching love to deaf ears. A wide median of desert sand, creosote, tumbleweed and Yucca plants separated her from oncoming traffic. Hubcaps, junk food, debris, and faded beer cans soiled the landscape.

Seven miles out, a bright chopper passed her going the other way at a high rate of speed. The loud straight pipes screamed at the desert openness and jackrabbits scattered for safety.

Sheila heard the muffled sound and looked around, but saw nothing, and nothing would stop her from the rampage that consumed her. At 100 mph, she whisked off the freeway and skidded to a brisk stop, then turned on the overpass to the station. She pulled up to the freshly painted service doors that were closed and locked. A large "Closed" sign filled the sundry store window. She cursed and pulled behind the dilapidated restaurant next door and shut off the engine. She yanked the .38 from her handbag and circled around the restaurant to the small Spanish cottage behind the station. She was sure a woman was with Chance and she fumed.

Her mind spun with sex-filled thoughts of the couple and her notion of justice. She kicked in the front door and stormed through the small house as the swamp cooler chugged in the back. In the bedroom she could swear she could smell their sex from the damp sheets. She spotted Chance's boxer shorts draped over a wooden chair next to the bed. She pulled her .38 and shot both pillows with deadly accuracy. Leaving the adobe home and slamming the screen door behind her, she stormed to the front of the truck stop.

««—»»

Chance shot along the freeway like a flaming locomotive on two wheels until he saw the lumbering '52 Ford pickup caressing the opposite slow lane at 55 mph. He tried to wave, but at over 110 mph, he passed her before he strained to reach his handlebars again. At that speed he hardly felt the heat. Suddenly, he was concerned. Rosa was a calm human being with a natural glow. He couldn't leave her at the station alone. What if Sheila returned? He searched ahead for a place to turn around. The next off ramp was 4 miles ahead, and he spun the throttle to the stops. He knew his motorcycle would do over 130 mph.

He wasn't sure how the chopper would handle at that speed, but he had to try. He would skim through the 4 miles in just over 2 minutes at 130 mph. The bike lifted slightly, but didn't hesitate to handle the speed. He felt for increased vibration but there was none. It seemed to relish the speed, and the 98 inches of pure V-Twin power drove him on. His eyes watered as he counted the seconds and the signs passed like stanchions on a picket fence. He screamed off the freeway, over the overpass and back onto the westbound lanes, where he pushed the vibrating throttle once more.

Without a thought of highway patrol surveillance, he pushed on. Soon, he was gaining on the creeping pickup, almost standing still as the constant 80 mph traffic whizzed around it.

««—»»

Sheila ran back to the Jeep, yanked the gas can out from behind her rear seat and ran to the house. She ran through the house pouring the quickly evaporating fluid. As she walked outside, the pilot light on the gas stove ignited the pungent fumes. With gas can in hand, she turned to face the door as the explosion expanded in the two-bedroom dwelling.

The screen door burst open and was ripped from its rusting hinges as a ball of flames shot from the doorframe. The front windows of the bungalow exploded, showering the front patio in glass.

The explosion threw Sheila against the back of the corrugated steel structure. The impact with the tin exterior wall split the gas can and spewed gas over the back wall and in the back door. It immediately ignited. Sheila fell to the dirt outside but wasn't protected from the shower of gasoline.

Rosa was just about to pull off the freeway when the speeding motorcycle skidded along side.

"Where were you going, speed demon?"

Rosa said, leaning out of the open window.

"I'm not sure," Chance shouted back over the noise of the stroker, "just looking after you."

Rosa looked at her station as she pulled to the stop. She had never been so proud of it or so hopeful. Then all of a sudden there was smoke behind the store.

"Chance, look!"

Chance dropped the stroker into gear and sped across the overpass to the station lot. He shut off the motor and ran to see what had happened. As he approached the store, the interior burst into flames and the front window exploded. He dove to the pavement, then scrambled to his feet. Rounding the corner was moving form in flames.

It was Sheila. He tackled her, driving her to the sand. Rolling her onto her back, their eyes met, and she attempted a smile. He pushed her legs down against the sand to extinguish the flames, but she fought against him, rolling and jumping to her feet. Just then, the service station exploded and drove them to the dirt once more. Again, Chance dove on the woman to protect her from flying debris.

Chance shoved a portion of collapsed wall aside and noticed that he too was on fire. Pushing Sheila out of harm's way, he dove into the sand and rolled.

When he got to his feet, the station was engulfed in flames. His work was destroyed and Rosa's home and income gone. He backed away from the searing heat and found Rosa standing alongside her truck at the edge of the lot.

She came to him with water and rags as the SUV screamed out of the parking lot and onto the freeway. The highway patrol arrived in minutes, but it was too late, the station was destroyed. Rosa told the officer about the woman and the word went out to stop the Explorer. There was no fire department close by, but one was called from Buckeye. The firemen arrived almost 45 minutes later, in time to chill the simmering embers.

Paramedics checked Chance and offered him a trip to the Hospital, but he refused. Rosa held Chance close and looked deeply at him.

"I own the land and I kept my insurance current," she said. "This could be a good thing."

"Where will you go?" Chance asked.

"I will go see my family in Phoenix," Rosa said, "And you?"

"Probably back to the coast. I can't take the chance she will ever return to hurt you again."

He picked up his smoldering vest that had saved him several times before, but not from a fire. It smoked in his hands. He removed a couple of pins he'd collected from motorcycle runs and tossed the vest in the rubble. He led Rosa to the highway patrol cruiser and she slid inside. The officer at the wheel put down his radio.

"They stopped the woman in the SUV. She's a mess."

"I will never forget the days we've had," Rosa said to Chance. She kissed him deeply and slipped some money into his denim pocket. She closed the door and the cruiser pulled out of the parking lot.

Chance watched and waved to Rosa when she turned and looked back. He walked to his stroker and stood there looking at the destroyed station smoldering in the late afternoon heat. The smell was pungent and the dosed gallons of water created a dense humidity. Chance was a wreck, his clothes torn and burnt, as he mounted his bike for the trip back to the coast. Another deck of cards gone bad.

-12-

BROKEN DREAMS

Sheila's SUV raced for the California border. The pain from the burns on her back and up her neck was excruciating and she almost lost consciousness. Then flashing lights in her rearview mirror distracted her. A highway patrol cruiser was rapidly gaining momentum. Looking in the mirror again, Sheila noticed a haze coming from inside the car and realized she was smoldering. The agony suddenly screamed up her spine.

She swerved off the road and into the creosote before her tires sunk axle-deep in the sand. She lurched forward in the seat, the air bag deployed, and she passed out.

The white Arizona Highway Patrol cruiser skidded to a stop near Sheila's vehicle in the sand. The SUV was still running as the patrolman lurched out of his car and lowered a 9mm automatic across the top of his hood. He could swear he smelled burnt flesh and gagged.

The patrolman could see that Sheila had her hands on the steering wheel and her head rested against the airbag. He reached for his radio and called headquarters.

"Unit 1042 to base, come in, over."

"This is base," the efficient female voice responded, "go ahead."

"I have the woman who was seen leaving Tonopah station. I'm 7 miles east of Quartzsite in the westbound emergency lane. We need backup and an ambulance."

"Right away 1042, thank you."

He returned the mic to its slot alongside the communications console and moved around the front of his cruiser to get a better vantage point on the woman. She was slumped over the steering wheel.

Fire had burned the hair on the back of her head and the clothes away from her back. Blood, hair, and smoky fabric stuck to the leather seat. He pulled the door handle gently, but it was locked. It was 110 degrees outside and her air conditioning was on. As long as the car didn't overheat, she could remain comfortably inside.

On the other hand, the smoke inside the car could kill her. The officer pondered the situation, holstered his weapon, and punched through the glass with his baton. He shoved his arm through the window and opened the door. He pulled her free of the vehicle and shut it off. She awoke and started to scream.

"Control yourself madam," Officer Sullivan said. "I've called an ambulance and if you will sit still, I will dress your wounds."

"I don't want any help," Sheila said, struggling against his grasp.

"I'm sorry young lady, but you are under arrest for arson in Tonopah," the officer said. "You have the right to remain silent, the right to an attorney…"

"Can I have my purse? I have some lotion in it for my burns."

She was wobbling on her feet but trying to make some sense. She attempted to break from the young officers' grasp and turn toward her smoking vehicle.

Sullivan was no chump. He spun the tall woman and slammed her against his cruiser. He drew his handcuffs and pulled her wrists together as he kicked her ankles apart. The cuffs went easily into place, but he was forced to look at her smoldering scalp, which was a gruesome sight. He shoved her to her knees and tie-wrapped her ankles in place.

"What are you doing?" Sheila shouted.

"Two things," Officer Sullivan said professionally. "Protecting you and protecting me. You are also under suspicion of murder and your injuries are substantial. You are considered a dangerous suspect."

He went to the trunk of his cruiser and got a first aid kit. He removed cream, gauze, and a pair of scissors. He cut away the back of her burned blouse and gasped at the third-degree burns. He dressed them to the best of his ability.

"Leave me alone," Sheila shouted and tried to squirm away from him. "I'm going to sue you if I'm hurt."

He couldn't fathom her level of anger. Most people under similar circumstances would have given anything to pass out and be cared for. This woman was obviously psychotic. He covered her injuries and was trying to shove her in the back of the cruiser when the ambulance arrived.

"I don't want to go in the ambulance. Take me to the station so I can bail out and leave!" Sheila shouted.

"No fuckin' way! I don't want you in my cruiser," Sullivan said, holding her firmly as the attendants removed the gurney and jacked it to full height.

"My God," the young female attendant murmured as she spotted Sheila's wounds. The officer stood in front of Sheila to ensure that she would not move while they inspected and dressed her burns. They strapped her face down to the gurney and loaded her in the ambulance for the trip back to the West Valley Hospital in Goodyear.

«« — »»

Chance stuffed earplugs into his ears and rode west on the freeway in a tomb of muted tones and the rumble of the stroker. He was dazed and brain numb. He couldn't figure out what the hell had happened. He didn't know if he had fallen in love with Rosa or with the solitude of the desert. Could she have been the best woman to ever enter his life? He'd never know. Did she give his wandering existence some meaning? He didn't know. He couldn't figure out what he was feeling. Was he mourning or in shock as he rolled through the hot desert toward Blythe and the California-Arizona border? All he knew for certain was that he had destroyed another woman's life.

Blythe was a terrible name for a town. It reeked of depression and despair. Quartzsite was just on the edge of Arizona before Blythe, and it smacked of a vast sandy swap meet full of booths and makeshift sheds housing quartz, turquoise and silver jewelry vendors. People who made strings of cheap chunks of turquoise for bracelets lived and attempted to survive there. Kitschy gifts allowed the creative to escape the city and abide like a tribe on the edge of the desert, undisturbed by the regulations and expectations of normal society.

Quartzsite was like some terrible omen of what was to come. Chance tried to ignore the road signs informing him of the distance to Quartzsite and Blythe. Although the ball of fire in the sky was dipping toward the west, it was still as hot as a skillet with the flame turned on high. The temperatures beat the earth into submission so that the ground was bleached white and little foliage grew. For as far as Chance could see, only a handful of cactus remained, surrounded by the resilient tumbleweed, creosote and fading debris. On a hot day, a man could die waiting for help on this fiery edge of the Mojave.

Chance was tempted to pull over and walk into the sand, praying that a diamondback rattler or a gang of tarantulas would take his life before the sun did. He sensed that his life was destined for a major change as the bike sputtered and he turned his petcock to reserve. He hadn't refuel the rigid since he arrived at Rosa's and the 130 mph blast up and down the freeway sucked more of his small supply.

The ride from Tonopah to Blythe was 110 miles and he still had 40 to peel off. His reserve supply was minimal with the shapely custom metal tank. His emotional doldrums were replaced with a tentative edge.

His desert suicide wish could come true. He still had 20 miles before he would reach Quartzsite. He slowed to improve mileage, but knew it wouldn't help much. Luck wasn't his strong suit on that blistering day as he passed a road sign that announced that Quartzsite was an unlucky 13 miles ahead as the chopped stroker coughed and died.

He pulled in the clutch and steered the long custom bike onto the emergency lane, over the ruffled asphalt meant to wake up nodding truckers. Just as he put his boots down on the hard surface, a caravan of trucks passed him at 80 mph, buffeting the lone biker and his machine. One of the truckers honked a biker salute but kept on rolling. Chance stepped off his machine and backed up a couple of steps.

He was a filthy mess of soot and dust. His sandy hair was matted and pulled back behind his head in a rubber band. As soon as he stepped off the machine, the full impact of the desert sun mingled with the heat of the engine. He gasped for breath, but even that felt hot in his lungs. He looked at his feet and the reality of the desert was suddenly closer.

At 80 mph, the world adjacent to interstates was an unreal blur of general landscape and landmarks. It was deceiving. The hot asphalt was scattered with the images of a society storming through nature without consideration for what it left behind. There were shards of broken glass from one terrible bone-twisting accident after another, bits of asphalt from hundreds of resurfacing passes, beer cans and faded whiskey bottles, diapers, and cigarette butts that never seemed to lose their shape.

The trash spread into the desert like a plague against the land.

Chance checked his bedroll for water. No such luck. He took everything into Rosa's house. He looked again and spotted a small bag that
once held his .38 and a small leather pouch of ammo.

It was also empty. In an outside pocket was some Chap Stick, which
he smeared across his lips, over his nose and along his hairline. As he
bent to return it to the pocket, he noticed something under the black
pouch and moved it to the side. It was a stack of paper bound together.

He pulled it free. It was a copy of Vince's screenplay. Chance
didn't have time to kick back and read. The sun was tearing at the
back of his neck. He needed water and fuel. He stuffed the manuscript
back into its dark place under the tool pouch and closed the Cordura
travel roll. He'd never told Vince he hid a copy.

Suddenly the hair on the back of his neck crawled and he heard
skidding tires. He looked up, his face a map of desperation. A car was
in the emergency lane headed directly at him and his motorcycle. It
was a convertible and a terrified woman was at the wheel. Chance saw
the fear in her eyes.

She saw the rider and tried to pull over, miscalculating her speed.
Chance motioned for her to get back in the No. 2 lane and go around
him, but the plume of dust billowing behind the compact indicated her
foot buried against the brake pedal and the vehicle was out of control.

Chance yanked at his drag bars and pushed his rigid chassis
toward a gully adjacent to the emergency lane. He dove behind it into
the tumbleweed and rubble. A billow of dust and ground rubber filled
the air as Chance buried his face in the sand and prayed that he
wouldn't feel the weight of the compact grinding him into the remains
of snake skins and tarantula carcasses.

The sound of a collision, the crying tires, the crumpling metal was
all consuming. Within that brief time duration, the world stopped,
while he waited for the outcome. Chance lingered, his face buried in
the earth. Then there was a silence. He bolted to his feet to see what
had happened.

Covered head to toe in sand, Chance stood to see the compact still
rocking in the spot where he'd just been. As the dust thinned, the
sound of a whimpering woman pierced the stillness. Chance climbed
out of the shallow gully to see if the driver was injured, but halfway
up he turned to look at his motorcycle. It lay, bleeding fluids into the
sand. He would need to return to it quickly.

"Are you alright?" he asked.

"I think so," the young girl said, still shaking.

"Were you trying to kill me?"

"No, no, I was trying to stop to help," she choked.

"Don't do that very often, do you? Listen, never mind that, do you have some water?" Chance said.

"Yes," she said more calmly. She was in her late 20s, with an athletic build and a mass of brunette curls pulled into a rubber band at the back of her head. Her face was handsome, not girlish or cute. She handed Chance an insulated container of cold water.

He took a long slug and handed it back to her. "Have some. It's hot as hell. You wouldn't happen to have some gas, would you?"

"Gas? I don't think so. Is that the problem?" she tried to compose herself

"It was," Chance said, trying to knock the big clumps of dirt from his clothes. "Oh shit, I've got to check my bike."

He turned and took two long strides into the bottom of the gully. Struggling, he righted his pride and found a beer can to support the kickstand. The bike was covered in sand, but appeared unharmed except for the leaking oil. He scrambled back to the car.

"Are you sure you're OK?" he asked gently. "I'm a fuckin' mess and you wouldn't believe a word of what I've been through today, so we won't go there, but I'm harmless. You may want to get out of your car and walk around for just a minute so we know you're all right."

"OK," she said and climbed out of the driver's side while Chance held the door and watched the traffic.

"Can you open the trunk and check for gas?"

"Sure," she said and bent over the door to retrieve the keys.

Chance's nerves were on edge. His eyes were drawn to the careening traffic looking east for another errant motorist who might come along and kill the both of them. He had enough mayhem surrounding his life.

"I hate to move you along, but let's decide what we're going to do and get the hell out of this emergency lane before we have another one."

Chance took the keys and opened the trunk. There was a clutter of suitcases, roller blades, gym bags and books, but no gas can. Chance picked up one of the books and looked at the wide spine, "Psychology of the Murdering Mind." He picked up another one, "Criminal Law, Vol. 5."

"No gas," Chance said. "Get back in the car."

She turned and Chance opened the door again.

"If you would like to help, "Chance said, "here's what I'm going to do."

"It's the least I can do," she returned to her seat and fumbled with her keys.

"I'll take the gas tank off the bike and we'll go get it filled."

He took another swig of water and offered the container to her again. "Drink."

He scrambled down to the bike and dug into his bedroll for tools. He removed the gas line, then the rubbermounted studs holding the tank in place. He pulled the empty tank free and climbed the hill to her car, placing it neatly on the floor of the back seat.

"That's it, let's hurry. Someone could take the bike while I'm gone. We need to haul ass."

She revved up the Mustang and dropped it into gear.

"What's your name?" she shouted over the buffeting wind.

"Chance Hogan," he replied. "And yours?"

"Kathleen Norton," she said.

"What's with the law books in the trunk?" Chance asked. "Are you an attorney or a cop?"

"I'm a junior cop," she said. "Just graduated and headed for my first job."

"Graduated?" Chance said.

"Yeah, I have a degree in criminal law from Phoenix. I could have become an attorney, but would really like to get into the FBI. I need some practical experience first, though."

Chance began to relax as she drove. She was hot looking but he was only interested in rescuing his motorcycle and returning to the coast.

"And what does Chance do?" Kathleen said.

"I'm proud and ashamed to say, not much of anything right now."

"Nothing, ever?"

"Oh, I've been everything from a welder to a magazine writer. I gambled for awhile, like my old man, but I guess you could say I'm a full-time biker rolling the dice on another adventure."

He was sure that would eliminate him from her wish list.

"I've always wished I could have a devil-may-care existence. I feel like we run at life trying to do so much for nothing. It's all bullshit."

She shrugged her muscular shoulders and drove on.

"Look," she said as they passed the smoldering Explorer in the sand with the highway patrol cruiser behind it, lights flashing and an ambulance. A gurney was being loaded.

Chance looked at it in dismay and turned away. He recognized the SUV. It reminded him of the terrible mess his life was in. On the horizon was Quartzsite and the plastic franchise gas station signs. Chance thought of Rosa and what they'd been building together and he shuttered.

They pulled off the freeway and into a station where Chance yanked the steel tank from the back seat and filled it. He borrowed some rags, wrapped the tank, and put it carefully into the trunk.

Kathleen peeled back onto the freeway for 10 miles, pulled across the freeway and made a U-turn into the westbound lanes until she was parallel to Chance's motorcycle. She pulled to a stop and Chance jumped out and retrieved his tank from the trunk. It was still hot as hell.

He mounted the tank on the rigid frame and hooked up the gas line. He dusted off the bike as best he could and fired it to life. He spun it around, kicking up sand and crap while trying to guide it out of the gully and back on the shoulder. It sputtered and slipped in the soft sand as he struggled to capture traction. He finally made it to the emergency lane and shut it off, then checked the bike from stem to stern. Sand was everywhere.

Kathleen watched the grubby biker with intrigue while kneeling on her seat. He wasn't half-bad looking, seemed like a hard-working, upstanding guy, and there was something else that she couldn't figure out.

Chance saw how she gazed at him, but he was too emotionally hammered to consider her. Besides, he wanted out of the desert in the worst way and back to the coast. He wiped down the bike as best he could. Everything seemed to be in place and ready to roll.

"Hey, thanks so much for the help," he said. "I'm going to get moving toward the coast."

"I'll follow you at least into Los Angeles," she said and sat back down in her leather seat.

Chance wanted to tell her no, but knew that she could save his ass if she was behind him, so he nodded.

"Thank you. I'll head on the 10 Freeway all the way to Los Angeles to the San Pedro freeway south."

He fired the bike to life and rolled onto the freeway. As he pulled up to 75 mph, it seemed cooler and he felt good with his shades on although his vest was gone and his clothes a mess. His bedroll bounced on the long front end and pushed some of the road breeze away from his torso. His earplugs kept the scream of the freeway out of his ears.

Chance pulled off the freeway in Palm Springs and filled up. She followed. He waved and pulled back onto the freeway with enough gas to deliver him back to Los Angeles.

He destroyed Rosa's life, or Sheila had. Sheila had also killed the girl he met in Phoenix. As Chance jammed past some bikini-clad babes in a sports car and they checked him out, he thought he was some sort of devil when it came to women. Now he had another one following.

"The luckiest thing she could do," Chance said to himself as he sped past Banning toward the city, "would be to turn off and never see me again."

He had no confidence in his San Pedro future, his new pad or in Vince's predicament. He just hoped he could get into his place, take a shower, and have a drink in peace.

-13-

DEATH BY THE SEA

Chance rode the entire distance across the state on Interstate10 because he'd promised the tight-looking brunette in the trailing sports car that he would lead her into the city. Finally, in downtown Los Angeles, he leaned south toward San Pedro and the coast. He could smell the salt air mixed with the automobile fumes that hung like a stale coffee-colored blanket over the coastline.

She pulled up alongside him in the bright red Mustang and shouted, "I want to see you again."

"No you don't," Chance shouted back. "I'm nothing but trouble, but thanks for the help."

"Please," she said, her dark hair flapping in the wind, her supple breasts bouncing in her slim athletic top.

Jesus, Chance thought to himself, she's going to kill the two of us in this traffic jam.

"Leave a message at Century Motorcycle in San Pedro," Chance screamed over his fiery exhaust tone. He spun his throttle, waved and split across two lanes and into the carpool lane at 100 mph. He never looked back and she never caught up.

As he crossed over the 405 Freeway, he felt a cooling salty breeze and smelled oil refineries through the smog. The downtown traffic lessened as he rolled toward the southernmost point in San Pedro where the freeway ended. He continued down the Harbor Freeway, closing in on his seaside home. He was still without employment and didn't know if his pad would be standing. It was custom-built in 1937 and sold in the early '60s to a woman who owned other properties around the point. She'd rented it out and never repaired it. Her last tenants were filth mongers and their pets ruled the roost.

Before Chance moved in, he ripped all the carpeting out of the small home, scrubbed the '30s tiled bathroom, ripped all the tile and appliances out of the kitchen, and bought a clean used refrigerator. Chance scrubbed the small pad that overlooked the main channel where cruise ships departed for Ensenada and beyond to Cabo San Lucas.

Two blocks over and a couple blocks east on Pacific Avenue was the historic Century Motorcycle Shop. It was more of a motorcycle junkyard than a shop or restoration source, but it had heart hanging from every dusty shelf. That included the gold pinstriped black Vincent tank holding the ashes of the former owner. His daughter, Cindy, a rambunctious redhead in her mid-40s, ran the counter, and managed the place. She was a wild stub of a woman with a joke sharing the heart on her sleeve.

Chance rolled off the freeway at Harbor and hung a right, his loud pipes rumbling against the pavement as he headed up Harbor Boulevard adjacent to the main channel. He loved the look of the ships on the harbor. His favorite restaurant was Acapulcos at the edge of the salty brine, where you could drink margaritas and watch the ships pass at 10 feet above sea level, less than 40 feet away. They were massive at that angle and ominous. He turned right on Crescent and rolled a couple blocks to the corner house. He shut off the bike in the street and rolled up onto the sidewalk to the gate.

Everything appeared in one piece. Then he noticed the card pinned next to the lock on the gate. He yanked the Century Motorcycle business card off the wooden fence and looked it over. On the back was a roughly scrawled note from Cindy. "Come down to the shop. It's Vince."

Chance looked at the card long and hard. He had been on hell's highway for six hours or six days. He was dying to see the inside of his pad and the bottom of a cocktail glass. He prayed that the cupboard still contained a bottle of Jack and the freezer, if his electricity wasn't turned off, had some ice in the tray. He pushed the clicking and cooling motorcycle inside the gate and kicked the chromed kickstand toward a chunk of concrete.

The back door was still locked and the house smelled of afternoon heat and dust, but it seemed in decent shape. He opened the chipped wooden cupboard to the left of the sink, where he kept his limited liquor supply. It contained a half bottle of Cuervo Gold and a bottle of Merlot, in case a woman arrived. Pushing the wine aside, he spotted his bottle of Jack Daniel's, with three fingers worth in the bottom. He went to the fridge, opened it and sighed. It was working. The freezer was badly in need of defrosting, but there was still ice in the tray.

Chance banged a handful of cubes out of the tray and poured a couple of fingers of amber Jack over the clinking ice. He sloshed the hard liquor around the cool glass and walked into the living room where he could see a container ship pushing its packed, beamy hull out of the harbor. He looked at it with escape in mind and wondered if he could find peace at sea. He knew the answer was no—no women. Just about to sit on the threadbare couch, he heard the whine of an unmuffled two-stroke screaming up the street.

His house was on the northwest corner of the block, so he looked to the left to catch a glimpse of the screaming metallic banshee. He spotted the bubbly redhead, Cindy, peeling into his small front yard on some mixture of a two-stroke Yamaha engine bolted haphazardly in an early rigid Triumph frame. She skidded to a stop in the center of the lawn and looked in the bay window.

"Get out here," she shouted, revving the engine and snapping the clutch, which caused the rickety cycle to throw a chunk of Chance's weed-filled lawn, dry as a popcorn fart, onto the neighbor's yard. Chance burst out his front door with the drink in his hand.

"What the hell?" he shouted.

"Gimme some of that," she snapped with a smile and killed the engine. She shoved the bike over until it leaned against the small concrete porch on the front of the house. It had no kickstand of any sort. She grabbed at Chance's drink and took a long slug.

"Take another swallow, you tall drink of water, you'll need it," she hollered handing the chilled tumbler back. "You look like hell. Where have you been?"

"You wouldn't believe me," Chance said. "What's up with Vince?"

"He's dead," Cindy said, suddenly somber and staring at the burnt lawn. Shufflin' her feet and looking at the strange red shoes she wore with stripped socks, she said, "He got in a fight at Harold's Saloon and someone killed him."

Chance took another hit on the tumbler and sat down on the edge of a concrete step.

"What the fuck?" he said. "Life can sure throw a deck full of bad hands at ya."

"I ain't one to give anyone advice," Cindy said, shuffling her flashy Wizard of Oz shoes. "Hell, my kid just got out of prison, for being in love with an insane bitch, but you're cool, Chance. Don't get involved in anything that will bring your life down."

She gave him a big bear of a hug and kissed him on the cheek. She was some 10 years his senior, but she wished she was younger.

"Take a shower and relax. There's nothing you can do."

Chance nodded and hugged her back. He stepped up onto the dilapidated porch and downed the rest of the drink. He tossed the glass across the street into the open field between him and the harbor.

"Sonuvabitch," he muttered and went inside, thinking about Vince and their friendship.

He knew the man was a hothead and prone to fights. Chance stripped off his sweaty, burnt, ruined T-shirt and Levi's and stepped into the shower. As the rusty shower head splashed him with luke-warm water, he thought about the time Vince rolled up to his pad drunk and shot a hole in the wall with the .45-caliber, because he didn't like the R&B music Chance was playing. Chance draped a picture over the hole and only showed it to people he could trust.

He got out of the shower and wiped himself down with the only towel he had. He went to his bedroom and put on a long-sleeved button down shirt and Wranglers with his charred brown cowboy boots that he wiped off and polished some. He pulled on the western belt and a buckle he made himself out of brass rod. It was in the shape of a spoked motorcycle wheel and matched the only ring he wore on his right hand. He dug through his jacket closet and found another leather vest designed by a Hells Angel and stared at his reflection in the mirror. He was tired to the bone, mentally and physically, but he needed some answers.

He looked around the beat-up old pad and something inside him wanted to stay, "Lie down and sleep, stupid." He shut the rickety door, pulled his chopper into the street and fired it to life. The bar was only a couple blocks away, but he rode because he had no idea if his next move would take him back to the pad for that much-needed rest or down the road in search of more answers.

The 2-inch exhaust slapped the pavement violently as he pulled into the alley behind the old seaport bar and coasted into the parking lot that held a rusting dumpster, several vehicles that needed to be towed to junkyards and two pickups. One had recently been painted, sans bodywork, over a severely dented body and bed. The paint job didn't help much. The other truck had smoother sheet metal, but was primered gray.

Both had Harley stickers in the rear windows. Two bikes were parked behind the rusting wrought-iron rear entrance. One was an old stretched black Shovel with a jockey shift that reminded Chance of one of his first customs. The other was another black chopper, a custom '46 Indian Chief with highbars.

Chance made his way inside through the rarely used small kitchen, where a couple of regulars ducked to smoke and talk shit. The bar was a local dump. From the floors to the ceilings, nothing was repaired. Even the Budweiser/NASCAR posters were disheveled and stained. Chance pulled up a bar stool next to Indian Joe, a local who rode the old Indian in the parking lot. It was the only possession he had. He no longer worked, since an accident destroyed his voice box and he was unable to speak. He wasn't educated and had a tough time writing messages on napkins to communicate with his fellow drinkers.

Indian Joe recognized Chance and immediately clapped him on the back, shook his hand in a biker grip and hugged him heartily. They didn't hang out together, but whenever Chance had the opportunity, he helped Joe out, getting him a gig riding as an extra in a music video, anything. Joe always wore his black fingerless gloves and a leather shirt over a black T-shirt and Levis. He wore shades night and day and a sweat-stained ball cap over a red bandanna tied at the back of his head.

After he grinned at seeing Chance, his mood turned somber and he looked at the rough, chewing gum-stained linoleum while pulling at his full black beard. He made some motions with his hand and spoke through a long mustache. No words came out but Chance could detect the mention of Vince and the terrible thing that happened to him.

"Can I get you anything?" asked Rachel.

Chance turned to her crooked smile but didn't smile back. "I'll take a Jack on the rocks," he said and returned his concentration to Indian Joe.

"What can you tell me Joe?" Chance said, pushing a cocktail napkin toward him and reaching into his vest for a pen. Joe waved his hand indicating no need for a pen, he always had one within easy reach. Joe shrugged his shoulders and waved his arms as he always did, while trying to communicate.

He turned toward the napkin and scribbled on the soft paper. "I wasn't here, but I heard that he fought three Mexicans. They didn't kill him."

Chance nodded, took a slug of the whiskey that was poured to the brim of the tumbler. The only benefit to drinkin' at Harold's Place was the depth of the drinks. It made all other bars appear chintzy. He turned and looked across the battered pool table to the shuffleboard that leaned at an odd angle and into the partitioned addition housing two more tables.

Two young Hispanics played on the back table. One had a black eye and he moved to the darkest corner of the bar to avoid Chance's gaze. His partner noticed his movements and turned to find the source of his concern. Chance stepped away from the barstool as the slightly taller Hispanic returned his cue to the rack. He attempted to put the cue away but the rack, like most of the bar, was in disrepair. Chance glanced at the table and noticed the game wasn't over.

The 6-foot Hispanic with narrow shoulders, wearing a long-shoreman's union T-shirt, tried again to put away the cue, but the retaining pins holding were bent or worn-out. In his frustration, he let the cue fall to the floor as he turned and headed for the front door at the same time Chance did. Chance moved quickly when another biker at the bar spied the action and grabbed his right arm. Chance spun and hit the old scooter tramp with a hard left. The biker collapsed. Chance stayed focused on the escaping Mexican.

The biker had slowed him enough to allow the young Hispanic to reach the front door. Just then, Hoss, the massive bouncer, entered the door from the street. Chance closed in on the petrified youngster, pulling his Beretta 3-inch knife from his rear pocket and snapping his wrist to unleash the blade.

The Mexican held up his hands and his partner ran at Chance with his cue, swinging it over his head.

"They didn't kill Vince," the biker shouted from the dusty deck, trying to pull himself up, his right eye swelling badly. Chance spotted the cue coming and spun to meet it, blocking and grabbing it with his left hand and pulling the little man toward him. The man's right arm flailed in the dim barroom as he saw the blade of the knife flicker and move toward his guts.

Chance's mind spun with alternatives before he drove the blade at the man's rib cage. If he hit him just under the last rib, he would cut main arteries to the man's heart and he would die instantly. Vince was his best friend, but he knew his mind was clouded. The young Hispanic's knees buckled in fear, and Chance closed his blade. The young man collapsed in Chance's arms.

"Who killed my brother?" Chance barked and let the youngster fall to the floor. He immediately turned to the other man who was trying to scramble to his feet. Hoss, a mountain of a man, helped the biker up.

"We no kill your brother," the young Hispanic said, half crying. "A man in nice suit shoot him."

"He drove off in a new BMW," Hoss said and stepped between Chance and the other Mexican. "You're out of line."

"I've been rolling the wrong set of dice for a couple of weeks," Chance said, helping one of the kids to his feet. "Vince was my brother, and I've got to find out what happened."

-14-

HOT WOMEN
AND COLD COPS

Chance woke with a start in his harbor home. He reached for his watch on the bed stand and was startled by the time: 10:30 a.m. He rolled over and tried to go back to sleep, but last night's events, Vince's death, and memories of Rosa haunted his consciousness with images of violence and love.

He sat up abruptly and stared straight ahead. He wanted to hide from the world, ride back to the desert, or find Vince's killer. He didn't know what to do. Then harsh reality set in. He owed the rent, the phone, the power, and electric. He had no food and only a little over a hundred bucks in his pocket. He needed a job. Besides, his Jack Daniel's supply waned.

He threw his long legs over the edge of the bed, scratched his scalp through the long sandy-blonde hair, and mused at the brightness of the day, with a sense that the psycho broad and the terror in the desert were behind him. There was no personal upheaval in San Pedro, no women beating him into the salt water of the harbor's main channel, and no cops after him.

He got up and stretched. He showered, dressed, and felt his stomach scream for chow. He'd only had breakfast at one joint on the harbor across the street from the Spanish fort-looking lath and plaster fisheries next to the busy channel. The stench was harsh, but it was one of the last of the old-time fish-and-chips joints.

Annette's Restaurant was next to an industrial marine store for the professional fishermen who moored their boats in the inlet next door. Chance rolled the chopper into the sunlight and took the cap off the taillight where the ground occasionally came loose. He tightened it down and fired the bike to life.

Even though it was dirty with desert sand, Chance rode his dicey motorcycle comfortably. He vowed to detail the bike later after some chow and a career investigation. He parked the bike in the diagonal slots out front of the cafe and walked past the nylon line and ship's anchor out front. It was a small joint, with walls painted the dark blue color of the water in the main channel. The bulkheads were scattered with photos of the historic harbor and days gone by, of captured fish, and devastating storms. The wood tables were covered with red-checkered tablecloths. Tin forks, knives, and paper napkins waited. Hanging from the ceiling was a square black chalkboard containing specials for the day.

A young lady was standing on a rickety wooden chair filling out the specials menu with her back to Chance. His eyes spied her long hair and the pleasant curve of her ass tightly embraced in form-fitting Levis. She took special artistic care with small caricatures of smiling fish around the edge of the chalkboard. A rotund Italian woman behind the counter with dark circles under her eyes called to Chance.

"Coffee?"

"Yeah, sure," Chance said, "black, goddamnit."

He pulled out a chair and began to sit when the girl standing on the chair spun and jumped to the linoleum floor.

"Hey," she snapped, heading for Chance.

Chance looked up, his eyes blinking in the morning sunlight billowing in the picture window. Her plump ass reminded him of his weakness for sex and his non-stop desire for women. He looked at her face and suddenly was reminded of the girl in the clapboard apartment a week ago at the Spot Saloon. His mind was cluttered with memories of the last week as if he was snorting a mental madness Slurpee.

"Suzanne?"

"You goddamn right," she snapped, her hands pressed firmly on her hips, bits of chalk crumbling in her tight grasp and falling on the polished floor beneath. "Where the hell have you been, damnit?" She mocked his use of "goddamnit."

Chance was hungry, but all of a sudden his mind was filled with the images of Suzanne nude on a small bed while her ex, the cop, pounded on the door. He shook his head violently and looked at her stern features surrounding those big dark eyes.

"I've been lost in the wrong poker game," Chance said. "Out of town for a week or so. Just got back."

"Am I suppose to believe that?" she said.

Chance's eye rode down her form over her small tits and white T-shirt-covered torso. She was young, real young and cute, even with no make-up.

"How's your boyfriend?" Chance said, not waiting for an answer. "You're still cute, though."

"Suzanne, chow's up," said the fat Italian women with the dour look as she pushed past the youngster to deliver a steaming mug of black Java to Chance.

"I'll be back," Suzanne said and spun to the galley at the back.

The Italian woman rolled her eyes and delivered the coffee and laminated menu to Chance's table.

The smells of the old-time fry joint filled the air and Chance was starving.

"Can I start with an order of wheat toast?"

"Sure," said the big woman without a smile as she wiped off his table and disappeared behind the counter again to glare at the young hottie as she dropped a couple of pieces of toast into the stained stainless toaster.

Suzanne burst out of the kitchen with an order for another table. There were maybe 25 people in the old joint.

"Why didn't you call me?" she spat, heading for a couple of retired longshoreman in flannel shirts and faded denims sitting at a nearby table.

"I don't know your number," Chance said. "Besides, we're not married. You didn't answer my question. How's your boyfriend?"

"I don't have a boyfriend," she said, slinging the plates of greasy food at the seamen. The customer looked startled and pushed back his chair as if she were yelling at him.

"I didn't come here to get bitched at," Chance said. "I was betting on having breakfast, and I thought this was a sure bet. Will you take my order?"

"Depends, damnit," she barked, tossing the other plate in front of her weary customer.

"Glad she's not pissed at me," he said, ducking for cover under his paper napkin.

"Hey," she snapped at the customer, then spun to Chance's table. "I was sorta thinkin' that I might see you again." She lowered her voice some, but everyone in the warm cafe could still hear every word.

"If you're going to starve me to death, I'll guarantee that you'll never see me again. Take my order, goddamnit. We'll talk later," Chance said, then waited.

She stared at him across the table, her fists pressed tightly against her hips again, her legs spread slightly. She was wearing a small blue apron with a fish hand painted in metallic inks over one pocket. She was steamed, but Chance wasn't interested in her reasoning. His stomach begged for nourishment.

"Whatta ya want?" she said, snatching her order book and a chewed-on pencil out of her apron.

"So you're horny?" Chance said as she put the pencil against the pad. She stopped abruptly and stared at Chance's green eyes.

"I'll take a half-dozen egg whites scrambled, a side of salsa, and a short stack."

She attempted to write, then stammered, "Uhhh."

"Just turn in the fuckin' order and get my toast with some jelly, will ya?" Chance said. She shook her head deliberately and backed away, then stormed into the kitchen.

Chance turned to the guys at a table across from him and said, "Sorry about the interruption."

"I'd hate to be in your shoes, buddy," the older looking of the two said.

"Hell, I only went out with her once. What if I had seen her for a week?" Chance said.

The two fellas laughed. One sported a gray beard, while the other had a full head of salt-and-pepper hair.

"You gentlemen know where a guy could find a job?" Chance inquired. "I can do most anything. I'm a good welder."

The two old guys sat and looked at one another. "You know you can't work much around here without being in a union," one of them said.

"Yeah, I know the drill," Chance returned.

The other old gent took a bite of his hash browns and turned toward Chance. "You can work for one of the marine supply joints. There's one at the end of Signal Street. I think they're hiring."

"I'll investigate right after breakfast. Thanks for the tip," Chance said, feeling his stomach turn and gurgle like a carburetor pulling the last fleeting drops of fuel out of a gas tank.

He sipped his steaming, chipped ceramic mug of coffee while watching the plump Italian woman butter his toast. As she turned to deliver it, Suzanne burst out of the kitchen into the area behind the counter. Chance watched her move.

She wasn't that good looking, but she was full of lust and youth. He could sense her sexual overload and he liked that. Her light brunette hair was thick and long, but he liked tits full and jetting, like missiles of love. He sensed an untamed horse wrapped in an artistic and creative soul. The thought terrified him as he watched her snatch the plate of toast from the older woman and head to his side.

She tossed it on his table and said, "What did you say to me?"

"Whatta ya mean?" Chance said, spreading strawberry jelly on the toast.

"You know what I mean," she spat.

"Oh you mean about getting fucked," he said.

"What?" she said, trying on the look of sheer disgust and dismay.

"You'd like me to fuck you a little, wouldn't you?" Chance said, rolling the sensual dice.

He put his hand on her forearm and began to run it gently up her arm. He looked her directly in the eyes as his hand slid off her arm and onto her lower back. Her agitated stance disappeared like a dense fog burnt off the harbor by intense sunlight.

As his hand reached the gentle curve just above her ass the older woman behind the counter shouted, "Suzanne, food's up."

At the same time, the front door opened with the clinking of a small bell and in walked a uniformed Hispanic Los Angeles Police Officer. His middle-aged face was stained with the pitted scars of youthful acne, which gave him a stern, tough look.

"Hi, baby," he said to Suzanne, as Chance took his hand from her ass.

Chance wasn't afraid of the man, but he had enough trouble in the spinning blender of his life. He didn't need a uniformed one. He looked up at Suzanne with a knowing gaze.

"What's up, honey?" the 6-foot officer said, following Suzanne into the kitchen.

Chance could hear the ruffled conversation from the kitchen but couldn't make out the words. She came out a couple of minutes later with Chance's plate of eggs and put them carefully on his table without making eye contact.

"No boyfriend, huh?" Chance said.

"I'll get the salsa, sir," she said and left the table, returning to the kitchen.

Some five minutes later, she returned with the salsa, the short stack, and syrup. Chance sensed that the officer may have recognized his motorcycle and was boiling, like old French fries left in the greasy cooker too long.

The chow hit the spot and he tried to focus on his low-level fuel situation. The officer came out of the kitchen as Chance took a long bite of the dripping hot cakes. He headed for the door.

As he pulled on the glass portal he turned back to Suzanne and said, "I'll talk to you later, baby." He then glanced at Chance and walked out to his patrol car with a bag of donuts and a full plastic mug of coffee.

Chance got up from his table and walked back to the cash register at the counter and paid the Italian woman as Suzanne stood in the doorway eyeing him.

"See ya later, baby," he said to Suzanne as he turned and headed for the door.

Outside, he straddled his scooter, hoping the cop hadn't seen it. Suzanne slipped up behind him.

"He's married."

"To you?" Chance said, starting the long chopper.

She stepped forward and handed him a slip of paper. "Call me, damnit."

"Only if I want to get shot or arrested," Chance said, backing out of the parking spot and rumbling up the street.

He could feel her watching him as he turned left on Signal and headed toward old warehouse number 1 at the end of the harbor spit less than a half mile away.

He parked his faithful scooter and walked up to a small temporary building at the end of the dock that housed Ships Services and Water Taxis. It was an odd prefab building, not much better than a motor home planted next to the oldest warehouse in the Los Angeles Harbor. The blue-with-white-trimmed wooden shed looked strange beneath the massive six-story concrete structure with giant metal doors on every floor surrounded by concrete lion-faced gargoyles. The taxi service was located at the end of the narrow spit with historic warehouses on each side forming a dark concrete dead end. A flier taped on the outside of the glass door read, "Now Hiring" in bold on the top. Without reading much else, Chance walked in.

A 25-year-old curly blond receptionist looked up with blue eyes and smiled at Chance. "Can I help you?"

"I need a job, goddamnit," Chance said.

"Here's an application." She smiled and looked Chance over. "You can take it over to that table and fill it out."

"What're my chances?" he asked, as he backed away from the small reception area.

"Depends," she said and smiled. "They need people. Guess it depends on your abilities and experience."

Chance filled out the application while occasionally checking her full, healthy cleavage while she bent over her computer keyboard. Her smile was irresistible and her boobs jiggled seductively in her iridescent blouse, but Chance had to put some bucks in his pocket before he could buy a girl a cup of coffee and a biscuit.

He slipped her the application while she took care of business on the phone and then walked back out to his bike. It was as grubby as it had ever been with the caked-on dust from the desert, and he was determined to detail it and check it out mechanically when he reached his pad on the bluff. As he slipped on his gloves, he looked up the narrow harbor peninsula from where he came.

He noted the two massive, football field long warehouses on either side, creating a trap at the end where he stood. His cautious nature noted that his only escape would be to run between the two prefab buildings at the dead end of the dock and dive into the briny harbor salt water. Not a great option.

Farther up the asphalt street strewn with railroad tracks were oil tanks and more warehouses. The street was desolate until he swung a leg over his bike and a car pulled out from between two buildings. It was a police cruiser, and it turned in Chance's direction.

Chance didn't pay it any mind and fired the chop to life, dropped it into gear, and pulled out of the parking spot and into his lane. The exhaust note reverberated between the two buildings as he pulled up to speed and hit second gear. He was about to hit third and pass the cruiser simultaneously when the officer hit his blinkers and pulled the patrol car directly into Chance's path. Chance clinched his front brake lever and the narrow front-end dove forward, the tire skidding against the rough asphalt. He leaned hard to the right in an attempt to stop and avoid slamming into the patrol car.

The car jerked to a stop and rocked in place, as if it was holding its ground. Chance hit his rear brake pedal hard and the rear of the bike slipped against the rough asphalt. The front wheel slipped against the slick steel surface of the multitude of criss-crossing railroad tracks, the harbor spur, driving the front wheel into the track groove and throwing the motorcycle off balance. Chance let go of the right pedal and rolled free of the motorcycle as he fell to the pavement. He jumped to his feet and shut off the Harley, lifting and pulling the handlebars and the front wheel out of the groove.

The motorcycle was the only thing Chance had to his name. It was his friend, his transportation, and his flag of freedom. The officer rounded the rear of the cruiser with his right hand on his service pistol and his left on the polished nightstick.

"Maybe you need to have your brakes looked at," the officer said.

"Did I do something wrong?" Chance said, ignoring the cop as he checked his front wheel and set the bike on the side stand. Then he turned toward the officer. "Is there a problem?"

"There could be," the officer said, pulling his pistol free from his holster and working the slide. "I don't want any harm coming to that girl."

Chance looked at the weapon and the sweaty pock-marked face of the officer and considered his options. No doubt the girl in the marine service building was watching. He needed that job.

"Listen, I went out with her once, buddy. I never date a girl who has a guy. So don't worry about me."

"Really?" the officer said, sensing Chance's sincerity.

"Look man, I just moved here. I need a job. I can't afford a girl in my life now, anyway," Chance said. "But I can't stop her. You need to do that."

"OK," the officer said. "She told me she doesn't want to see me, but...OK."

He muttered something and returned to the driver's side of the car, started it up, and pulled away.

Chance shook his head and got back on his bike. He watched the cruiser roll up the street and turn left on 22nd. He thought to himself that if he was looking at a poker hand, it wouldn't amount to much.

-15-

Got a Job, Babe

Chance spent the rest of his day working on his pad and going through the mail, where he discovered a small check payment for a motorcycle tech book he wrote. Not much, but enough to get his phone turned back on and the rent paid. It felt good to take care of business and relax.

Chance woke the next morning with a start at 5:15 a.m., the phone blaring in his ear. The voice on the other end of the line was soft and dreamy,

"This is Julie from Harbor Taxi. We've got a job for you if you want it. You need to be here at 7:00. Can you make it?"

Chance shook his head in dismay. He needed a job, but this was against the biker code. Bikers get up and arrive at work when they're good and ready.

"If you want me, I'll be there, Goddamnit," Chance said. "Anything else I need to know?"

"Nope," Julie said, "Just be here and prove you can do the job."

"Not a problem," Chance said, "See ya at 7:00."

He rolled out of bed and hopped in the shower. He backed his motorcycle out of the garage and sprayed it with a cleaner and quickly wiped it down.

As he pulled it into the street, an old mid '70s Impala squealed to a stop beside his faded pad. The car was wider than most trucks and heavy metal music screamed out of the passenger window. The vinyl top was scratched and torn and the body covered with a chalky looking Royal Blue faded paint job. Chance looked inside and was hit with the image of the wrecked single apartment on the other side of town. The floor of the car was strewn with crushed soda cans, cigarette butts, scraps of paper and kids' toys.

He knew immediately that it was Suzanne. "Looks like your pad, goddamnit," Chance said.

"Shut up, damnit!" She spat, "I hate getting up this early for work."

"I'll stop in for a cup of coffee, if your boyfriend won't arrest me," Chance said.

"I'm not going out with him anymore," She said emphatically.

"He's not on that program just yet," Chance said,

"I'll see you at the shop."

Chance turned to walk back to his bike as the sun was breaking over the harbor and the mist over the boats and ships lifted.

"Are we going out, or what," She shouted.

"No, go to work. I'll talk to you there," Chance said, thinking that this girl was a time bomb that had been ticking for a week. She was as dangerous as a stacked deck.

«« — »»

Sheila McBride awoke in a prison cell in Phoenix.

"Wake up missy," a tough looking dyke officer shouted, dragging her nightstick across the steel bars. "Your arraignment is this morning at 8:00."

Sheila rolled back and forth in the slim bunk clutching her stomach. The jail food wasn't bad, since she was released from the county hospital, but the chlorine smell nagged her. She felt like shit.

"Your bail will be set," the officer sneered, "but arson and murder claim tall bails. Better be prepared."

Sheila looked up at the face of a man attached to a woman's body and began to turn green. She lurched for the stainless steel toilet and puked.

"Something's wrong with me." Sheila said trying to look concerned.

"We know somethin's wrong with you," the officer snorted, "Just be ready for the judge."

Sheila stiffened and got to her feet. Her attorney recommended a lengthy hospital stay, but her act wasn't working.

"My God," she said looking at herself in the slice of polished stainless steel used for a cell mirror. She was drawn. She had no makeup, and they shaved her hair off in the hospital. She also felt, but couldn't see, the burn bandages on her back and the back of her head. She screamed and hammered the mirror with her small hands.

"I can't stand it, I can't stand it, I can't..." Sheila stumbled and collapsed on the bunk.

She dated Chance for a short period, but the relationship was intense. She sensed that he was the one, but his past haunted her like a deadly disease. She couldn't put his other marriages out of her mind. She couldn't omit all the women he knew and loved out of her twisted mind. She was constantly jealous and tossed in a rage that drove him away.

Chance also loved her and was captivated by her desire to please him, but her angry abuse was something he had never dealt with and never intended to. It was as if he was playing a game of poker he had never tried, and didn't like. It had new rules and sharp uncomfortable edges to it.

She kicked at the slick concrete floor and pounded her fists against her knees. The tears flooded her features and trying to shake the feelings only seemed to make them stronger. The judge was less than an hour away.

«« — »»

Chance pulled up in front of Annette's Cafe and shut off his scooter. He went inside and sat near the window looking out at the professional fishing boats along a narrow spit. Suzanne came to his table immediately in bouncy form.

"Can I help you, sir?" She said mocking him. "Are we going out tonight?"

"I just got a job, goddamnit," Chance said. "We'll go out just as soon as I have the bucks to buy you a beer. Besides, I don't know how long my shift will be. This is my first day on the job; in fact, I'm sorta in a hurry. Bring me some scrambled egg whites, wheat toast and some salsa."

"How about if I buy?" she said, ignoring his order. Just then, a police cruiser pulled up and in came Officer Joe Fernandez.

"Your husband's here. Thought you weren't seeing him," Chance said. "If I was betting on this deal, my money would be on the guy in the uniform."

"Oh bullshit," She muttered as the officer came in the door.

"Hi baby," Fernandez said. "I'll have my usual."

Chance just shook his head and held his ceramic mug up for the rotund Italian woman to fill with steaming hot coffee.

"Make me some wheat toast, will ya?"

She nodded sullenly and moved onto another table. Chance ate his toast and drank hot coffee while waiting for the rest of his order. It never came, but a myriad of sideways glances did. He plopped some change on the table and got up to leave. Suzanne followed him outside.

"Am I gonna see you, tonight? She said.

"Where are my scrambled eggs?" Chance said. "Don't answer that. Tell your husband to have a nice day."

He fired the bike while she dashed back inside. He revved the pipes, made a u-turn in the street and headed down Signal for the job site at the end of the docks. Chance checked in with Julie and was told to go outside and introduce himself to Carl Beard, the dock boss. A balding guy wearing a sweatshirt and bib overalls wheeled a dolly of packages onto the dock when Chance rounded the corner.

"Hey Carl," Chance said, "I'm the new guy, Chance."

"What kind of fucking name is that?" Carl said spinning toward Chance and ignoring his outstretched hand.

"It's my fucking name, asshole," Chance said, "If you don't like it I'll promise to go for a ride, have a drink or two, and not work for you today."

Carl was big and round, where Chance was tall and tight. Carl assumed that every asshole, who worked for him was a non-stop derelict, some good for nothing wino with only enough desire to work for another bottle. He busted out laughing.

"Well at least you're a biker, but talk's cheap. "Let's see if you can work," Carl said. "We're gonna be runnin' scared today. One day we're starving, and the next I've got enough work for twice the boats I own and no pilots or mechanics to run them. Clean up that baby over there. Can you steer a fuckin' boat?"

"If I can't, it will take me 15 minutes to learn," Chance said. "Where's the cleaning gear?"

"The oil rig crew will be here in a half hour," Carl growled, "fuel 'er up, clean it, check the oil, take 'em out and get your ass back."

"Aye, aye, cap," Chance said and headed for the 25-foot fiber-glass, diesel-powered skiff.

He scrubbed the decks, the hull, polished the windshield, checked the oil, and inspected the bilge. It wasn't overflowing. He made sure the batteries weren't on their last legs, cleaned the terminals, and replaced the fuel filters. A half-dozen guys came to the docks right on time and he fired up the boat for passage to one of the offshore oil rigs, just a couple of miles beyond the Los Angeles breakwater. He was back and forth all day.

As the sun set, he enjoyed his final passage, bringing another crew back from a rig. He watched the sky turn crimson and blast the harbor with warm ruby light bouncing off the water. The boat tossed and turned on the ocean side of the breakwater, and as soon as he cleared the channel, the swells smoothed and he scooted along over calm currents, pulling up easily at the docks. He tied it up securely and washed the skiff down, then jogged to the office. Julie was preparing to leave.

"How was your first day?" She asked.

"Hell, I don't know," Chance said washing his hands. "How did I do?"

"Couldn't have been too bad. The old man wants you back tomorrow," she said slipping into her light jacket.

She checked out Chance, but he wasn't going to give the slightest signal to a girl at work. He had enough troubles with women.

"Have a good one," Chance said as she walked out the door.

He cleaned up and headed to his bike. It fired right to life and he dropped the long chopper into gear after warming it. He rode it past his pad up to Pacific, where he pulled into Mando's Mexican food for her five-taco special and a Diet Coke.

Back at the house, he showered and trimmed his scruffy beard before he sat down to eat. He turned up the stereo and poured a shot of Jack in his Coke. He was tired, and by 9:00 he was ready for shut-eye. He dropped his worn out Levis on the bed and turned on the television.

About 9:30 he heard a car screech up to the curb outside. Two minutes later there was a terrible clamor at the front door. He got up to see what the fuck was happening. He didn't know anyone in town. As he rounded the corner, he spotted Suzanne through the glass. She was holding some sort of bottle in a paper bag and a bright smile lit up her face.

"Ya gonna let me in or not?" She shouted through the glass.

"I shouldn't," Chance muttered opening the door.

She was clean, cute; her make-up was fresh and she reeked of sex. Chance couldn't talk himself out of it. She pushed passed him into the kitchen where she found a couple of coffee cups and poured two shots of coffee liquor.

Chance sat down with her on the couch and lit a candle on the coffee table. They looked out at the harbor when Chance picked up his cup.

"Well, here's to a clear night and you," he said.

He took one sip of the sweet liquor and put the heavy cup on the table. Suzanne took a swallow, empting the ceramic mug and set the cup next to Chance's.

"Are you going to tell me what you said?" she asked with mock directness.

"When?" Chance said.

"The other day when you came by," she said. "You know."

"Oh, was that something about you being horny and wanting me to slide my hands up your thighs?"

She scooted closer to him and put her hands on Chance's thighs. She had big hands with long colorful fingernails, yet small perky tits.

"Go on," she said.

"How about we go in the bedroom and I'll demonstrate," Chance said.

She didn't say anything, just stood, and began to walk toward the back of the house. As he followed her young ass, he wondered what the hell he was doing, but he was doing it just the same. Chance folded the bedspread back and plumped up the pillows.

"Would you like another drink?" he said. He wanted to know if she was the kind of girl who had to be drunk to fuck.

"No, not right now," she said sitting carefully on the edge of the bed. Chance ignored her and walked around the bed lighting candles,

"You have how many kids?"

"I've got two," she said.

"So you have a pretty tough life trying to make a go of it?" Chance said, "Is the cop the father?"

"No way," she replied.

"Do you have any child support?" Chance said.

"Not from either dad," she said warming to the candlelight.

"Why don't you roll over on your belly and I'll give you a massage," Chance said. "Don't worry, I won't hurt you. It's your time to relax."

With the lights dimmed, the music soft old R & B, Chance remove his shirt and broke out his massage oil. He pulled up her blouse slightly and began to rub her lower back from the spine out.

"So there are two fathers?"

"Yep," she said. "One is in jail."

"And the other?" Chance said softly

"Rehab," she said disgustedly.

"So you're carrying the load yourself," Chance said massaging her legs.

"Yes, I…,"she began to speak when Chance interrupted her.

"Are your kids all right tonight?"

"Yeah, sure," she said, "they're with my neighbor."

"You're a mess and your back is tight," Chance said leaning down close to her exposed soft lower back. "You need a break."

He kissed her right above the waistband of her Levis. He kissed along the waistband in both directions then rolled her over. She was beginning to relax as he pushed off of the bed and unlaced her shoes, removed them, and sat on the bed to rub her feet.

"How long have you worked at Annette's?"

"Oh, I suppose…" She lingered on about her job, while Chance gently massaged one foot after another. While she told him about her love of art and doing the little creative stuff around the restaurant. Chance moved up her legs to her white cotton blouse. He unbuttoned it slowly and she leaned forward so he could remove it. Then he kissed her tummy and her chest between her breasts and up to her neck. Her hair was thick and full like a lion's mane. He moved it aside and kissed around the base of her neck and up to her lips where they kissed for the first time. The kiss was soft and sensual, but not overtly passionate.

"If there's something you'd like," Chance said softly in her ear, "I'll try to take care of you. I'm not the rough type, though."

They kissed again, but this time she came alive, and their tongues clashed and dove for the core of each others' being. Chance pressed his exposed chest against her bra and pulled her tightly to him. Her hands walked all over his muscular torso, and her nails occasionally dug into him. She pushed off and tore at her bra straps, removing it quickly and throwing it against the wall. They hugged again, crushing torso to torso, her nipples hardening.

Chance tore away long enough to suck on one tit after the other while she moaned, and then grappled to strip off her pants and panties. Chance did the same and they collided in an embrace, grinding in tune to the blues coming from the stereo.

Chance pushed her back and spread her legs. He kissed her full on the lips again, but pulled his tongue from her warm mouth, dragging it over her chin and down her neck along her softness, over her nipples and down her soft stomach to her mound, breathing heavily on it, then allowing his tongue to slip deeper. She spread her legs and arched her back.

"I want you, please. Now," she moaned.

Chance pulled himself up and allowed his cock to slip between her legs and slid up and down the lips of her pussy, tempting her.

She grabbed him and shoved his hardness inside her. She screamed as he began to feel all of her gradually, moving slowly with shallow strokes, then deeper until he was all the way in, pulsing against her. She erupted like a volcano.

Chance slowed, to allow her to catch her breath. He lifted his body so he wasn't crushing her and she could relax, but as her eyes opened, he slipped deeper inside once more and kissed her around her mouth without laying on her. She began to respond again, and Chance moved with more fervor, building with her. While fucking her, he leaned down and kissed and sucked her nipples. She began to scream again, and Chance groaned in unison. For long moments they lay together while the world faded back in.

"Sex takes me to another place," Chance said.

They kissed for a while, and then she leaned forward. "I've got to go back to my kids. I don't want to, but you know the drill," she said as she pulled away and sat up.

"I don't know what to say," she muttered. "Can we do this again?"

"Of course," Chance said, knowing he should say no.

Chance walked her to her car barefoot, kissed her good night and watched her drive away. The cold of the pavement brought reality back. He shouldn't have anything to do with this one. He didn't date girls with kids, but what a night. He also didn't date girls who went out with cops.

Chance went back into the pad and dug Vince's screenplay from his bedroll, then headed to the bedroom. He missed his riding partner and needed to know if the screenplay had anything to do with his murder.

-16-

San Murder

Suzanne drove her battered Impala toward her one-bedroom apartment on the west side of San Pedro. She enjoyed what she felt between her legs after making love to Chance and it made her want more. She knew that Chance wasn't one she could hold down, but she would love to change him, if she could. She wanted a man with a place big enough for her two kids, a guy who was good-looking, and loved to fuck as much as she did.

She knew that her legacy was her downfall. She was born to a tramp and abandoned when she was 10. By 12, she was working in bars. Sex intrigued her. It consumed her like a drug that took her away from all that was less than splendid in her life. She was engaged the first time at 13, to a 25-year-old man, and was pregnant at 15.

She'd decided that she wanted to keep her man, so she stopped taking the pill and immediately got knocked up, just about the time the short Hispanic kid, with no particular profession, turned into a drug addict. She didn't know whether he had a propensity for drugs before he knew of his fatherly responsibility, or if the news drove his insecurities over the top, so he lunged for something to help him escape.

Suzanne had the baby on welfare and was launched into another chapter of her young, unprepared life. She dropped out of school to work and fuck around. But she needed an education for her child and the ability to bring home the bacon. Her first job was working for Tony, a married Italian, who had a small delivery business. He was big, with wavy black hair, and his presence and support were comforting. He also couldn't keep his hands off her round, young ass, and soon she was being screwed in the storeroom behind her receptionist desk.

She was pregnant in a couple of months. For fear his marriage would be destroyed, Tony let Suzanne go with a teary promise that he would help her. Tony controlled her with stories of his mob connections. She had a second child, no job, and no support from Tony.

She had to admit to herself that she had a weakness for sex. When a man touched that button between her legs, she was gone. Unfortunately, she had no notion of how to handle her addiction, but she was trying desperately to learn.

She pulled her lumbering slab of rusting tin to a stop in front of the picket fence separating the sidewalk from the five clapboard cottages. There were two, one-bedroom units on either side of a center walk way and one lone unit at the back, facing the '40s bungalows. She lived in the second one on the right, and her kids were staying with the Hispanic lady in the second unit on the left. As she stepped up to the fence, she could sense that someone else was near, in the dark. She spun, then stopped and smiled.

《《 — 》》

Chance woke up to the jingling of his phone next to his ear. As he answered, he reminded himself to turn off the ringer. It was too close.

"Time to get up, baby," Julie said, "we've got work for you."

For a split-second, he thought the voice might be Suzanne and was relieved that it was not. He didn't want another woman immersed in his life just yet. He wanted sex but no involvement, especially from her.

"I'll be right there, honey," Chance said and hung up.

As he lifted his arms above the covers he noticed the screenplay at his side. He struggled through reading it. His late riding partner had an unceasing attitude about many things and they were apparent on each page as Chance read his screenplay, "Agency Discount."

It was apparent that Vince was hitting hard at some of the business aspects of mainstream advertising agencies. Each colorfully detailed grievance was tainted with greed. Money was king and Chance could read between the lines after listening to Vince pour his guts out over several bar tops before he was killed.

Chance knew someone had hired a hit on Vince and it would be tough to fetter out. On the other hand, Vince was his brother rider and Chance believed fervently that he had to find answers, the source and make it right, even though Hollywood was not Chance's territory. He knew the streets and how to handle them. He could walk into any joint in town and comfortably kick up a conversation with anyone, but he would stick out like a sore thumb in a posh Hollywood nightclub.

He needed a contact. He mused about it as he showered and dried off. While he dressed, he looked through his tattered phone book, to no avail. He was about to leave when it dawned on him to check a small tin box where he stashed business cards. As he flipped through it, he thought about the businesses imprisoned in the box, riders he hadn't contacted in some time, and some of the companies he knew were gone. He tossed one card after another into the wicker trash basket under his desk. Then he came across a card that intrigued him.

"Mark Lonsworth, CQBI." He remembered this guy.

Chance looked at the clock. He shoved the card in another old leather vest, as he made his way to the garage for his bike. He rolled to a quick stop in front of the harbor fish and chips joint, swung off the warm motorcycle and walked inside. As usual, the tables were full of dockworkers and retired stevedores. Suzanne did not meet him at the door. Instead, it was the rotund Italian woman, who seemed to be in an especially dour mood.

"You wouldn't happen to know where she is?" the woman asked as she poured Chance a cup of coffee.

"No," Chance said, looking around. "Does she miss days like this?"

"She misses the plot constantly," she said. "Wheat toast and scrambled eggs?"

"Sure, that will be fine."

He sat down at the table and sipped his coffee, wondering what the hell had happened to the bouncy broad. As he put the jam on his toast, he remembered Mark's card in his vest and pulled it out. He recalled hanging out with a group of riders in Hollywood and this big rider showing up from time to time. He knew a couple of the other guys as acquaintances, but conversations were light. Mark stood out because he didn't wear a leather rider's jacket. He wore an army camouflage jacket, black Levis, and military lace-up boots. His bike was a black FXR with only performance modifications and a small muscular green frog painted on the tank.

Green on motorcycles was always the kiss of death, but Chance scoffed at the old taboo, and evidently, Mark did the same. The rest of the riders were upscale with bright paint jobs and wallets full of cash.

Chance didn't have the budget to stick with the group. At a gas station on Sunset Boulevard, Chance approached Mark for the first time.

"Name's Chance Hogan," he said, extending his hand. "What's the meaning of the frog?"

Mark was pale and his thinning hair was laced with gray, though his smile was youthful and playful.

"I started a dive team once called Frogmen," Mark replied. "That's one of my many nicknames."

"I've only seen you a couple of times. You ride much?"

"I'm in and out of this godforsaken town on business," Mark said. "Besides, I can't ride too often with these RUBs. Their boots are too shiny, if you know what I mean."

As Chance shot the shit with Mark, he discovered that he trained at the Gold's Gym in Venice, and Chance needed a place to work out. Mark had a background in various training regimens, including Tae Kwon Do and military Special Forces training. He was 35 and from New Zealand. He came to America for the Olympics as a sharp shooter and didn't ever want to go back. To stay in the country, he took a job as a bodyguard for a studio executive. He wrote a book about being a proper bodyguard for an estate that included guards, travel and security systems.

He self-published five books on security, sniping, and close-quarters combat. That was the acronym on his card, CQBI, with an international designation. Through one of his bodyguard assignments, Mark had the opportunity to play a walk-on part in a movie, and then he started learning the stunt routines and picked up parts from time to time.

Mark was Chance's contact. Besides, if he was going to go after a hit man, he needed some weapons training. He finished his breakfast and headed to the dock house on the end of the peninsula. He pulled up, chained his bike, and jogged inside the office.

"Hi, beautiful," Chance said.

"Hi, baby," Julie said with a tinge of flirtation in her voice.

"Can I make a quick call?" Chance asked.

"Sure," Julie said, motioning him to another office. "Use that phone over there."

Chance dialed Mark's number and waited.

"It's too early," Mark said at the other end of the line.

"I know," Chance said. "Just needed to know if this number was still good. This is Chance."

"You ready to train?" Mark asked.

"Yep," Chance said.

"See ya Saturday," Mark said and hung up.

Chance looked at the phone. He liked the no-bullshit directness of this guy. He set the phone down and went to work.

Chance hauled two loads of oilmen to offshore rigs in company skiffs. The sun was breaking to the east and cascaded deep orange streaks through radiant stratocumulus clouds that seemed to rest on the water's edge.

Each trip to the rigs was different. Morning hauls were always the best. The sunrise, the glassy water until he reached the breakwater, which led to a mellow or wild ride to the base pylons of the rig. As the afternoon approached, so did the swells. After he unloaded the men to their workstations, he saluted them away and hauled ass back to the harbor and the docks.

Carl, the owner of the sea taxi agency, was away on business, so Chance cleaned and detailed each of his four boats, checked the fluid levels, and topped off the fuel tanks. He cleaned the docks and started to work scrapping, sanding and painting the rusting railings on the gangplanks.

Julie watched him work from the office. She admired his resilience and work ethic and hoped that he would stick around. She got a call from West Marine, an industrial ships supply and parts yard. They were loading a truck full of ship-sized engine parts for a ship anchored in the Long Beach Harbor and need someone to deliver the parts post haste.

"Come on down," Julie said, "we have a boat ready." She hung up and leaned out the window to the dock below. "Chance?"

Chance turned in her direction. The air was filled with the fresh scent of salt watery brine on the harbor.

"We've got a parts shipment on the way," Julie said, leaning out the window and revealing her succulent cleavage to Chance's delight. "Can you operate the crane?"

"I'll figure it out," Chance said and hustled up the gangplank to the small one-ton crane bolted to the concrete foundation in a pad of concrete. He fired up the electrical circuit and operated the various levers until he felt confident with the system.

He went to the storage area and unlocked the shed. He found a milk crate full of cables and clevis pins for wrapping cargo and pulled the box into the open. The truck showed up in 15 minutes and he had the heaviest boat tied to the dock waiting cargo.

"Is this the place?" the driver shouted from the cab of the truck.

"If you were any closer, you'd knock me into the bay," Chance said, indicating to the driver where to face the truck.

With the trucker assisting, they strapped a valve crate for a 15,000-horse diesel engine. The single intake valve was nearly as tall as Chance. Another crate carried a set of five springs. More crates carried miscellaneous parts and fasteners.

Chance put the smaller boxes on a single pallet and lifted it with the crane, carefully lowering it into the hull of the harbor skiff. He sent the driver inside to handle the paperwork and invoice from Julie, then jumped to the helm of the skiff. He untied it from the dock and pulled a U-turn in the green sea heading toward Long Beach.

The run was effortless and the freighter was prepared with a crane and hook hanging over the side of the hull as he approached. Chance handled the drop and the paperwork, and buzzed back to the seaside docks. While tying up the skiff, he looked up toward Julie's office, hoping for another view of her cleavage when she leaned out the window. She was sitting at her cluttered desk, stoically looking up at two police officers. They both turned in his direction. Chance finished tying up the boat and headed up the gangplank.

There were two patrol cars in the parking lot. As the two officers hurriedly rounded the corner, Chance noticed that they both had their hands on their side arms, and the leather straps were removed from the hammers. Both officers were tense.

"Chance Hogan?" one officer asked as he headed directly for Chance. The other officer dropped back. He was the one who had jacked up Chance the previous week.

"Yes sir," Chance said.

"You're under arrest for suspicion of murder. You're going to go downtown with me."

Chance looked at Officer Fernandez then back at the young black officer.

"Who died?"

"Suzanne Cross," the officer snapped. "Turn around."

Fernandez pulled his pistol and was pointing it at the middle of Chance's head as his partner cuffed him.

"Why don't you take him?" Chance said nodding in the direction of the officer Grey. "She's his girlfriend."

The officer ignored Chance's comment with a fleeting glance at his partner, and pushed Chance toward his patrol car. He was taken across town to a two-story building on the edge of the port. It was a modern glass and steel structure with chain link surrounding it.

Officer Grey pulled his patrol car into the parking lot adjacent to two swinging doors, up several wide concrete steps affectionately known as the loading dock to the officers of the sub- department of the Los Angeles Police Department. They were actually known as the Harbor Division. If a prisoner was out of line, he often didn't make it up the stairs without a violent stumble and fall. The steps were often scrubbed after a long Saturday night after payday.

Two officers burst out of the doors as officer Grey arrived. They weren't forced to deal with many murders in San Pedro and this one was particularly brutal, plus the victim was a young woman who was known by some of the officers on the force. Joe Fernandez was married, but some of the crew knew that he had Suzanne on the side.

"This the guy?" asked Officer Myer, a stout redhead, as Grey lead Chance from the car.

"This is the guy, but..." Officer Grey said, pushing him forward.

"Maybe he should taste the loading dock," the red-haired officer was practically foaming at the mouth as he approached.

Chance purposefully kept his head up and eyes on Lt. Myer, but tightened his abdominal muscles as the fireplug of a man slugged him in the guts. Chance bent hard against the blow to recoil from it quickly.

"You murdering fuck!" Officer Myer shouted.

The following officer, also glaring at Chance, pulled Myer back as Chance attempted to stand and take another step.

"I don't think this is the guy," Officer Grey said, pulling Chance away from Myer.

"Fuck he's not," Myer said, red-faced. "Biker fuckin' trash. We'll see. Get him inside."

Several other officers stood at the windows looking out at the asphalt scuffle. Two detectives, Callahan and Norton, were called into the department head's office. The head was a long-time Harbor officer who enjoyed the generally harmonious district. His main objective was drug-running out of the harbor, which he dealt with in conjunction with the Coast Guard. He was a big Irish man named Reed, an ex-boxer with a crooked nose to prove it, and preferred to be called lieutenant over chief.

"Sit down," he said to his two investigators.

Callahan was an old hand in law enforcement. Kate Norton was highly educated but a rookie. She was studying for her masters. She wasn't well liked in the unit because of her high-end education, her lack of street experience, and her heady ambition.

"Callahan, this is Norton's first murder case," the lieutenant said. "I want you to take her under your wing and give her a shot at learning from the streets."

Callahan had been on the force as long as Reed. He was experienced, but a loose-canon emotionally, and Reed was hoping that some of Kate's scientific education would rub off on him. He could only hope.

"They brought in the biker for questioning," Reed said. "See what you can find out, but do it together."

Callahan and uniformed officers spent most of the morning with the coroner after the body was discovered down by the fish docks.

"Why was he brought in?" Kate asked. She was one of the few officers who was referred to by her first name because she was a woman. She didn't mind unless there was attitude wrapped around the word.

"He could be the one," Callahan said abruptly.

"Can I read your crime scene report?" Kate asked Callahan, who was in his mid-40s and bristling with attitude.

"Of course," Callahan spat, "when I'm finished. He was the last one to see her. I'll bet we find his semen in her."

Kate knew only what she heard as evidence.

"I don't think I should be in on this interview," she said to her boss.

"What's wrong?" Callahan interjected. "You afraid of a biker? Probably couldn't interview a black. Scared to death," he scoffed.

Kate ignored the snipe and said, "I need to see shots of the crime scene and read the report before I question the suspect. I wish I had been invited to the scene. It would have been a lot of help."

Officer Callahan crossed his arms across his beer belly and chewed on a toothpick that combed his mustache back and forth.

"I understand," the lieutenant said, looking hard at Callahan. "We will see that you have full access to this case from now on, won't we, Detective Callahan?" Reed raised his left eyebrow in a gaze that would melt butter in an icebox.

Callahan avoided his radar-like gaze as he got to his feet.

"Yes sir," he said and headed for the door.

"As for you," he turned his attention, "we want to see the level of scientific knowledge you learned in school. A number of officers on this staff want to stay on top of cutting edge investigations."

"I need access to the crime scene to be effective, sir," Kate said as she got to her feet.

She wore slacks but her athletic figure was still profoundly visible through the carefully creased pants. Her top was professional and form fitting. She looked like an executive in a gas station as she followed Callahan into the questioning room where Chance had been placed. He was still cuffed, and Officer Grey stood in the corner eying him.

Callahan came in the room followed by Kate, who looked knowingly at Chance but didn't give any indication of their previous acquaintance near the Arizona-California border. Chance's eyes followed Callahan, then came to rest on Kate's form, widened briefly, then narrowed again.

Kate sat in a wooden chair back behind Callahan's and maintained a deadpan look as Callahan began questioning.

"When did you last see Suzanne Cross?" Callahan asked.

"Last night about 10," Chance said. "She left in her car."

"Do you want an attorney?" Callahan said.

"Nope, don't need one," Chance said.

"How long did you know Suzanne?"

"That was our first date," Chance said. "I had a run-in with her at a bar a few weeks ago, and I saw her at Annette's, where I went for breakfast. That's it."

"We're you involved with her?" Callahan asked.

"No, but one of your officers was," Chance said.

"Where were you the rest of the night?" Callahan asked, shuffling his feet.

"I went to bed," Chance said.

"Did you kill her?" Kate asked, moving her chair forward.

"No," Chance said, looking at Kate with a disbelieving gaze.

"Would you mind if we took a blood sample and fingerprint you?" Kate said.

"Not at all."

"Can we search your home?" Kate said.

"Sure," Chance said. "Look, I didn't do anything except go out with the girl. Is someone taking care of her kids?"

"Well?" Kate asked, looking at Officer Callahan.

"I didn't know she had kids," Callahan spat, frustrated. "Goddamnit, get him out of here. Don't leave town, motherfucker. We'll be seeing you."

-17-

KATE, THE COP

Chance followed Kate to their crime lab and technicians drew blood. He was holding his own, but cop shops scared the living shit out of him. He wasn't wealthy, so he knew that if they decided to put him away for as little as having long hair, his life was shattered, and they could keep him as long as they could manipulate the courts to do so.

His knees seemed to rattle between his thighs and his calves. He couldn't bail out his cat if it was arrested for shitting in the park. He didn't plan to be broke forever, but sometimes, if a guy has some cash, that just means he's got something the Man can take. He shuttered as they wandered down the long polished linoleum hallway with bare high gloss enamel walls.

Kate gazed at Chance over her shoulder and they glanced at one another, but didn't utter a word. Big Detective Callahan was following, and Chance felt the corporate vibe, so he decided that it was best that no one know of his and Kate's previous encounter.

"Do you want to search my place now?" Chance said to Kate, but Callahan answered the question.

"Of course we do, you idiot," Callahan shrugged. "You fuckin' bikers are real brain trusts."

Chance ignored the smear, but mentally put Callahan on his disliked list. He turned to Kate.

"Here are my keys. Search my place whenever you like. Just take me back to work. Have your boy bring me the keys when you're done."

"I'll give you a lift," Kate said and turned to Callahan. "We'll meet at Mr. Hogan's residence in a half hour. Will that work, detective?"

"We'll be there and if I find so much as a seed, I'll tear the place apart," Callahan muttered.

Sweat was beading on his brow as his pot-bellied gut hung over his belt and he tried to hitch up his pants. He tried to look tough, but his age and obesity destroyed any underpinnings of ruggedness. Chance didn't bother to look back, and followed Kate to her unmarked cruiser in the parking lot.

She let Chance in the passenger door and went to the driver's side of the car. The weather was typical balmy southern California, with the smells of the harbor permeating the freshness of the sea. Diesel trucks pulled out of the China Shipping yard across the street. The area contained city blocks of stacked dull shipping containers. The smell of diesel fumes never stopped drifting around the police station unless an offshore gale pushed the pungent aroma inland. They rolled out of the asphalt parking lot and bumped onto Pacific Avenue.

"Nice bunch of guys," Chance said.

"They're edgy over this murder," Kate said. "Do you know what happened to her? Did they say anything to you?"

"No," Chance said.

"I can't tell you direct evidence, yet," Kate said nervously, "I haven't even had the opportunity to see the corpse myself, but I know she was a mess. Whoever did this was an angry sonuvabitch. Did you fuck her?" Kate asked and glanced at Chance.

"Yep," Chance said.

"I'm sure that will show up," Kate muttered as they rolled down Harbor Blvd. "I heard they were picking you up, and I know you work down here somewhere, but you'll have to give me directions."

"Sure," Chance said, "Just keep going straight. Do me a favor. Try to prevent them from tearing my place apart. Hell, it's already a mess. I just got started on it."

"They know what they're looking for," Kate said. "There shouldn't be a problem."

"Damn," Chance said, "I just want to be left alone. I can't catch a decent hand of cards."

"Did you know Vince?" Kate asked, shifting to another case on her list.

"He was a wild-eyed hot head, but my best friend and a brilliant writer," Chance said.

"What happened to him?" Kate said. "I heard it was a hit."

"Could be," Chance said. "Vince had written some bad shit about the advertising industry and his boss, but I haven't pinned anything down just yet."

"Be careful," Kate said, "Where there's one hit, there can be another. That kind of stuff is easy to get away with. This is the kind of murder that shakes up a community."

Chance thought about the officer who was so protective of Suzanne, but didn't mention him. Being a snitch was against the Code of the West, and Chance didn't want to pursue that line. It wouldn't bode well coming from him anyhow. Cops need to deal with their own, just like he preferred to deal with his own problems. He actually didn't want to discuss Vince's death with Kate, but sensed that she could be a valuable resource. On the other hand...

"She was a wild woman," Chance said, "Maybe she had some druggie boyfriend."

"I'm going to go over everything, later," Kate said. "We'll run DNA tests on anything we can find. Hopefully, it will point us in the right direction, before this sonuvabitch gets another chance. I'll call you when I know more and can release it. If I can help you with Vince's death, call me."

She handed him her new business card.

"Are you enjoying this police work?" Chance asked.

"This is what I was educated to do," Kate said. "Some of the politics are a pain, but a case like this is what I was trained to handle. We'll see. It's too early to tell."

She looked at Chance with a curious gaze. She was hot looking, even in her professional attire, and Chance let his eyes dance along her form like a painter touching up a painting.

He didn't want her, but recognized good form and a handsome woman. She was dressed impeccably, and her body was that of a female athlete. Chance pointed for her to turn down Signal to the end of the old industrial warehouse peninsula.

"Let's stay in touch," Kate said as she pulled to a stop.

She looked at Chance close like she wanted to read something more from his facial expression.

"Are you seeing anyone else?" she asked, and it was the sternest question asked.

"No," Chance answered uneasily, "I'm not."

"Let's go to lunch," Kate said, "when all of this is over."

She touched his arm and he remembered her earnest behavior in the desert. What was it about this woman?

"I need to put a couple of things behind me," Chance answered honestly. "Need some money in the bank, my house fixed, and Vince's case solved before I would feel right about going out with anyone."

"You don't need..." Kate said and her radio began to squawk.

Chance leaned over and kissed her on the cheek and touched her arm.

"I'll talk to you soon," he whispered and got out of the car.

"23 we're at the suspect's house." Callahan's voice was even irritating over the radio. "We're going in. Are you coming?"

"I've got the key," Kate said into the handheld mike.

"That's not stopping me," Callahan barked.

"I'll be right there," Kate said waving at Chance standing in front of the Harbor Taxi temporary office. Spinning the car around, she headed back up the peninsula for a mile and a half to Chance's small rental home overlooking the harbor.

Callahan stood on the concrete porch with a couple of uniformed officers who had already wrapped the front yard with yellow police tape. Kate pulled up across the street on 19th and jumped out of the car.

"What the hell do you think you're doing?" she shouted running up the short concrete walk to the narrow steps front of the house. "This is not a crime scene yet."

"I think the neighbors ought to know the kind of people they got in the neighborhood," Callahan said indicating for the officers to continue.

"I need to see the real crime scene before all the evidence is destroyed," Kate said.

"Sure, sure," Callahan said. "If we find the shit we need here, this case will be over."

Kate opened the rickety front door into a tight turret shaped foyer leading into the small stucco home. Callahan stormed through the house like a bull in a china closet.

The house was clean, but old and worn. The furniture was limited, since the place was being remodeled. Chance had a few items with motorcycle seats mounted on exhaust pipes for small chairs, a barber's chair in his living room, and a chair lifted from an insane asylum used for dental work in the '40s. A small couch faced a plastered-over brick fireplace.

The officers opened and searched every drawer. Two officers
went out the back door to the garage and searched it. There was no
indication of foul play. His bed was neatly made; Kate could smell a
woman's cheap perfume in the bedroom. One Jack Daniel's tumbler
was beside the bed, which she carefully lifted and bagged for prints.

Kate put on latex gloves and indicated for the other officers to do
the same. Callahan ignored her request and continued to dig through
drawers barehanded. Chance didn't have a lot. His furniture was
sparse, and his clothes minimal. Levis and t-shirts filled one of the
shaky old dressers.

Walking up the ramp to the seaside Taxi service, bubbly Julie met
Chance at the door.

"Do you always have that effect on female cops?" she said a wry
smile crossing her face.

Chance was dulled by the whole experience and unable to immediately respond. He looked at Julie's voluptuous curves and thought
to himself that her wide hips and plump breasts were much more
alluring than Kate's sophisticated, trim sexuality. He looked at her
body and a smile crossed his dour features.

"Something to do with the way she searched me," Chance said
and nudged her.

Julie blushed at the thought.

"What happened?" she asked, her peach-soft features disturbed
with wrinkles of concern.

"I went out with the girl who works at the restaurant at the
corner," Chance said. "She was killed last night after she went home
from my place. Of course, they wanted me to take the fall and wrap it
up. They're searching my place right now."

"That Suzanne girl?" Julie said, and Chance realized that Julie
had probably been into Annette's any number of times.

"Yep," Chance said heading across the small reception room for
Carl's office.

"She was a nut," Julie said. "You must have been hurting for a
date?"

"I'm not an old hat in this town," Chance said. "Besides most
girls want to go out with a guy who has something going for him.
Hell, if I owned this business, I'd want you."

Chance paused before he opened the door.

"She was a nut, but didn't deserve to die."

Julie nodded again and blushed. She wanted to add something about the two of them dating, but his last statement stopped her. She sat down in her chair and looked after Chance as he stepped behind the door to Carl's small glassed in office. He explained the interaction to Carl.

"I'm sorry about the delay. I'll work a couple of hours late tonight. What do you need me to do?"

"Don't let the cops run over you," Carl said. "They'll use any excuse to put a guy away."

"Scares me just to talk to one on the street," Chance said. "When I get behind the door of a cop shop, I can't wait to escape."

Chance went to work servicing the boats and making runs. At 7:00 p.m., he checked out just after the sun dropped over the Palos Verdes Peninsula and into the Los Angeles Harbor blanketing the container ships and warehouses with an orange hue. Just as the sun dipped under the horizon, the light-sensitive sensors switched on terminal and crane lights and the harbor lit up. Chance was amazed by the sight and magnificent sunsets.

He had an adage about sunsets and it rolled through his mind as he unchained his motorcycle and slipped his gloves on. When he was stressed, one glorious sunset would snatch him from the doldrums. He couldn't imagine creating anything more beautiful than a woman or the next multi-hued, cloud-streaked sunset.

As he looked on in amazement, he was centered by the revelation that man can bust his ass to create, but can never equal the simple beauty of one sunset. He reveled in it as it filled the sky with warmth, then faded into dusk. His bike fired to life and straddled it for the short putt home.

On the way up 22nd street, he reflected on Suzanne's brutal death. It disturbed him and he began to think about some of the other girls in his life. With each bump in the road, he was immersed in a relationship flashback, many of them bad. He had left more women than he cared to admit. He tried to be honest with them about his unrelenting desire for freedom, but few would listen and all endeavored to tie him down.

He loved to love a woman, but his freedom was dear. As they took it away, they crushed his love until the open door was more tempting than the touch of a woman, and he walked. Each time he turned his back on a woman, there were tears. Each time he walked away, a new life began. He took a chance once more. It was always a roll of the dice.

From time to time, he relished in a friend's long-term relationship, wherein two people built themselves a life and all the material crap that went along with it, but for some reason, Chance couldn't stick if the feeling wasn't right. Every day was precious. If two people weren't happy, he was willing to take the risk and walk. He pulled up to his battered house and rolled his bike into the back yard. In the house he checked for phone messages. There was one from Kate.

"Hey, are you working late? Call me at home tonight. I'll give you a report. It's not good."

Chance pulled her card out of his flannel pocket and turned it over. He dialed the number and waited for three rings.

"Hello?" Kate said.

"Hey you," Chance said, "You're breathing heavy, should I go?"

"I'm working out," Kate said. "Not that kind of heavy breathing."

"Wanna call me when you're done?" Chance said. "I need to work out myself, but not tonight, and that reminds me. I need to make a call. I worked late to make up for today."

"No, No," Kate said. "I was just about finished. You need to know what's going on. Gimme five minutes and I'll call you back."

Kate had a Stairmaster installed in her upscale condo, so she could perform her cardio workouts at home. She also trained at the Gold's Gym in downtown Long Beach a couple of times a week and went for a 3-mile run on Saturdays.

"I'll call you back as soon as I get out of the shower," Chance said and hung up.

He showered and inspected the house for police brutality. Furniture was shifted and he could tell that all his drawers had been rustled through. He didn't have much, so it didn't matter. He showered, pulled on a pair of workout shorts and a sweatshirt and thought about getting something to eat, but decided to pour himself a shot of Jack and return her call. He dialed her number, but there was no answer. Her machine picked up and he assumed that he caught her in the shower.

"Hey you, it's Chance. I'm somewhat clean and available," Chance said. "Call me when you can."

He sat down in the living room, sipped his drink, and looked out at the harbor. He was intrigued about the outcome of her investigation. For a moment, he felt it would be strange, romantic justice if he took the fall for the murder. He had hurt enough women in his life; he deserved to atone in an abstract way.

Another side of him felt that men weren't afforded enough access to women for their natural drive. The business about getting hooked with one woman for the rest of his life seemed absurd. A man thinks about sex every seven minutes and probably thinks about sex for seven minutes each time. He needed the right to exercise those thoughts and not feel tied to the same bedpost forever. Chance realized that attitude had scuttled several relationships.

He turned on his CD player and some old Temptations tunes filled his pad. The drink relaxed him when he heard a tap on the windowpane of dining room. He got up and rounded the corner into this tattered room. Standing on the other side of the window was Detective Kate Norton, holding a bag of take-out Chinese food and a bottle of wine.

Her smile was full and warm. Her bright, even teeth and calm demeanor reminded him of something pure, something he didn't deserve. She was an angel standing at a gunslingers door, holding a basket of fruit. He paused and looked at the sight as if a church group had come to his door with a winning raffle ticket. It's the wrong fuckin' address, he thought. The phone rang, bringing Chance out his reverie. He opened the door quickly.

"Come in, Come in," he said as he turned toward the kitchen and the phone on the wall.

"You didn't have to…" he paused, "there's a table in the breakfast nook."

He motioned to the oval table with a Formica-looking cover and a 4-inch aluminum band around the edge, with tuck-and-roll chairs. It was like a table and chairs from a '50s coffee shop.

He picked up the black wall phone, "Yeah," he said.

"This is Rosa," she said. Her voice trickled out of the phone like the touch her soft hands left on his body after a hard day's work in the desert. She was a voice from the not too distant past, and suddenly Chance was caught off guard with two women in his house.

"How are you?" Chance said, but she could pick up the flat unemotional tone in his voice.

"Is this a bad time," Rosa said, "I can call back."

"No wait," Chance said, "It's not a bad time. I'm just sitting down to eat. Let me have your number. I'll call you back."

Nervous sweat beaded on his forehead. He had a code with women. He always treated the one he was with as if there were no other women in the world, even if he was dating five. It was his rule and he made every effort to abide by it. Again, an edge of discomfort flooded over him as if a cop walked in while he was rolling a joint. He wrote down the number.

"I'll call you later."

"Please," she said, "I have lots to tell you. It's good to hear your voice."

"You too," Chance said, his voice softening. He hung up.

"An old friend?" Kate asked.

Her investigative training and nature had the entire conversation pegged. It was another woman, she knew for sure, and a woman Chance had been intimate with.

"You could say that," Chance said his wandering expression filled with memories. "What did you find out?"

Kate laid out the food on two plates, his filled high with fried rice, Kung Pao chicken, and beef and broccoli. Chance opened the bottle of wine and grabbed a couple of plain water glasses. He lit a candle on the table and turned out the bright light in the kitchen.

The room was located at the front of the house opposite of the living room with the dining room in-between. The living room had a bay window that looked out over the harbor and out to sea. The small window in the breakfast nook also overlooked the harbor, and at night by candlelight, he could see the glitter of lights on the harbor, but he wanted to change it to another bay window to expand visibility and match the living room design.

"I knew you worked late and hadn't eaten," Kate said, "I needed something to eat and also needed to discuss this with you, so I thought, what the hell. Am I interrupting anything tonight?"

"No, no," Chance said, "I knew that girl in Arizona. She owned a gas station and someone burned it down. I'm glad she called. I wanted to know what happened to her and her station."

Kate nodded with relief as she took a small bite of fried rice. She wasn't threatened with any woman in another state. She dished up small portions of the steaming food on her plate. It looked like small samples to the big eater, Chance.

He looked at Kate, his emotional cement mixer spinning. He sat up slightly straighter. His hair was freshly shampooed and pulled back into a ponytail, although it was still wet. His mustache was full and his beard hadn't been shaved for a couple of days. He looked naturally haggard. He liked the look of being up for three days straight.

"I hope this investigation goes quickly," Kate said putting her chopsticks down, "for your sake."

"What do you mean," Chance said.

"I have a feeling about this case, but no real basis for it. Let me tell you something, you were all over that girl and in her." Kate said. "All fingers point at you, except that you didn't run. They found your DNA in her hair and on her clothes. Your fingerprints are on her car. Her DNA and fingerprints are in your house. There is proof that she was drinking. Your semen was in her. Yet, I know you didn't do it. She was raped and beaten, then her wrists were slit and she was tortured while she died. Some very sick person did this. She was dumped in her own car, in the trunk, down that dirty lane of fisheries."

Chance set down his fork full of food. "I don't get it," he muttered.

"This sonuvabitch was pissed off," Kate said lowering her glass of wine. "I'm just wondering whether he was pissed at her, women in general, or you."

-18-

BEVERLY CRIME

The phone rang at 8:00 on Saturday morning. Chance rolled over and picked it up.

"Yeah," he mumbled, half awake.

"We working out today or what?" Mark asked, demanding an affirmative answer.

"You goddamn right."

Chance shut his eyes again. He was feeling inundated again and couldn't figure out why he was in the crosshairs of so much insanity. Was he creating it? Could he let his partner's death go unchecked? What really happened to Nicole? Who killed Suzanne? There was far too much death around him. He couldn't decide if solving one crime would eliminate the problem or cause more. His eyes burst open. His blood pressure peaked.

"See you at ten," Mark said and hung up.

Chance's gaze darted around the small bedroom. The raggedy window curtain over the north wall was his gauge of the morning's climate. The simple white curtain was mounted on a cheap sprung tube that snapped into the chipped wooden window sill about a third of the way down the window, leaving the top 8 inches of window exposed. From the bed, all he could see was blue sky. It was clear as cut glass and the white window framed the perfect sky as if someone had spray-painted it with five coats of hand-rubbed acrylic a magnificent baby blue hue.

The house was small enough that if the sun was shining over the harbor, it flooded the entire pad like a tsunami invading an Olympic swimming pool. The light rushed down the hall and into the bedroom.

The rental was a piece of shit, but outside, the sun was shinning. Chance rolled his ass out of bed and jumped in the shower. He rinsed off and dressed.

Chance knew that it would be a good 80 degrees on the coast, so he dressed in old stained sweats and running shoes, threw on his leather vest and went to the kitchen for a protein bar and a glass of milk. He was ready.

Chance wiped his bike down hurriedly and rolled it into the street. In the sunlight from the east, it glistened, even in all its dull, coffee-brown hue. He fired it to life and rolled along Harbor Boulevard toward the freeway. It felt good to be in the sun with the smell of the salt water drifting off the harbor as he rolled along on the light rigid. Then he heard the bark of a police siren and checked his review mirror.

"Goddamnit," he said, spying the black and white dead on his ass. He leaned slightly and pulled to the side of the street overlooking Ports O' Call, a seaside village, below. He knew he wasn't speeding, but suspected something worse as he stood and started to throw his leg over the saddle.

"Stay on the bike," a bullhorn voice growled.

Chance sat back down and waited. He waited nervously for a good 10 minutes until an unmarked cruiser pulled up in front of him. Callahan got out of the tan cruiser and attempted to heft his belt as he stood. He was wearing a cheap dress shirt and a ridiculous plaid tie that couldn't reach his belt because of the curve of his beer gut. Even in short sleeves, he already had sweat stains under his arms and his collar was too tight. He pulled his tweed sport coat off the back of the bench seat and threw it on over the shoulder holster that held his Smith & Wesson snub-nosed .38. Not exactly a state-of-the-art weapon. He was a big doughboy waddling toward Chance with a bleak look on his face.

"Where the fuck do you think you're going?" Callahan blubbered.

"What's it look like?" Chance held his arms out to his sides, revealing his workout attire and running shoes.

"Don't be a smart ass," Callahan snapped. "You're still the one as far as I'm concerned. I'm going to watch you constantly. You won't be able to breathe without smelling my cigars."

"Listen pal," Chance said disgustedly, firing the Evo back to life. "I didn't touch that girl except where she wanted. I'm going to the gym. I'll be back in a couple of hours, if you want to take a shower with me."

He revved the motor and snapped the clutch. The uniformed officer behind Chance yanked his polished nightstick from his belt and darted forward. The long front end lunged and startled the big sloppy cop. Chance released the clutch and Callahan jerked. The uniformed officer, Joe Fernandez, closed on Chance, who pulled around Callahan and into the street. He jockeyed the throttle and pushed the revs in first through a red light, snapping the bike into second while spinning the throttle for a wheelstand before dropping it into third.

"I can't stand that sonuvabitch," Callahan said as he yanked on his waistband again.

"I'll get that cocksucker," Fernandez snarled.

A bead of sweat ran down his temple and across his pockmarked cheek as he twisted the nightstick in his hands. Callahan looked at Joe with a questioning gape.

"Just keep an eye on him, Joe," he said. "I'll get him when the time is right."

Chance rode up the freeway on-ramp, shaken. He respected cops on one hand and feared them on the other. He knew they had one of the shittiest jobs on the planet and appreciated the bullshit they dealt with daily. On the other hand, he didn't want to have a goddamn thing to do with them.

He pulled onto the 405 Freeway northbound, goosed the chopper, and peeled through lanes like wire through cheese. He ripped past Los Angeles International Airport and pulled off the freeway in Santa Monica. He fought traffic down Santa Monica Boulevard to a series of side streets named after major universities. He turned left on Princeton and pulled up to the condo complex where Mark owned one of the units toward the back. He rang the buzzer on the gate.

"It's about time," Mark hollered and hit the button to release the gate.

Chance was still pumping adrenaline as he entered Mark's dark, two-story brick condo. At the foot of Mark's dark green door was a Beretta doormat with crossed pistols formed in the rubber. As Chance walked into the cavern, he discovered a cache of arms, knives and training equipment. He couldn't help but be consumed by the vast assortment of weapons and diving gear. There were dumbbells on the fireplace hearth, knives on the bookshelf, military books and Soldier of Fortune magazines on his coffee table and black leather couch. All the windows were covered with closed blinds.

"I got popped trying to get over here," Chance said.

"What was that all about?" Mark asked.

"I'll tell you later," Chance replied looking around the room at all the armament, impressed. "Let's get to it."

Chance pulled Vince's screenplay out from under his vest, then took off the vest and his sweatshirt.

"Read this over. This will give you some background on my deal with Vince. That's what we need to discuss."

Mark grabbed a canvas bag full of equipment and they headed into the underground garage area. Beneath the two-story condo complex were three double-car garages and an area large enough for cars to pull under and turn into their respective garages. Leading to the outside was a massive automatic cell door with vertical bars that opened like a garage door to a driveway that curved up and out of the tunnel to street level. The area reminded Chance of some massive underground holding cell and gave him the chills. There were no windows, just concrete walls, and sewage pipes running along the ceiling.

Mark opened his cluttered garage, which housed two Harleys, training equipment, tools, and a reloading bench for making his own ammunition. Mark grabbed a rubber knife and dragged a 25-pound heavy canvas punching bag out of the corner. Chance lifted it and Mark chained it over a steel grating covering a rain drain from above. A small cylindrical beam of light filtered into the concrete tomb.

"We'll begin with a warm-up and knife defense," Mark said, demonstrating how to move away from a knife threat. They warmed up, then he took Chance through knife defense, then to blocking and taking the weapon away.

"You can use these motions with all forms of defense, whether it's a gun, knife or stick," he explained.

He made Chance run through the moves several times. Mark was nearly the same size as Chance at 6-foot-2 and 225 pounds. Mark studied various forms of martial arts and combined them into his own regimen of close quarters combat. No foo-foo dancing or acrobatics; it was designed strictly for life and death situations.

After the training session, he led Chance through a series of punches and kicks until Chance couldn't lift his arms and legs anymore.

Sweating profusely, they both knocked off.

"Let's get a protein shake and talk about your case," Mark said. "Run your bike down to the garage. We'll take my Bronco."

Chance drove while Mark thumbed through the screenplay. "Your partner knew how to push peoples' buttons, didn't he?" Mark said.

"Like no one else in the world," Chance said. "He was a master."

"Are you still wearing Wranglers and flannel shirts with your brown vest?" Mark questioned.

"Yep," Chance said. "Never liked black much."

"You will now," Mark spat, turning the pages of the screenplay and shaking his head. "That's all people wear in Hollywood anymore. We need to fix you up. Pull over there."

He pointed to an open parking spot next to a meter. While they drank protein shakes inside, Mark continued to thumb through the screenplay.

"This guy can write, but I'd kill him, too, if he said shit like this about me."

Mark tossed the screenplay into the rear seat of the black Bronco and they walked down the promenade. There was a collection of restaurants, clothing shops, and movie houses under the glistening Southern California sun. Mark dressed like a man who knew nothing of style, only security and practicality. He wore sweatshirts with his leather jacket and either jogging pants or black Levis with his running shoes. Mark drug Chance into a Miller's Outpost and pointed him at black shit.

"This is what you need," he said, "you might as well go for it."

"It's not my style," Chance said, pulling out a pair of black Levi's and a shirt to match.

"You want to find out who killed your brother?" Mark pointed to the boot shop across the street. "I'll take you to a party tonight that will put you right in the middle of that crowd."

By the end of the afternoon, Chance was decked out. Mark told him that he would loan him a HAL black leather vest for the time being. Chance even stuck his head in a kitschy shop full of dice earrings for women and fuzzy dice for cars. He bagged a set of bad-assed black sunglasses from the counter and paid the girl who was wearing black eye makeup and lipstick. Her bright red hair was pulled into two ponytails and tied with black bows. She wore a white T-shirt with red dice over her tits, a black patent leather mini skirt, black patent leather boots with 6-inch spikes. She sported a massive stainless steel bobble bouncing on her pierced tongue. Mark drove back to his place.

"Take this shit home and throw it in the washer. Be back at my place at eight," Mark said. "This will be a learning experience."

Chance stuffed the clothes into Mark's black backpack and headed home. As he pulled up to his house, he could see a black-and-white on the corner. He rolled the bike into the back and closed his gate. His anxiety had returned. He needed to try to get away from all the pressure.

He couldn't do anything for a few hours. He dropped down into the small, cramped, cinderblock basement of his house and threw the new pants and shirt in the laundry, then went to the garage.

Chance had one more black item to develop before he attended the evening's event. He knew he had a couple old black belts, but no buckles. He liked to wear something custom, so he dug out his belt buckle jig and dug out the brass rod and went to work. He donned welding shades and fired up the torches. He used to make a buckle or two for pals.

His jig consisted of a 6-by-4 inch plate of half-inch steel welded to a plate that could be clamped into his vice. There were two hand-made clamps brazed to the plate to hold the hub of the wheel and the brass rod rim. A hole was drilled in the end of the plate for bending the belt strap. A rod was welded to the bottom of the plate and made a 90-degree turn upward. It had a quarter inch round disc welded to it, 3 inches in diameter. It was used to wrap the 1/4-inch brass rod to form the rim of the wheel buckle.

Chance spent an hour brazing each thin brass rod spoke to the rim and hub. Then he brazed a post to catch the belt holes and the bridge to snap the leather strap through. He dropped the red hot buckle in a coffee can full of rusty water to cool it, then turned on his buffing wheels and carefully polished the handmade buckle until it glistened.

He took the finished product into the house and dug through a chest of old motorcycle shit until he found a black belt that a rider made for him in exchange for a buckle. He made sure that the belt would fit through the loop on the back of the buckle. On the back of the wide leather belt a pair of dice were tooled into the leather and dyed red with white spots. Chance rubbed the belt down with leather conditioner on a rag to soothe the dry hide. Chance returned to the garage, dug out his bike cleaning kit, and went to work on it. He didn't own a cage, and no sedan would ever be parked in his garage. This was the Code of the West for many bikers.

He opened a can of tuna, chopped up a carrot, some onion, and made himself a sandwich. Then he jumped in the shower. As he showered, the evening got to him the way beetles eat a pine tree. In a matter of weeks, a 100-year-old tree was dead.

He tried to shake his concerns for the missing broad and Vince, but they were like a blanket wrapped around him so tightly he could hardly breathe. He blasted out of his pad dressed in all black, with a shiny new brass buckle and his matching gold ring. The sun was down and he arrived at Mark's place early.

"You're early," Mark said through his speaker box on the front gate.

"No time to lose, goddamnit," Chance said, leaning against the electrical gate. The new boots were already pinching his feet.

Mark's door was open and Chance walked in. Mark was sitting with his back to Chance, wailing on his computer. He was writing another military training manual on mountain rescue.

Mark recently returned from a trip to the base camp of Mount Everest. Skiing equipment was perched against the wall leading to the tiny kitchen at the back of the condo. He had no food in the dusty cupboards, only protein drinks and a couple of beers. He wasn't interested in cooking and needed a break from his work, so he strolled out to one of the busiest boulevards in the city where restaurants were stacked, several to each block.

"I'll tell ya why I'm early," Chance said, looking at the weapons and equipment around Mark's living room. "I don't wear black much. I don't do Hollywood parties. I want to find the sonuvabitch who killed Vince and go back to San Pedro, and I want to do it now. I've got enough bullshit in my life on the coast. This is an unfinished chapter."

"Women?" Mark said, shutting off his computer. "I got all set to get married about five years ago. I was hooked bad and she dumped me, after I spent five grand on the bitch. That was it for me."

"Sure," Chance said. "Where there's trouble in my life, women are generally involved."

"Look," Mark said, "I'm glad to help. A good fight always winds me up, but the chances of walking into this party and finding the bastard who killed your brother are slim. In fact, it's more likely that whoever did it will find out you're looking and take you out. Done deal."

"I gotta roll the dice," Chance said.

"I figured," Mark said, ascending his carpeted stairs. "I'll jump in the shower and we'll go get a bite to eat, then investigate."

Chance paced Mark's living room, looking at his book collection of military material and training manuals. He had a series of gun shooting awards from several competitions. Chance thought about his probability of finding the hitter and taking care of his brother's assassin. He was very aware that he could never bring the mad biker back.

In a sense, Vince had it coming. He wrote the screenplay that perhaps would destroy numerous careers and influence an industry for all-time. The conclusion would be for the good, except for the advertising industry. Chance kicked the carpeting in dismay. He liked life to be simple, black and white. He didn't like all the dull edges that turned a wrong into almost a right. He pondered his options, but his heart only hollered for one: justice. But even justice could take several forms. Mark came storming down the stairs.

"Let's ride. You know, it might piss them off more if you got the movie made," Mark said, as he jogged out his front door and down the stairwell to his underground garage.

"That's one of the reasons I brought the screenplay to you," Chance said.

They fired their bikes and rode out to Santa Monica Boulevard.

"How about a killer burrito?" Mark shouted over the noise of their engines.

"Just make it fast," Chance said as they shot across the intersection.

Chance didn't ride with a lot of bikers. He recognized immediately that Mark could ride. He wasn't a squirrel behind his black FXR bars. He also wasn't scared to death like some riders, especially in the city. City riding was like playing football naked against full-suited pros. There's armed and dangerous treachery everywhere.

Mark cut over to Wilshire, then Montana Boulevard, and pulled into Rico's Mexican joint. It was small and on a side street, but the parking was open and they slid up to a spot in front of the restaurant's windows, a necessity for bikers in the city. If they couldn't watch their bikes, they'd be stolen before they finished their first beer. The two bikes clicked and squeaked as they walked into the restaurant and ordered a couple special burritos and two beers. The air was warm as they left the bikes at the curb, but it cooled as the sun departed. The shadows from the square stucco and steel buildings turned from hard dark shapes reaching across the street to soft opaque forms. Then darkness took over.

Night changed the city from shorts and sports to nightlife, drugs, and thugs. Bikers were meant for the night. Harleys run well in the heavy, cool evening air. Their chrome glistens, and they take on the appearance of evil sabers slashing through the nighttime traffic.

After the brief chow stop, they rolled out to Wilshire Boulevard and rode under the freeway, cutting through Westwood, where the UCLA students hang out and the streets are crowded with bars, restaurants, theaters, and action all night long.

They shot up the four-lane boulevard to Beverly and hung a left into Beverly Hills. The evening had taken over the streets and the home-folk stayed safe inside. The night crowd ruled the saucy streets. Mark led as they turned up Benedict Canyon for a home on a hill. Mark motioned Chance to slow as he turned right up a narrow driveway to the top, where it leveled out.

There were two Porches, a Ferrari, and a Corvette parked at the plateau of the asphalt. A series of garages faced the parking section, which was bordered by a back yard of brick decking and grass. The house was old and overlooked a curve in the canyon below. Mark knew the owner, a single man named Cronin who owned a high-end Los Angeles printing company, Monarch Litho. He was responsible for printing top-of-the-line advertising agency jobs, brochures, and quarterly reports. He also enjoyed antique motorcycles and was a member of an exclusive motorcycle group in Hollywood that was made up of producers, several actors, and agents.

Mark made his way through the patio and into the sprawling kitchen at the back of the house. People were mingling throughout the house and Chance felt uncomfortable. Crowds made him feel ill at ease, but the girls were hot-looking in their slinky black dresses dancing over curvy bodies. Mark took off his jacket and threw it on an antique wooden chair just inside the door. Chance followed Mark as he wandered through the kitchen into the dining room. The antique oak dining room table was covered with a fine lace tablecloth and a buffet of appetizers.

Chance had no appetite, although the food looked delicious. Mark wandered into the foyer of the house painted all white with hardwood floors and a wild series of art hung on all the walls and up the stairs to the second story.

"Cronin," Mark said. The host was a short man with salt-and-pepper hair who wore Levis and a denim shirt, unlike all his guests adorned in all-black evening attire. Denim was his uniform. He looked like he was working on the house not living in it. Cronin had owned the home for 20 years. It was a work in progress that he'd restored and packed with antiques.

"Hey stunt man, how are you?"

"I'm good. This is a buddy rider," Mark said, gesturing to Chance.

"Chance Hogan," Chance said. "Good to meet you."

"You ride?" Cronin said and Chance nodded. "Let me show you something I just got back."

Cronin roamed back through his house. Chance could tell as he moved along that the small man was also uncomfortable with his slick audience. His tall, voluptuous girlfriend cornered him in the kitchen.

"Baby," she said, her eyes brightening as she looked beyond Cronin to the two big guys behind him.

She was a sizeable woman in a long black gown that was cut low. Her ample breasts pushed and jiggled in the v-neck of her dress. She had a wide mouth with succulent lips and she smiled broadly.

"I need some more ice. Mark, how are you? Who's that new guy with you?"

Her wavy blond hair was similar in color to Chance's, but not as rugged and stiff. It was full and soft. Chance blushed as he moved forward and took her hand in his,

"Chance," he said.

"Chance?" she said her eyes wandering along his form. "Interesting name. I'm Carol."

Chance could feel the seduction in her warm breath, the wet glint in her eyes, and the turn of her succulent lips.

"Damn good to meet you, Carol," Chance said.

Then, turning toward Cronin, he said, "Mark told me you're working on an FXR." He needed to stroll quickly out from under Carol's gaze.

Cronin paid little attention to Carol. He grabbed one of the caterers by the arm.

"I've got more ice in the garage," he said.

The three walked into the cool evening air that smelled of pine trees mixed with the exhaust fumes from the constant cars buzzing below. Cronin opened his garage and led them inside, flicking on a bank of 8-foot fluorescents bulbs.

The garage was packed with motorcycles, walls of tools, parts hanging from the rafters, and a hot rod covered with a canvas tarp. On the left side of the garage was one open area with a motorcycle covered with a black cordura cover. Cronin walked to the bike and carefully lifted the cover.

"This was restored by Steve Huntson up north," Cronin said. "It's a 1913 Model F Harley-Davidson. I waited for a year for him to finish it. Only 49 of these ever built."

Huntson was noted for some of the finest over-restorations in the world. His sense of detail was beyond what any factory ever dreamed. Simple pinstriping became ornate gold leaf. Factory engine cases became highly polished or machine-turned works of art. Chance and Mark wandered around the bike treating it with museum respect.

"Incredible," Chance said. "But where's the FXR?"

"Oh," Cronin said, carefully re-covering the rare motorcycle. "It's right here."

"This is the one Billy West was building?" Chance asked.

Billy West was a customizer of magic proportions in the Los Angeles region. He was a persnickety bastard who worked at his own pace, in his own time, with whomever he chose. He ran off more customers than he kept.

"He's been working on this bike for ten years," Cronin said. "It's still in primer."

Chance reviewed the bike with Mark. Billy was an artist with classic deco flair. His talents were spent hand-forming handlebars with the levers built in. Nothing was fabricated using a CNC machine or even a lathe. He welded, pounded, and sanded forever. Each side cover was reformed. The exhaust was altered from a mechanical object to a piece of art with flairs and art deco highlights. The taillight housing was hand-made, along with the lens. Chance was stunned by the workmanship. Billy took pride in building a bike and having the owner show-off the primered workmanship.

"It could take me a couple of years to convince Billy to paint it," Cronin said.

Mark and Chance both thanked Cronin for the tour and complimented his taste. Cronin wasn't bashful about his wealth but he was humble. He led them out of the garage and turned off the lights. It was obvious that the garage was off limits to the other guests.

As they headed back toward the house, Chance looked through the French doors into the kitchen and the living room beyond. He spotted a blonde, about 5-foot-7, walking with her back to him. She wore a black, backless evening dress. She was model slender with a snake-like rhythm to her stride.

Chance was suddenly mesmerized. She looked like Nicole, Chance thought, Vince's missing girlfriend. "It couldn't be," he muttered to himself.

"Cronin," Chance said politely, but he could feel his voice quake. "You should be proud of what you've accomplished here. Please excuse me for a second."

He patted Cronin on the shoulder and walked around him in the direction of the blonde. She was on the arm of an older guy, maybe 45, who was wearing a thick gold bracelet and a Rolex watch. Chance entered the archway and stopped. He watched the couple cross the room. Several eyes followed her, and two of the other guests rose out of their chairs and greeted the man. Chance picked up his first name, Barry.

"That's Barry Macintyre," Cronin said, coming up beside him, "and his new squeeze."

A butler approached the couple and offered them glasses of champagne. Barry, 6 feet and good looking with salt and pepper sideburns and black curly hair, picked up two slender glasses. Their shape mirrored the shape of the woman but lacked the moves. He turned his back to Chance once more and touched the blonde's bare arm.

She turned to accept the glass. It *was* Nicole. She was a natural from the tips of her painted exposed toes all the way up the slit in her dress that showed enough leg to lick. Her waist was hand-holding narrow and her bust just ample enough to still be a model. Her neck was long and tender, and she had a slight tan. She was born with thick, wavy Nordic blond hair. No need for dyes. It was fantastic, just the way it was.

When she said, "Danka," Chance knew he wasn't dreaming. She took the slender glass from her man's grasp and several men watched as she lifted it to her ruby lips. Cronin stood admiring at Chance's side as she took pleasure in each man's attention. She scanned the room, then her gaze met Chance's. The glass dropped from her hands, shattering on the floor, and she turned away.

"You have this effect on all women?" Cronin joked. When he looked up at Chance's hardening features, he knew something was wrong. Nicole turned to run, but her boyfriend grabbed her arm and jerked her back. He spun in the direction of her terrified gaze, but only Cronin stood in the doorway, slightly flushed.

"Who was that?" Barry asked, attempting to keep Nicole from

fainting. She couldn't speak as he lowered her onto the deep white leather couch and propped her head with a fluffy pillow.

Two motorcycles rumbled to life in the parking area. Chance noted the license plate of a mid-'50s Bentley that said "BARRY II" as they jammed down the hill.

-19-

NICOLE'S LAST PARTY

The two bikers motored to the bottom of the steep Beverly Hills driveway and stopped, both bikes rumbling in the night air.

"Are you thinking what I'm thinking?" Chance asked Mark.

"I know what you're thinking," Mark said. "I saw how she reacted."

"Let's press 'em," Chance said.

"Let's move somewhere to talk," Mark hollered against the crackling engines.

They putted down winding Benedict Canyon, turned down a side street and pulled over.

"I want to go back," Chance said.

"That's his old, missing girlfriend, isn't it?" Mark asked.

"That's right," Chance said. "They both had something to do with Vince's death, and I've got a shot at taking care of it, tonight."

"What are you going to do," Mark asked, "go break into his car and wait for him? You know the bastard's car is alarmed. It's a wonder the bikes didn't set it off."

They pulled off a dark side street and there weren't many cars lining the Beverly Hills lane. Chance stood so he could see the canyon weave past.

"Moot point, brother. There it goes," he said, pointing at the Bentley.

They fired up the bikes, darted to Benedict, and then leaned right. They could see the Bentley making a left on Sunset. The car's exterior glistened in the lights on the boulevard as the big whitewalls turned into the left lane.

"Let's bear down on them," Mark hollered over the rumbling engines.

Chance enjoyed being a loner, but he also was happy to have an expert to help in a potentially deadly situation. Mark's experience as a mercenary and an estate security organizer for major companies and ambassadors gave him a substantial edge, and Chance was relieved to allow his experience take the lead. At the next light, they stopped four cars behind the glistening Bentley.

"Let's split lanes and jump right on his tail," Mark suggested.

Mark was a wise, cagey sort and honest about his feelings. Chance nodded, slipped to the left between a Beemer and a Porsche, and blasted up to the Bentley bumping the rear bumper. He liked the sparkle of the upscale cars on the glittery street, but it wasn't his part of town. He didn't belong there.

Mark gassed his chopped FXR and rolled up behind the Bentley on the opposite side. They both revved their engines and tried to see inside through the small rear window. The Bentley jolted and weaved in the lane. The car jerked to the right beside a high-rise, then right again down a narrow street, which seemed odd to Chance.

Chance and Mark cut across the right lane to stay right on the Bentley's tail.

"Follow me," Mark shouted, scooting alongside the building. It turned left on another street directly behind the structure and dropped down a long slope to Doheny Boulevard.

Pulling up to the intersection, Mark and Chance watched the Bentley roll down a block, pull right and stop abruptly against the curb. The car door burst open and the tall blonde dove out onto the grassy parkway. She screamed at the driver. In the lights of the oncoming vehicles, Chance could see the driver raise a pistol. He snapped his clutch lever, lurched forward, purposely banging into the rear bumper. The sedan lurched, the gun went off, the door slammed shut, and the car sped away.

Nicole tried to run to a high-rise apartment across the street, but Chance cut her off. She ran down a side street, kicking off her high heels. The Harleys followed.

Chance spotted a circular driveway and jammed into it to cut her off. She ran into the front yard of a large Colonial home and headed for the front door, but he beat her to it. Lights came on in the house as Chance shut off his barking motorcycle.

"Go ahead," Chance barked at her. "Knock on the door, call the cops. Let's see how you explain Vince's death."

Nicole stopped dead in her tracks.

Mark rolled up on the sidewalk, shutting off his bike and stepping off it. He moved to the edge of the lawn closest to Doheny in case she tried to break for the street.

"You can talk to us or the cops, your choice," Chance said.

"Nice line," Mark said.

Chance glanced at him, then at Nicole. Her makeup ran down her face with tears and she stumbled in her bare feet. Chance looked at the mashed platinum blond hair and saw Hollywood painted all over her. He got the chills looking at her in the dim light with the cars speeding past on Doheny, as expensive houses around him glowed. The cops were probably on their way. He scanned the windows of the spacious house to see if anyone was looking. He knew his time was short.

Nicole stood facing him in the center of the walkway. He wanted her to confess, to tell him everything. She was a product of the dreamy neon environment and obviously her world had crashed at the party.

"What happened to Vince?" Chance asked.

"Somebody in the house called the cops," Mark muttered. "I can sense it."

"I hate dat guy," Nicole's said. "He promised me big time. I got nuttin'."

"I don't give a fuck," Chance snapped. "You didn't have to kill him."

"I didn't," Nicole blubbered. "I swear, I swear!"

Chance gazed at her million-dollar figure and perfect features. He usually melted in front of women who looked that good, but in this case, he lost all compassion as a patrol car screeched around the corner. Nicole stood there like a kitten caught in the headlights of an approaching car. Her disdain for Vince was turning against her and Chance sensed it in her gaze. She was breaking down.

Mark trained cops in close quarters combat and had a series of business cards he could flash on them to calm the situation. With red lights flashing, the car jolted to a stop. The patrol spotlight beamed on Chance and the girl. The doors burst open and the officers jumped out. The cop on the passenger side drew a .357 Magnum and aimed it at Chance. The other officer slipped his billy club into his belt ring and stepped around the front of the car into the light.

"Is there a problem here?" he asked.

Mark stepped forward and handed the officer his card as a member of the Los Angeles County Sheriff's Department's Emergency Dive Team. The officer looked at the card knowingly.

"We received a disturbance call," he said.

He was a young officer with muscular arms that fit snugly in the short sleeves of his crisp uniform. He stood as tall as Mark at over 6 feet.

"It's a long story, but we wanted to ask this girl some questions about the death of a friend. That's the bottom line," Mark said. "It's a murder case in San Pedro."

Meanwhile, Nicole shivered with fear, consumed by her knowledge of Vince's death. As one of the officers approached her, she broke down and fell to her knees on the smooth pavement.

Chance was bothered by what he saw. He didn't want the cops involved. He wanted to take care of this himself. He was also aware of the consequences if he did. Another aspect of the scene bugged him; a woman was involved. He loved women, but in the last couple of months, he'd faced a number of terrors with the opposite sex. The whole scenario perplexed him. Chance couldn't figure it out, yet he was sure the murder of Suzanne and acts of the psycho bitch, Sheila, haunted him for some reason. He wasn't sure he wanted to know why.

Officer Taylor, the black cop, approached Chance.

"We can't hold this girl for murder. How do you know her?"

"She was my best friend's girl," Chance said. "Somebody contacted him and told him she had been kidnapped. The next day, he received a threatening note. Now he's dead, and she doesn't appear to be kidnapped. Why don't you give this investigator, Kate Norton from the Harbor Division, a call? She'll explain or come down and question her."

He handed the officer Kate's card.

"I'll do that," the officer said. "You're free to go."

"Thanks, officer," Chance said and nodded to Mark.

They mounted their bikes, fired them up, and rode down to Santa Monica Boulevard. Chance was relieved. He would still have to keep an eye on the case with Nicole and her boyfriend, but he suspected that she lost her ability to hold the story back. She knew Chance would hunt her down again if the law didn't sort it out. He was also glad to be rolling out of the upscale end of town. It wasn't for him.

At the first red light, Chance pulled up beside Mark. "Hey, wanna grab a cup of coffee?"

"I suppose," Mark said as the light turned green. "Then again, hanging with you could be dangerous."

"Shit, look whose talkin'," Chance hollered as their bikes split lanes heading for the freeway.

They stopped at the California Café, a couple of blocks from Mark's condo, drank coffee and ate muffins, while discussing the next workout routine.

"Let's go for a ride one of these days," Chance said.

"How about to Sturgis this year?"

"Sounds good to me," Chance said.

"See if you can make it next Saturday," Mark said. "We'll hit the gym."

"If I'm not arrested or shot by then," Chance said, starting his bike and rolling to the curb.

"I won't hold my breath."

As Chance headed up the brightly lit Santa Monica Boulevard toward the freeway, he thought about Suzanne and a cold chill rushed over him. Something in his bones told him that his San Pedro problem wasn't over. As he leaned right and felt the bars in his hands shake over a couple of potholes at the base of the freeway on-ramp, he was hit with a sense of uncertainty. He enjoyed living near the ocean in the union workers' community near the docks. He enjoyed the quiet harbor at night, no rushing boulevards or screaming freeways within earshot, just the whistle of a ship leaving the harbor or the bright lights of a cruise vessel coming home.

He was lonely in a sense, and he knew as he flew past LAX on the long chopper that there would be another woman. He would try to hold back, clear the deck and let the dice collect dust for a while. But he didn't know how long he could wait before he took another gamble at love.

Something told him women were danger signs he should steer clear of for awhile. He revved the engine, dropped it into fourth, and spun around a sports car with a buxom blonde behind the wheel. As Chance passed her, she looked up startled, then smiled. Their eyes met and that unnerving chill returned. He twisted the throttle hard.

-20-

BAKED GOODS

Chance awoke abruptly Sunday morning, pulled on a pair of shorts, and ran next door to the neighbor's pad. He didn't brush his teeth or comb his long hair; he needed to look at the paper first. The neighbors were a couple of geologists who bounced from job to job in the unpopular environmental industry.

He popped open their rusting gate and grabbed the Los Angeles Times off the stoop. There on the front page was a photo of Vince's girlfriend and one of the partners of the McIntyre agency. The headline read, "Lovers Linked to Murder."

He read the article through to the end. The cops had a confession from her and the dude was trying to play innocent. In the advertising industry, he understood and knew the press, but had never been the focus of its attention.

Chance refolded the paper and set it on the porch. As he walked back to his little house on the corner, he looked out at the harbor, and for the first time in awhile, enjoyed the comfort of the bay and his view of the lapping Pacific. Nothing in the newspaper report would bring his brother back. Vince and Chance would never share another ride. He realized then that his efforts were hollow, that he had lost his riding partner forever.

Chance pulled on his running shoes and ran around the docks at the marina for a half-hour. He was off his routine and wanted to kick it in the ass again. After the workout, he rode his bike to Mando's burrito joint and ordered a breakfast burrito. He ate it on his porch overlooking the harbor as the sun blazed into the blue sky. Chance was tired of the turmoil and violence in his life, and hoped the negative spell was broken. He washed the burrito down with a protein drink and took a shower. While rinsing off, he thought about Suzanne and decided to call Kate and find out if the cops had picked up the perpetrator.

"Officer Kate here."

"Officer Chance here, reporting in."

"I can't thank you enough. Did you read the paper, congratulations," Kate said. "You put me on the map with the department. I'll tell you more in the near future."

"Thanks for handling that," Chance said. "What about Suzanne?"

"They're still looking at you, so stay clean. They know it wasn't you, but they have no one else to beat on. What are you doing today?"

"I suggest that you steer clear of me until you catch the guy behind that killing."

"I'm a trained professional," Kate said, "I can handle myself."

"Ya got any drug-dealing prostitutes you want offed? Let's test the waters. Gimme her number and I'll go out with her."

"That's bullshit," Kate said. "Besides, I wouldn't want to wish that torture on anyone."

"Least of all you," Chance said. "Gimme a couple of weeks, then we'll share Chinese food again. Keep me posted if you hear anything."

"Call me once in awhile," Kate said and hung up.

Chance couldn't figure out the tight little officer or his own perplexing feelings, but he was determined to stay away from her as much as possible. He was just a tramp biker who roamed from town to town. She was highly educated and a cop. The two would never mix.

Chance showered and dressed in denims, a sweatshirt, and his vest then rolled his bike into the sun. It was a blistering morning, and he decided to ride to Walker's at Point Fermin for a beer and to see if anything was going on. He didn't hang out much, but he liked to check the bikes at the old bar and walk across to the park, home to the inoperable Point Fermin lighthouse and cliffs overlooking Catalina Island.

He pulled up out front and found a spot to squeeze into. The sun glistened on the scooters. The tattered striped canvas awnings flapped in the breeze. The hand-painted sign above the door contained two hand-painted buxom mermaids surrounding a ship's life ring in the center.

The sign was cracked and faded, but well known as home to most of the guys who rode in Southern California. It was a small clapboard breakfast joint dating to the '40s, with only seven wooden tables coated with layers of hippy resin from the '70s. It had a small bar and was run by the old man, his wife, and two buxom, surly waitresses. One, the blond, was the fry cook and the other, a raven-haired woman in her late 30s, moved from table to table. Pa was the supply clerk and ma was a kindly old waitress with a streak of meanness that surfaced anytime a rider stepped out the door with a beer in his hand. She was on him like chrome on exhaust pipes.

Chance strode into the café and ordered a Corona while eyeing the bikes. The assortment ranged from rice-burning road racers to antiques, choppers, and stock Harleys. The dark-haired waitress smiled at Chance and her bare nipples seemed to harden against her white Walker's T-shirt.

She had big swaying boobs, which Chance would have liked to cup in his hands, but he knew that it would lead to a slap, or worse. He squeezed a lime into his Corona and took a long swig, the perfect chaser to an afternoon ride on the coast. He shot the shit with a couple riders. A blue-collar worker admired his bike, which needed some tender care and maintenance.

After the beer, Chance rode to the Blue Café in downtown Long Beach for a killer salad while listening to the outdoor blues band. The bike felt strong and easy roaming along Harbor Boulevard, then over the Vincent Thomas Bridge between San Pedro and Terminal Island. His waitress was a short knockout with flickering blue eyes and rich brunette hair. She pranced up to his table and set the menu down.

"Can I get you something to drink?

"Sure, I'll take a Corona with a slice of lime, thanks."

"Yes, sir. Is that your bike?" she asked, gazing across the promenade.

"Yep, that's mine," Chance said.

"I used to ride before I had my daughter," the waitress said.

He could tell her mind was working, wondering if he had a decent job, whether he liked kids, and how he was in bed.

"That's too bad," Chance said. "I'm on the road most of the time. "How old is your daughter?"

He could see the wind flap right out of her sails.

"Oh, she's only two," the pretty girl said. "Are you going to want something to eat?"

"Yep, that's why I'm here. I'm not much of a drinker. I'll take that California salad." He watched her eyes brighten again.

"I'll be right back with your beer," she said and disappeared inside the Blue Café.

Chance thought about calling Mark to see what he was up to, but he didn't want to ride deeper into the congested city. Ever since discovering San Pedro, he enjoyed the coastline, just minutes south of the hectic atmosphere, the blight and violence of the inner city.

The waitress returned with his beer as Chance looked at mostly newer bikes parked across the promenade from the patio. Then he noticed a figure lurking in the parking lot behind the bikes. The dark-haired individual wore an overcoat and was hanging around between the parked cars, but Chance dismissed it as a homeless nut.

On Sunday, the downtown area of Long Beach was alive with people, tourists, and homeless panhandlers. Nearby Pine Avenue was lined with restored old buildings housing chi-chi restaurants and upscale shops. Downtown Long Beach, perched on the bluffs over some of the most pristine beaches on the California coast, was once on the verge of collapse. Homeless folks and druggies roamed the streets with sailors from the now-closed Naval base. But times changed and downtown came alive again.

Chance ate a terrific salad of grilled chicken, greens, avocado, pine nuts, mandarin orange slices, and mango dressing. He finished the Corona, paid his tab and said goodbye to the waitress as he headed for his scooter. It felt good to be able to ride along the coast without being engulfed in urban mayhem.

He had to admit that he wanted a woman in his life, but he feared it would never work. He felt trapped in that regard as he buzzed over the Vincent Thomas Bridge and cut to Pacific Avenue to Ramona's Bakery for a couple of morning muffins for the week ahead. He hoped he still had a job at the docks, and that Julie would call him in the morning and invite him to come to work.

He pulled up in front of the bakery and dismounted the warm motorcycle. It was running as sweet as it could, and he enjoyed every fleeting minute of his time in the saddle. He stepped away from the bike and entered the old bakery on Pacific Avenue. It was one of those few fleeting businesses run in the old school fashion.

It wasn't a franchise joint, but a traditional one-shop enterprise. Many of the businesses in that area of San Pedro still maintained that air. It was one of the area's traits that Chance enjoyed. The wallpaper was faded and the linoleum worn, but the girls were friendly. A luscious Hispanic girl bagged his muffins for the ride home. She was slender and her white uniform fit her like a leather bra over the nose of a Corvette. Her skin was olive and her lips were blood red, outlined with black liner. As she came around the counter, Chance saw that the zipper in the front of her uniform was down to her tits. Her breasts weren't too large, but they formed a natural cleavage that sucked Chance's gaze to her soft flesh.

"Can I see your bike?" she asked.

Without thinking about it Chance said, "Sure." He opened the door and held it for her.

"It is a beautiful bike," she said. Chance noticed the nametag on her uniform said Mari.

"Thanks, Mari," Chance said. "How long have you worked at Ramona's?"

"Not long," Mari said. "I'm the daughter of the owners. I work here in the summer when I'm not in college."

"What's your major?" Chance asked.

"I'm a senior in business administration," Mari said. "I will go for my master's beginning next year."

"I might need to pick your brain about business," Chance said.

"Anytime," Mari said. "What type of business do you have in mind?"

"What do you think?" Chance said. "I'd like to open a bike shop in town."

"What about a restaurant, a cantina? From what I've learned, retail is difficult at best and prone to cyclical changes. Some 85 percent of all retail outlets go out of business in the first year," she said, and her eyes were bright with enthusiasm.

"That's the level of knowledge I'll need in the future," Chance said, amazed by her furtive grin and the soft words flowing from her delicate lips.

"Bars are business no-brainers, and coupled with restaurants, they are the most profitable retail outlets," Mari said. "Put a bar and restaurant together with a motorcycle motif, add some T-shirts and style and you might have something."

As she spoke, she moved closer to Chance.

"I'd like to talk to you again about this," Chance said. "I need to know all I can. Will you work at the bakery all summer?"

"Yes," she said, standing so close to Chance he could smell her perfume on the breezy street. "Are you involved?"

"No," Chance said, "I'm not, and you're a knockout, young and intelligent. I would be a fool not to go out with you."

"Well?" she said, looking him directly in the eye with an assuming gaze.

"This is not the time," Chance muttered. He wanted her in the worst way. He could have torn that dress off her in a hot second.

"Because I'm Mexican?" she snapped.

"Don't go there," Chance said. "That's not the problem. I need a week to get my job in order to be acceptable."

Then he smiled at her.

"Look, I would like to take you in my arms right now, but I need to take care of something that you will completely understand when the time comes. Is that clear or do I need to bend you over my bike and spank you?"

"Promises, promises," she said with a glimmer in her eyes. She turned her body so that Chance looked down her soft lower back to a very narrow waist and at the curve of her knockout bubble butt. Chance could feel a lump growing in his throat and elsewhere.

"Don't pressure me," he said, "I can't handle it."

"You've got a week." Mari stood on her tiptoes and kissed him gently on the lips.

He felt his knees weaken. He placed his hand on her waist as her lips touched his like a flesh-eating magnet.

"I'll call you," Chance said and backed away from her as if he had just won a million dollars at a roulette table.

He staggered and tossed a leg over his bike. He looked around once more and watched her strong, shapely legs in high heels as he fired the bike to life. He was in trouble already and he knew it.

As he peeled down the street, a tan sedan pulled away from the other side of the street facing the opposite direction.

Chance floated an inch above his saddle as he rode home. He pulled his bike in the back and stood looking at it, as if his steel brother had a life of its own.

«« — »»

The bakery closed at 8:00 on Saturday night. Mari's mom and dad came out of the back of Ramona's, slid into their business van and drove away. The ovens were set, the cash registers cleared, and the neon on the front of the building turned off when Mari came out of the back of the shop, set the alarm, and closed the door.

There was a small parking lot behind the building, shared by three retail businesses on Pacific. The sky was gray, with the glow of the streetlights looming over the buildings, as she lightheartedly strolled to her car, a compact Honda. Another car was parked next to it, a nondescript faded tan sedan that almost looked like an undercover police car. It had no chrome strips on it and the wheels had no hubcaps. Rust was beginning to push the paint from the sheet metal at the corners of the wheel wells like an angry mold.

So many of the cars in San Pedro were in bad shape that Mari paid no mind to the car next to hers, although there were rarely cars in the lot at night. She pulled her small, patent leather purse to her front and undid the small gold clasp to reach for her key, but she never touched it. Something narrow and hard like stainless steel cable slipped around her neck and jerked like someone slamming a door. Immediately she couldn't breathe and was yanked off her feet and thrown into the trunk of the sedan.

She grasped at the unrelenting pain in her throat. Filled with terror, she tried to turn but a strip of duct tape covered her eyes and another covered her mouth. The cable was released, but she felt her hands being yanked to her back and handcuffs being snapped into place. Then her ankles were wrapped in the duct tape. She heard the lid of the trunk slam shut. Less than a minute passed in abject fear. Then the trunk opened again and she felt her purse hit her in the face. The trunk slammed again.

«« — »»

Chance pushed his bike into the garage and up on his lift. He hadn't had much time to check it over. He unlocked the house, poured himself a Jack on the rocks, and returned to the garage. Turning on his old dusty ghetto blaster, he walked around to his Snap-On toolbox, pulled out a handful of wrenches and began to tighten and wipe down various fasteners. He checked his brake master cylinder for fluids, then the transmission oil level. He checked the air pressure in the tires and his clutch cable adjustment. He was still dancing on air as he thought about the girl at the bakery.

The night slipped away, so he shut off the 8-foot fluorescent lights and headed to the house. It was nearing eleven o'clock as he crawled into bed, hoping for the early morning wake-up call and a full day on the job.

At three in the morning, he awoke with a start. He heard something and sat up. He listened carefully, then heard what he thought was his gate close. He threw his legs over the side of his bed and jumped to his feet.

He rounded the corner of the bed to reach the window looking out at the patio. As he gazed out he heard a car pull away and made his way down the hall to the front of the house. Staring out, all he could see were the taillights of a sedan speeding down Crescent Avenue toward Harbor Boulevard. He picked up the phone and dialed Kate's number.

"Officer Norton," Kate said as if she had been awake for an hour.

"Chance here," he said. "Someone was just in my back yard."

"Do you know a girl named Mari?" Kate asked.

"Met her today at a bakery," Chance said. "Spoke to her for 10 minutes."

"Don't move, don't touch anything. She's dead."

-21-

THE GUILTY BIKER

Before Chance could hang up the phone, Detective Callahan and a troop of uniformed cops stormed his house, kicked in the front door and turned over everything they touched. Callahan came directly at Chance, clad only in his boxer shorts, and threw a warrant at his feet.

"You're under arrest for murder, motherfucker," he shouted. "And we can search this joint until we find anything we want!"

A big, muscular black officer named Grey stormed in behind Detective Callahan, yanked his handcuffs from his belt, and said, "You know the drill."

"Can I put on a pair of shorts?" Chance asked.

Callahan erupted. "Fuck you, sonuvabitch," he screamed. "Cuff the cocksucker. He'll get prison blues at the station."

Chance turned his back to the black officer and presented his wrists for the cuffs. Officer Grey led him out to his black and white and shoved him into the back seat, just as another plain-clothes cruiser arrived in the dark with red light flashing. Neighbors peered through open windows and lights flickered on as cop cars surrounded the small stucco house and officers strung yellow crime scene tape around the premises.

Morning coolness lay over the harbor in a dank, foreboding mist. Chance thought about that evil blanket as he looked through the cruiser security screen and out the windshield toward the harbor. He saw one tug motoring out of the main channel to meet a freighter, when an image of Mari flashed into his consciousness. His sense of loss was profound and disturbing. She was a thing of beauty, grace, and intelligence. She was a unique, fragile doll who was destroyed for no conceivable reason. He began to grind his teeth in anger.

Kate jumped out of her car and ran to the black and white housing Chance. She eyed his bare, muscular torso and smirked.

"They got to you before you could dress?"

"I just hung up the phone," Chance said.

"Where was the prowler?" Kate asked. "I want to get to that area before they do."

"Check around the back of the house or in the basement," Chance said.

Kate headed to the back gate. The lock was cut. She called for the officer with a camera to take a shot of it and bagged the padlock for the lab. Chance's back yard was nothing to shout about. A portion at the side of the house was concrete with a 6-foot wooden fence that led to the separate garage facing 19th Street to the north. The cement extended past the small garage side door to the rear of the structure, where it ended. Five feet beyond was the only foliage in the back yard: a dry, hopelessly scrawny citrus tree on its last legs. Other than the starving tree, the ground was covered with hard-cracked clay and a handful of diehard weeds capable of growing in an oil spill.

Kate flashed her Maglite around the base of the house and inspected the vents. She looked for footprints, anything. Between Chance's house and the one next door was an eight-foot expanse of low weeds. She studied the area along the edge of the house carefully. The small picket fences between the two houses had rotted so badly that Chance tore it down and piled the remains in the corner of the lot.

Kate crept around the side of the building and through the back yard, then worked around to the north side of the house. Moving along the house from back to front, she came across the one and only window on that side of the house before the kitchen, and the basement door. The lock was gone and the door stood ajar. Without touching the knob, she pushed the door open, turned on the fluorescent lights, and descended the five wooden steps to the concrete floor. She studied the steps closely, and on the bottom rung she spotted a fresh drop of blood.

There was another dark, almost black drop still shining on the dusty concrete. If it had dried, it would have collected enough dust to diminish its glow. She summoned an officer to tape off the doorway and take photos and samples. The basement was plain, rectangular, and built from cinderblocks. Chance used more cinderblocks and unused doors to make shelves for storage. Across from the shelves against the north exterior wall sat his washer and dryer. To the east was one long shelf that housed tools like Skil saws for working on the house, but Chance had little time to use them.

The west wall was adjacent to the stairs and Kate flashed her light over the edge into the three-foot dirt pan between the structural underpinnings of the house. There were more drops of blood on the top of the basement wall. She bent carefully over the abutment and discovered bloody pieces of clothing. She called the police photographer, and asked him to set up several shots and collect the material.

Kate entered the house from the back door and discovered Callahan tearing drawers open and throwing them on the hardwood floor, scattering the contents. She went back outside.

"I want you to take shots of every room in the house," she said to the photographer.

She went back inside the house and studied the interior, the windows, the doors, and the ledges.

"I found a joint," Callahan said, "You find anything?"

"Bloody garments," Kate said, rapidly losing respect for the fat goon with seniority.

Callahan was a wild man, out of control, and had no business in investigations. The new philosophy in the police world was to place science well above attitude. They were discovering that the science of crime far outweighed emotional outbursts. In fact, the wrong attitude or behavior in handling a case can lose a conviction quicker than conflicting evidence. Science was cut and dry.

"Where?" Callahan spat.

"In the basement," Kate said.

Callahan charged past her down the hall toward the back door. He burst out the back and down the stairs. He was convinced that the biker was guilty and already running the persuasive crime scenario in his mind. He stepped on the blood drops and reached over the cinderblock wall and grabbed the clothing before the photographer could crawl under the house and set up a proper shot of the evidence, much less tag and bag it.

Callahan ran to the cruiser at the curb with this handful of torn and tattered clothes, a bra, and panties dripping with blood.

"You sonuvabitch," Callahan screamed. "How could you do this? Are you ready to confess?"

"No sir," Chance snapped at the detective, "But I'm ready to kill the sonuvabitch who killed her."

Officer Grey and another officer followed Callahan into the street and tried to pull him back from the cruiser.

"I knew that girl," Callahan shouted, "I've known her mom for 20 years!"

Kate also followed, opened her briefcase, and recorded the outburst. Neighbors were beginning to spill onto the street around Chance and the officers. A van pulled up. A reporter jumped out and began to take photos of Chance's house and the wild detective swinging his arms at the longhaired biker cuffed in the back seat of the car.

Chance instinctively kept his head high, but wasn't sure that was the right move. He was innocent; at least, he thought he was, and no tirade from a detective changed that. On the other hand, Chance didn't know if the rules to this poker game were in the book of Hoyle.

Kate told Grey to take the prisoner back to the station immediately, and then approached the detective.

"The press is here detective," Kate said calmly. "You need to straighten up your act."

"I don't need to do shit," Callahan spat. "Thatsonuvabitch did it and I want the world to know it!"

"That's what our judicial system is designed to do," Kate said.

"Fuck the judicial system," Callahan erupted. "He'll get off if it's up to some fat Jewish lawyer."

"You're burying yourself," Kate got in Callahan's face and hissed in harsh tones, "You'll be out of a job if a line like that is printed in the press. You're a fuckin' idiot."

Callahan's face reddened as he tried to pull away from the officers holding him. He jerked his arms from their hold, straightened his jacket, tucked in his dress shirt over his substantial beer gut, and yanked unsuccessfully at his waistband.

"Where's the body?" Kate asked.

"It's near the same spot as the other one by the Spanish fisheries near Annette's restaurant," Callahan said, and waddled toward his car.

Kate mentioned to one of the officers to stay at Chance's house. She took the cameraman and lab guy with her to the body, which was near where fish were unloaded from the fishing boats, cleaned, and loaded onto trucks for market. Several officers surrounded the area with yellow tape, while another held a cameraman from KTTV television at bay. Kate approached the area cautiously, having the photographer take continuous shots. The lab man collected samples of everything in reach. Kate approached the television reporter who was arguing with the uniformed officer.

"Can I help you?" Kate asked the reporter professionally.

"I'd like access to this crime area. The people demand to know what's happening here."

The reporter was Chinese but reasonably tall and extremely good-looking.

"I can't let you have access right now," Kate said as softly as possible, "but I will give you a report in a half hour, after we've processed the scene and the coroner has removed the body. I will try to get a live shot of the girl for you to use on your program. Please bear with us. If we disturb any element of the scene, it could mean that we destroy critical evidence. You know that."

The reporter, Henry Cheung, backed away, "So I can interview you here in a half hour?" he asked pressing for a commitment.

"Yes, of course," Kate confirmed, "Unless something to do with the case demands my immediate action."

It was a terrible situation for investigation. There was death and the smell of fish everywhere. The body had been tossed in a dumpster behind the fisheries. Kate donned a plastic protective body suit and gloves. The girl's wrists were cut. She had deep ligature marks around her throat. Kate asked the photographer to take as many shots as possible and the lab guy to collect samples of even the water under the dumpster. Fish blood, fish guts, and scales mixed with human blood.

As she returned to her cruiser and removed the hazardous waste garment, Henry Chueng approached her.

"Can I interview you now?" he asked respectfuly.

"Yes," Kate said.

But she was worried that Chance was back at the station being punched around, and he wasn't the killer.

"Is there a serial killer loose in San Pedro?" Henry asked, sticking his KTTV embossed mike in her face.

"Yes," Kate said, "I believe there is."

"What can you tell me about the murders?" Henry asked.

"I can tell you that they are angry, hostile murders of young women and that's about all we know," she said, still mulling the sketchy evidence in her own mind.

"We see that you have a suspect," Henry said, showing her a Polaroid shot of Chance in the back of the cruiser. "Is he your man?"

"I wish I could say yes and put an end to these horrible cases," Kate said, "but in all honestly, I don't believe so. This is a man who recently went out with or met these girls, but we're checking all the angles."

"The people of San Pedro and Los Angeles will be very concerned about these attacks," Henry said, pressing Kate. "What can we tell them?"

"For the time being," Kate muttered and briefly looked at her soiled shoes, "I would warn women to be much more cautious about their whereabouts when it's dark. Stay close to friends or have someone walk you to your car after work or in shopping areas."

Henry began to step forward and she suspected that the next question would delve into the efficiency of the department or some past failure or blunder.

"That's all I have time for Henry," Kate said holding a card out for Henry to take. "Call me if you have any questions and if you would give me your card, I will call you if there are new developments."

Henry walked away, but a small hawk-nosed producer approached and handed her one of Henry's cards.

"Thank you," he said, "for your openness. We appreciate it. We'll air our first segment this afternoon. I hope you can find the guy quickly, before anyone else is harmed."

Kate took the card and nodded. "Me too," she said and walked to her car.

Her blonde hair was ruffled from the Haz-Mat outfit, but she still looked sharp in her tan suit and thin cashmere sweater. Her car radio was bleeping as she approached.

"710/base come in," it squawked rudely.

"710 here," Kate said into the mic.

"This is Lieutenant Reed," he said, "I heard you were talking to Henry Cheung."

"That's correct," Kate said.

"We have PR people trained for that purpose, detective," he snapped.

"Then that staff member should have been here at the crime scene to deal with the press so I could work, sir," Kate said. "I believe I handled it correctly. You'll have to be the judge of that. On the other hand, I wouldn't hold my breath for a glowing report in the news. Callahan is the one you need to be scolding. Have they questioned the suspect?"

"They're about to," Officer Reed said, "You better get your ass back here."

Kate quickly wiped her shoes down and climbed into her cruiser. Rolling quickly back to the station, the smell of dead fish filled her car, and she ran her fan on high with all the windows open on the cool coastal morning.

Chance was shackled in the interrogation room, awaiting questioning. A tape recorder was placed on the oak table. He was dressed in prison overalls, his hair was a mess, and he hadn't brushed his teeth, but mostly he was nail-biting mad.

Officer Grey was already in the room monitoring the prisoner as Callahan entered with Kate. Kate sat down and Callahan pressed the two buttons on the recorder to start the process.

"Are you ready to confess?" Callahan said and tossed a shot of Chance kissing the girl in front of Ramona's on the conference table. "Don't deny that you know her."

"Knowing her and killing her are at opposite ends of the spectrum," Chance said and looked at Kate. "Have you found anything?"

"You're here to answer questions, Mr. Biker," Callahan interrupted. "We ask the questions."

Chance ignored Callahan. He gazed at the wall covered with a sound proofing material, at the one-way mirror on the wall, and at the barred door at one end of the room. He knew he was in deep shit, but it wasn't his doing. He was hoping for the first time in a long time he could live in an area and enjoy himself without a lot of bullshit, but not now. He was again in the midst of something ugly, but it was different. Innocent girls were being murdered and he wanted it to end immediately.

"Ask me anything?" Chance said. "Anything that might assist in putting an end to this bullshit."

He coolly looked Callahan in the eyes. "Detective, if I thought you could end this shit by putting a bullet in me, I would tell you to go for it, but I'm afraid that won't do the trick. I met the girl once at Ramona's. We discussed dating and I told her that I couldn't see her because of that last mess. Now this."

Then he looked at Kate. "I would suggest at the risk of losing my job that you keep me here for a week while you investigate."

Chance sensed where he was and knew that the tape recorder was running. He wanted to talk to Kate alone, but knew if he told her what he suspected, she would also be in danger. He was stuck between the proverbial rock and a hard place.

"I will contact your work," Kate said.

"I'm not convinced he's not the one," Callahan snarled. "Do you want an attorney?"

"No," Chance said, "there's no need. Do your checking and book me. I can't afford to get out of bed, much less bail myself out for murder."

Kate got up and left the room. Callahan asked a bunch of useless questions then left, and Grey took Chance to the back of the building where a dozen cells were arranged along a wall for temporary housing.

The Harbor Division didn't have a full service jail, just the holding cells and one large holding tank for drunks. Everywhere Grey took him, Chance noticed that Officer Fernandez was watching. Chance mulled over the hands that could be played in this game. He figured one of the options was that Fernandez would kill him in his cell. His death might end the murders for awhile.

-22-

TROUBLE IN PARADISE

Chance woke up in a Harbor Division cell a week later to the racket from a baton beating on the rungs of the door. There wasn't a more irritating, harsher noise on earth as Chance woke up from a fitful slumber.

Officer Fernandez stood at the door, beads of sweat dripped off his oily brow. It was warm in the cellblock, but not that warm. Fernandez had unsuccessfully stuffed his 50-year-old frame into a navy blue Los Angeles Police uniform that was better suited to a cop half his age. He peered at Chance through the bars.

"What is it?" Chance said.

"A cell will be your home someday soon," Joe Fernandez said threateningly.

"Not if I can help it," Chance said. "Did you enjoy killing Mari?"

He watched the man's grip on his polished lacquer baton tighten.

"You have no business breathing in my city…"

Fernandez's voice was cut short as the door to the cellblock opened and Detective Callahan lumbered down the hall, tugging at his pants. His face was beet-red and he seemed to be steaming.

"Let him out," Callahan barked.

"Yes sir," Officer Fernandez said, and inserted the key.

The door slid open on an iron track and Chance cautiously stood up, eyeing the men suspiciously as he stretched and gathered the few personal effects they allowed him.

He huddled for a week waiting for a vigilante cop, or even Fernandez, to off him while he sat in the cell. He was the prime suspect in both murders, with only Detective Kate Norton as an ally. Each murder was horrifying. Many of the officers on the force who witnessed the gruesome photographs or experienced the crime scene first-hand assumed Chance was the guy.

The case was a blight on the department. They had evidence against the jailed suspect, but not enough. Chance's face was spread across every newspaper in Southern California. He considered leaving the country, but he was determined to crawl to the bottom of this treacherous cesspool and clear his lousy fuckin' name.

Without a word, he left the cell and walked through the booking area. Fernandez purposely led him through the squad room, as if to remind each detective of his or her lack of evidence to hold the pre-judged biker. Chance held his head high, but he knew if he appeared cocky, someone would cap him. He rolled the dice every time he made eye contact with an armed officer.

Kate jumped to her feet and grabbed his arm, and without a saying a word, led him to the checkout area at the back of the building.

Approaching the counter, she said to the officer behind the counter directly, "Let me have Chance Hogan's things"

"Why?" asked the obese female officer behind the desk. "He'll be back in a week for good."

"If you can make a case, do it," Kate said. "We all want this to end."

She signed the form, took a 9 x 12 manila envelope off the counter, and led Chance out the back door to her car. She unshackled him, opened the passenger door and let him in, then walked somberly around the car to the driver's side and got in. A mist of fog hung over the harbor and the smell of salt air filled the air.

"I don't know what to say," Kate muttered visibly upset, "You should have been out of there the day after you were booked. I know you wanted it that way, but nothing has happened and we don't have any more evidence."

"It's bullshit, but I wasn't capped by an over-zealous cop, either," Chance said. "I'm still alive."

He lifted his hands to his mouth and drew his fingers across his lips to indicate for her to be silent. She drove out of the lot slowly. Officers at their patrol cars and in the windows stood and glared at what they considered a scooter bum, guilty of several heinous crimes, allowed to run free.

"Where do you want to go?" Kate said.

"Let's get a cup of coffee," Chance said then noticed another cruiser pulling out of the lot behind them and following.

"Maybe not. Just take me home and wander through the house with me."

"Sure," Kate said and turned onto Pacific and passed 1st street, then 2nd and continued down the worn pre-WWII street packed with old buildings. Restaurants were constructed next to mechanic's garages, tattoo parlors, Hispanic video stores, and burrito joints.

She turned left on 19th and continued down to the corner, where she pulled to the right and stopped. Locals had thrown beer cans, trash, tomatoes, and crap against the side of the house and fence that lead from his home to the garage. There was graffiti on the fence that said, "Murderer lives here."

"Welcome home," Chance said mostly to himself.

The police tape was torn, but it was still wrapped around the house haphazardly. It was early and there weren't many people on the street. The fog hung over the harbor below and loomed around the bluff like a gray death cloud. The kitchen window was broken where someone tossed a rock through it.

"The house is bugged," Kate said.

"I figured," Chance said crawling out of her sedan and stepping into the growing weeds.

Kate swung her shapely legs out the driver's side and walked around the car to the curb. Together, they walked onto the lawn and Chance looked up at his smashed front door. A rough slab of plywood was screwed over the opening with drywall fasteners. He could see a little of the interior and it wasn't pretty. His house was torn to shambles. Out the corner of his eye, he saw a black and white pull up to the curb behind Kate's sedan. Chance turned his back on the house and walked to the edge of his weed-covered lawn facing Crescent Avenue and the harbor.

"You shouldn't be here. You need to stay far away from me." Chance said thinking about Officer Fernandez and the black and white.

"Look," she said turning to face him, "this is my first investigator's position. I'm fresh out of school, but I was never trained to bury innocent people. You're in a tough spot, but I'm your friend above all else."

Her pretty pale blue eyes filled with tears. She briefly touched his arm, wanting to hold him, and then turned to face the harbor.

"I appreciate that, but someone is going to off me if they continue to think I'm the guilty sonuvabitch," Chance said. "We need a way to communicate without being scrutinized. Now act like you're pissed at me and leave. We're being watched."

"I'll look into the communication part of the deal," she said, and then raised her voice. "Don't even think about leaving town. We'll have someone on your ass daily. Have I made myself clear?"

She poked an index finger at his chest fervently.

"I may need to disappear for awhile," Chance said, and then raised his voice in return.

"Now get the hell off my property. I'm innocent and you know it."

He turned and walked up to the destroyed front door as Kate stormed to her sedan and drove away. Chance turned on the short concrete step and looked out at the harbor briefly. It looked calm and serene, but his life was anything but tranquil.

He was forced to enter the house from the back door. The door jam was split and the door popped openly easily. Everything was out of cupboards and on the floor. He didn't have much, but they had made a mess out of what he did keep.

He strolled through the house, thinking and picking up as he went, until he reached the bedroom and found the bed in shambles, the mattress ripped and torn. He couldn't even sleep in his own fucking bed. Anger brewed in him, but mostly he was consumed with fear and uncertainty.

He remembered the first time he was arrested as a kid. It was a misunderstanding, but he went to jail anyway. He was just a biker in the wrong place at the right time. The girl he packed belonged to another rider. A California Highway Patrolman pulled him over for speeding. His buddy pulled up a minute later. Without a word, the young babe slipped into his car and they sped away. The cop, a paranoid type, surmised that she was carrying drugs or was underage, but since they couldn't find her to confirm anything, they booked Chance for reckless driving. He spent the night in the county lockup.

The more he looked around the house, the more depressed he became. He ran to the garage and opened the unlocked door. The lock had been clipped and was lying on the concrete at his feet. His heart jumped to his throat as he pushed the metal door open. There stood his motorcycle, unharmed and Chance's knees buckled.

That Harley meant everything to him. It was all that he had for transportation or to escape the blight that hung about him. He treasured its sleek lines. For some odd reason, that Harley was his sanctuary, his sword, his protection. No relationship lasted the length of time his companionship with a single motorcycle did. He placed his hand on the smooth tank and then returned to the house.

Each ransacked room reminded him of every shattered relationship he had with a woman - the good, the bad, and the ugly. A broken Mexican plate on the kitchen floor reminded him or Rosa, and he wondered if he still had her number. He hadn't called her back since the last time she rang. His ripped and shredded bed reminded him of the wild sex he had with Sheila. When they parted, his heart was torn like the covers on his bed. He grabbed the phone and called Harbor Taxi. The usually bubbly Julie answered the phone.

"Harbor Taxi," she said in a flat voice.

"Come in, over," Chance said.

"Chance?" Julie said, her voice brightening. "Are you a serial killer like they all say?"

"Nope," Chance said, "but promise me one thing."

"What's that?" Julie asked tentatively.

"Don't ever go out with me or even to lunch," Chance said, "not before we get this straightened out."

"So marriage is out of the question?"

"I'm afraid so," Chance said. "Is Carl in?" Chance said.

"Sure, but he's in a bad mood," Julie said. "We need you and he's had to work too hard."

"Okay," Chance said, "Put him on. I don't think I can come back to work just yet, but let me talk to him."

"Chance," Carl said in a strained voice, "What the hell is going on with you?"

"How about I bring a couple of burritos down and we have lunch?" Chance said, "I'll try to explain."

"I can't do it, buddy," Carl said, wiping his bald head, "I don't have the time to breathe. Bring them down to the office. We'll talk on the run."

"You got it, I'll see you at noon," Chance said and hung up.

He moved around the house in a daze, trying to straighten up. He wasn't sure what the hell to do next or how to do it. He didn't want to make a move that would be the harbinger to his demise, but he was uncertain as to what the next step would be.

Chance showered and dressed in his cowboy boots, denims, a sweatshirt, and his vest. He rode down over to Mando's for quick burritos. He was followed, but knew that would be the drill, until he could surreptitiously shake his tail.

He rode down 22nd street along the Cabrillo Marina and turned right on Signal Street to the end of the peninsula and the Harbor Taxi Service. Julie saw him pull up, jumped up from her desk, and ran out of the prefab mobile home office used temporarily at large developments. He jumped off the bike as she burst into his arms.

"You shouldn't even act like you might like me," Chance said.

"I don't care," Julie said holding him, "It's good to see you."

"I've never had the pleasure of this embrace," Chance said kissing her on the cheek and pushing her away. "This must be my lucky day. I'm outta jail and the best looking chick-a-dee in San Pedro kissed me. Life can't be all that bad."

Chance followed her plump ass back into the harbor shack with the burritos in a plastic bag. He had to admit to himself that he would certainly like to have a night with her.

Carl came out of his glassed office and greeted Chance. "How you doing?" he said.

"Not exactly a banner week at the roulette tables, but I'm still here to talk about it," Chance said, smiling at Julie who returned to her desk.

"Let's go outside," Carl said, as he led the way out the side door and down the steps to the dock. The boats were dirty and bouncing irreverently against the dock.

"I can't keep them up," he sad, gesturing at the boats. "Can you come back to work?"

They leaned up against a couple of dented and rusting 50-gallon drums and broke open the burritos.

"Maybe I can," Chance said. "I just had a thought. How about I come at night and service the boats whenever I can. Listen, I've got to get to the bottom of these murders or die trying. The cops or someone will kill me if I don't and my love life is shot until I do, but it's going to be touchy. One day, I'll be here and the next I won't."

"Anything will help," Carl said chewing on the burrito, but his eyes bounced around the dock hurriedly, as if he should toss the burrito and get back to the chores at hand.

"I may need a place to hide," Chance said. "Do you have any access to these warehouses?"

"Yeah," Carl said perking up. "These buildings were controlled by the mafia for the longest time. Now, they don't do much, but they still own them. I'll make a call."

"My house is a mess," Chance said, "It leaves me wide open for target practice."

"Can you work today?" Carl asked.

"I'll be right back," Chance said and jogged back to his chopper, straddled the seat, rode back to his house two miles away and grabbed a couple of changes of clothes. He shoved them into his Bandit's Bedroll, strapped it to his handlebars, and bungeed his work shoes on top. He jammed back to the dock and went to work cleaning and servicing the boats.

As he moved around the building to the tool shed, he kept an eye on the long corridor of warehouses that led up to 22nd street, where Annette's Restaurant was located around the corner. He thought of Suzanne and grimaced as he pulled out the pump for changing oil on the boats. He kept an eye on the black and white at the end of the block and thought about how he could shake the surveillance. When one cruiser left the end of the street, another replaced it.

"They're not taking a break on you, are they," Julie said in her usual perky fashion from the office window.

"Nope," Chance said, "If you notice that they're out of sight, holler. I need to stash my bike so they think I'm gone."

"Will do, baby," Julie said, and went back to her computer bookkeeping work.

By the end if the day, Chance serviced two of the boats. They were ready to rock as Carl steered another craft along side the docks and tossed Chance a line. He tied up the boat as Carl lumbered up the ramp to the dock. He was worn and haggard looking. He wore a ballcap that covered his monkish hair. His eyebrows seemed to sag over his coffee brown eyes, pushing his eyelids down. He was as tired as an old hound after a fox hunt.

"Chance," he said breathlessly, "you've got to find the sonuvabitch who is killing these girls. I'd make you a partner if you were free. On the other hand, I may have to fire you if they keep pointing the finger at you. My customers are talking."

Chance nodded and looked out to sea. The afternoon wind whistled through the harbor and kicked up whitecaps as the sun set. The sky was rich with crimson streaks and the salt air was cool.

He turned to Carl and said, "Thank you." I'll do all I can. I'm playing at a poker game I'm not familiar with."

"I don't know what to tell you," Carl said and patted Chance on the shoulder before struggling up the stairs to the office.

"I asked Julie to cut you a key, and the family who owns this old warehouse on the right says it's open all the time. You can duck in there whenever you want. Just don't let us down."

Chance could tell by the way he said each word that he wanted to help, but doubted the outcome. Julie bounded out of the pre-fab and kissed Chance on the cheek and handed him the key to the office.

"He's glad you're back," she said smiling a broad clean smile with fresh lipstick. "We need you around here."

She held onto his arm for a long moment, but could see that Chance was riddled with concern.

"You'll figure it out," she finally said, and jogged to her little VW and waved as she drove away.

Chance went down the ramp to the dock, locked all the skiffs in place, and secured the lines and bumpers between them. Mesmerized with grizzly thoughts, he turned and looked down the darkening lane at the police cruiser. They were still watching him.

He turned back to the cherry and gold sunset and wondered what to do next. His guts tugged at him to leave San Pedro forever. He was a biker first and all he needed was his scooter and an open road.

Something more nagged at him as he watched the golden orb of the sun fall into the mighty Pacific and the harbor changed colors once again. Chance didn't like cops. He never had. He rode on the wrong side of the law most of his life, and he gambled with one relationship after another. He may have been a tramp who walked away from one too many relationships, but he never beat a woman, plus he suspected the cop. On the other glove was Kate, and he was terrified that she would be next, or if he confided in her he would jeopardize her life. He paced the dock. He wanted to talk to Kate in the worst way.

Chance gave up trying to stash his motorcycle in the warehouse, locked up the office, and rode his scooter up Signal Street to 22nd and over the hill to the pad. It was still in shambles. He was still confused as he showered and started to make a pot of Top Ramen with a handful of vegetables and a chicken breast. He poured himself a Jack on the rocks and took a slug when the phone rang.

"Chance?" It was Kate.

"Yep?"

"How are you?"

"I'm okay," Chance said, "They gave me my job back."

"Good," Kate said, "We're still unable to pin anything down except you. Keep your nose clean."

"It's cleaner than it's ever been," Chance said, knowing his phone was tapped. Kate knew it too.

"Don't leave town," Kate said and Chance seized the opportunity.

"I won't," he said, "The farthest I'm going this weekend is the Lobster Festival at Port O' Call, Friday night."

"That's all right, just don't leave town," she said, and hung up.

Somebody drove past the house and threw a beer bottle that shattered against the hard exterior stucco. They screamed obscenities in Spanish and peeled down the street. Chance looked around the house and began to button up the old windows and secure the broken ones. He called the agent who found the pad and told him to put his sign out front that the place was for rent.

Chance ate the noodles from the saucepan while packing up much of the house. He rearranged the garage. Then he started making trips from the house to the garage and to the basement. Before the night was over, he had moved into the garage, where he set up an old armchair and a space heater to keep him warm. In the house, he was an easy target with all the windows. Hell, he was a biker and didn't have the coin to buy frilly curtains.

He worked until 2:00 in the morning moving the last of his crap into the garage. It wasn't a lot, and since the warm summer was coming, he could hold out in the garage and still protect the only thing that meant a hill of beans to him in the world, his chopper.

He crashed in the chair and slept for four hours before the phone began to ring. Chance stumbled out of the lounge chair and fell over a box trying to get to the wall phone.

"Good morning criminal," Julie said, her voice as bubbly as a teenager on her birthday. "Time to get up and come to work. We need you."

"Damn," Chance said trying to wake up. "Your voice would drive any man wild."

"This is your wake-up call," Julie said. "Are you comin' in?"

"I wouldn't miss seeing you for the world," Chance said.

"I like that," She said, "see you soon."

Chance stretched and got moving. He snuck back in the house with a handful of work clothes, showered, and dressed. He rolled his bike out of the backyard and took off for the dock. It felt good to get up and go to work almost like a normal Joe. He picked up a quick breakfast burrito and a Diet Coke and hauled ass to the port.

It was Thursday and the following evening, he was hoping to see Kate at the Lobster Festival in the harbor. He knew that for every minute that he rolled around town, the real murderer was out there planning another victim, and he needed to be as on-the-ball as much as possible. He tried to keep his mind on the job, but his nerves were on edge as he moved around the dock, changing oil in the boats and making runs to the offshore oilrigs.

"Hey handsome," Julie said out her side window, "You're in trouble again. You've got a call and they don't sound happy."

Chance jogged up the steps to the office and picked up the receiver. "Yeah?"

"This Chance Hogan?" the voice snapped.

"Yep, what's up?" Chance said.

"What do you mean what's up?" the woman on the other end of the phone began to shout in his ear. "We represent the house you live in. It belongs to our clients and you've destroyed it."

"It's not destroyed," Chance said, "I just needs…"

"You're full of shit," the woman continued to scream. "You'll pay for the repairs!"

"How about if I buy that joint?" Change said, "The fuckin' place was a mess when I moved in."

"It's not for sale," she spat back. "Besides you'll probably be in jail. Just fix the place fast!"

The phone went dead with a snap. Chance looked at it. Never a dull moment, he thought.

"You're right," he said to Julie, "I'm in trouble again. I keep rolling bad dice."

"It's not all bad," Julie said reaching across the counter and touching Chance's hand. "You're here with me."

Her blue eyes sparkled. She reminded Chance of the good witch from the Wizard of Oz. He tingled in her cape of goodness, which engulfed him, plus that milky cleavage that could melt stone…

"You sure make a bad day worth celebrating," Chance said. "Thank you."

He bowed and went back out to the dock.

«« — »»

By Friday at noon, Chance helped Carl pull the business back together. The boats were serviced and cleaned. His small dock was scoured and Carl invited Chance to Annette's for lunch. They both had tuna melts, french fries, and Diet Cokes.

The cops were still watching Chance, the real estate agency was still harassing him to fix the house, and he was still living in the garage. Another car passed the house the night before and another rock was thrown through the front bay window.

He couldn't take on the entire neighborhood, and the more shit that poured into the newspapers, the more the public hated Chance. He remained the only suspect, thanks to some overzealous cops and a gullible press.

"What do you think is going to happen with this case?" Carl asked over lunch. Two officers, including Joe Fernandez sat at a table across from them in the small seaside café.

"I hope they catch the slimy sonuvabitch who is doing this," Chance said loud enough to be overheard.

"They better make it quick," Carl said.

Chance couldn't say a word of what he suspected, but he was losing patience with his inability to move on something he felt strongly about.

After work, he said good night to Julie, and she tugged at him like dessert to someone on a strict diet. He rode home quickly and showered as the sun set over the harbor. He put on running sweats and shoes and took off down the path along the Marina, then cut over railroad tracks toward the little rundown fishing village of Ports O' Call and across the crowded parking lot to ensure that he wasn't followed. His hair was pulled back in a ponytail and he pulled his hood over his head as he passed a van idling toward the entrance. He paid at the makeshift gate manned with several volunteers sitting at two long portable tables. He kept his face hidden as he entered the fenced-in area that was dedicated to the Lobster festival.

In a carnival-like atmosphere, there were bright lights and booths set up in rows, with a stage at the far end. The festival was designed to draw more traffic to the shops in the village, since business had been down for quite some time. The parking lot was jammed and families and young couples paid $15 to enter. Cops watched the gates.

Chance wandered up and down the rows of business booths, art displays, crafts, and food vendors, looking for Kate. With his 15-buck ticket, he also received a lobster dinner. He wandered from stand to cubicle, checking the antiques, art, and ceramic lighthouses.

Near eight o'clock, a mist formed on the asphalt, and incoming fog filtered over the buildings on the main channel into the parking lot. Chance's stomach was beginning to growl. He did his best to stay out of the limelight, yet knew Kate would be able to find him if she arrived.

He kept himself busy for another 45 minutes, and then turned in his ticket for a shellfish feast. He took his paper plate stacked high with lobster, coleslaw and corn on the cob into the overhang set up for dining and moved to the back, where he dug into the food, washing it down with a beer. From his vantage point, he could see everyone who came to the end of the isles or toward the bandstand. He was certain that she would show, but she didn't. Finally, at 9:45, he walked out of the area and started to jog toward his house.

As he ran along the broad Harbor Boulevard toward 22nd street, he could see his little rental on the bluff. There was something wrong. Cops surrounded the joint with their lights flashing. As he looked down Harbor, he saw an ambulance emerging from Signal Street and it rolled past him toward the city, the siren wailing and putting a dismal tint on an evening clouded with fog. He started to run the other direction then stopped dead in his tracks.

The cops answered one question. He knew where Kate was. It also told him that another girl might be dead. The ambulance came from the direction of Annette's and the docks—Julie. His knees quaked and he stumbled. A lump formed in this throat. He couldn't run to the warehouse next to the taxi service. He couldn't run home. He had no alibi.

He wanted to run back to his house, but if Fernandez was behind the killings, he would gun for Chance. Chance kept running toward town.

-23-

Running for Julie

Chance ran faster and faster as the adrenaline pumped through his veins and fear for Julie's life intensified. She was a dream, and voluptuous with a personality as light as a feather. Her hair was that of a blond queen's with eyes from the goddess of the sea, who made life comfortable for all who knew her. Carl would be destroyed, Chance's job on the docks gone. It would never be the same without her there.

Chance cut up a residential street and saw a cop car cruising along Mesa Street. He cut to the right toward downtown, where the homeless roamed the streets constantly. He passed Beacon Street, the whorehouse district from the '40s, which once housed speakeasies and gambling parlors.

The old tenement buildings were now halfway houses and rehab shelters for drug addicts and alcoholics. Prime property relinquished to the down and out. When not housed, the derelicts roamed the area, panhandling passers-by for their next drink or fix.

Chance sliced up one street after another until he reached the edge of downtown and a phone booth. He dumped in a quarter and dialed Mark's number.

"Yeah?" Mark answered abruptly. He was the only other person Chance knew who answered his phone in the same manner as he did.

"What are you doing?" Chance said.

"Working on Vince's fuckin' screenplay," Mark said, "It's going to be made into a movie, his legacy. Why?"

"I need you to pick me up and put me up for the night," Chance said.

"I take it you're in trouble again with a woman," Mark said.

"So to speak," Chance said, "but it's not a relationship deal. Goddamnit, I'm not going to explain. You comin' to get me or not?"

"Yeah, yeah," Mark said, "But first, you better tell me where the fuck you are."

"Just pull up in front of the post office in San Pedro," Chance said, "and bring a cell phone."

"I'll be there in a half-hour," Mark said and hung up.

Chance ducked into a parking lot behind an abandoned Wells Fargo bank on 7th Street and hid between a couple of parked cars that were always in the same spots when he arrived to use the ATM. In front of one car was an angle-iron made trailer with old faded and warped plywood sides about two feet high. It was packed with junk and chained to one of the posts. It had been parked in that very spot since he first moved to San Pedro.

Chance huddled between the rusting truck and an old station wagon, minus its hubcaps, and looked at his watch. There were no overhead lights in the parking lot and it was dark except for the glow from the streetlights on 7th filtering between the buildings to the alley, and the parking lot behind.

Chance waited 20 minutes in the shadows before starting to move through the cars and across Broadway into a park beside a dark church. Another black and white cruised passed and flashed a brilliant halogen spotlight down each sidewalk and between the houses. Chance hid behind one dark car after another as he made his way over five blocks to the 1930s-era post office. It was a magnificent dark ornate granite building facing the main channel of the harbor. He jogged down 9th to Beacon, checked around the corner of the hard concrete building, and bolted across the street into the dim park overlooking the harbor facing the post office. It was grass-covered except for scattered palm trees.

Crouching down, Chance moved from tree to tree. Unfortunately, homeless perched under most of the trees. Some kept shopping cart households full of plastic bags; others out of bedrolls or just a stained sea bag full of crap. He found an uninhabited short palm with wild unruly fronds that formed a shingled roof in all directions. He crouched low. Fortunately, the edge of the park overlooking the main channel was on a bluff 40 feet above Harbor Boulevard. He saw Mark's black Bronco pull up in front of the Post Office and shut off his lights. Chance watched the street as another black and white passed. He darted across the street and crawled in the passenger side door.

"Get in the back seat," Mark said, "you're wanted all over the city."

Chance jumped in the back and scrunched down low. Mark checked the street, fired up the raised, all-black SUV, and rolled around the block and back to Harbor Boulevard, where he swung left toward the freeway.

"Who is Julie MacGreagor?" Mark said.

"Julie!" Chance exclaimed.

"Yeah," Mark said. "They found her in a warehouse right near your work, and apparently, you were given access to the building as a place to hide."

"Julie didn't deserve this," Chance said ignoring the accusations.

"What the hell are you going to do now?" Mark asked.

"Fuck, I don't know," Chance said. "Open a new deck, deal a new hand, and try something new. Did you bring your cell phone?"

"Yeah, here," Mark said, handing him the Nokia.

Chance pulled Kate's card out of the pocket to his sweats. It was soggy with sweat and smelled some. Mark turned on his overhead light as he turned onto the freeway onramp.

"Detective Norton," Kate said, and Chance knew that she was surrounded.

"I waited at the Lobster Festival," Chance said.

"It's been a tough evening," Kate said, "Can I call you back in a half hour?"

"Of course," Chance said, "did you get this number?"

"Yes, thank you," Kate said and shut her phone down.

"She's going to call you back?" Mark said.

"Yeah," Chance said.

"Don't pull me into this mess," Mark said and looked at him over his shoulder. "Jesus, they want to tag you for three murders."

"I won't need you for much," Chance said, "It's only my fuckin' life they want. I think I might know who is behind it. It's a cop."

"Oh, that's bitchin'!" Mark said. "The community wants to hang you, and you want to tag a cop with this shit. How about I take you to the Santa Monica Pier and you walk off the end and try to swim to Catalina?"

"Listen asshole," Chance barked from the back, "This sonuvabitch is killing innocent women. I've got to find out who for certain and stop him, because the cops damn sure won't."

"Yeah," Mark started as he swung off the Harbor freeway onto the San Diego Freeway heading north. "You just wanted to find the people who put the hit on your partner, too. That was cool, but this is a rat trap and you're in the center."

The night was clear and the fog rarely crept this far inland. It was a Friday evening on a Los Angeles freeway streaming with thousands of cars rolling in both directions. The freeways were just as crowed at 11:00 p.m. as they were during rush hour. Chance couldn't figure out where the hell everyone was going.

They were a couple of miles from the Santa Monica Freeway when Mark's cell phone rang.

"Kate?"

"You won't believe it," Kate started. "I know you didn't do it, but they want you anyway. I'm sorry I couldn't meet you, but I got the call on Julie."

"I'll bet it was a fax without a return address," Chance guessed.

"You're right," Kate said amazed. "Did you know Mari wasn't raped?"

"I'm going to tell you something," Chance said, thinking about what she said. "Are you alone?"

"I'm in my car," Kate said.

"Get out of your car," Chance said, "And get a new car. Make up some excuse."

"Just tell me," Kate said.

"I think it's a cop," Chance said, "and you could be in terrible danger. You would be the next one he'd hit."

"Well," Kate said, "It's been nice talking to you. I'll give you a call tomorrow." She hung up.

Chance didn't know what to make of her conclusion as he clicked off the cell phone and handed it back to Mark.

"Keep it," Mark said as he rolled off the freeway and drove down the busy Santa Monica Boulevard. "Give it back to me when you get this worked out."

"It better be soon," Chance said, "or they'll be buryin' my ass with your cell phone."

"Nope, that won't do," Mark said. "I want you to return it."

The phone rang again. "Yeah?" Chance said.

"It's me," Kate answered. "I'm in a public place."

"Where's Fernandez?" Chance asked.

"He's back at your place."

"Are you sure?"

"I think so." Can I come to you?"

"That might be best; just don't let anyone follow you. I'm in Santa Monica, 1534 Princeton. Take Santa Monica Blvd South from the 405 Freeway and left at Princeton. Just a block on the right."

"On my way."

Chance decided to check his messages at home. He had four. The first one was a crank call threatening his life. Then a call from Carl.

"You're fired. She was the best thing that ever happened to me. I don't give a fuck if you're innocent, don't come around here."

The next call was a heavy breather and Chance listened carefully, trying to make out any sounds in the background. He saved that message to listen to later. The final message startled him.

"Chance, you didn't return my call. This is Rosa, I see you're in another fix. The insurance company is building me a new gas station and they want me gone for a while. I'm coming to LA. My number is (602) 404-1554. Call me."

Chance grabbed a pen out of Mark's counsel and wrote the number down. He called her immediately.

"Hello," Rosa said, and Chance instantaneously recognized her buttery warmth.

"Rosa, it's Chance," Chance said. "I'm sorry I didn't call."

"Don't apologize, Chance," Rosa said, "I saw the reports in the newspaper. You're in trouble again. I'm coming to LA tomorrow."

"You can't," Chance said abruptly. "I can't even say hello to a girl on the street. She'll get murdered."

"You need help," Rosa said, "And Chorizo and eggs for breakfast. Think about it. I'll leave in the morning and call you from the road."

"It's too dangerous, Rosa," he said, but she had already hung up.

"Another girl?" Mark said over his shoulder.

He spun a left across two lanes of fast-moving traffic onto Princeton and pulled into the parking space in front of a garage next door that he rented. They both jumped out and rounded trimmed bushes for the redwood gate to Mark's condo. He plugged in his code and they jogged inside. Mark's condo was the third one down the narrow walkway.

"Since you've got that cop coming over, we'd better straighten up the guest bedroom. You need a shower, too." Mark said. I'll get you some shorts and a t-shirt."

Chance followed Mark up the stairs past the ski equipment, diving equipment, and weapons scattered on the stairway and hall. If

cops raided the joint, they'd assume that it was the underground headquarters for a subversive militia group. The spare bedroom was the
same but worse. Gear was stacked everywhere. They scrambled to
shove some of the stuff in the closet and clear the bed.

"It's not like she's staying," Chance said.

"Yeah, sure," Mark spat at him. "She's driving all the way to
Santa Monica to have a beer with a couple of guys and go home.
Right. What the hell are you going to do with this other broad?"

"I don't have the slightest," Chance said. "Hell, I don't know
what I'm going to do with myself. I want to go on the offensive, but
how the hell can I do that with cops around me like flies on shit? The
bastard can shoot me anywhere at anytime, and if I get caught stalking
the sonuvabitch, I'm done. They have all the resources and I have a
loud motorcycle."

"That's one thing she'll have," Mark said mockingly.

"A car?" Chance said.

"Maybe she can get a place in Long Beach," Mark mumbled.
"Then you'll have a couple of places to hide out."

"Now, you're thinking," Chance said.

Mark's mercenary background was coming into play.

Chance hit the shower and shaved his beard, leaving the bushy
mustache. He slipped on the black jogging shorts and t-shirt Mark
gave him. His long, thick hair was still wet as he jumped down the
stairs and went out to the gate as Kate came down the street on foot.

She put her hand on his arm as she approached and pushed herself
up on her toes and kissed him lightly on the lips. He was startled. It was
like a kiss from a long-term spouse just coming home from the office.

"Mark, this is Kate," Chance said introducing the short, athletic
sandy blond to the salt-and-pepper big guy. For a man who was a 24-
hour-a-day outdoorsman, his skin wasn't the open-air consistency of
a surfer. Kate had a tight body and he watched Mark admiring it.

"How do you do," Kate said extending her hand. "Thanks for getting this criminal out of San Pedro. For him, it's the most dangerous
town on the planet."

They all chuckled at her wry humor and the ironic truth within it.

"He's the dangerous one," Mark said.

Inside the condo, Mark offered Kate a drink. When she declined,
he sat down at his computer with his back to the two of them and hammered at the keys. They sat close on the long black leather couch.

"Tell me about it," Chance said to Kate.

"It was the same as the rest," she said. "She was strangled and tortured as she died slowly. Whoever it was took bloody clothing to your place again. Your turn; tell me your thoughts."

"I had one night with Suzanne," Chance said about the first victim. "Fernandez was going out with her and came over while we were going at it. It was my first time with her. I didn't know if she was seeing anyone. He tried to pressure me to stop seeing her; then she was killed."

"I'm sure he's the guy," he continued. "I watched him while I was in jail, saw the way he moved around the station. I thought he might kill me while I was locked up. The sonuvabitch has a touchy twitch and sweats constantly."

"Why didn't he?" Kate said. "He could have left your door unlocked and shot the escaping prisoner."

"Maybe," Chance said, his green eyes meeting Kate's. "After he killed the first girl, he discovered that he liked it, or maybe he was jealous of me. I don't have all answers, but to my way of thinking, he's the prime suspect. He's the only guy in town I know who would have any reason to fuck with me."

"Somehow," Kate said, "I'll have to keep an eye on him."

As she spoke, she moved closer to Chance and touched him on his bare knee. Mark was right. Chance's mind spun out of control. She was attracted to him and he to her in a different sort of way.

She was sharply attired - a perfect pert hairdo and a light sand-colored, button-down blouse, dark tan slacks, and a matching ivy-league over sweater. Her feet were small and petite in professional looking soft leather pumps. She was the perfect Nordstrom model and in great shape with sparkling baby blue eyes that sought appreciation and affection.

"I want to solve this case so bad," Kate said and a tear broke from one of her soft eyelids and ran down her bright cheek.

Chance slipped his arm around her shoulder and she slid against him neatly. His reaction to her was one of soft comfort and desire, but conversation cemented her resolve to get to the bottom of this bullshit before another girl was killed. When Kate looked up at him, he bent down and kissed her and she molded herself into his arm like clay into the palm of a potter on a spinning wheel.

It was all happening fast. Chance didn't feel he deserved a woman like her. He was just a biker and she was a cop, a beautiful cop - but still a cop.

Mark glanced over his shoulder and took the hint. Quietly, he rose from his desk chair, grabbed a book on automatic weapons and went upstairs to his master bedroom.

Kate wrapped her arms around Chance's taut frame and drew herself toward him. Their kiss went deep as he sought to taste her very soul. It wasn't a sexual passion, but something emotional and rewarding, as if they both had just crested Mount Everest or had just surfed the perfect wave.

With each kiss, their determination to drive the fear from San Pedro heightened. She wept silently as they parted, and Chance kissed the tears from her cheeks. He was kissing her neck when her cell phone vibrated in her purse.

"Hello?" Kate said, and paused.

"Yes, Lieutenant; right away." She hung up and turned to embrace Chance again. "I must go, but maybe someday."

"Let's put and end to this deadly poker game first," Chance said and hugged back.

-24-

THREE MURDERS AND LOVE

Chance walked Kate to her sedan. "I didn't expect that," Chance said.

"I was hoping…" Kate replied bashfully. "But it's best. There would be hell to pay from several angles."

For the first time, he saw a soft, compliant side, beyond her professional drive and ambition. Although they were only forty miles from San Pedro, the murders seemed far away.

"What the hell are you going to do?"

"Good question," Chance said, thinking to himself. A chill ran up his taught spine. Suddenly the onerous burden of three murdered women returned. "I'm wondering what you're going to do. I was thinking about turning myself in."

"They've torn up your house again," Kate said.

"I thought being a biker was tough on pads," Chance said, "but being a murder suspect is just as bad when it comes to keeping a home up."

"Did you lose your job?" Kate asked.

"Yep," Chance said, "It's gone." Then Rosa dawned on him and he started to piece something together. "I've got to tell you something."

"Who is she?" Kate said.

"Did I tell you about Rosa, from the desert?" Chance said.

"Not entirely," Kate answered, and her tight smooth features scrunched up like a wrinkled peach.

"I helped her in Arizona, just before I met you," Chance said.

"She called yesterday; she's coming to LA. But I just had a thought. If I have a woman with me constantly, I can watch her, and it might give you some time to work on this bastard. It's only temporary, then she's going back to Arizona."

"She'll be in terrible danger," Kate said.

She knew another woman would come along, but she was hurt nonetheless. A tinge to jealousy spread across her soft features, but she didn't let go of the bottom line.

"I told her," Chance said, impressed with Kate's ability to handle Rosa. He saw her flinch, but she recoiled fast.

"But she insisted."

"It might work," Kate said, "Let me go to the station and see if we can't put you under house arrest."

"For murder?" Chance said.

"They still don't have concrete evidence against you," Kate muttered, still holding him tight, "except this bastard tries to pin it on you each time, unsuccessfully. I'm afraid he'll get it right one time and you'll be in trouble."

"Fuck, I felt like a million bucks a little while ago," Chance said, "but it's all so goddamn fleeting. Just over the hill is another poker game gone bad."

"You know," Kate said, "My mom has an old friend who teaches college out here who loves to work on homes. He might be able to help fix your place up."

"I need all the help I can get," Chance said. "Get me a number." Then he turned and ran back to Mark's condo and picked up his sweat-soaked running outfit.

"I told you," Mark said coming down the stairs in a bathrobe.

"Remind me to thank the blackjack dealer in the sky, but we didn't do anything," Chance said. "Then again, you're a pain in the ass, but thanks for the help."

"When are we going to train again?" Mark asked.

"I don't know. I've got a couple of bullshit items to work out and a wonderful helper on her way to town, plus my place is a mess. Fuck, I don't know if I'll be on the streets tomorrow."

"If I'm in your neighborhood tomorrow," Mark said, "I'll stop in and give you a hand."

"Thanks, brother," Chance said, and meant it as he headed out the door.

As Kate drove toward San Pedro, they moved along through the evening traffic in silence. Chance thought about Rosa, his landlord, his job, the murders, and his house, and wondered what more could surface.

Kate checked her beeper and she had a number of pending calls. She liked the closeness with Chance and she wanted more of it and the tranquility it brought. He made her comfortable and contented. She wanted the freedom to fall in love, but knew it wasn't there, at least not yet.

She pulled up to his house in front of a black and white parked at the curb. Officer Grey stepped out of the cruiser.

"What the hell?" he said to Kate. "Where did you find him?"

"Never mind. He's under house arrest until further notice."

"I understand," the officer said, "but some of the higher-ups won't like it."

"I'll deal with that," Kate said. "Call me if anyone comes around. I mean anyone. Don't let them bother him."

Chance started to unlock the back door, but the jam was destroyed. The door swung open on its own accord and he walked in apprehensively. The cops had once again trashed his humble abode piece by piece looking for evidence that wasn't there. The linoleum in the kitchen was shredded. The stove was pushed into the center of the room and the cupboard around it hung loose from the wall. The refrigerator was displaced from its bulkhead, so they could inspect behind it.

The place was a bigger mess that before and it depressed Chance. He made a drink and carried it into the back yard. His garage was in shambles, too. He was beginning to wonder why he didn't grab Rosa and return to the desert. It was a humble but wonderfully solitary existence. He sat in his tattered recliner and fell asleep.

The next morning, Chance found himself in one of those situations too catastrophic to even consider, like a mobile home after a tornado. The damn place was so destroyed he didn't know where to begin, or even why. He despised thinking about it, because he couldn't stand another murder or the outcome. He cleaned up and made a cup of coffee. He sat on the porch drinking the coffee and looked out to sea as another cop car pulled in front. Joe Fernandez got out.

That broke the last straw. He was the slimiest sonuvabitch Chance knew. Chance's favorite target for the murders, a jealous cop who was past his prime and looked it. As Fernandez walked around the corner of the yard and up 19th, Officer Grey got out of his car and headed him off. He knew there was something between the two of them, but wasn't sure what it was, other than Chance knew that Fernandez had once dated one of the murdered girls.

Grey was younger and well-built, a strong black man.

"I've been told to keep people away from him," Grey said. "He's under house arrest."

"I don't care," Joe said. "I want that piece of shit."

Officer Grey raised his arm in a half-assed attempt to block a brother officer, but Fernandez pushed past him and pulled his service pistol as Chance jumped off the porch.

"You sonuvabitch," Joe said lunging toward Chance with his gun pointing directly at his target. "I'm going to blow your fuckin' head off."

Chance was trained by Mark to act afraid but to be aggressive. He raised his hands in mock fear and tossed his cup of coffee. Officer Grey was stunned by the action, and drew his Browning 9mm, snapping the safety off. The coffee splashed against Joe's chest and face as he tried to side-step the hot liquid.

Chance realized at that second Fernandez could pull the trigger less than a yard from his target. He also knew that he hated this sonuvabitch more than any living creature on the earth and wouldn't back down, even if he had five armed officers with him. He didn't give a fuck. The cocksucker was a representative of society's law gone wrong. He was the lowest of the low.

Chance dipped his torso and came up under the arm holding the pistol just as Fernandez fired, shattering the window in the breakfast nook. Chance parried the weapon aside with his left hand and hit Fernandez forcefully in the neck with the web of his right hand. He stepped forward with his right leg, slipping his foot behind Joe's leg, while driving his fist into the man's neck again. Chance then snapped the weapon free from the officer's grasp and drove the officer over backwards to the pavement, where his head smacked the concrete with a nasty crack.

Chance followed through with his attack, dropping his right knee into the cop's ribs, and Fernandez exhaled in pain. A hammer fist strike broke the cop's nose. Grey was stunned by Chance's forceful attack, and discovered quickly that he had to change his own direction.

"That's enough," Grey spat as Chance prepared to strike Fernandez again. Chance stopped and bounced to his feet, kicking Fernandez' fallen pistol from the sidewalk onto the grass.

"This will make you even more popular with the crew," Grey said.

"Whatta ya bet while he's in the hospital, I could go out with any number of girls and no one would get hurt?" Chance mouthed, breathing heavily. He needed to keep up the workout routine.

Grey paid little attention to Chance's comment and reached for his radio.

"Officer Grey to base. I have an officer injured on the corner of 19th and Crescent. Send an ambulance. No backup necessary."

"Go inside and stay there," Grey said. "You might call Kate and tell her to get over here quick before three or four of the guys attempt what Fernandez failed at."

Chance picked up his busted coffee cup and turned to go back inside. His heart was pumping like a high-speed piston in his chest. He felt good for the second time in 24 hours. Once inside, he dialed Kate's cell phone.

"Yes?" Kate answered sorta joyfully.

"What the hell was that?" Chance said. "What happened to Officer Kate?"

"I'm still buzzing from last night," Kate said lightly, "plus they found none of your DNA on or near Julie's body. She also wasn't raped."

"Did you start anything on Fernandez?" Chance quizzed.

"I took Lt. Reed aside," Kate said. "I have to trust someone."

"I need you to get your cute little ass over here," Chance said. "Fernandez attempted to shoot me, but I kicked his ass badly. He'll be in the hospital for a week."

"I'll be right there," Kate said and hung up.

Within ten minutes, the place was surrounded with police cars and an ambulance. Fernandez nose was broken and his cheekbone fractured. A couple of ribs were busted and he had a concussion. The EMT's wrapped him up and slid him in the back of the ambulance, but not before Callahan and a couple of uniformed officers and Detective Myers told him that they would back his play and take out Chance any opportunity they had.

Myers, the stout redhead, called to Chance in the house over his bullhorn, "Hey biker trash. Come on out here. Let's run through your moves again and see if you're as successful."

The house was surrounded with detectives and uniformed officers leaning over their cars with weapons at the ready. It smacked of the

SLA in downtown Los Angeles in the '70s. At the drop of a hat, the house would become a crushed box of Chinese toothpicks.

Kate skidded up in her sedan and jumped out as another officer put another rock through the plate glass window in the living room.

"Hey chickenshit, let's play," he shouted before ducking back behind his black and white. Kate ran up the concrete porch and knocked on the cracked plywood front door.

"Chance!" she hollered.

The ambulance pulled away, siren blaring, and the officers lifted their weapons from a firing position as Kate beat on the door. She took the heat out of their attack and they scoffed and cussed, but knew they were in the wrong.

"Come around back," Chance said and met her behind the house.

"I don't know what to say," she said expecting Chance to react to her conversation with her boss.

"It may be a blessing," Chance said. "You can get some DNA testing going, and maybe even search his place while he's in the hospital."

Kate moved closer to Chance but didn't dare touch him. The place was still surrounded by angry cops.

"You're right," she said quietly. "I hope Officer Grey took the report on this incident. He's the only fair cop of this bunch right now."

"He was here for the entire strike," Chance said, "No one could handle it more accurately. Hell, some of it's a blur to me."

"I'll get you a copy," Kate said, then a frown crossed her delicate features. "When will Rosa arrive?"

"Probably early this afternoon," Chance said. "Listen, I'm not sure what to make of last night, but it was terrific and I won't ever forget it. You never know when we might roll the dice."

Kate smiled and wanted to kiss him. A bounce came back to her feet as she danced out of his beat and bruised home. She wasn't gone five minutes when the phone rang.

"Chance?" Rosa said.

"Yeah, babe," Chance said, "Are you sure you want to come to this hole?"

"I'm almost there," Rosa said, "no turning back now. You've got to give me directions."

"Can you get this down?" Chance said.

"Just give me the highpoints," Rosa muttered, watching the road in front of her. "I'll call back when I'm closer."

"Do you have a map?" Chance asked.

"Sure," Rosa confirmed.

"You just need to get to the 110 freeway and head toward the coast or south," Chance said. "Then get off on Harbor Boulevard and turn right, then call me again. Where are you?"

"About an hour or so out," Rosa said.

"Are you sure you wanna do this?"

"Yes, goddamnit," Rosa said, mimicking Chance. "I can't wait to see you. We'll work it out."

She hung up and Chance stood in his destroyed kitchen, perplexed. He didn't know which way to turn. The phone started to ring again.

"Yeah?" Chance said.

"This is Jake," he said his voice light and friendly. "Kate asked me to call you. You've got a project?"

"It's more like a disaster," Chance said.

"I'll come over and take a look," Jake said.

"Right now?" Chance muttered confused.

"Bad time?" Jake returned, concerned that he was interrupting.

"Ah, no," Chance said, thinking about Rosa and traffic, "Where you comin' from?"

"I'm in Long Beach," Jake said. He lived in a small beach area. He was a college professor, an accomplished artist and loved being a handy man. "I'll be there in 15 minutes."

"Have you read the newspapers?" Chance said.

"That's how I know where you are," Jake said.

"See you then," Chance said.

Christ, he thought, one minute he was under the impression all was lost and all he had left was to fight or be killed; then suddenly he was kissed, Rosa called and someone was going to help him with his dump. If he could buy the joint, it would top off his day, but he didn't have a job.

Chance picked up the phone and decided to share the good vibes with someone close. He called Harbor Taxi. He didn't have Carl's weekend number, so he called the shop and waited for the answering machine to pick up the line. He knew Carl was reacting to Julie's death, but Carl also was aware that Chance was innocent.

"Carl, it's Chance. You know I didn't have anything to do with Julie. I'm terribly sorry, but I know you need the help. I'm coming back to work on Monday and I'm bringing a woman who can fill Julie's shoes for the time being."

He hung up and started hurrying around the house, trying to pick up and make the place look more inhabitable than it currently did. The windows were wood-framed, cracked, and old, and in most cases, no longer fit well in the runners, and some were cockeyed. Each room needed fresh paint and new light fixtures. They were all 40 years old, if a day.

Chance brought in a throw rug and threw it over some of the stains in the hardwood floor in the living room. He tried to drag in a chair or two, and swept the kitchen floor. Ten minutes passed and a rusting, faded Toyota pickup pulled along side the house next to the cop car and Jake got out.

The pickup had a common camper shell with windows in the side that needed cleaning badly, which Jake ignored. Jake was a short 5'7" and thick, but not stout. He wore plain work boots, faded Levis, no belt and a tattered t-shirt. He was in his late 40s with a clean-shaven face that looked childlike with smooth features. His hair was mud brown. It was disheveled and thick, but not long. He pushed his glasses up his nose as he walked alongside the house to the front, a large sketchpad, a ruler, tape measure, and pencil in hand. Chance saw him coming through the busted kitchen window and went to the front door.

"Hey," Chance said in the sunlight as Jake stood on the lawn and looked at the front of the house.

"I didn't know we had an Alamo here on the coast," Jake said, scratching his head. "Who are you at war with?"

Officer Grey had stepped out of his car as he watched Jake stroll inquisitively onto the lawn.

"The Harbor Division of the Los Angeles Police Department," Chance muttered dejectedly. "Excuse me for a second."

"It's okay," Chance said approaching Grey. "He's might help me with repairs. I'm also expecting a Mexican woman to arrive in about an hour. Is that cool?"

"As long and nothing happens to her," Grey said, staring at Chance eyeball to eyeball.

"As long as Fernandez is in the hospital, nothing will happen," Chance said. "I'm not the guy and you know it. I don't want anything to happen to any woman. Do me a favor, keep me informed of Fernandez's location."

"He's my brother," Grey said with lackluster in his eyes. "I can't turn on him."

"Can you watch another woman suffer and die?" Chance said.

"Of course not," Grey, said fumbling with his nightstick.

"Then let the chips fall where they may, but don't lose another woman in the process," Chance said, and walked away.

"Hey Jake," Chance said again, greeting him on the lawn. "I'm under house arrest. Don't you read the papers?"

"I didn't catch that part," Jake said and scribbled on his pad.

Jake looked at Chance as if he was coming out of a deep sleep. He took off his bifocals and reviewed Chance like a schoolteacher eyeballs a tardy student.

"I hate cops," Jake said, sizing up Chance, and then his eyes brightened as if reality sprung from a textbook.

"My God," he said, "You're the murderer."

He took a step back and dropped his large artist pad on the ragged lawn, then turned to pick it up. As he bent down to retrieve the pad, he collected his scattered thoughts.

"Why the hell would you fix up this dump," he began, "If you kill women in your spare time? I felt from reading the accounts that you were primarily guilty of being a biker."

"I'll confess to that one," Chance said. "I'm hoping to buy this joint, if the cops don't kill me first. I think it's a cop behind the killings. In fact, he tried to off me this morning. He's in the hospital now and I'll bet as long as he's there, you won't see a killing."

"When do you think you'll hear something about the house?" Jake asked, moving around the house, looking at the broken windows, and taking measurements. "I'll bet this shit is putting a damper on your action in town."

"Action is treacherous until he's busted or I can catch and kill him myself," Chance said, following the short but agile man through the weeds between his house and the Spanish house next door.

"I'm a Vietnam veteran," Jake said. "I spent time in 'Nam and Okinawa, and between smokin' all the dope I could get my hands on and the whores, I trained in the martial arts. I kept it up for a while when I returned, but then let it slide. You wanna burn a fattie?"

"Too risky with cops poised outside my door," Chance said. "They search this place and tear it up every other day, whether I like it our not."

"Oh yeah," Jake said, handing Chance the end of the tape measure, pacing off the side of the house, and noting the placement of each window and its size. The phone started to ring in the house and Chance could hear it readily through the tilting and broken windows. He excused himself and jogged around to the front of the joint, up the stairs and into the kitchen, and snatched it from the black plastic cradle.

"Yeah?" Chance said.

"Baby," Rosa said, "I just rounded the corner onto Harbor Boulevard."

"You're just up the street," Chance said. "Stay on Harbor through a couple of lights for a mile, then turn right on Crescent. I'm on the corner of 19th. You won't miss it. There's a cop parked beside the house. I'll see you in five minutes."

"I'm looking forward to it," Rosa said and hung up.

Chance was both excited and apprehensive. He jogged out front to where Jake was measuring the porch and the bay window at the front of the house.

"I've got a babe arriving in a couple of minutes," Chance said. "I'm nervous as shit."

Jake turned and faced Chance. "Am I in the way?"

"No," Chance said, "Not at all. She may be living with me for awhile. I have been poison to too many women over the last couple of months. Hell, a psycho in my life burnt Rosa's old gas station down in Arizona. I've already been bad news to her once."

"Take care of her," Jake said, "she obviously wants to see you. I'll keep myself busy. Okay, if I go in the house?"

"Sure," Chance said.

"Call the real estate asshole," Jake said, "and see if you can cut a deal. This place is all right, overlooking the Harbor and all."

"I will," Chance said rubbing his face.

He ran in the house and combed his long mussed hair. He hadn't shaved, and smelled from the fight and sweat from the sun. He washed his face and chest quickly and slipped on a clean sweatshirt. As he ran out the front door, he saw Rosa pull up in a new pickup. She parked in front of Officer Grey's cruiser. She jumped out of the cab as Chance rounded the corner and hugged him.

" Chance," Rosa said, "it's been too long."

The cop got out of the black and white and came forward.

"Officer Grey," Chance said breaking the embrace hesitantly, kissing her one more time. "This is Rosa. She'll be living with me for awhile. So see that no one harms her, will ya?"

"Hi, Rosa," Officer Grey announced professionally while his eyes danced along her voluptuous body with concern. "You are aware that this gentleman is under house arrest for terrible heinous crimes against women?"

Rosa tucked herself against Chance's body and held him close. "Yes sir," she said, "I'm aware that this outlaw is a dangerous sort, but he's not the man you are looking for. It is good to meet you."

Chance helped her with her bags.

"What the hell brings you out here?" Chance asked as he led her into the messy house.

"We had a good time, didn't we?" Rosa said, "I know you need help, and you helped me a great deal. I will have a new station when I return. I have a new truck and money. All is well."

"But it's treacherous here," Chance said.

"I will help," Rosa said, "When can we make love?"

Chance was startled by her directness. He stumbled with his thoughts of Kate and Rosa's bountiful breasts jiggling enticingly in her loose blouse before his eyes. Although he was nervous, she was an absolute delight to his senses and he pulled her close.

"I better show you around first," Chance said, pulling her inside. Rosa's eyes widened as she gazed around the dump at the police destruction and disarray, and the poor general condition of the house.

"How long have you lived here?" she asked

"Actually, I've never had a chance to live here for more than a week. Every time I try, something went to hell, but generally, I like the joint. It has been a rental for years and the last people who rented it were pigs."

"I can see that," Rosa said, moving through the house until she saw Jake measuring the bathroom. "Oh, excuse me."

"This is Jake," Chance said. "He's a friend of a friend who might help me clean this place up."

"Buenos dias," Jake said and bowed slightly. "Hey, I have a clean stove that I just took out of a rental. I'll bring it by tomorrow."

"Thanks."

"It is a pleasure to meet anyone helping Chance at this time of need," Rosa said, and turned to head toward the kitchen.

"She's a knockout," Jake said, measuring every inch of the bathroom and taking notes.

Rosa returned with a somewhat sour look on her lovely Hispanic features.

"Where's the market and Home Depot?" she asked.

"I'm a goddamn biker," Chance said, "I don't have the slightest."

"Just head up 19th to Pacific and turn right," Jake said. "It's the main drag. There's a hardware store just down the street on the left."

Rosa kissed Chance on the cheek and scooted out the door. She was a blooming flower in the center of a desert as she disappeared out the door to her truck.

Jake pulled a small pipe out of his Levis pocket, slipped a piece of a bud into it from a matchbox and lit it. Chance stepped back.

"Jesus," Chance said.

"Ah, fuck 'em," Jake said, coughing billows of smoke and shoving the pipe toward Chance.

"No fuckin' way! I'm a nervous wreck now. There's too much going on for me to get high. Hopefully, she'll return with a bottle of Jack for later."

"Call that agent," Jake said. "This place is worth going after, if you can get the right price."

Chance picked up the phone and dialed the number to the office of Harbor Real Estate.

"Harbor Real Estate?"

"This is the tenant at 19th and Crescent," Chance said and was cut off.

"Are you repairing that house, murderer?" she spat.

"Have you found out if it's for sale?" Chance asked, trying to maintain his anger level. He had about had it with this bitch.

"No, and I'm not..." she tried to continue her harangue.

"Listen, bitch," Chance spat into the phone, "If I don't have an answer and terms in an hour, I'm coming to visit you. How about that?"

The phone went completely silent as if she had passed out. The breathing in the background came is gasps.

"Yes, yes, sir," she said. "That won't be necessary."

By the time Chance ended the call, her voice was as soft as a down pillow. He turned to Jake, who was still sketching and making notes on his pad. Jake was like a mad scientist, scribbling with wild abandon. He clipped the tape measure to his waistband and shoved the pencil in his pocket. He had no cell phone or pager, just a pencil and the large industrial tape measure.

"I'm taking off," Jake said. "I'll see you tomorrow. I may bring my wife over to see the project. She's better at some of this shit than I am. Besides, she'll want to meet the criminal."

Chance stood dumfounded on his porch and watched Jake drive away. He didn't understand what was happening to him. He didn't have any idea if he could buy the house in the first place. He had no expertise at working on houses and couldn't keep a job. He was a fuckin' biker under investigation for murder and on the run from one woman after another. He didn't know diddly about settling down, but he had to admit to himself that the notion at the minute seemed damn nice.

Rosa pulled up in her pickup with a brand-new refrigerator in the back. Between the two of them and officer Grey, they threw out the old filthy, scum-coated refrigerator, the stove, and the grease-soaked shelves around it. Rosa swept and cleaned the kitchen the best she could, then loaded the cupboards and the new fridge with groceries. Then she turned her attention to the garage and the bedroom and moved stuff back in, and Chance helped her turn the mattress upside down. She remade the bed with fresh sheets and placed four votive candles around the bed, but didn't light them. She jumped into the truck and drove up to Mando's for Mexican food and returned. As the sun dipped into the harbor, she poured Chance a stiff Jack on the rocks.

He opened her bottle of wine, let the bottle breath for a few minutes, and then poured it into a small wine glass, which she just bought. They took their drinks and tacos to the porch and sat and watched the sun set over the harbor. They sat and drank quietly as the sun drifted behind the Palos Verdes Peninsula and the lights of the harbor twinkled on. A large Carnival Cruise high-rise tourist ship slipped out of the harbor, music playing, and lights aglow from every porthole.

"This is a lovely place, Chance," Rosa said. "I can understand why you like it here, but oh, this house is a mess. We have our work cut out."

"I'm not sure whether to run," Chance said, "or stand my ground. I like it here." He was going to say that he had thought of her place in the quiet desert often, but held back.

"Don't you think it's time see if that bed works," Rosa said raising her eyebrows.

Chance looked in her smiling dark eyes and smiled, then took her soft tan hand and pulled her to her feet.

-25-

ROSA WARMS SAN PEDRO

Chance rolled over as the alarm went off and touched Rosa on the shoulder. He was filled with memories of their short time in the desert, and it was wonderful to pull himself against her curvaceous backside and cup her form like two spoons nestled together in a velvet-lined drawer.

Emotionally, he was wrapped in the terror of the three murdered women and watching out for Rosa. He wished he could jump out of the sack and go to war with the bastard, man to man. On the other hand, he wanted desperately to be free to make love to Rosa all day. They'd never had the opportunity to dig into their sexual fantasies and explore.

As he ran his hand up her soft leg and over her supple ass, he wished he had the time and free spirit to kiss her body from her olive toes to her dark, responsive nipples. He pushed her thick black wave aside and kissed her neck.

"Is it time to go to your new job?" she asked as she rolled toward him and nestled against Chance's hairy chest. He melted inside.

"Not just yet," Chance said, kissing her full on her soft mouth and rolling on top of her. She spread her legs eagerly and rocked her pelvis so her mound could welcome him inside. She never had yielding, comfortable sex from her abusive drunken ex and Chance felt so good. She rocked slowly, feeling her breath come in short gasps as she reached above herself to the bed frame and held on in anticipation.

Chance pushed himself up on his strong arms. His chest was hairy but his arms and back were smooth, and she watched his pecks flex as he slid inside her so slowly. She felt him enter her as if his body was

French kissing her for the first time. He didn't jam in and start pumping her like a water pump behind a barn. He moved in slowly, tenderly, and her body wanted more, but he would not allow it, even as he began to swell. The more she arched and spread her legs, the more he resisted, looking down at her large quivering tits. Then he slid inside her fully, and she screamed and grabbed his waist, pulling him to her deeply, swelling, pulsing and crying for more. Her climax came quickly and violently. She shuttered and screamed, and he slowed until he was still, his swollen cock still pulsing deep inside her.

"What you do to me," she murmured contentedly.

Chance held himself with one arm and ran his hand down the side of her face, along her olive-contoured neck to her curvy tit from the side and lifted it gently as he began to back out of her.

"No," she said realizing what he was doing. He continued down her body with his hand and backed away. Then he leaned down and kissed her stomach and flicked his tongue into her navel.

Her pulse quickened as she could sense that her pussy was still throbbing, anxious and tender. Soon, his mouth was above her mound and she could feel his soft breath on her as his kisses teased her madly, and her passion flowed like a river over the bed. He slowly kissed around her lips, then up to her clit, touching it so lightly with his tongue that she wasn't sure he had caressed her at all. She was tingling and jiggling like sleigh bells on a troop of horses running from a winter storm.

Chance kissed her tenderly. He knew that she was still on a sensitive cloud. He kissed the place where her hips met her mound with grace and gentleness. It was one of the softest, most delectable places on earth to him, and he relished the time he spent there. He kissed each side and allowed his cheek to touch her inner thigh, another special place.

He breathed a warm sigh against her pussy and watched as she arched to reach his mouth. Then he kissed her like he would kiss her mouth. The deep kiss that consumed her lips, his tongue slipped inside of her, and she moaned. Then he backed off slightly and explored each lip, slowly working closer to her clitoris.

Rosa was in the midst of heightened sexuality, yet completely relaxed. His tenderness allowed her to release every muscle as his tongue explored her, then reached her button that clicked all systems to pleasure alert. She grabbed her tits and touched her nipples as muscles trembled and she approached another climax. His tongue flicked her gently, consuming her on her path to delight and she started to pant, then scream, as he slid his hands under her soft ass, and she arched and quivered against him.

He held her close, his mouth securely encircling her love button and holding on until her last spasm had passed, then withdrew slowly, so as not to jar the perfect sensation. Again, she was tranquil, like a small boat in glassy waters. He let her rest.

"Baby," Rosa said as if she had to force the words to come, "Please. It's your turn."

Chance moved between her legs again and touched her with his cock, rocking slightly as he swelled, then guided himself inside her once more, rocking slowly then faster. Rosa ran her hands up his muscular arms and raised her head to see his cock thrust inside of her, and once more, her body cried out for release.

"Don't stop, Chance," she whimpered as she began to explode.

Chance felt himself near his climax and moved with her as she began to shake beneath him before releasing himself inside of her and they burst into each others' arms grasping deliberately, clamped to one another for a long moments. Their hot breath created a warm moist fog in the small bedroom.

"Unfortunately we gotta move," Chance finally said, disappointed that they couldn't remain in bed all day. Simultaneously, they jumped out of bed and ran to the shower. Chance cleared it with Kate for the two of them to work at Harbor Taxi. There was no way that Chance was going to let Rosa out of his sight, which struck him as odd. Generally, he wanted freedom, and to feel totally connected to a woman in any circumstances, other than in the bedroom, was confining, but it was the last thing on his mind while a murderer was loose.

His chopper would remain in the dilapidated garage and they would take Rosa's new truck to work. As the two of them started for the door, the phone rang.

"This is Shirley from Harbor Real Estate," she said, her voice trembling with apprehension. "You were right, they want to sell. The lady who owns it wants $240,000."

"Work up an offer for $185,000," Chance countered. "This place is a dump. I'll be by to sign it at noon." He hung up.

"Good news, this dump is for sale," he said to Rosa, whose lip jutted out slightly. Chance could tell she was already hoping to drag him back to the desert. "Come on, baby, let's go."

He kissed her full on her tender lips and pulled her toward him. He had to wedge the front door closed and a chair against the back one. There was no way he could lock the damaged doors.

They drove over to Ramona's Bakery where Mari had worked. Chance stayed in the car as Rosa went inside and ordered muffins and large cups of coffee. Chance felt like a chickenshit sitting in the car, then noticed that someone was pointing a finger as him and the conversation became long and heated.

Rosa was followed out the door by a big, older Hispanic woman who was wearing an apron like Mari did the day he met her, but it didn't fit anything like Mari's. It hurt Chance to think about it. He leapt out of the truck and onto the grimy sidewalk to face the murdered girl's mother. He didn't know what to except but bowed respectfully.

"I'm humbly sorry," Chance said, and just looking at her sad face brought a tear to his eye.

The plump, gray-haired older woman's face was a roadmap of grief. Her emotions spilled from her eyes and Chance embraced her.

"She was so happy the afternoon that she kissed you," her mother said, and burst into tears. "I miss her so." They wept together on the sidewalk .

"I will not rest until I find the man…" Chance said, trying to suppress his tears.

Mari's mom pressed her flour dusted fingers against his lips. "Let's remember, not talk of another death." She kissed him on the cheek. "Please come see me often."

"I will," Chance said, looking at Rosa who held the woman's puffy and wrinkled hand for long moments and looked at Chance with admiration.

The woman waved and returned to her shop as they climbed in Rosa's pickup and rolled down Pacific toward 22nd street. A black and white followed. They pulled up in front of the prefab office on Signal Street, which was quiet except for the sound of a phone ringing. As Chance got out of the truck, he noticed that Carl's truck was in its usual parking spot. A lumped formed in his throat as Rosa rounded her truck. Chance held the cardboard container of tall paper coffee cups and the bag of muffins. Rosa took his arm and looked up at Chance.

"This also will be tough, won't it?" she said.

The blond office manager was the latest victim. Each time a girl was killed, Chance became the prime suspect. Each time, he was forced to overcome the heat and pain.

"He'll either hug me or shoot me," Chance said.

"Come on," Rosa said, tugging at his arm with her soft hand.

She had dressed colorfully in traditional Hispanic attire, like the dress she was wearing when they first met. There was something festive about the embroidery around the base of the white cotton dress and around the gathered sleeves. Her jet black hair was pulled away from her pretty face into a full ponytail, and her lips were carefully painted with traditional red lipstick. She was a knockout and walked like the entire world was having a party. She reeked of confidence as she walked up the steps toward the front door. They strolled into the lobby area, mussed and unkempt from the previous week. Nothing had been accomplished since Julie's death.

They could hear sobbing from behind the glass cubicle of Carl's office. He was a big man, almost bald, with his face in his hands, weeping. The job, the business, the accounting, bookkeeping, marketing, everything, was shared by the two of them. The loss of Julie's buoyant attitude and unflinching ability to pour through one chore after another, always with a smile, was hard for him to bear.

"You go first," Chance said. He wasn't afraid, but he knew that just the sight of Rosa in these grim surroundings would make any man perk up. Chance disliked that about industrial atmospheres. He loved a woman's touch everywhere. Rosa moved quietly to the open door in front of Carl's tiny, glassed-in office.

"Carl?" Chance called from behind Rosa's shapely form.

Carl was bent over in tears behind his small Formica desk. He was holding a framed shot of Julie and himself standing on the dock the day the business opened. Behind them was the freshly painted Harbor Taxi sign in blue and white against the gray mobile home-like wooden structure. He looked up slightly, his brown eyes puffy with tears. He saw Rosa's fluffy white dress, the colorful embroidery, her narrow waist, amply endowed chest, and a face so full of joy she brightened the room. He pushed himself away from the desk and to his feet.

"I'm sorry," Carl said as he reached out his hand.

Rosa extended her hand as Chance said, "Carl, this is Rosa. She's going to help out for awhile."

Rosa was so moved by Carl's features that instead of shaking his hand she took him in her arms like she would a small wounded child.

He wept again and Chance moved away to Julie's counter and set the muffins and coffee down. He went outside and down the steps to the cold concrete dock.

Damn, he thought to himself. Would his life ever float on an even keel again? He moved to the edge of the dock and looked out at the boats, still lined up and secured. His big hands were stuffed in his jeans as he leaned against a tar-soaked pylon and watched a tramp freighter enter the harbor, lumbering against the gentle swell.

He had a burning desire to handle this situation in a hurry, but he wasn't sure how. He was relieved that Fernandez was in the hospital and out of action, but that was only a temporary fix.

Chance moved out onto the dock and began to unlock the power skiffs and prepare them for action as a van pulled up packed with oil workers. He shook the doldrums free from his consciousness, ran down the dock to the last boat, and jumped onboard. He plugged in the key and fired it to life. The fuel gauge popped to full and he signaled the waiting clan of young oil workers to climb aboard.

The roar of the engine filled the morning as the sun warmed the day while reflecting light on the water through a stringy array of stratus clouds. Chance put the boat in reverse, backed away from the dock and spun the wheel before shifting it into forward. Then he pulled back on the throttle knob as the engine roared and the boat spun in line with the rocky jetty.

"Hey Chance," one of the dark oil workers hollered, "are you going to set a new record today?"

The man was dressed in heavy work boots stained with crude oil, navy blue overalls, and an oil-stained ballcap. Other than his clothing, he was clean and freshly shaven, and carried a large canvas bag that housed extra clothes and a sizeable lunch.

The men worked in a tough profession that paid handsomely, but few hung with offshore oil rigs for long. The harbor water surface was mild, but the seas outside the jetty were nasty with 4-foot swells and 10-knot winds whistling and churning up whitecaps. It wasn't the whitecaps that were dangerous, but the dark deep blue waves beneath the spray.

"Should we roll the dice today?" Chance asked.

The boat chugged along, fighting against the currents until he reached the jetty and the wall of swells. He turned and looked at the oil rig crew, who shook their heads in unison. There would be no race.

He rumbled forward, pushing over one swell after another until he reached concrete pillars covered with sharp barnacles, like rusting razor blades growing from the side of each post, protruding down from the steel floor of the rig.

"We'll try again for a record tomorrow," the worker shouted, grabbing the ladder from the rig and pulling himself out of the rocking boat. His compadres followed

"Be careful, guys," Chance hollered while trying to control the 30-foot skiff in the rough seas. He shoved the throttle forward, and the boat, which felt as though it was being sucked under the treacherous pillars and braces of the towering oil rig, suddenly lurched and sped away. His ability with the controls was enhanced with each exercise. As quickly as possible, he returned to the Harbor Taxi docks, grabbed a line and jumped off the bow of the tilting skiff.

No sooner had he landed on the floating extension of the concrete boat dock than Rosa called to him from the window.

"Not so fast, boat boy," she said and smiled.

He looked up startled, yet satisfied. She leaned out the window much the same way Julie did, except her cleavage was more forthright and teasing. Her smile was just as broad and positive, yet she looked nothing like the bouncy blond. Chance grimaced and he looked at the gray-painted wood slats at his feet for a second, then mustered a half-hearted smile and looked up again. She noted his hesitation and suspected that he might have had a flirty relationship with Julie.

"Chance, they need a supply boat at the Cabrillo Marina. They need an engine hauled to the South Shore Marina."

"I got it," Chance said and threw her a kiss. How's Carl?"

"He'll be fine," Rosa said. "Wait just a second."

In a minute, she was at the ramp with a cup of Ramona's coffee and a muffin. Chance met her at the top and kissed her deeply.

"Thank you, babe," he said. "You reminded me of Julie in the window."

"Bittersweet, huh?" Rosa said. "I could see it in your eyes."

"I better move," Chance said and turned toward the swaying ramp.

"Not so fast," Rosa said, "Jake, your helper, called. He wants to meet at the house at noon today. What should I do?"

"Call him back and tell him none of the doors are locked," Chance said. "If the cops will let him in, he can go for it."

"Okay," Rosa said and turned her rounded rump toward Chance, who slapped it and backed toward him. "Hmm, do I deserve another?" she said.

Chance spanked her hard and he could tell that it tuned her on. He kissed her again and pushed her back toward the office.

-26-

SECURITY AND SEX

Each morning, Chance and Rosa tooled to the docks and Harbor Taxi to work. The business began to flourish. The evenings were consumed with crazy Jake, working on the dumpy harbor pad. Carl, Chance and Rosa attended Julie's funeral the following weekend. A Forrest Lawn affair, her family and friends were somber and remorseful. An ex-boyfriend from high school, who chased her ever since, glared at Chance from the grassy knoll surrounding the coffin before it was lowered on squeaky wheels to the bottom, where the pastor gave his final eulogy.

Chance was skeptical about attending. In some circles, being a biker was bad news enough, but being a biker under investigation for the woman's murder over-stepped the bounds of being at home with the family. It could have been treacherous, but Carl, who knew the family, attempted to clear the course for the afternoon.

This vista contained a terrible emotional twist and Chance wasn't sure how to play his hand. He worked and flirted with the girl. He had every right to be there, except that half the community thought he killed her. The tenuous day lingered longer than he would have preferred, but he stood tall and ignored the hurtful stares and under-the-breath murmurs. He was also the only male attendee at the funeral in Wranglers, cowboy boots, a long sleeve shirt, and a worn brown leather vest.

A wispy fog filtered through the trees as if reaching for Chance, pulling him back to the coast. Finally, the boyfriend approached with his chest puffed out. He was stocky, with a wide face and a long dark mustache that curved around his pursed lips. He was wearing shades and Chance watched his hands for weapons as he moved closer.

"You the guilty motherfucker?" the man grumbled under his breath.

"Some think so," Chance said, and left it at that.

"I think you're fuckin' guilty," the thick man said and his feet shifted, as if he was moving into an attack stance.

"I'm not, or I wouldn't be here." Chance said turning to face the man directly. "What are you gonna do about your opinion, pal?"

He deliberately stepped closer to the man. If the bastard moved, he wanted an inside shot. The man's face turned crimson. He was wearing a dark suit that looked as if it might split wide open. Carl spotted the clenching fists and twitching arm muscles, and quickly approached him from the left. The service was almost over and the somber affair was as quiet as a mouse quivering along side a freeway. The only sound was the harsh rush of traffic on Western Blvd 100 yards to the east.

"Jimmy," Carl said quietly, "he didn't do it."

"Prove it," Jimmy spat. He was looking up at Chance's wide form and beginning to doubt his fighting confidence. Carl broke the ice. He grabbed Jimmy's arm and tugged him back from the confrontation with Chance.

Chance knew that if he kicked the pushy bastard's ass, it wouldn't go well with the local cops. All they wanted was one stinkin' excuse to take him down. The reverend made his final gesture to lower the coffin and people lined up to shovel soft turf on the ornate polished casket. The service was over and the crowd moved toward their cars.

Rosa took the opportunity to depart and pulled at Chance's vest. He turned away from Jimmy for the first time and faced Rosa's warm lovely features. She stepped up to him and their lips met. The touch took the fire out of Chance's eyes like a sponge sucking up spilled whiskey.

From time to time, Kate Norton pulled up to the office to report on the case and see Chance. It was awkward for Chance, but he couldn't avoid the meetings. Rosa knew little of his flirtatious relationship with the cop, but suspected that there was some chemistry brewing.

Chance didn't know how he felt about the buttoned-down cop. He didn't know whether there was deep attraction or he was more concerned for her welfare. She was a friend and his only inside connection to the police force and source of any information that surfaced on the three murders he was accused of committing. If anything happened to her, his life would turn to hell.

After work, Chance headed home with Rosa in her pickup and met squirrelly Jake at the house. Rosa made a large pot of wonderful soup while they tore the doors off the house and replaced them. Everything had to go. A small cylindrical turret contained the battered front door and a tiny foyer. With sledgehammers and pry bars, they ripped the form, the door, and the flooring off the front of the house. Jake rented a jackhammer, and Chance spent an afternoon beating the three concrete steps, leading to the door, into gravel. Jake drew up sketches of the stucco Spanish home without it.

His sketches showed French doors replacing a small window looking out at the harbor and a deck for afternoon relaxation, and evening drinks. Rosa kept the kitchen functional while removing the tile from the counters, which Jake's wife planned to replace. Chance could almost sense his life settling, yet terrifying uncertainty surrounded it. He enjoyed finishing a project, but the thought that he might end up in jail for the rest of his life for murders he didn't commit ripped at him. He relished accomplishment, no matter how small. He enjoyed learning anything about the harbor from Carl, or carpentry from Jake.

A new door and frame were carefully fitted into the living room, surrounded by glass blocks, and together, they knocked out the dining room window. Chance learned the ugly job of tearing away stucco that rattled at the structure of the home until there was enough room for the French doors to be installed.

Like many young men stumbling into the vast realm of life's endeavors, Chance was insecure. Harleys were his first path of learning. He may have looked like a grubby biker on the outside, but inside, he was a student who learned through welding, rebuilding carburetors, fabrication, and engine rebuilding. Each bike he built nurtured his creative nature and abilities. Jake's wife, Marge, came over on the weekends and worked on the kitchen. Rosa helped with every aspect of the operation and made fabulous Mexican lunches or sandwiches, which kept the crew nourished and on the job. The evenings were full of restful affection and lovemaking.

"We need more time," Rosa said as they slipped into bed at midnight on Sunday night. They spent the entire day tearing five layers of linoleum off the kitchen floor.

"You're right, baby," Chance said, crawling into bed and into her for some warm lovemaking before they drifted off to sleep. Rosa tugged on Chance as he moved on top of her. His arms were tired but he held himself high and moved into her slowly at first. The evening air was warm on his back as he slithered deeper into her and she began to relax and release a powerful orgasm. She pulled Chance closer and they melted together. She was arching and crying out. She enjoyed his size and weight like a sexy blanket that gave much more than warmth.

Chance kissed her neck softly as his cock French kissed the very depths of her body. There was something about her climaxes that turned Chance on even more. It had to do with the way their bodies meshed and held so tight, the manner in which her pussy enveloped him, and the tender touch of her flesh against his. He could feel himself rocking to an explosion as she screamed and simultaneously they fired sensual rockets into the starry sky.

Chance lifted himself off her carefully and comfortably slid to her side. He held back the covers and watched her naked form breathe, the shape of her lovely round globes panting against the night air and her dark eyes as she turned to him, a look of deep satisfaction and love caressing her lips and sparkling eyes.

"I want more," Rosa said breathing heavily.

"So do it," Chance said running his hand softly over her thigh.

"But we can't tonight," Rosa moaned, "We need the sleep for work tomorrow."

"Oh, screw it," Chance chided, "let's party."

"We can't," she said poking him in the stomach, "You know that."

"Jake has classes the first couple of days of the week," Chance said. "Let's take a break from the house tomorrow night."

"Please," she said, rolling against him. They were asleep in minutes.

The next morning began as scheduled. Rosa got out of bed and they showered together. While she put on make-up, Chance pulled his bike out of the garage and fired it to life. They putted over to Ramona's for muffins and coffee, and shared a breakfast burrito at Mando's. Chance made a point to go inside Ramona's every morning and hug Mari's mom. Carl was waiting with a list of clients to service when they arrived at Harbor Taxi.

"Hey," Carl shouted, "we got shit to do."

"Yeah, yeah," Chance said, pulling up to his designated spot and anchoring the bike to a loop he welded to a steel support. "I suppose we're burnin' daylight."

Ten minutes passed before the oil rig workers arrived and Chance made a record breaking run to the offshore rig through murky swells. As he returned, he recognized Kate's unmarked sedan parked on the wharf. She was standing on the bottom of the ramp on the swaying landing.

"Hey," Chance said jumping off the tire-protected transom to the dock,"what's up?"

"He's out of the hospital and home," Kate said somberly.

Together, they walked up the ramp and toward her car. For the first time in a week, an evil spell of uncertainty and insecurity engulfed him once more.

"What have you found out?" Chance asked.

"I can't get much support from the crew," Kate muttered dejectedly. "They want to believe you're the one. They won't pursue him. They've all worked with the guy for 20 or more years."

"Has anyone been to his home?" Chance said.

"That's another problem.," Kate kicked at the dust at her feet on the concrete, then looked at Chance.

"He's married. We don't know how much his wife knows about his affairs. He must have another place somewhere and we don't know where it is."

"Is he on duty yet?" Chance asked, watching a black and white pull to a stop at the corner of a warehouse a quarter mile up the street. "Does he know you're investigating him?"

"There's another problem," Kate said. "He knows, somebody snitched us off, but no, he's not on duty yet. He went home to recuperate."

"I suppose you're the brunt of all the accusations," Chance said, studying her body language. She looked mentally beat.

"I missed you this weekend," Kate said, "I would like to be able to call more."

"You wanna have a threesome?" Chance said with a smirk on his face.

"Goddamnit Chance!" Her features brightened and she blushed. "I didn't mean that."

"Let's have lunch tomorrow," Chance said. "Whatta ya say?"

"I'll look forward to it," she smiled, but there was still concern in her usually bright blue eyes.

"What kind of shape is he in?" Chance asked, turning the conversation back to Fernandez. "Is he mobile?"

"I don't know," Kate shrugged reluctantly. "They took him home in an ambulance. A couple of officers were there to meet him."

"You're on your own with this, aren't you?"

"That's the way I feel. Even Lieutenant Reed is holding his mud."

"What the hell are they waiting for?" Chance spat in the direction of the cop car at the end of the block. "They wanta see another girl murdered?"

"I don't know," Kate said. "I'm sure they don't want that. They're under a lot of pressure from the city, but they want you to fall, so they don't have to think about it anymore. It's the easy way out."

"Are there any women on the squad other than yourself?" Chance asked, trying to get her investigative juices flowing. "Maybe a woman would be more responsive?"

"I can't talk to anyone without arising suspicions. Anyone who talks to me is automatically a traitor."

"You need to be very careful. "Stay in touch with me constantly. It's okay to call."

He pulled her behind the Taxi building and hugged her. She held him tightly, not wanting to let go. They walked quietly back to her sedan. As she slipped into her cruiser, she lowered her window and Chance leaned on the doorframe. One more inspiration came to mind, but he wasn't sure how to approach it.

"You know, a good investigator always finds a way around a problem. Hell, don't you want to join the FBI?" He patted her door-frame and headed back to the office.

"You're right," she muttered, starting the car. She pulled out of the parking space and he watched as she rolled up the street.

"Is everything okay?" Rosa asked as he entered the office.

"The cop is out of the hospital," Chance said. "I'll tell you the rest at lunch."

Rosa touched Chance's arm across the tall counter in the office of Harbor Taxi. He leaned over it and kissed her.

"Does she want to see you?"

"I asked her to have a threesome with us."

Rosa jumped out of her chair and came around the counter after him.

"You bastard!" she shouted, knowing that he was joking. Sorta.

«« — »»

Joe Fernandez wasn't a bad cop. He was as corrupt as possible within his means for 30 years on the force. The ambulance pulled up in front of his two-story stucco box in Torrance, a track home on a cul de sac. It represented so much, yet so little happiness to Joe. Officers Grey and Stengle were waiting by the front door with his white wife of 25 years. She was still in a bathrobe and her hair was in pink curlers. She visited Joe in the hospital daily, but was still upset over his injuries. As soon as Grey pulled up, she started on him.

"Why wasn't that man arrested for attacking Joe?" she sputtered through puffy lips. She was grossly overweight, and had been for the last 20 years, ever since their third child was born.

"It's still under investigation," Grey said indicating a great deal of concern. It was a common phrase used to ward off further questioning by family members or citizens asking stupid questions. He didn't know what Joe was telling his wife.

Grey was more concerned about the allegations that Joe might be involved in the murders. It bothered him like finding out his son was a car thief. Joe was a co-worker and there was a code in those circumstances, but what happened to the girls was unacceptable.

Margaret Fernandez stood on the short square lawn while the EMT's moved to the stern of the ambulance and prepared to remove the gurney with Joe securely strapped in place. She was wearing fuzzy pink slippers, a slip, and a terrycloth bathrobe over it. She had no makeup on and held her fifth cup of black coffee in her pudgy hand. She was mad, mad at Joe for what happened, mad at the suspect, mad at the force for not forcing Joe to retire, mad at all the women Joe had, and mad at her kids for being slugs, like she was. She grew up in a middle class family and did poorly in school, knowing full well that she would land some sap, get pregnant, marry and watch television and eat donuts for the rest of her life. Her every wish came true.

She was especially ecstatic to score a cop, who was fooling around on his fiancée when they met on a cool California morning in a donut shop. She was just 19 and it was the only time in her life she looked hot. Her boobs were full and erect. She had 19-year-old skin that was soft and supple, and her curves were already on the voluptuous side. From the very minute they met, she lied about birth control and shortly after their second encounter, she was pregnant.

He wasn't particularly attracted to her. She was a hottie with large breasts and a prime ass, but it was growing. She was his "nooner" a couple of times a week in odd locations, like a garage he was sent to investigate, or a drug dealer's apartment. She felt good, but didn't have a damn thing to talk about, wasn't going to college and had no ambition or talents, just nice tits and a soft ass. His fiancée, Maria, was about to graduate from two years at Long Beach Community College and move onto nursing school. She was bright and articulate, loved to watercolor and exercise. Margaret made a point to announce her pregnancy at the station and word spread to Maria, who immediately broke off the engagement.

Joe bought the home in Torrance shortly thereafter, and they move in just before his first son was born. She constantly harangued him about love, then a home for his son, then marriage. He avoided the marriage end of the bargain until the second kid was born, then he attempted to make a deal with her. No more kids and they would get married. During the costly extravagant get together to impress her high school friends and family, she announced that she was pregnant again, to the congregation, not him. He was locked in for life.

They hauled him out of the ambulance and the wheels automatically lowered beneath the gurney. He was strapped securely and given a painkiller before leaving the hospital. His ribs needed five weeks to heal and the slightest movement was terribly painful. The EMTs carefully rolled the suspended gurney to the curb and lifted it onto the sidewalk.

"How you doin', brother?" Officer Grey asked.

"Smarts some," Joe said, looking at him as if to say that he wanted to know more, but he didn't dare start asking questions. He was nervous and in pain.

"We're still watchin' that guy," Stengle said, moving to Joe's side.

Stengle was a white blond. Most of the force was made up of Indians, blacks or Hispanics. He was a young white guy with a false notion of the force and politics, but he was learning and stumbling as he went.

"He won't get away with this shit."

A bead of sweat formed on Joe's forehead from the pain and stress. He sensed he couldn't trust Officer Grey and the new kid could be a loaded cannon pointed in the wrong direction. He needed help, but wasn't sure which way to turn.

"That new cop is trying to bury me," Joe said.

"Yeah," Stengle mouthed, "she's a real bitch. I been watchin' her. No one talks to her anymore."

"Too bad she can't have an accident or be transferred," Joe said, then wished he hadn't said it in front of the big black officer.

"Yeah!" Stengle said. He was tall and gangly, and had a bright youthful face that registered every emotion.

Grey and Stengle helped lift the gurney into the wide front door and up the stairs to Joe's master bedroom. The house was basically the same as when he bought it, except harshly worn from three kids ripping up and down the stairs, jumping on the furniture, and rolling on the carpeting. The kids didn't really know their parents. Joe abandoned the house emotionally after the third kid was born. He didn't even take the time off duty to go to the hospital. From that point on, he came home late at night, got up in the morning and went back to work. The more his wife complained, the more extra hours he took. There were plenty of fresh squeezes on the streets. He didn't need the ever-increasing fat at home.

Margaret accepted her fate. Her life revolved around coffee, donuts, soap operas, and taking the kids to school. She had no education to share with them and didn't choose to learn, even from her kids, although initially each kid tried, but couldn't get through attention grabbing soap operas. Her only saving grace was her willingness to allow her kids to seek the companionship of others. When they wanted to go someplace with another family, she never stopped them, and she was always home to make sandwiches or to run them to the doctor. Her desire to have a home and kids became her solitary confinement.

By the fifth year of their marriage she started to fight with Joe, to bitch and moan about everything. When vacation time rolled around, he took "fishing trips" with the boys. She was never invited.

Joe dreaded being stuck in his own master bedroom for five weeks and plotted escape plans immediately. During the years and the bimbos he chased, caught, and fought, he became wary of women. He wanted nothing to do with them except sex. Broads came to the station, told their folks, tried to find out where he lived, and wrote letters to his boss and wife.

Suzanne caused him similar headaches. The girls were another reason his career never advanced much. The officers said goodbye while Margaret tapped her ugly toe in the corner. Nothing about the broad was attractive. She smoked and drank coffee simultaneously. He looked at her disgustedly.

"Hand me the phone," he barked at her.

She bent over and put out the cigarette in a tray cluttered with butts. She went to the bed stand and lifted the phone.

"This is just peachy," she grumbled, and Joe knew that it would lead to a lengthily sniveling harangue. "Two beds in the same bedroom. We don't sleep together anyway, what difference does it make?"

It wasn't really a question.

"I need to make a call," Joe said and indicated for her to leave. "Is there anything to eat?"

"Donuts," she said, turning her back to Joe as she walked out and closed the door behind her.

-27-

Not All Bikers Are Cool

Two weeks passed uneventfully. Investigator Kate Norton rolled toward home in her unmarked sedan. She was in a strange, disconnected emotional state. She knew that Chance was supportive, but she couldn't be seen with him. Her coworkers turned against her, and her family wasn't in the area. She was alone, unaided, and on the wrong side of the issue.

In intellectual circumstances, it could be indicative of a simple disagreement. In the corporate world, it could mean a job loss. But between cops, it might become a measure for deadly force. She believed in the biker, even if he was the San Pedro Police Department's number one murder suspect.

In her studies, she came across similar situations within the Mafia or outlaw motorcycle clubs. Members turned up on the wrong side of a quandary and ended up capped in the desert or wrapped in chains and tossed in a bay. It gave her chills to think about it happening to her by a fellow officer. She needed a compadre on the inside and she thought about Chance's previous suggestion to ferret out the women on the force and see if one was willing to stand against the tide of a potentially lethal dispute.

It was a treacherous challenge she faced nervously. She certainly didn't want to jeopardize another officer's career, or worse, her life. The whole notion of brotherhood within the ranks of police officers was crumbling before her eyes as she drove along Ocean Blvd toward her apartment. She was young and unknown on the force, still an outsider in her co-workers' eyes. Brotherhood was one thing. Young women being raped and perhaps murdered by a cop was another. They suspected the biker; she suspected the cop.

She missed her contact with Chance. She felt that Rosa was good for him in the short term, but that the warm sexy Hispanic was a deterrent to her ability to reach out to him. It was a gut feeling she couldn't deny. It usurped a connection she wanted and needed to foster. She questioned whether her feelings for Chance were clouding her vision of the case.

"That's ridiculous," she muttered to herself as she drove along the coast.

Kate lived in Belmont Shore in a small duplex near the beach, where she could run and even walk to the gym on 2nd Street. Restaurants, coffee shops, and stores were abundant. The area was a packed mass of small homes on straight narrow streets surrounded by bays and the broad oceanside beaches of Long Beach. As she neared downtown Belmont Shore area, Ocean Blvd split, and one leg continued along the coast down a three-block-wide peninsula that ended where Alamitos Bay flowed into the Pacific. To the left, Ocean Blvd wove across the interior of Belmont Shore between the lowlands and Belmont Heights, where large homes were securely planted on wide, palm-lined streets.

She usually drove along the quiet peninsula strip and turned left on her street, but occasionally, she scooted into the center of the Belmont Shore commercial area to hit a store or the gym on the way home. As she was pondering her decision to work out, she heard the buzz of a sport bike near her car. It didn't have the threatening rumble of a Harley like Chance's scooter, but a terrible whine like a monster bumblebee bearing down on an unsuspecting target. The bike came so close, the rider's black leathers filled the window on her left. Then there was a crack and her window shattered.

She veered to the right and her car struck a broad grassy medium and crashed into a thick robust palm in the center. It all happened so fast that the motorcycle was gone before she had the opportunity to look for a license plate

The sedan struck the curb with a violent impact, snapping the pinion shaft on the front right wheel, crushing the wheel face down in the grass. At 40 mph, without a split second of braking time, the vehicle center-punched the palm with tremendous force, throwing

Kate forward in her seat. The entire bench seat ripped from its foundation. The right end of the seat careened forward as the air bag inflated. The radiator was driven into the engine, spouting streams of steam gushing as the copper tubing buckled and snapped.

Kate slammed into the airbag and her hand slipped from the steering wheel. Just as quickly, the airbag deflated and she bounced back, snapping her spine like a bullwhip. She reached for the door handle and yanked it. The door popped open violently and wrenched against the hinges as it rocked back and forth. Kate snapped her seat belt free and dove to the grassy surface beside the car. She rolled clear then laid very still. She was in shock, stunned, and unable to discern the level of her injuries. She could smell gasoline and heard terrible screeching as other cars collided in the street. A young man ran to her side.

"Are you all right?" he shouted as much in shock as she was. "I saw that biker. There was no license. What the hell was he thinking?"

Kate lay very still, then turned to her first aid training and began to analyze her own condition. She tried to relax as much as possible.

"Can I get you anything?" the young man asked.

"Not yet," Kate said. "Gimme a second to see how I'm doing."

She started to move her limbs and test for pain or broken bones, nothing so far. She could hear the sound of a siren approaching in the background. She began to pat herself down as she tried to remain very still, when she felt a lump in her side. It was her sweater pocket and her cell phone. She yanked it out quickly and handed it to the young homosexual quivering above her.

"Here," she said, "Press the arrow until you see 'Chance' in the display. Call that number and tell him where I am."

"Gladly," the young college man said in his light effeminate voice. He stood up and looked at the phone as he scrolled through a couple of names before reaching Chance.

«« — »»

Chance and Rosa arrived at the construction-battered house. Chance showered as Rosa scrounged up supper. She worked in the tattered kitchen without the use of a counter or sink.

Jake's wife reworked the underpinnings of the counter to apply new tile. The stovetop would have to suffice for the time being. The daylight savings time weather was still warm and the sun was just beginning to change the colors of the buildings and boats on the harbor. She was pleased and excited. She enjoyed her time with Chance and hoped for another long night filled with titillating love-making. She tingled with anticipation.

As Chance showered, he pondered the myriad of projects and threats facing him and his new abode. The threat of prosecution hung over him like a poisonous veil. On the other hand, his home repairs were similar to building a bike. He thought about the various aspects, the budget and what he needed from the hardware store. Then a cop would cruise by, and he wondered if his freedom was in jeopardy.

Tonight, he planned to put it all out of his mind and concentrate on Rosa. He was torn by his nature. The two most important aspects of his jangled life were dangling before him: sex and creative accomplishment. Sex always won. He admitted to himself that the touch of a woman beat the touch of chrome any day. The seaside abode fell into the same category. Compared to sanding and painting primer on a door jam, sex was the winner. The phone rang in the kitchen and Rosa answered it.

"Hello," the voice said in a strange quivering tone." Is Chance in?"

"Yes," Rosa replied. "Hold on for a second."

"Baby!" Rosa hollered, "There's a call for you."

Chance picked up the line in the bedroom and Rosa hung up.

"Yeah?" Chance said.

"Hold on," the voice on the phone said almost shaking.

"Chance," Kate said, "I've been in an accident. I think I'm okay. Can you come?"

"Of course," Chance said. "Where are you?"

She gave him the address as an officer from the Long Beach Police Department ran to her side.

"I'll be right there," Chance said and hung up.

He threw on some clothes and headed toward the kitchen.

"Let's go, baby,"

Chance said, grabbing Rosa. "We'll be eating out tonight. Kate's been in an accident. I hope it was accident."

"You can go," Rosa said, "I'll wait here."

"No way," Chance said, pulling her toward the door. "I'm never leaving you alone again until we get to the bottom of this."

"Okay, okay," Rosa said, and grabbed her purse. "Will you drive?"

"Sure, babe," Chance said, heading toward the door.

«« — »»

"How do you feel?" Officer Applegate asked leaning down toward Kate.

Kate blinked and looked at the soft features of woman officer staring down at her.

"I think I'm okay," Kate said, "I'm resting. You might want to check my purse."

The officer turned and went to the car still smoldering with steam hissing out around the crumpled hood, and the smell of oil and gasoline was permeating the area.

"You're a cop?" Applegate asked. "Would you like me to call an ambulance?"

"No, no," Kate said with a deep sigh, "a friend is coming. I'll get up in a second. I work for the Harbor division as an investigator."

"Do you want me to call them?" Applegate asked.

"No, that's okay," Kate said. "I will, in a bit."

Kate held her hand out to indicate that she wanted a lift to her feet and officer Applegate obliged.

"How long have you worked at Harbor?" Applegate asked.

"Not long," Kate said, "I'm on my first murder case."

"Don't tell me," Applegate said.

"Yeah," Kate said, "that's the case. You'll meet the number one suspect if you hang around. He's the only friend I currently have, and a damn good one."

"I don't get it," Applegate said pushing her hat back on her head.

"It'll take a while to explain," Kate said.

"I know one of the officers in that department," Applegate said, and her awkward gaze indicated that there was something more to the statement.

"Wouldn't be a female officer?" Kate asked, hoping for a connection.

"Yes," Applegate said.

A tow truck pulled up as Kate gave the slender officer the rundown on the basics of the case without any mention of Joe Fernandez.

"So what's the problem?" Applegate said.

"What do you mean?" Kate responded.

"What's the problem with the case?" Applegate said, as a motorcycle cop pulled up and spread flares in the street. "Who killed the girls if your friend didn't?"

Kate looked at her tea-like brown eyes. She was still stunned from the accident and leaned against Applegate's black and white somberly. She couldn't distinguish whether she was thinking straight or not.

"Have you ever had a problem with the department?" Kate asked, "How long have you worked there?"

"I've been on the force for five years," Applegate said, but suddenly her confidence waned. She looked around like someone who wanted to find busy work. She was avoiding the question.

"Listen," Kate said, "thanks for your help. Chance will be here anytime to give me a hand, if you need to get moving. Here's my card. Call me, if you ever need a Pedro investigator."

Applegate brightened, relieved to avoid the question and handed Kate her card. Just then, Chance pulled up with Rosa in her white truck.

"Are you all right?" Chance said, coming to her side.

"I'm shaky," Kate said. "This is officer Applegate."

"How do you do," Chance said, extending his hand. "Thanks for looking after her."

"No problem," Applegate said shaking his hand with the force of a guy. Chance noted her manly grip. She had a pretty face, but was plump in a muscular way.

Applegate raised her eyebrows at Kate regarding Chance. "Hope you're okay," she said, "and call me if I can help with anything."

"Thanks," Kate said, with Rosa on one side and Chance on the other, leading her to the truck.

Chance pulled away and jogged to the driver's side. Rosa slid Kate into the center and she appreciated the warmth and closeness.

"Let's take you to the hospital and get you checked out."

"I don't know," Kate said. "I just need some rest."

Chance didn't like the smell of the accident. "Let's take a cruise past your house first. I want you to pick up a couple of things and stay with us for a couple of days. Which street do you live on?" Chance asked, watching the cluttered traffic of the busy beach area.

"I live on Clairmont," Kate said.

"Is there an alley and a rear entrance?"

"Sure," Kate said, "we'll go in from the back."

They pulled up a couple of doors from her duplex and Rosa got out of the cab.

"Don't get out just yet," Chance said. "I want to look around first."

Chance wandered between two old Spanish-style buildings on the narrow streets. He ran up the stairs to the apartment and inspected the door. He couldn't see any sign of forced entry. He didn't try the door, but slipped back down the steps. A blue-haired lady was watering her plants next door. She was wearing a smock that was as bright as the flowers she cared for.

"Excuse me ma'am," Chance said. "Have you seen anyone going upstairs?"

"She's hardly home," the woman replied. She was evidently permanently bent over, but tried to straighten some to look up at Chance. She was no more that 5-foot tall with thin white hair that still contained a magnificent wave.

"A motorcyclist came by earlier and went in. She's not there?" She was immediately concerned she might be talking out of turn.

"No," Chance said, "she's not home, but she's okay. She won't be home for a week. Could you keep an eye on the place for her?"

"Oh sure, sure," the woman said, curious as hell.

Chance walked back to the car. "Do you have a biker boyfriend?" he asked Kate.

"Not until today," Kate said, "and he's pissed at me."

"He stopped by," Chance said. "Let me have one of your cards. I may have an old woman who can keep an eye on your place."

They drove Kate to the ER at Long Beach Memorial Hospital, where she was thoroughly checked over. She was tired and terribly bruised, but would survive. As they pulled away from the hospital and the sun dropped from the sky, another warm night engulfed the city.

"I'll be okay," Kate reported as they drove along Anaheim Boulevard toward the Long Beach Freeway.

"I'd like to say that it would be safe to take you home," Chance said, "but I can't and you know it."

"You're staying with us," Rosa said. Chance and Rosa had already shared the sexual disappointment while waiting in the vast sterile hospital lobby.

"Rosa said that she'll take you to work in the morning," Chance said, "but that's the only time I'm letting her out of my sight."

"We want you to stay with us for a week," Rosa said.

"That's impossible," Kate said, "I can't do that."

"We may need to stick together," Chance said, "at least until we get to the bottom of this. He may have an accomplice. That's not a good sign."

"I need you to find out about sport bike clubs, or where sport bike riders hang out," Chance said. "Let's move as fast as possible. If we can wrap this up before Fernandez is back on his feet, we may save a life. You need to work on a connection in the department."

Kate pulled Officer Applegate's card out of her pocket and examined it. "I have a remote connection," she said, "that I need to follow up on."

"That female Long Beach cop?" Chance said, "is she a lesbian?"

"I never thought of that," Kate said, "but maybe that's the connection with the Harbor Division she wouldn't mention. I'll call her from the house."

They drove over the Vincent Thomas Bridge in silence. Chance was concerned about his pad. If the rider had been to the Kate's apartment, he knew where Chance lived, and with only a couple of doors repaired, he had easy access. Chance thought about checking with his neighbors. He also reminisced about the quiet days he had before Fernandez was released from the hospital. He knew things were going to heat up like a 4th of July party in New Orleans. On one hand, he was looking forward to the confrontation; on the other, he was terrified for the two women sitting next to him. He couldn't tolerate either one of them being injured.

He knew in his gambler's heart that if something happened to either one, he would go off like an Uzi on full automatic. There would be no trial. Gut instinct would prevail.

The Palos Verdes Peninsula was aglow with sparkling lights beneath them and a Carnival Cruise ship slowly motored out of the harbor like a party afloat, but they weren't in a partying mood. Chance pulled up to the house. The usual black and white was gone. He asked the girls to wait in the truck as he ran across the street and asked his neighbor if he'd seen any activity around the house.

Tony was a retired stevedore who had two sons, in their 30s, living with him. It was cool with him. He enjoyed the company. One of his sons worked on the docks and the other was an architect in training. He poked his head out and said he hadn't seen anything out of the ordinary.

Chance jogged around the rundown home, looking for anything out of the ordinary. That was a tough call, since the place was already a mess. Some of the windows were still broken; others wouldn't stay shut unless you nailed them. On a wild hair, he lifted one of the living room windows slowly. There was a terrible natural gas smell permeating the interior of the house.

Chance moved from window to window, carefully opening one after the other. There were few screens left. Those remaining were torn and rusting. After airing the house, he climbed in a window and carefully moved through the dump. The flexible stove gas line had been clipped and he discovered a pack of matches duct-taped to the bottom of the back door, so if they had opened it, the matches would have ignited and the gas-filled house would have exploded. Chance removed the matches and turned off the gas.

He let the house air out for another five minutes before signaling the girls to return.

"Is everything okay?" Rosa asked.

"Smelled a little like gas in here," Chance said, "but I aired it out."

Kate looked at him inquisitively, but didn't question. She didn't need any more bad crime news. She had enough for one day.

"Make yourself comfortable," Chance said, "If that's possible in this dump."

He was perplexed. He needed to get to a hardware store and replace the malleable line between the stove and the wall valve, but he didn't dare leave the girls alone. He picked up the phone and called the local take-out Chinese food joint and ordered some chow to be delivered. Rosa fixed up the bed so that Kate could sit and be comfortable. Kate reached for the phone and called Applegate.

"Hello?" Officer Applegate said.

"Officer," this is Kate Norton. You helped me with my accident today."

"I remember," Applegate said, "How are you feeling?"

"Just tired and bruised," Kate said. "I was lucky."

"You were," Applegate said. "did you hear the rest?"

"What do you mean?" Kate said.

"You're apartment exploded about an hour ago," Applegate said. "You must have been at the hospital and didn't get the message."

"You're kidding!" Kate said, shocked.

"Someone has it out for you."

"That's what I want to talk to you about," Kate said, shaking with fatigue and emotional stress.

"I'm off tomorrow," Applegate said. "Why don't you come over for lunch?"

"I'll call you once I have a new cruiser," Kate said.

"That sounds like a plan. I'll look forward to it," Applegate said, her voice audibly brightened, and she hung up.

Kate looked at the receiver. She didn't know whether her feelings were real or if she was just lost after a tough, out-of-control day. A new edge to the mayhem took place. Her rental was destroyed, her car wrecked, she had no support from the SPPD and a murderer had her in his sights. She wondered if she could sleep at all.

-28-

One Wrong Move

The morning emerged like the crack of a whip to a bound prisoner. Chance awoke with a start and jumped out of bed. Rosa stirred and her big dark eyes fluttered open.

"Is everything alright?"

"Yep," Chance said. "No time to lose today. We've got to roll."

"I'm right behind you," Rosa said and tugged on his hand.

Chance turned and looked at the gorgeous Hispanic woman in his bed. For a lingering moment, he was at peace, snagged by her form, those beautiful shapely tits peeking out from her nightgown. He leaned down, pulled the nightgown aside and kissed one of her large round nipples, then kissed her lips deeply. Her flickering eyes told him volumes. She was there to assist at any cost.

Another lump in the king-sized bed moved and groaned, and then Kate sat up immediately. She turned and saw Chance in his boxers standing over Rosa on the other side. Chance looked at her and smiled briefly. Kate was wearing one of his T-shirts.

"Good morning," Kate said instinctively, although she suspected the morning wasn't going to be all peaches and flowers.

"Good morning," Chance said. "We best get moving."

Rosa looked at Kate as she eyed Chance's muscular form. She saw the same longing in Kate's sparkling blue eyes and tugged at Chance's hand once more. Chance looked at Rosa's naturally tanned features and she nodded toward Kate and whispered, "Give her a hug."

Chance moved around the corner of the bed and caught Kate in stride. As he pulled her close she looked up at his gruff but kind features, and she melted into him for several long moments. She held the big man for all he was worth. Her apartment was destroyed and someone had attempted to kill her. She was far from home, family, and friends were non-existent, except for Chance and his girl.

"Together," Chance said, "we'll get this bastard."

The thought was encouraging, but her presence in his arms was touching a different, deeper chord. She liked the man and her thoughts reached way beyond the terrifying obstacles that filled her life. She liked his smell, the form of his chest and his drive, but his comment brought back the plight of the day. She squeezed him once more, gazed into his seaweed- green eyes, stood on her tiptoes, and kissed his unshaven cheek.

Chance scratched the back of his neck in wonderment as she darted into the head. Two knockouts in his bedroom at the same time, yet he felt so many emotions rushing around the room, he couldn't comprehend them. Some were so good; others so treacherous. He had to get to work. Rosa would drive Kate to the police station, and blast back to work. He needed answers and was concerned about leaving his pad unprotected. He didn't know which way to turn, but he needed to take a piss something awful. Rosa slipped by him and into the kitchen. The stove still didn't work, but she toasted wheat bread and sliced fruit for protein shakes, one of Chance's mainstays.

Chance hit the head and then went outside to check the perimeter. Nothing seemed odd or out of the ordinary, but he knew better. He pulled his chopper out of the garage and into the back yard. All three moved around the construction site he called a home without a word. Kate dressed in her only clothes and thought about finding another undercover car, her pending lunch with Applegate, and her destroyed apartment. Rosa fixed breakfast and pondered how she could help. Chance showered and wondered about the sport bike rider and how to find the sonuvabitch and his connection to the cop, if there was one. He burst out of the shower still dripping and wrapped in a towel.

"Hey Kate!" he hollered down the hall. "How can we keep an eye on Fernandez's home? I'd love to catch a rice grinder parked out front."

"I'll check into it," Kate said, putting on make-up and sipping coffee. "The complexion of this case is changing."

"Yeah," Chance agreed, walking briskly into the kitchen while pulling an old run sweatshirt over his head. "Let's roll."

Rosa leapt up from the table and darted to the back of the house to change, carrying her protein shake with her. Chance pulled his wet hair back and gulped at his coffee.

"Do you ever shave?" Kate asked kidding him.

"Once a week, whether I need it or not,"

Chance said gobbling his toast. "Let's see how the cop shop handles you this morning."

"Could be interesting," Kate said. "Somebody is nervous about this case. They're breaking down."

"We need to find that biker," Chance said, "and hope that we still have a home after work. He was here yesterday, cut the gas line to the stove and set a spark-trigger on the back door."

"I wondered what took you so long to get into the house last night," Kate said.

Rosa emerged from the trashed dining room like a bright star on a cloudy night. She appeared as fresh as a new blossom, bright and upbeat, in her form-fitting Levis, a colorful top, and brilliant candy-red high heels.

"I'm ready," she said.

"Wow!" Chance said, and led them to Rosa's truck. He kissed them both goodbye and straddled his scooter. He fired it to life and thought about following them to the police station, but Kate was armed and trained for these situations.

Chance pulled the rapping and popping chopper out of his backyard and into the street. It felt good to let out the clutch and sense the freedom and oneness with his machine. Nothing in the world felt like that motorcycle. He could aim it in any direction and just peel out, but not now, not today. He'd be shot if he left the city limits and tagged with murder. He turned right on Signal and rode to the end of the peninsula. Carl met him at the wooden porch.

"Big day," he said, gleaming with enthusiasm . "Where's Rosa?"

"She'll be right here. She had to take Kate to the station," Chance said. "We'll explain at lunch. What's up?"

"I've got two runs to the oil islands, first thing," Carl said, and pointed to several boxes of supplies.

"I'm all over it," Chance said, locking his scooter to his heavy welded ring sunk into the pavement.

He bounded down the ramp to the dock with an armload of boxes. He checked over his 35-foot water taxi and fired it to life, as it rocked in the mild seas, moored to the equally swaying wooden dock. Chance grabbed a dolly out of the back of the idling boat and made another trip to the top of the ramp.

The cop shop was less than three miles from Chance's home, opposite the China Seas shipping yard. She pulled into the parking lot and Kate stepped out of the cab.

"Will you be all right?" Rosa asked. "I can hang here as long as you need me."

"No," Kate answered, "I'll be fine. Just do me a favor. Call me when you get to work. I think we all need to stay in touch."

"Sure," Rosa said. "I need to get some gas, but then I'll drive directly to Harbor Taxi."

"Thanks for everything," Kate said and shut the door. She entered the station from the rear entrance and met the female clerk, changing in the locker room.

"Kate, are you all right?" she asked as she buttoned up the starched collar to her navy blue uniform. It was the first time, since the first girl was murdered, that this woman spoke to her.

"Yeah, I'm fine; just some bumps and bruises," Kate said. She grabbed a clean blouse out of her locker and dressed.

There was a knock on the locker room door. "Norton? The chief wants to speak with you," came a male voice.

"I'll be right there."

Lt. Reed had the face texture of a stale prune. He had wrinkles on wrinkles and he wasn't that old, maybe 58. He looked at Kate across his wooden desk with a somber glare.

"What do you make of what happened?" he asked.

"What do you have on it?" Kate returned, eyeing him quizzically. She cleaned up the best she could, but wasn't comfortable in day-old underwear. It pissed her off that it took someone to nearly kill her before she received a modicum of compassion from her co-workers.

"Goddamnit, Norton," Lt. Reed snapped, "I'll ask the questions."

"You're the fuckin' boss," Kate said and stood up abruptly. "I've had the ass around here for too long. Why should I tell you anything?"

"Listen," Reed stumbled. The other officers watched over their cubicle barriers and through blinds into the office. "I know you've had a rough go of your first major case."

"That's a goddamn understatement," Kate muttered.

"Look, I'm only going to take so much of your shit," Reed hissed through clenched teeth. He wasn't one to give in, but he knew she had a break coming.

"I don't have much on your attack or the guy who blew up your apartment. We're running numbers and cases to find out if we have anything on any similar attacks. Do you think it has anything to do with the other girls?"

"In a distant sense," Kate said. "I hope this takes the heat off Hogan?"

"In a distant sense." Reed said, trying to pry thoughts out of her.

"That figures," Kate said, looking directly into Reed's watery green eyes. His eyebrows were bristle brushes of white.

"I know you have something on this case, " Reed sputtered, "and we need to know what it is?"

Kate slid forward in her chair and leaned on the edge of his desk. She had the face of a bookworm angel. She had a direct edge about her nature. It was beautiful, but not all soft and feminine.

"I don't know anything about the sport bike rider who ran me off the road," Kate said. "He blew up my apartment—I know that. Yep, I have some thoughts that I can't tell you or anyone on this force. I need some time, and I'm scared. Another girl is going down if I can't move as fast as possible."

"Look, I've got the media all over me about this case," Reed said almost pleading.

"I've got women dying, and I could be the next one," Kate spat and walked out of his office.

The young uniformed officer who graced her with niceties in the locker room approached. "We're running sport bike owners, explosive attacks, anything we can find."

Kate looked at her and nodded appreciatively. "Let me know if anything pops. I need a car."

"I'll requisition one right away," she said and returned to her desk.

Kate checked her cluttered desk and read the report on the explosion that rocked her apartment. A glob of C-4 was set near the stove with a cheap timer. It took out most of the small apartment kitchen and set the gas stove on fire. If the blast hadn't killed her, the smoke and fire would have. She set the report down in dismay. She was fearful, but even more tenuous about her co-workers. She wanted out of the station, but the streets also held treachery.

«« — »»

After dropping off Kate, Rosa peeled down Channel toward Pacific Avenue, then up to Gaffey, the next boulevard inland, to find a gas station. She was anxious to get to work. Gaffey was lined with signs of the franchise world. Every corner was plastered and plastic with Mac Donald's, Jack in the Box, KFC, and pizza joints. She pulled into Mobil station, slid out of the cab, and slipped her credit card into the pump. She whistled a light Hispanic tune while pumping the gas and watching the bustling morning traffic, taking workers from San Pedro to the maze of freeways snaking into the city. The sun was brilliant from the east and warmed her rosy cheeks as she put the nozzle back into its holster and turned to get in the truck.

As she slid in the driver's seat, a young wiry Asian kid snatched opened the passenger door and jumped in.

"Drive," he barked, pointing a stainless Walther PPK at her curvy chest. She started the truck and pulled out of the station lot.

«« — »»

Chance bobbed and weaved the crew taxi vessel back to the swaying Harbor Taxi dock. Carl was waiting at the edge. Chance threw him the bowline and noticed immediately that his facial features had changed. He shut the flathead six engine down then threw Carl the stern line.

"What's up?" Chance asked, hoping for the best, but fearing the worst.

"Rosa's not here yet," Carl said with concern.

"Did you call the cop shop?" Chance asked and his voice faded. He mentally kicked himself for letting Rosa out of his sight.

"Yep, she dropped Kate off over an hour ago. "They have every unit out looking for her truck."

"Never a dull moment," Chance said, jumping off the skiff onto the gray wooden slats of the gang plank. He embraced Carl like a son embraces his father.

"We'll find her," he said and ran toward his bike.

-29-

Duck and Run

"You don't have a prayer," Rosa said to the sweaty Asian poking the shiny pistol in her side.

"Shut up and turn left at the light!" the kid snapped with one hand grasping the dashboard.

"I just left the police department," Rosa said, flinching from the hardness of the barrel bruising her ribs. "Every cop in the city will be looking for this truck."

That startled the kid. He grimaced, as if a car had hit his dog.

"I told you to shut up!" he spouted throwing anger-induced spittle at the dash. "You had no business there. Stay where you belong." His eyes flashed from the road to her in a dismissive manner, as if she should be the out back with the cleaning ladies.

Rosa was also pissed off. She knew the kid couldn't kill her while she drove, but she didn't know their destination, and that troubled her.

"Where we going?"

"Shut the fuck up, bitch!" he said, jabbing the weapon into her ribs.

He wanted to scream. His nerves were over the edge and already colliding down a shear precipice. He thought he was helping a friend, but everything went wrong. Now he was up to his fishy gills in a mess he couldn't escape. The truck suddenly lurched and skidded, and he hadn't fastenened his seatbelt after he abducted Rosa. His torso slammed into the dashboard. She hit the brakes, and the anti-locking system jerked. He spun facing the woman he instantly determined was his warden.

The gun went off and the bullet sliced between Rosa's thighs and taught arms clutching the steering wheel as his body flew forward. He didn't intend to fire the pistol, yet. The safety belts reacted to her jolting motion. The whizzing bullet sliced through the hem of her blouse below her bra-cupped tits and slammed into and through the driver's door and out the exterior plate, splaying the tin.

Rosa grabbed the door handle and her belt release simultaneously. The cab of the truck instantaneously filled with the smell of gunpowder, which burnt her eyes. She was making the turn on 17th and hit the brakes between Gaffey and Pacific Avenue, one of the many dour sections of the long shoremens' town.

The dash caught the young man's impact and he recoiled form the shock and the blast from the pistol. He lurched at the sleeve of her frilly blouse. He snatched a handful and yanked with all he had, using the fabric to pull himself back onto the seat, while jamming the pistol into her thigh.

"I won't miss next time!" he snapped. "Drive!"

She yanked the door closed and put her hands back on the wheel. She couldn't lift her leg to press her foot on the gas, from the pain of the barrel pressed against her soft thigh. For the first time, she looked at the man who kidnapped her. In his mid twenties, he was slim and slight, but semi-muscular and wiry. His face seemed slimy and evil; his dark eyes taunted her to move. He wanted to shoot her, but he wouldn't succeed if he did. He was blistering mad and distrusted all women. She turned forward once more, avoiding his icy gaze and drove down the wide 1930s residential street, jammed bumper to bumper with middle class cars, from cheap compacts to lowered '70s primered customs. Her eyes darted from one side of the tree-lined street to the other, as if she could find someone she knew. There was no Chance.

The light was green at Pacific, and the Asian kept the barrel of the gun pressed against her. The pain was almost staggering and she grimaced at every bump in the earthquake-cracked concrete. They passed Mesa Street heading directly toward Chance's pad.

The kid pulled Rosa out of the cab and into Chance's back yard quickly. He drug her up the steps into the kitchen, but Rosa fought back, trying to break free. He slammed her against the stove and ripped her dress away from her soft boobs. She fell to the hardwood deck. He dropped to his knees and punched her in the face.

"I hate you, bitch!" he shouted and ripped her bra away, attempting to wrap it around her neck.

Rosa fought back, but he pistol-whipped her into unconsciousness. He stood up panting, looking at her bloody features. He had one chance to clear his tutor. He witnessed Joe's pain and had to do something. If he could kill the girl, the crime would surely clear the officer. He saw the anguish in his brother's eyes and had to help, but all his attempts to eliminate obstacles had failed. He had only one shot at success left.

The Asian kid stumbled down the hall dragging Rosa, his fingers digging into her upper arm like vice-grips into soft wood. Time was running out. Nothing worked. His plans crashed around him like a suicide bomber touching himself off on an empty bus. He wanted to be a cop bad. That didn't work. He wanted desperately to assist his mentor, the only man who ever believed in him, and he couldn't fail. He shoved Rosa onto the bed.

He read all the newspaper reports several times. He knew how each murder was committed, but he couldn't find it in himself to cut Rosa's wrist. He wasn't a rapist, and torture was out of his realm of thinking, but he was mad, mostly mad at himself for his lack of guts to finish the job.

Rosa's perfume was soft and warm, which piqued the kid's guilt. The sounds outside from the port and sirens in the distance drove his paranoia through the ceiling. He was as scared as a rabbit in the center lane of a freeway, who knew he could not outrun the thundering traffic bearing down on him. There was nowhere to run, nowhere to hide. Rosa was passed out on the bed, face down.

It wouldn't take any bravado to pop a cap in the back of her head and crawl out the window, like an escaping dog. He lifted the weapon, but his life was colliding around him.

«« — »»

Chance jumped on his scooter and fired her to life. The Avon tire grabbed the asphalt on the peninsula and his front 21-inch wheel jumped off the pavement in a wheelstand. He didn't know where he was going, but he was scrambling. Rosa had endured her own hell; she damn sure didn't need a taste of his. He peeled up to the intersection of Signal and 22nd Street when he felt Mark's cell phone vibrating in his vest pocket. He slammed on his rear disc brakes and the light chopper skidded to a stop.

"Kate," he said, grabbing at the phone with gloved hands.

"Every car in the city is looking for Rosa's truck," Kate said, jumping into her new unmarked unit.

"I don't know what the fuck to do!" Chance said. "I'm going to the bridge. "I don't want that bastard to get out of town."

"No, no," Kate stammered, trying to hold the phone and insert her key in the ignition. "Go home," she said instinctively. "I'll call. The bridge is covered with our units and the Highway Patrol."

"I've got to do something," Chance shouted, fumbling with the miniature phone over the rumble of his Harley.

"I'll call you in 15 minutes," Kate said. "We should have found her by then."

"If it's not too late," Chance spat and ended the call.

He was furious. He shoved the phone in his vest and peeled through the red light toward the hill directly in front of him. It was a straight stretch for a quarter mile and he flew through the next light at over a 100, then slammed on his brakes, smoking the tires for a block before hanging a right on Mesa. As he turned, he calculated that he was on 22nd and he was heading for 17th, only five blocks away.

He blew through each four-way boulevard stop and slid to the corner of 19th and Mesa, where he turned right for one block. As he spun around the corner losing traction and tearing the chrome off his exhaust, grinding it against the concrete. He saw what looked like Rosa's truck at the curb. He twisted the wick on the chopper to the stops ripping up the street, then roared up a driveway and his foot pegs clipped rotten picket fence posts, scattering wooden slivers into his exhaust fumes playing hard rock against the sidewalk.

He rode right into the front yard and laid the motorcycle down in the weeds. He jumped off the chopper and ran toward the front door when the first bullet shattered glass and whizzed into the street past him. He dove in the rubble of the construction site he called home, grabbed a chunk of old plaster, and threw it through the window.

"Fuck you! Sonuvabitch!" Chance shouted. "You're cooked and I'm going to light the goddamn stove."

Chance ran at the front door, kicking it down. Bullets sliced through the air around him as he crashed into the living room.

«« — »»

With one bullet left, the kid heard Chance scramble to his feet in the rubble and thunder down the hall. He took the weapon in both hands and pointed it at Rosa laying face down on the bed. Chance's heavy boots collided with the hardwood floor a split-second away.

Rosa awoke and tried to crawl over the bed. With sweat running into his eyes, the young man couldn't sight the weapon at her head as Chance entered the small bedroom on a dead run. The punk tried to rub his eyes and clear his vision. He held the pistol with one hand and blocked Chance's attack with the other. Chance dove as the gun exploded. With his right, he caught the Asian's block and forced it aside. With his left, he grabbed the weapon and collided with the slight man, too small to be an effective policeman, and drove him out of the bedroom window.

The two men split the rotten, termite-ridden, vertical sliding window frame and careened through the glass, falling to the weed-strewn hard clay surface five feet below. Chance used the small man to break his impact with the tough surface and rolled over him, but the kid was on his feet and fighting before Chance could straighten. He kicked with soft training sneakers at Chance's ribs.

Chance, continued to roll to avoid the attack, then jumped to a crouching position. The Asian turned and ran for the six-foot wooden fence surrounding the yard, like a cat trying to escape a rabid dog. He was lithe and his agility took him up and over piles of lumber and the woodworking supplies Chance had mustered to rebuild his home.

Chance scrambled after him with every ounce of energy, adrenaline, and anger he had, but the kid hit the fence fast, clawing to the top edge. Chance couldn't catch the agile Asian, who was running on pure nitrous fear. He grabbed a lawn chair and flung it with all his might at the leaping man's spinal cord. The kid grabbed the top edge of the planks with both hands and kicked his feet to the right over the fence in a scissor kick. Mid-stride, the flimsy chair struck his lower back, throwing him off balance. Chance was right behind him, leaping the fence.

The kid tumbled to the pavement. Chance landed on the sidewalk as the kid leapt to his feet and darted for the end of the block. Chance was right on his tail as the young man rounded the corner, jumped a four-foot chain link fence, and cut between two old stucco garages for an alley separating two San Pedro streets.

Chance cleared the fence and pumped his legs for all he was

worth. He wanted the kid alive. He didn't know whether Rosa was still alive or needed him. He stumbled. She could be bleeding to death in his bedroom. He took another long stride. The kid gained distance, adrenaline pulsing through his veins.

The alley was cluttered with trash containers and debris. This kid was directly connected to the worst ordeal in Chance's life. He couldn't let him escape. Chance ran with all he had, snatching a small empty galvanized trash can, he heaved it at the kid and caught him in the calves. The kid went down and Chance gained on him. But the agile youngster regained his feet and peeled around the corner at the end of the alley.

Chance scrambled less than 10 feet behind him. The kid rounded the corner, hauling ass for all he was worth down 18th toward Crescent, over the boulevard, diving onto the dirt bluff leading to a recently built jogging path along the ridge overlooking the harbor's main channel.

Chance narrowly missed a passing tan sedan as he ran into the two-lane street and onto the sandy decline to the jogging trail below. The kid jumped to his feet at the edge of the wide path and Chance tackled him as he reached for the railing, driving the kid's torso into the steel railing. His narrow neck slammed against the top rail, killing him instantly.

Chance rolled him over immediately and dug through his pockets until he discovered his cell phone and wallet. He clicked the cell phone open and called Kate.

"Rosa's home, get there quick," Chance said, snapped the cell phone closed and ran toward his home on the bluff.

A black and white and an undercover car skidded to a stop in the middle of the street, lights blazing, and sirens wailing as Chance ran up the bluff. One officer tried to stop him at the split front door.

"It's all right," Kate called from her cruiser as she skidded to a stop and Chance, who was sweating profusely, scrambled down the hall.

"Rosa!" Chance hollered breathlessly.

He rushed into the trashed bedroom with Kate on his heals.

"Where's the kidnapper," Kate hollered as Chance scooped Rosa into his arms.

"He's on the jogging trial between 17th and 18th," Chance said, and Kate hollered for some uniforms to go find him.

Two officers jumped in their car, called for backup, and screeched up the street.

"Rosa, baby," Chance said. The bedroom scattered with broken class and still filled with the odor of gunpowder. She was alive.

"She's okay," Kate said, relieved. "An ambulance is on the way."

Another young female officer entered the room, looked at Chance's long mussed hair, and disheveled appearance. She bowed her head in respect and stepped out of the room.

"The kid on the path is dead," she said.

Chance sat on the edge of bed and put a trembling hand one of Rosa's soft thighs. She leaned against him and began to sob. Chance knew as she put her warm arms around him that he had lost her. The fear, the treachery and the uncertainty had reached her limits. She would return to the desert.

"I can't stay," she muttered between tears. "I'm scared."

"I understand, baby," he said, but his heart was heavy with the impending loss of this nascent relationship. She was terrified, and for her safety, he was forced to let her go. As much as she was his elixir for life as well as Carl's, he had no choice, much like the other dice he rolled with women in San Pedro. The disappointment was overwhelming, yet she was safe. That was foremost to Chance.

Chance turned to Kate and handed her the kid's wallet and cell phone.

Would the shit ever end?

-30-

Can't Win for Losing

Chance watched Rosa leave his war-torn pad, as she was assisted into an ambulance. She assured the cops that she was alright, but they requested a full examination, a report and photographs of her injuries. The bullet fired at close quarters may have damaged her eardrum. She may have suffered a concussion. His bedroom was a wreck, with bullet holes in the lathe and plaster walls, shattered glass on the hardwood floor, and the window blown out by the two bodies crashing through it.

"Chance," Grey, called from down the hallway.

"Yeah," Chance returned. "They found the kid?"

He pulled off his ripped and torn t-shirt and threw it on the floor. It was littered with glass fragments. He grabbed another faded, cycle shop sweatshirt, from the closet, and pulled it over his mussed hair. He immediately felt the chips of glass, the thick shirt, raked from his full sandy hair.

"Shit," he said, and yanked the shirt off and tossed it in the corner. He stepped into the head and brushed madly at his wild frock of hair.

The big cop met him in the small narrow hall. "He's dead."

"I figured," Chance said. "They'll peg me with the murder and we lost our only connection."

"Connection to what?" Grey said perplexed.

"You don't think he had anything to do with the other murders?" Chance asked.

"You're guilty of those," the cop said with a wry smile.

"Funny," Chance said. "Kate is checking out his cell phone and wallet right now."

Chance was relieved that Kate was on the job. He had ultimate faith in her, but he knew they were burnin' daylight. Something else was going to happen and he needed to head it off immediately.

«« — »»

Officer Joe Fernandez lay alone in his dank bedroom, recuperating from his Chance-busted ribs. Another two weeks of bed rest was required, but he itched. He felt like a house-arrest prisoner. He wanted out. His ol' lady drove him crazy with her constant bitchy harangue, and another woman was bothering him. He watched soap operas and ground his teeth all day. His only contact with the outside world was diminishing reports from the station and his constant phone calls from the Asian kid. Suddenly they ended and he didn't know why?

He was a nervous wreck and his wife could tell each time she waddled into the room with stale coffee and tired donuts. She was a mess. He hadn't spent this much time with her since they first moved into his two-story stucco cage, and he wrote her off to chase younger broads. It was as if they were strangers.

His demeanor was disjointed. He generally treated her as if she was a clerk in a train station, selling tickets to his kids. He just moved through, spoke an occasional nicety, and was gone. There were no romantic pleasantries flying around his home, and no flowers on the mantel. Since the fight, he grimaced constantly. When she asked him questions or tried to converse, he mentally escaped to a wild woman he met about a month ago. It took him long moments to come around and he constantly asked his wife to repeat herself, sometimes twice.

When he finally picked up the gist of the inquiry, he wanted nothing to do with it or her. He dismissed her quickly, but the pain in his pockmarked Hispanic features was evident, glowing and growing. She couldn't figure it out. She asked over and over, if he was in suffering. She had no idea. She didn't understand the depth of his pain.

She hesitated to enter his room to pick up his breakfast dish that consisted of a sweet roll and a black cup of coffee. He was gaining weight, another item that disgusted him.

"Do you need anything?" she said.

"Huh?" Joe said, staring out of the window.

"Do you need anything?"

"No, no," he said, not looking at the chubby couch potato, still wearing a bathrobe at noon.

"What would you like for lunch?" she said.

"What?" Joe snapped.

"What do you....? Her frustration was rising.

"Nothing from you!" he spat. She incensed him.

"What the hell is wrong with you?" she screamed.

The phone began to ring as he turned slightly and looked at her for the first time in two days. His mind spun with evil images of torturing every bone in her body. His intense stare was so foreboding, she backed toward the door. She could hear a kid screaming in the background and was relieved for an excuse to escape. Her gaze fell to the old shag carpet at her feet, and she turned to depart, slamming the door behind her. Her one final fearful act of rebellion.

Relieved at her leaving, Joe picked up the phone. "Hello?"

"That fuckin' biker did it again," Officer Myer barked in the phone.

"Whatta ya mean?" Joe asked, his anxiety cresting.

"He killed someone else," the biker-hating officer said. "Another biker this time. He broke his neck."

"Was the kid an Asian?" Joe asked wound to the stops.

"Yeah, how did you know, Joe?"

Joe was stuck, caught by his own limiting frustration. Sweat immediately beaded on his forehead. "I pulled over a local Asian sport bike rider once."

"Uh-huh," detective Myer said with doubt in his voice. "That chick detective thinks he's connected to the Harbor murders."

"Whatta you think?" Joe asked guiding the conversation away from himself.

"That kid didn't have anything to do with those murders," he said. "He had the broad who was living with the biker and couldn't do her. Didn't have the balls to cap her. He had a cell phone and Kate is running his records now. How you feeling?"

"I feel like shit." Joe said it without connecting his brain to his quivering vocal cords. He didn't know what to say. His blood pressure was peaking.

"I'll bet you'd like to get the hell out of there," Myer said.

"You don't know the half of it!" Joe exclaimed.

"I better get back to the beat," Myer said. "I'll try to stop by."

"Thanks for the call," Joe said and hung up.

He sat up in bed gingerly. The pain wasn't that bad. He was using the head and could move around his room, but he felt a painful tinge in his chest and fatigue prevented mobility, but not now. He took two more Vicadin and sat up. He yanked off his pajama shirt and reached for a roll of Ace bandages on the side table. He began to twist the tape around his chest, pulling it as tight as he could without incurring excruciating agony. He wrapped layer after layer of Ace bandage and tacked the ends with the aluminum clasps. Then he started the process again.

He sat on the edge of the bed and panted. The pain of sitting up was sharp and jagged, but once upright, it wasn't bad. He could feel sweat rolling out of his pits into the bandage as he struggled to get to his feet. He was forced to move. His world was crumbling and anger engulfed him. He had no choice, he felt physically terrible as he struggled to pull on a pair of slacks. He couldn't bend to tie his shoes so he wore sandals and a sweatshirt over the bandages.

He picked up the phone, dialed hurriedly and waited. No one answered, then a soft sensuous voice asked for a message.

"Sheila," Joe said pleading. "I need to speak with you."

In the head, he washed his face and attempted to comb his disheveled hair. He looked at himself in the mirror and was startled by his pale semblance. He couldn't figure out what caused his ghost-like appearance. Perspiration broke out on his temples once again as he made his way toward his bedroom door, then he turned back, opened his top dresser drawer and pulled out his service pistol. As he tucked it into his waistband, pain shot up his chest, and he ground his teeth with bitterness and anger toward the biker.

«« — »»

Kate called Lieutenant Reed and reported her findings. He excitedly put staff on searching the kid's apartment, running phone records and digging into his criminal past.

For the first time since she was given the job, she felt supported and was relieved to maybe break the case that haunted her, Chance, and the people of San Pedro. She was running on adrenaline when she pulled her undercover car next to the pad on 19th. Chance was loading his motorcycle into the back of Rosa's truck. He needed to attend to Rosa at the hospital and take her back to Arizona.

Kate was excited to see Chance. "We are breaking this case wide open," she said, running to his side.

"That's terrific," Chance said, "but there's a glitch."

"What do you mean," Kate said apprehensively.

"He's still out there," Chance said. "Be careful."

"You still think it's Fernandez?" Kate said. "The last two girls weren't raped. That's been bothering me."

"He's got something to do with it," Chance said, looking over his shoulder for other cops still gathering evidence around his house. "He still has friends and I don't. We need to watch our backs. Get those phone records. I'm going to see Rosa."

"Is she all right?" Kate muttered, holding Chance's arm

"She's cool but going back to Arizona, and I'm glad," Chance said. "I've got to get her out of here. I wish we could plant someone in front of his home."

"We still don't have proof," Kate said.

"That's the scary part," Chance said. "It's as if we are playing out the final hand and we don't know who has the cards."

"I feel good." Kate said. "We'll have all the connections in a matter of hours. I can feel it."

"Listen," Chance said, "I'm going to load up Rosa's stuff, pick her up at the hospital and roll out of town. We need her out of Dodge safely. That leaves you as the sole target. You've got to stay safe until I return. Can you do that?"

"Nobody knows where I'll be," Kate said. I spoke to Officer Applegate in Long Beach. I'll stay with her."

"I need 24 hours," Chance said. "You know as well as I do, that as soon as cops start turning up the cards, all the evidence will surface, then the shit will fly, unless you jump the bastard first. You must stay clear and let the shit fall, at least until I return. Got that?"

"I got it," Kate said and stood on her toes to kiss Chance's rough cheek, but he turned his head and kissed her full on the lips instead. Kate liked the touch of his soft lips and the connection to hers. It was the electricity she had always hoped for.

"Be careful and get back here quick."

«« — »»

Fernandez took several pain killers and hobbled down the stairs to the living room. Two of his kids were mesmerized by the television and didn't look up. His wife came out of the kitchen and was startled to see him out of bed.

"Where are you going?" she said, but truly didn't want to know.

"See you later." He ignored her question and headed to the garage. He opened his gun safe and yanked out his High Standard, 12-gauge, sawed-off shotgun and a box of shells. He snatched a 9mm Browning automatic pistol and all the magazines he had. Two were empty. He stood on the cold cement floor and snapped in rounds until they were packed. He opened his car door and tossed the shit on the passenger seat and floor. There was no order to his movements or thoughts. He pressed the automatic garage door opener and started the car. He jammed down Pacific Avenue toward 19th. Once he was rolling, the pain intensified with every crack in the streets.

He wanted to be back in bed, but something had to occur before the rest of his life collided into him. He held onto the plastic wheel, as if he could crush it. He stared out the windshield with the intensity of a vampire under a full moon, chasing the bastard with the silver bullets.

-31-

THE DICE ARE STUCK

Chance jammed his chopper into the back of Rosa's white F-150, leaving the tailgate down because the bed was too short. Kate hauled ass back to the station, confident her murder case had exploded wide open.

Chance felt like the dice were sticking to his hand. He didn't share Kate's positive vibe; in fact, the opposite. His emotional side was stuck in the corner of a bad-ass bar, his back against the wall, surrounded by all the wrong guys. His hands began to sweat.

Strapping his beloved ride securely to steel eyelets in the corners of the pickup bed, he ran through a mental checklist. He packed a quick bedroll with just enough duds to take him across the Golden state and into the Arizona desert, 83 miles to Tonopah, where he would make absolutely certain Rosa was secure and out of harm's way. He moved quickly but a dense cloud of uncertainty engulfed him. Jumping in the cab, he looked at his bedraggled shed, still wrapped in yellow crime scene tape. He pulled away abruptly.

Jamming across town, his mind wandered as if he was a novice prepping for a shuttle launch, clicking through a vague, unreliable checklist. His directory had no organization, no rules, a gambler's guess list.

«« — »»

Officer Fernandez called the Harbor Division from his Jeep.

"Callahan?" Fernandez said.

"Why aren't you in bed?" Callahan retorted. He detected sounds of traffic and a moving vehicle.

"I have a hunch," Fernandez said, driving fast, his eyes intent on the road as he spoke into the cell phone. "That biker killed that kid for no good reason. He's trying to implicate someone else. I'll bet he'll attack the Mexican broad."

"We're checking the kid out now," Callahan said.

"You don't need to," Fernandez said sweat building in droplets on his dark brow. "Hold off, will ya? I'm going to question the broad. She'll tell us that Chance is your man."

"You're nuts," Callahan said. "Go back to bed. We'll handle this."

"Just give me 20 minutes," Fernandez said, quickly turning onto Gaffey.

"Okay, okay," Callahan said. "I'll hold it up until you talk to the woman."

"Thanks," Fernandez said, rolling quickly passed the new Home Depot block building at the base of town.

«« — »»

Kate ran up the stairs of the San Pedro Police department and tore into the offices. The female cop snagged her at the door to the change room.

"This may be the day," she said hugging Kate.

"Damn," Kate said, looking at her eyeball-to-eyeball. "It better be."

"It's too bad Chance killed that kid," the officer said averting her gaze to the polished linoleum floor.

"It was self-defense," Kate said, looking at the officer with questioning eyes.

"He was just a kid, and that biker broke his neck," the officer said. "Something fishy about that."

"Is someone running the info on the kid and his cell phone?" Kate asked, realizing that this officer wasn't on the latest investigative page.

"No," she said, perplexed at Kate's response.

"Why?"

"We just heard that Fernandez got out of bed to question Rosa," the officer replied. "Orders from Callahan."

"That's bullshit," Kate said.

She stopped, as if time had ended. She stared at the officer and dealt a hand in her mind. Chance was rubbing off on her. She pondered her options, as a poker player figures the odds in his hand.

Should she attempt a conversation with Lt. Reed? She turned and ran back to her car. Burning rubber, she peeled out of the parking lot and hit the speed dial button for Officer Grey.

"Officer Grey?" she said into her phone.

"Yes, Norton," the big black uniform returned.

"What the hell is going on?" Kate spat.

"I'm not sure. Fernandez spoke to someone in the investigators' pool."

"We need to dig into the kid's past, his phone records, everything," Kate said anxiously while speeding down Gaffey toward 7th street where the San Pedro Peninsula Hospital was located on the hill over-looking the harbor. "I'm going to the hospital."

"I'll try to get it moving," Grey said, and hung up.

"Don't they know?" Kate screamed into the phone as the line went dead.

«« — »»

Five minutes passed and Joe's cell phone rang as he entered downtown.

"Fernandez, Callahan here. That Norton broad was just here and she's pissed that we held up the investigation on the kid. She's headed toward the hospital."

"Fuck," Fernandez said numbly into the receiver and hung up. He spun right on 6th Street and sped up the hill toward the backside of the hospital.

He tried Sheila's number again. No answer. He met this sexual goddess just a short while ago, and ever since, his life was in shambles. Where the hell was she? She swept into town like a sexual drug lord spinning a lustful web over Joe, like a hungry black widow. She enticed him with her massive bolt-on boobs, and her unceasing desire for sex, any place, at any time. His life was upside down with infatuation. He wanted to leave his wife, the kids, the force, and the country to be with her, but he sensed a different agenda in the woman.

She had an edge, like a knife too sharp to touch. He couldn't figure it out, until the second girl died. He lost it with Suzanne, and felt that if he just remained in the shadows, the force would bust the biker or the investigation would dry up. Then the next girl died and he wasn't involved. But after the girl from Harbor Taxi died, her sexual hold lost its grip. The murders had to stop, one way or another. He had to get to Rosa before Sheila did.

«« — »»

Kate's mid-sized cruiser, red light flashing, siren wailing, skidded around the corner of Gaffey and 7th, screaming up the wildly steep hill, lunging over the speed bumps and ripples in the 80-year-old cracked concrete. A two-lane road aimed directly at the top of Palos Verdes Peninsula cut from commercial and retail on Gaffey into a residential area surrounding the hospital region, consisting of single-story doctors' offices and high-rise medical buildings. The only bog in the lane was a series of four-way boulevard stops positioned every other block in her scrambling path to the top and the hospital.

She let off the gas for a split second at the first intersection before blowing through it. She did the same at the second one on the steep rise. To her left, the intersection was empty. Her eyes spun right as her foot left the gas, hesitated above the brake pedal then returned to the gas pedal. As she wavered, a red Jeep Cherokee rolled one foot past the broad line in the adjacent street.

She didn't understand. Her emergency lights flashed, and her siren screamed, why didn't the driver see or hear? He or she would surely stop, but didn't. She hit the brakes and the rear end of the sedan skidded to the right.

The Jeep sped forward, then suddenly there was a blast. Shotgun pellets slammed against her passenger window and windshield, shattering both. Her car, out of control, careened toward the opposite northwest corner. She slammed onto the curb and crashed into a block retaining wall surrounding an old Spanish duplex. Two red ceramic roof tiles snapped loose and fell crashing into her hood. She smacked against the airbag that blocked any remnants of vision she might have.

Kate popped the door handle. It burst open, and she tumbled to the sidewalk stunned, but not injured. She rolled and pulled her service pistol. Another shotgun blast rocked the opposite side of her car. She jumped to her feet and spun to lower the 9 mm across her hood. She fired at the driver's door, then recognized Fernandez at the wheel. He tried to pull away.

Kate leapt over the hood and ran after the Jeep. Fernandez' frustration, pain, and anxiety peaked. His driver-side window was open and the shotgun barrel protruded into the open. Her second shot shattered his windshield and he collided with a parked car on the right.

He pushed his door open and attempted to step out of the SUV, but stumbled and fell to the asphalt. When he rolled over Kate was standing over him with her pistol aimed at his head.

"Don't move, you sonuvabitch!" she spat.

«« — »»

At the hospital, Rosa rested in the emergency room on a bed. The duty doctor looked her over, administered a CAT scan, cleaned her bruises and cuts, and blessed her departure. Shortly after he left, a tall nurse entered her area and offered to help her into a wheelchair and out to the waiting area.

"How are you feeling?" the tall nurse asked.

"I'm feeling better," Rosa said. She was still in a daze and the doctor had given her something to help her relax.

Rosa turned slightly and placed her legs over the edge of the bed, while the nurse rolled a wheelchair to the side and helped her stand up, turn and sit in the chair gingerly.

Rosa was out of focus, but noticed that this girl had a dry, direct demeanor and a very large chest. She seemed out of place, like a Barbie/nurse doll left in a box full of toy soldiers. As Rosa sat comfortably in the chair, she felt the girl's hand on the side of her face, then smelled something pungent and chemical. Then she passed out.

«« — »»

Five minutes later, Chance also rolled up Gaffey from the opposite direction, but was held up from making a left on 7th while emergency vehicles careened up the street. He backed up slightly, changed lanes and drove to 6th Street before turning left. Another five minutes and he was behind the hospital parking the truck. He jogged around to the front of the hospital and the automatic glass doors slowly slid open. At the reception area stood officer Stengle, leaning heavily against the glass counter.

Chance looked at him with questioning eyes then turned to the nurse behind the cluttered desk. "Where's Rosa?"

The nurse looked like a teenager caught with a handful of her mother's jewelry.

"She's gone," Stengle said and no customary sarcastic smile crossed his lips or raised his blonde eyebrows.

"Fernandez?" Chance muttered in a low fretful tone.

"No, he's under arrest," Stengle said.

"Rosa was with him?" Chance looked at the officer, as if Stengle just shot him in the foot.

"No," Stengle said.

He looked at the receptionist. "Any clues?"

She shook her head dismally.

"Do you know where she might be?" Officer Stengle hollered after him, as Chance bolted for the door.

Chance didn't know, and that was the worst part. As he ran back to the truck, the thought of driving like a mad dog with his faithful chopper in the bed disturbed him. He snatched the ramp, slapped it against the pavement, released the tailgate and unleashed the dicey chopper. Burning rubber, he peeled out of the lot and across Alma Avenue to 8th Street.

He had no inclination where they might go, but he was burnin' daylight, and by nightfall, which was just around the corner, Rosa would be dead. At Beacon Street, he hung a right and rattled windows in halfway houses and rundown rehab centers as he headed toward the old warehouse district on the south end of the harbor, where most of the bodies were discovered.

The sun dipped over the Palos Verdes bluff and golden colors of the harbor changed to rich warm hues. In a half-hour, dusk would hinder vision, then night would blanket the dank warehouses. A chill ran up Chance's spine as the motorcycle peeled along Crescent in front of his house, reminding him of the warmth Rosa brought home and the chaos surrounding his life.

He gulped at the salty air, downshifted and ran the boulevard stop at Crescent and Mesa. He hit a left, then another left on 22nd Street as it dipped along the Cabrillo Marina in the direction of the old concrete wharves.

He peeled up and down each wharf, along the east channel, beside the sinking waterlogged docks in the original Cabrillo Marina. He searched abandoned fuel barges at the end of the peninsula and through the rusting boat hulks on dry docks in the San Pedro Boat

Yard. He gripped his bars like an innocent man in a jail cell and kept looking. Nothing made sense. Fernandez was in custody. Who had Rosa? He thought about running at top speed off the end of any pier.

At Signal Street, he skidded to a stop and looked right. Shadows leaned heavily against the cracked black asphalt. The Harbor Taxi building was bathed in darkness. A brown sedan was parked at the end at an odd angle. Chance's cell phone rang in his vest. He could barely hear it for the rumble of the big Harley.

"Do you know a girl named Sheila McBride?" Kate asked urgently from the hospital emergency room.

"Oh no!" Chance said. "I mean yes, and I'll bet she's in Warehouse number 1 on Signal. There's a familiar sedan down there."

"Don't go, she may be armed," Kate said. "I'll send the troops."

"This card game will be played one on one," Chance said and hung up.

He down shifted into first, grabbed all the throttle possible, and snapped the clutch like a bullwhip. Dust and debris floated across the concrete canyon of warehouse walls. Snake-like unused railroad tracks crisscrossed the old street built over San Pedro Bay. The smell of salt water and diesel fumes wafted in the evening air as the long chopper roared toward the Ford like an arrow toward its prey, peeling past Berths 58, 59, and 60.

The pent-up threats of criminal prosecution, the smiles of three women who perished of terrible torture, the lies, the slam against the police brotherhood, and the cop gone bad drove Chance insane with fury, but it wasn't all Fernandez.

Rosa couldn't die, not before Chance, and not because of him. Out of his mind with unleashed anger, he peeled through four gears directly toward the building at the end of the wharf. As far as Chance was concerned this was it, his last wild ride. His straight pipes ricocheted his intentions off the surrounding walls.

As Chance nailed it down Signal Street a head popped up behind the sedan at the end of the block. Carl, his trusted, middle-aged employer, crept around the back of the new vehicle and pointed at the building. Chance smacked his disc brakes and slid up behind the car, jumped off the seat and crouched down. Fire spurted from inside concrete Warehouse #1, the oldest abandoned warehouse in San Pedro. Chance ducked as bullets whizzed around the old undercover cop car Fernandez gave to Sheila.

"I saw her drag Rosa into the warehouse," Carl said, panting while loading a pump shotgun. "I haven't fired this in years."

"How long has she been in there?" Chance asked, looking at the sweat beading up on Carl's nearly bald head.

"Just a few minutes," Carl said as several rounds of ammo came spewing out of the building and crashed into the corrugated steel warehouse behind them.

"Stay here," Chance said. "Cops will be all over the place shortly. Do you have a flare? I may need a distraction. I've got to go in."

"I'll take care of it. Don't let anything happen to Rosa," Carl said and his white beardless face quivered in fear.

Chance crouched behind the Jeep, then jumped back on the rumbling chopper. He leaned it hard, revved the engine, and dumped the clutch. The rear wheel broke loose and burned in a circle until he spit the motorcycle alongside the gray concrete to the opening of the historic Prohibition-era warehouse and raced inside. It was cold as death. He sped into the abandoned building scattered with immense concrete pillars and laid the bike down in a shower of sparks on the damp cement floor.

"She's dead, you low-life sonuvabitch!" Sheila screamed, her icy voice reverberating in the cement tomb. "You killed her! You killed all of them!"

"That's bullshit!" Chance shouted. "Come and get me!"

Terror ran up his spine, but he rolled away from his chopper behind a chipped concrete post. He didn't care anymore. He would rather be dead than to deal with the death of another beautiful woman. He dove in the dust behind a pillar as Sheila fired, clipping the right heel of his cowboy boot. He couldn't return fire. Where was Rosa? He couldn't see, only smelled the gunpowder in the air mixed with rat piss.

Chance tucked the .38 Stengle offered him back in his vest and stood up behind the concrete and steel pillar. Darkness engulfed the vast cold building constructed in 1948, except where slivers of fading light leaked into the interior. Suddenly, a marine flare rolled into an opening and filled the room with a blood-red glow of sparks and smoke—Carl.

Chance pulled the .38, glance around the pillar, found his moving target running for a stairwell. Another form was slumped in a chair at the dark end of the building. He ran firing the snub-nosed weapon.

Pungent phosphorescent smoke filled the room and Chance crouched as the flare hissed. He moved to another pillar, but gunfire traced his path. He couldn't reload the revolver. He only had two shots left. Darkness engulfed the interior again as Chance slipped from pillar to pillar toward the lonely chair in the distance.

He prayed Rosa was alive and unharmed as he ducked Sheila's bullets and attempted to reach the chair. He fired once more, but he was out of ammo, and Sheila was reloading. He tried to keep track of her firing cycles. He stumbled over rusting tracks in the floor, and counted four out of six rounds. Then he slipped in something wet and fell to the slick concrete. Terror swept over him as his busted boot touched her naked foot. He was sure he was lying in a pool of Rosa's blood. Two more bullets split the concrete around him and something caught fire. He heard the snap of a firing pin against an empty chamber and he scrambled to his feet.

He could hear sirens in the distance, wailing for all they were worth. A patrol car careened into the wide wharf door and bathed Chance with headlight illumination. He was lying in a pool of motor oil at the feet of Rosa's body tied to a rusting metal chair. Her mouth was securely wrapped in duct tape but her dark eyes were alive with fear. Chance snatched the chair and dove with Rosa behind a protective cement barrier.

Officers bounded from their vehicles with guns trained on Chance. Patrol cars fanned out around the building. A creaking freight elevator began to climb through one floor after another.

Chance looked up at Rosa's unnaturally pale features.

"Chance?" Kate's voice called from the edge of the door. "They know you're innocent."

Chance jumped to his feet, slipping in the oil. He snatched his Beretta folding knife, snapped the blade open, cut Rosa free and pulled her to momentary safety behind another thick concrete post. He ran toward the stairwell.

"Wait," Kate hollered. "She's armed."

"So am I," Chance muttered to himself, scrambling up the corroded expanded-metal stairs. The elevator continued to creek toward the 6th floor. Chance ran with all his will. At the fourth floor, he stepped through a rung of the eroded metal stairway and collapsed against the jagged step. He hurried to pull his leather boot free, but he was trapped.

As he kicked the rusting craggy hulk of steel with his other boot, someone stepped out of the darkness behind him. Chance was bleeding, his leg was snagged like a fishhook barb snagging its prey. He turned to face the muzzle of a .38.

"You took my life," Sheila said, raising the 2-inch barrel of the smoking weapon as Chance faced her.

"Kill me, you piece of shit," Chance spat in Sheila's angry face. "You didn't need to kill any of those girls."

He remembered the first time he gazed at the sexual goddess. He remembered how she exuded sex in every touch, but this time her blue eyes were iced with hate.

"You're nobody, a fuckin' biker," Sheila said and squeezed the trigger with sweat-soaked finger. "You had no business with any of these women. Why would any of them want you?"

She was psychotic, but her eyes warmed and Chance knew that at any second she could and would snap.

"Now I know why the other girl's weren't raped," Chance said grinding his teeth.

He twisted abruptly and the blast ran parallel to his gut taking shreds of his vest. He jammed his hand under the barrel of the revolver as Sheila attempted to fire again.

"You had your chance, bitch," Chance shouted, and drove her forearm against the rusting railing. The revolver snapped free of her grasp and fell to the harbor brine below. Cringing in pain, she reached into her waistband for something.

Chance attempted to pull his leg free again, and felt the rusty serrated steel slicing his calf. Sheila yanked a grizzly, stained, wood-handle knife from her waistband. Her eyes became pools of Satanic hatred, like a rabid wolf salivating over wounded prey. She slashed at Chance as if slicing meat for a meal.

"Don't do it," Kate ordered, rounding the corner on the steel stairwell. "Drop the knife." She held the pistol on target as she approached Chance.

Chance knelt to pry the steel rungs away from his boot and slipped it free. Sheila paused, looked at Chance's muscular back as he freed his foot, and remembered the many nights they once had. Then her gaze switched to the short athletic detective in the form-fitting professional suit, then back at Chance. She immediately noticed the soft manner in which the beautiful female cop looked at Chance. She lowered the weapon, but nodded, as if some psycho realization struck home.

In their close proximity on the steel landing, Kate tried to slip past Chance. She looked at him, his bleeding leg, then back at Sheila.

"She's another one," Sheila screamed and charged forward toward Kate.

Chance stood up, spun and blocked the knife attack before Kate could raise her weapon once more. He slapped Sheila, twisted her wrist and the knife fell to the grating. He drew his fist back and adrenaline rushed to every limb.

"Don't do it," Kate hollered, and shoved Sheila against the railing, where she cuffed her. "We need her alive."

"Where are you going?" Kate asked, as Chance turned to hobble back down the stairs.

"I need a long ride," Chance said, "I'm taking Rosa home."

K. RANDALL BALL is an old grubby biker and a so-so writer, who's hung around with many of the greats in the custom motorcycle world. He's built a handful of bikes, set Bonneville records and traveled around the world. He spends most of his time working in his Wilmington, California shop, writing for his web site, Bikernet.com, and wondering why he's so attracted to redheads.

Other works by K. Randall Ball

Prize Possession
Outlaw Justice
Sam "Chopper" Orwell
How to Build a Bonneville Salt Flats Motorcycle

www.ingramcontent.com/pod-product-compliance
Lightning Source LLC
Chambersburg PA
CBHW070315260626
47160CB00003B/848